Praise for Jaye C

"Filled with laughs"

"A round of applause . . . a captivating, feel-good story
that you want to go on reading"

Mayo News

"Rattles along at a very readable pace, but has an
underlying depth to the story . . . If you liked her
previous books, *If the Shoe Fits* and *The Sweetest Feeling*,
then you'll love this."

Sunday World

Praise for Jaye Carroll's *The Sweetest Feeling*

"A definite talent for the witty one-liners . . . A tight
little story that will keep you reading all night. A real
page-turner."

Irish Farmers Monthly

"Fun and very readable . . . perfect holiday escapism
reading."

Irish Independent

Praise for Jaye Carroll's *If the Shoe Fits*

"What really makes it stand out is the consistent humour
with which the author imbues [the] characters . . . An
interesting and entertaining first novel"

Irish Immigrant Newsletter

Looking for Mr Wrong

Also by Jaye Carroll

Loving the Stars
The Sweetest Feeling
If the Shoe Fits

Looking for Mr Wrong

jaye carroll

POOLBEG

Published 2004
by Poolbeg Press Ltd
123 Grange Hill, Baldoyle
Dublin 13, Ireland
E-mail: poolbeg@poolbeg.com

Typesetting, layout, design © Poolbeg Group Services Ltd.

1 3 5 7 9 10 8 6 4 2

A catalogue record for this book is available from the British Library.

ISBN 1-84223-114-6

Typeset by Patricia Hope in Palatino 9.6/13.5
Printed by
Litografia Rosés S.A., Spain

www.poolbeg.com

About the Author

Jaye Carroll can trace her family tree all the way back to her parents.

As well as being the author of several bestselling books, Jaye is widely acknowledged as the world's foremost expert on the different types of little stones that come up when you're mowing the lawn.

An avid amateur photographer, Jaye Carroll is also the proud owner of a large collection of photographs of fingers and camera straps.

Jaye would like to take this opportunity to categorically deny that there is any truth in the rumours about her and the postman, despite whatever that nasty old wagon on the next street might tell you.

Acknowledgements

Contrary to what some authors would like us to believe, books are not written in a vacuum (mainly because it'd be too dusty) . . . so I'd like to thank the following people for their unwavering support and friendship (the list is in alphabetical order, so no fighting!): Alix, Amanda, Angie, Anita, Anna, Aveen, Ben, Brona, Catherine, Catriona, Chris, Claudia, Crystal, Deirdre, Denise, Doreen, Elaine, Elvis, Frank, Frank, Gabi, Gary, Gaye, Harry, Helen, Jack, Jackie, James, James, James, James, Janet, Jim, Jo, John, John, Kawen, Kerrie, Liam, Marian, Martin, Martin, Martina, Mary Jo, Mike, Mike, Mike, Morgan, Owen, Paddy, Paddy, Pádraig, Pádraig, Pat, Paul, Paula, Peter, Rachel, Rhona, Robert, Robert, Sally, Shane, Sheelagh, Stef, Tanya, Theresa, Tim, Todd, Tríona, Willie, and Zach.

Thanks also to the fine people at Poolbeg, to the booksellers (who are all incredibly sexy and clever), to the reviewers and journalists who have spoken well of my previous books (who are guaranteed a top spot when I establish my New World Order), and to the readers (who make all this worthwhile).

Also thanks to the many phone company representatives

Jaye Carroll

for the large number of cheerful and unrelenting phone calls and visits, and without whom this book would have been finished a lot sooner.

A special mention goes out to Jenny Chapman, who promised me money if I mentioned her name in this book.

Love and cuddles,
Jaye Carroll
Dublin, April 2004

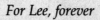

For Lee, forever

Chapter 1

There are times in your life when all you want to do is crawl into bed and have a damn good cry.

But I couldn't even do *that*, because my bed was missing.

This was Monday at about two o'clock in the afternoon, a week after Des had ever-so-casually made the suggestion that I go away for the weekend . . .

* * *

I'd been up for about an hour, and was in the process of manoeuvring the stepladder up the stairs so that I could do a little work on the spare bedroom – I'd already stripped the ceiling and now it was time to start filling in the cracks – when Des came wandering out of the bathroom. He stopped in the doorway, wearing only a towel about his waist. He still had little drops of water clinging to his chest hairs. "Orla, how do you feel about spending next weekend with Killian and Claire?"

I wasn't really paying that much attention to him, because I'd just had a brainwave. You know how sometimes something occurs to you and it's so blindingly obvious that you feel like kicking yourself for not having thought of it before? Well, it was one of those.

There I was, halfway up the stairs, carefully holding on to the wicked stepladder, when the thought came to me that I must have done this a hundred times. I need to do some work upstairs, and where's the ladder? It's downstairs. And if I need to do some work downstairs . . . well, you can guess the rest. It's not that the ladder was heavy; it was just awkward. It was a simple A-frame, two metres long, made of aluminium, and polka-dotted with years of paint-brush dropping – your basic stepladder, in other words – but it was tricky to person-handle the thing up and down a staircase. It didn't help that I was usually also carrying paint buckets or a toolbox at the time. The wall beside the stairs was covered in little scratches and gouges where the ladder had suddenly developed a mind of its own and decided to go wandering.

Not for the first time, I said to myself, "This would be a lot simpler if there was some way to have the ladder upstairs without having to actually carry the thing up, or downstairs without having to carry the thing down." Unfortunately, that would have meant having the ladder in two different places at the same time.

Then out of the indigo, I realised that the solution was very, very simple: you *can't* have one ladder in two different places at the same time, but you can have *two* ladders in two different places at the same time! The solution to my great problem was to buy another stepladder: then I'd have an upstairs one and a downstairs one.

"So what do you think?" Des was saying.

I stopped and stared at him, one hand carrying the tub of Polyfilla and the other holding onto the stepladder. "Sorry?" I felt a little bit annoyed with him for not noticing that I'd just become a genius.

"Yeah, you should do it. Give yourself a few days off and go and see them. I mean, you could do with a break, right? And you've been saying that you're due a few days off work. Give you a chance to recharge the batteries before the new term starts."

I wondered where he was going with this. "I suppose so. It's been a while since we saw them."

He hesitated a little. "Only, this weekend I'm going to be absolutely *swamped*, so it's probably as good a time as any."

Ah! I said to myself. He doesn't want to go himself, he just wants me to go. He's up to something.

Normally I stand my ground when my suspicions are aroused – and in this case, they weren't so much aroused as they were kicked awake by someone with hobnailed boots – but the coming weekend marked the anniversary of my birth. So far, Des hadn't mentioned any potential birthday presents – usually he'd drop a few hints just to gauge my reaction – so I was pretty sure that he had something planned.

Des leaned back into the bathroom, grabbed a hand-towel and began to dry his hair. "You could give Killian a call, see what he thinks," he said from under the towel.

That only made me more suspicious, because Killian

and Des had never quite got on, and this was probably only about the tenth time the Des had even mentioned my brother by name.

"But next Sunday's my birthday," I said. Internally, I'd already decided to go, but I knew that it was my role now to not have already guessed that he had an ulterior motive.

He looked up. "Oh shite, yeah, of course it is. Sorry." He put on his guilty expression. "I can't change the plans now. I've got the contractors and the major investors all coming in to the site. Look, we can celebrate the weekend after, how's that sound?"

I've never been one for celebrating birthdays, so I wasn't all that bothered about missing my twenty-seventh. "Okay."

I set up the stepladder in the spare bedroom, and – as I was doing my best to fill in the cracks between the ceiling and the wall – Des stood in the doorway gallantly not offering to help, and explaining his work plans for the coming weekend. He needn't have bothered, because I could never make head nor tail of contracts and management stuff. I knew it was important, though, which is another reason I didn't kick up a fuss.

For well over two years, Des had been trying to get the new shopping centre built. By that, I mean that he'd spent that time organising everything; from negotiating with the landowner and her solicitors, to applying for government grants, searching for investors, dealing with construction firms, and so on. It was all maddeningly complicated, but he was well able for it: Des seemed to be able to hold about a thousand different things in his head at any one time.

And now, after countless delays, everything was finally coming together. Lots of money was about to change hands, contracts would be signed, and if all went well the ground would be broken in a couple of weeks.

So even if I had been upset that Des was too busy to spend time with me on my birthday, which I wasn't, there wasn't much I could have done about it. The new shopping centre would create hundreds of jobs in the area and generate vast amounts of money. Any protests on my part would be selfish and pointless – it couldn't all stop just because Orla Adare's birthday was coming up.

And on top of all that, I was certain that it was all a ruse anyway, and that Des had something very special planned for me. I was right.

* * *

For a little over a year, I'd been slowly renovating the house. It was a large, three-bedroomed semi, inherited from my parents. The house hadn't been properly decorated since some time in the 1950s, so I'd decided that to make my house look young and fresh again I would do the structural equivalent of a bit of cosmetic surgery: I was giving my home a house-lift.

I was doing this partly because it was now my house and I wanted to give it my own look, and partly because any designer worth her salt really shouldn't be living in a dark, crumbling old shell that's still packed with thousands of old knick-knacks that her parents had accumulated over the years, and with some rooms still lined with the same woodchip wallpaper that had looked ancient to her when she was a kid.

5

One of the reasons it took me so long to get around to remodelling the house was that I simply didn't know what I should do with all my parents' stuff. The house was full of old chests of drawers that were packed with several lifetimes' accumulations of, well, crap: newspaper clippings, tiny little ornaments, jamjars full of screws that my dad had taken out of things that were to be thrown away, mouldy books and periodicals that had belonged to my grandparents, acres and acres of old curtains that my mother had refused to throw out "because they might come in handy one day". All that sort of thing.

My brother hadn't wanted any of the stuff, so he'd generously told me that it was all mine. I didn't want it either, but I just couldn't see myself throwing it all out.

So instead of putting my energies into clearing the house, I put them into designing how I wanted it all to look like once I'd cleared it. The walls of the spare room were covered in sketches – all genuine Orla Adare originals, almost worth their weight in paper! – that showed a perfectly remodelled house that my parents would probably have hated.

Before I took over the house, "redecoration" had consisted mainly of painting over the old wallpaper, with the result that when I started *my* redecoration, I discovered that the best tool with which to strip the walls wasn't a paint-stripper, but a large screwdriver: I had to gouge holes in the walls and prise the bits off with the screwdriver.

I'd been involved in enough redecoration and restoration projects to know how easy it is to get so completely bogged down with little tasks that you never get anything finished, so with my own house I'd decided to tackle the rooms one at a time, more or less.

The first room I'd completed was the bathroom. Before, it had been the home of a huge iron bath with cracked enamel and rusty streaks running from the taps down to the plug-hole. After the carpet – who in their right mind puts a thick carpet in the bathroom? – that was the first thing to go, replaced with a corner unit and a power shower. I didn't do the plumbing or the electrics myself, but I did everything else. Next came a new toilet and hand basin – matching the bath – then I stripped, sanded and sealed the floorboards. All by myself, and all by hand. That was a tough job, but it was nothing compared to tiling the floor and walls. After that, the new light fittings and cabinets were a doddle.

Finally, in the middle of an ancient ruin of a house, was a bathroom that wouldn't have looked out of place in *Vanity Fair*. The whole job had taken me about seven months, but it was worth it.

There's something very satisfying about completing a DIY job; for months afterwards you keep looking at it and thinking, "*I* did that!" And when friends are over, you show it off to them, but you keep putting it down. "I missed a bit there," and "That's not perfectly horizontal." Of course, you can only do this with friends who don't know anything at all about decorating, because they'll be impressed anyway. Ideally, if you want to show off your DIY skills you need to select people who don't actually know how to get the lid off a tin of paint, or who – if they manage to achieve that feat – then suddenly realise that they don't have anything to stir the paint with, so they end up using a wooden spoon. Their paintwork is always patchy and streaked because they never clean their rollers properly, and their brushes have bristles that stick out all over the place, a bit like Patrick Kielty's hair. In other words, the sort of people who'd call in an expert to hang a picture for them.

Though I considered myself to be a good designer, I wasn't really a DIY expert, and doing the bathroom had been a learning experience – it was definitely a lot easier to design how a room should look like than to actually physically *make* the room look like that – but after that, doing the main bedroom had been a piece of cake. I stripped the room of everything, borrowed a belt sander to do the floorboards, bought a book on plastering and re-rendered one of the walls, then hired a real plasterer to come in and finish the job properly.

Aside from that little setback, I was pleased with the bedroom: bare polished boards, hidden lighting, minimalist furniture, topaz walls with amber bedclothes on the new bed. I'd uncovered and restored the long-blocked-up fireplace, and on cold winter evenings there was nothing more cosy than being curled up in bed with the fire blazing.

So that was two rooms completed, and now I was starting on the spare bedroom. After that, I'd do the box room, then the attic conversion, then the landing, and then begin work on the downstairs rooms.

Okay, so I wasn't doing it on a strictly room-by-room basis: some things had to be done all in one go, like the rewiring, the plumbing and the windows. In fact, stripping the window frames had been the least successful project. It had seemed like a good idea at the time, but once it was done I discovered that the many layers of paint had been the only thing stopping the windows from rattling like crazy every time a truck went past. And we weren't even that close to the main road. My ultimate plan was that one day I'd replace the old sash windows with something a little more modern, and a lot more heat-efficient, but right now the budget didn't stretch to that.

On the whole, things were coming together pretty well. The biggest job was converting the attic, and I'd been putting it off for a long time. It had been the first job I'd planned – my sketches were now so old that my design had gone out of fashion and back in again – but it got nudged aside fairly quickly; I'd made one trip up to the attic to sketch out the layout of the crossbeams, and despaired at the hundreds of old boxes up there.

It wasn't that we needed the extra space that an attic conversion would give us; I just wanted to do it.

* * *

I waited until Des had gone off to the site before I phoned Claire. After the usual opening salvos about how the kids were, how each other's job was going, and all that, I mentioned that since I hadn't seen any of them in ages, maybe I could come and spend the weekend with them.

Almost before I'd got the words out, Claire said, "That'd be great!" I knew then that something was definitely up; Killian and Claire normally needed a couple of months' notice before visitors were allowed anywhere *near* the house. I know this because once Des and I showed up unexpectedly – we'd been on a sort of making-it-up-as-we-went-along driving holiday of the south-west – and

Killian and Claire's house was a complete mess. I didn't mind that myself – with two young kids in the family they'd have a tough time trying to keep it permanently tidy – but Claire had been mortified. For the entire duration of our visit she was surreptitiously rearranging cushions to hide stains and nudging stuff under the sofa with the back of her foot.

She continued: "You can stay in Niamh's room. I know she'd love to share a room with you. She's always going on about wanting a big sister!"

Claire and I had been friends since we were in primary school; I knew she was rubbish at keeping secrets, so – just chancing my arm – I said, "Great, thanks! But where will *Des* sleep?"

"Des? But isn't this the weekend that he's finalising all the contracts and everything?"

"A-ha!" I said. "And how would *you* know about that?"

Claire muttered a few choice swear-words into the phone. "Just don't tell him I let it slip, okay?"

"What's going on then?"

She hesitated for a couple of seconds, then gave in. "You're getting your attic done. It's sort of a birthday present from Des. He phoned us last week to set it up. It's costing him a fortune, so it is. He said he's taken copies of your designs and shown them to the builders. They're going to do it exactly as you'd planned."

"You're not kidding?"

"No. I think he's got a few other things planned too, along the same lines."

"So all that stuff about him having to work this weekend . . . that's not really happening?"

"No, I think it is. Des said that he can't change that, so he decided this would be a good time to get the attic done too. So when you go back home next Monday, you have to let on that it's all a complete surprise."

I told her that I thought I could manage that. After a few more pleasantries, plus me telling Claire about ten times that I wouldn't give Des any hints that I knew what was really going on, we said good-bye and hung up.

I spent the rest of the morning cleaning the kitchen. Our friends Justin and Mags had been over on Saturday night, and I still hadn't got around to cleaning up after the event. There were mugs and glasses all over the sitting-room – you'd think that four people would only use four mugs and four glasses, but somehow it never works out like that – and while I said I don't mind things being untidy, it does bother me when things are dirty. My mother had been just the same: there had always been piles of, well, anything and everything, tucked away in the corners and forever in danger of toppling over, but she'd been fanatically obsessed with cleanliness and reacted to a used tea bag left in the sink with the same horror that most people reserve for an overflowing toilet.

As I worked away with the mop and the dishcloth – though not at the same time – I started going over the conversations Des and I had had about the work on the house. Or at least the ones I could remember; a lot of the discussions seemed to have taken place when I was pretty drunk, so I was a little nervous about what *else* he might have remembered and planned to put into action. I was pretty sure that one alcohol-inspired scheme had to do with an indoor barbecue, which hadn't seemed even nearly as good an idea once the Alka-Seltzer kicked in the next morning. And I could also remember a drunken theory that if we painted the kitchen in luminous paint we'd save a fortune in electricity.

* * *

My parents had married quite late in their lives; they'd been in their early forties by the time I was born.

My father died when I was nineteen; he'd dozed off in the pub one Saturday afternoon, as he often did, and simply didn't wake up again. I suppose it would be a nice way to go, surrounded by your mates, even if your mates didn't immediately notice you were dead. By the time his friends realised that something was wrong, Dad had three full pints on the table in front of him.

My mother succumbed to a heart attack three years later, which to be honest came as no surprise to anyone who knew her. She'd been a very heavy smoker and drinker, which was bad enough, but it was her diet that killed her: one of the last remaining followers of the "if it was good enough for my ancestors" school of thought, she'd always cooked with lard, refused to eat anything that wasn't steeped in butter – though on special occasions she'd be willing to substitute cream – and doused everything in salt or sugar. Or sometimes both.

When Mam died, she left the house to me and Killian, but by then he was already settled in Tipperary and wasn't inclined to move back to Dublin. I wanted to stay in the house, so I took out a small mortgage and bought Killian's half of the house from him. That had been seven years earlier, and I was still paying it off.

Until a couple of years ago, I'd had a nice steady job as an assistant designer in a firm called Desire and Design, where we specialised in working with shop-fitters – we had some nice contracts with a few of the larger chain stores – and with wealthy people who wanted us to remodel their homes. I soon grew frustrated that I was never allowed to cut loose and do my own thing rather than fill in the details on someone else's designs, so I decided that I could do a lot better on my own.

I was dead wrong about that; I wasn't able to take on any small clients because it just wasn't cost-effective, and the large clients were just too much for a one-woman operation, as I found out the hard way. I was forced to close down my own company, but I wasn't able to go back to the old job, because I'd kind of said a few things I shouldn't have said when I left. Nor was I able to get a similar job elsewhere, because there were a lot of designers looking for work, and most of them didn't come with the stigma of a failed company.

I'd had a tough time paying the mortgage. It used to amuse me quite a bit when the threatening letters from the building society arrived at the same time as their junk mail that wanted to know if I had considered taking out a second mortgage on the property.

At least I had Des, though. I'd met him when he was working as a project manager for a large shop-fitting firm, and I was assigned to help out the senior designer. This meant that I'd had to spend quite a lot of time with Des, working out plans and costings, colour schemes and features, all the usual.

One day, just as the project was coming to an end, Des

held me back as a meeting was ending, and then asked, "How'd you like to come out for a drink tonight?"

I'd just come out of one of those short-term but intense relationships – the sort where you call each other three or four times a day for the first month, and then never want to even *hear* the other person's name again – so I wasn't sure. "Maybe some other time."

"Ah, go on. It'll do you good. Well, it'll do *me* good, I know that for sure."

"All right, then."

So we went out that night and had a pretty good time, but made no further plans. And then he phoned me out of the blue a few months later, we got together and within four months Des had moved in.

* * *

So that Monday evening, when Des got back from the office, I couldn't say anything that would give him a clue I knew about the attic plans.

"How was everything today?" I called down to him. I was in the spare bedroom, one foot on the ladder and the other on the windowsill as I applied my trusty scraper-'n'-damp-sponge combination to the more stubborn bits of wallpaper.

"Great," he called up. I heard him dump his briefcase in its usual place under the little table in the hall, then he clumped his way up the stairs to see me. "Yeah, it's great. We're very nearly there now. Remember when you were a kid and you were waiting for Christmas and it always seemed like it would *never* arrive, and then one day you

14

realise that Christmas is only a couple of days away? That's how it feels like now."

I knew exactly what he meant. I'd felt the same thing when I was redecorating the bathroom; it seemed to go on forever, until I suddenly realised that I only had about another day's work left on it. "So when do *you* get paid?" I asked Des.

"Pretty soon." This was one of the awkward things about his job: since very little money would change hands until all the contracts were signed, and since Des's role was administrative more than anything else, he wasn't actually employed by anyone, so he worked on commission. This meant that he'd only get paid when everyone else did.

He'd never actually said how much he was going to make, and I'd never asked, but I knew it was a *lot*. The total cost of the shopping centre had been estimated at just over twenty-four million euro. If Des only got one per cent of that, that was two hundred and forty thousand. But I suppose when you consider Des had spent the best part of three years working on the deal, it wasn't really *that* much.

But it was clearly going to be enough to cover the cost of doing the attic and getting the garden landscaped. Maybe there'd even be some cash left over to get the windows properly done.

He was right about it being like Christmas coming: ever since I'd had to shut down my company, we'd been getting by on a few small consultancy jobs Des had managed to get, plus my part-time job working in

Flanagan's Bistro and the evening art classes I'd been teaching in the local secondary school.

But now it seemed that Mr Claus had decided to put us on the "good" list: not only would Des soon be getting paid, but the following night – Tuesday – was enrolment for the new term. There would be fresh supplies of money coming in soon!

* * *

"So . . . what would I learn, then, exactly?"

I smiled up at the old man who was peering short-sightedly at the flyer. This was the fifth time in the past ten minutes that I'd had to answer that question.

We were in the assembly room of the local secondary school, enrolment night for the autumn term's evening classes. Potential students – most of whom were either retired or well on the way there – milled about, dithering between courses like "Computers for Beginners" and "Basic Car Maintenance".

I started to explain the nature of the course, but he interrupted me.

"Exactly what will I get for my money?" the old man asked.

That was a little more direct than I was used to. "Over the course of the – uh – the course, we'll start off with basic sketching and then move on to figure drawing and watercolours. That's two nights a week for twelve weeks."

"Yes, but . . . ." he tapped the flyer, "it says a hundred and twenty quid plus forty for supplies. What supplies would we need?"

"There's a couple of books, but mostly it's paper, pens and paint."

"And if we bring our own supplies, then we get the forty quid off?"

"Not really . . ."

He rattled his upper dentures about in a thoughtful manner. "It doesn't sound like it's for me, pet. Thanks anyway." He folded the flyer neatly and tucked it into his pocket, then headed over towards "Beginning Cross-stitch".

I wasn't that bothered about losing his custom; I'd learned from the previous enrolment evenings that a lot of people came along just to see what it was about and never signed up for anything. Besides, I already had twenty-two people signed up.

There was a lull at my table for a moment, so I had a look at the others. As always, the computer courses had filled up the quickest, though that didn't stop people from badgering the poor chap who taught them. Right now, he was in the middle of explaining the nature and purpose of a spreadsheet.

Across the room I spotted Peter Harney, owner of the local hardware store, whose "Restoring Old Furniture" class wasn't exactly swamped. Peter was in his early thirties, with skinny arms and huge hands. I didn't know him that well – I bought most of my redecorating paraphernalia at the larger chain stores – but Peter had worked with Des in the past and he'd always promised me that if anyone ever needed a designer he'd send them my way. He'd been saying that for a couple of years now and it still hadn't happened.

Peter spotted me looking at him, and held up his enrolment list. It had one name on it. He smiled and shrugged, then gave me a look that meant, "How many have you got?"

I showed him my list, and he came over. "I'm beginning to think I'm in the wrong business, Orla," he said. "I can't see myself teaching only one student."

"Maybe you should cut your rates," I said. "Or tell them that you'll give your students a discount in your shop."

"That's not a bad idea . . . What do you think? Five per cent?"

"Make it ten," I said. "Most of them here are pensioners, and they're already getting a good discount at B&Q."

"All right then. Ten it is." He walked back to his desk, cleared his throat and took a deep breath. In a loud, clear voice he said, "Can I have your attention, please? Thank you! As a special offer, anyone who signs up for my furniture restoration course will be entitled to a ten per cent discount at my store, Harney's Hardware, on the main street." Within seconds he was swamped with potential students.

Afterwards, Des came to pick me up – there was no way I was going to walk home with almost three thousand euro in cash and cheques – and we stopped to chat with Pete for a few moments.

"So how many did you get?" I asked.

"Fifteen. That's three times the number I started with last term."

"Do you have a high drop-out rate?" Des asked.

Pete snorted. "This time last year it was a hundred per cent after four weeks. How about you, Orla?"

18

"Usually about half of them make it through to the end."

"Still," Des said, "at least they pay up-front."

* * *

For the rest of the week, Des was in and out of the house quite a bit. Maybe it was because I was watching out for it, but it seemed to me that he was looking for reasons to visit every room in the house. And of course I couldn't say anything about it.

Early on Friday afternoon I started packing for the trip to Tipperary. Since Killian and Claire were real stay-at-home-and-watch-the-telly types, I didn't bother packing anything much. A spare pair of jeans, a couple of tops, a change of underwear, and that was pretty much it. There was certainly no point in packing any glamorous going-out clothes.

As I was finished up, Des wandered into the bedroom and said, "You know the coffee table in the sitting-room?"

"Yeah . . ."

"I was thinking that it could do with a new coat of varnish. It's looking pretty tatty."

I was tempted to say something along the lines of, "No, leave it. I like everything just the way it is," to see how he reacted, but I felt that would be just too cruel. Funny, but cruel. Instead, I said, "I know. But there's a few things with higher priority on my list. I'll get to it eventually."

"I thought you didn't much like varnishing?"

"I don't mind the varnishing at all. I just hate stripping off the *old* varnish."

Des looked out the window down to the back garden.

19

"We'll really have to give the shed a clear-out one of these days."

"Sure," I said. "I'll have a look through it when I get back on Monday. See if there's anything that can be thrown out."

He nodded, still looking out the window. It took me a couple of seconds to realise that he was waiting for me to go, so that he could get started on clearing the attic. For all I knew, there was van packed with builders around the corner, waiting for the "all clear" signal.

Des finally turned back to me. "So, do you have everything?"

"I think so. Money, keys, phone, clothes, presents for the kids."

"What did you get them?"

"A doll for Niamh, and a dinosaur for Sean. All boys like dinosaurs, right?"

"Probably, yeah. Are you sure you don't need a lift to the station?" He said that like he was hoping I'd say no.

"I'll be fine on the bus."

"What about work? Flanagan didn't give you any hassle about taking the weekend off?"

I shook my head. "No. Sure I'd already booked Sunday off." I worked Friday, Saturday and Sunday nights – and a couple of lunchtimes most weeks – in Flanagan's Bistro.

Then Des said, "I think I'll take the coffee table and the big chest of drawers down to Pete. He was saying yesterday that they've just had a big order delayed for a couple of weeks. He says that his lads are sitting around all day just reading the paper. He'll fix up anything we

LOOKING FOR MR WRONG

want just for cost. Unless you're really keen to do it yourself?"

"Sure it'll be years before I get the time to do it. No, I'm happy enough for someone else to do the work. I can tick it off the list then."

While I finished packing, Des loaded the coffee table and the chest of drawers into his van, and added a few old chairs.

He came back in as I was carrying my bag down to the hall. "Okay . . . I'll see you on Monday, then." He seemed a little nervous.

I smiled at him. I desperately wanted to tell him that I knew about his plans, and that he wasn't to worry; I trusted him not to put a swimming-pool in the kitchen. But of course I couldn't say anything – the surprise was the biggest part of the thing.

He wrapped his arms around me and give me a hug, then kissed the top of my head – he's eight inches taller than me – and said, "Have a good time, okay? I'll miss you."

"Oh, sure! I know you . . . you'll be too busy working to even think about me."

"That's not true." He stepped back. "Okay . . . I'd better get this stuff down to Pete's place, then I'm off to the site." He kissed me good-bye, and I stood in the doorway, watching him go.

I had a few minutes before I had to leave for the bus, so I went up to the spare bedroom to get my stepladder, but – naturally – it was downstairs, so I dragged a chair from the junk room out to the landing, climbed up onto it and was about to push open the trapdoor into the attic

21

when I spotted all the dust and cobwebs on it. I stopped: I'd wanted to peer into the attic to see how it looked, but if Des noticed that the trapdoor had been opened, then he'd know I'd been up there, and he'd know that I knew about the surprise.

So I got back down and put the chair away, and instead had a wander through the rest of the house, wondering about the other surprises Claire told me Des had planned.

It was a pretty big house, and would probably be worth a fortune when I'd finished doing it up. It was about eighty years old. Just as I'd inherited it from my mother, she'd inherited it from *her* parents, who had been very well-off but somehow hadn't managed to save any money.

I guess in that sense they were just like my parents, and me. Though the reason that I didn't have any real savings now was because I'd sunk so much into the company and into the renovations. Now, I made just enough from working in the bistro and from teaching the classes to cover the mortgage and pay the bills, with a little left over.

But my grand plan, you see, was that when I'd fully restored the house I'd sell it for lots of money and buy another old, rundown house and do the same. I figured that if I spent three or four years working on the house, restoring, repairing and repainting, I'd increase its value by at least a hundred thousand euro, possibly a lot more. It would be a lot of work, but the alternative was to quit the restaurant and get a nine-to-five job somewhere else, and I didn't want to do that. It wasn't that I was mad about spending pretty much every weekend waiting tables in the restaurant, but I only had to do three lunch-shifts a week and I liked having my mornings off.

When I got to the gate, I turned back and took one last look at the house as it was. I couldn't help smiling: the conversion of the attic would be another major piece of work done, one of the most difficult. In a way, I felt a little sad that I wouldn't actually be doing the work myself, but then my carpentry skills didn't go much beyond putting up shelves, so if it had been left to me it might never have been done.

I slung my bag over my shoulder and headed towards the bus stop.

I never saw Des again.

Chapter 2

So I spent the weekend with my brother and his family. It was okay, certainly not as bad as it could have been. The kids were on pretty good behaviour. On more than one previous visit I'd had the misfortune of witnessing them tearing lumps out of each other, screeching at the top of their voices and throwing toys about, while Claire and Killian made rather pathetic attempts to appeal to reason: "Niamh . . .! What would your friends think if they saw you behaving like that?" "Now, Sean! Haven't have I told you before about trying to poke your sister in the eye with a fork?"

My own instinct in such situations was to follow my mother's example and dispense justice at the business end of a wooden spoon, but since physical punishment had never worked on Killian, he hadn't seen the point of introducing the concept into his own home.

Killian and I had never really been close. He's a couple of years older than me and I don't think he ever got over the horror of learning that he was going to have a little sister – my mother once told me that he'd been holding out hope for a brother, or, even better, a puppy. Apparently he sulked for weeks after I finally appeared, but that was more because my mother gave him hell for speculating on whether I'd land on my feet like a cat if he dropped me off the roof of the shed.

My mother also once told me that I'd learned to walk earlier than any other child she'd ever met, and that was because it was faster to run away from Killian than to crawl away from him.

Not that he was completely responsible for the animosity between us; I'm sure I take at least half the blame. I'd learned very early that I could get away with almost anything by accusing Killian. My parents copped on pretty quickly, but that didn't stop me from trying.

It wouldn't be true to say that as we grew up Killian and I fought like proverbial cats and dogs – that would have taken too much effort. Instead, we did our best to avoid each other unless it was absolutely necessary. So we kept out of each other's way, like, well, like *actual* cats and dogs.

And it's not that Killian was a bully or anything, he was just a loner. He'd never had too many close friends, and that suited him. He liked to do his own thing in his own way, and since other people tended to want things *their* own way, Killian quickly decided that other people were usually more trouble than they were worth.

But that changed, for a while, when we reached our teenage years. When my friends called over to the house Killian would make excuses to talk to me, usually about something fairly neutral, so that we wouldn't fight. I knew he was only doing it so that he could check out my friends, but that's okay because I did the same when his friends were over.

When he was about seventeen, Killian came to the conclusion that girls liked men who could fix things, so whenever me and my friends were sitting in the front garden, Killian would reverse Mam's old car out of the garage, open up the bonnet and rub his hands all over the engine to get them nice and greasy. He'd poke about a bit, examine things like he knew what he was doing, then start the car up, make a frowny face, take out the spark plugs and pretend to "adjust" them somehow, plug them back in and start up the car again, then look at it with a satisfied expression, as though he'd managed to iron out a particularly difficult problem.

He performed this sort of trick several times until it backfired, in more ways than one: he fiddled with some part of the engine that he shouldn't have, started up the car and then a few minutes later – "bang!" – a huge cloud of white smoke, followed by "clang!" as the exhaust fell off, then "rattle" as a few other bits decided to abandon the car, then "Oh crap" as Killian realised how much trouble he was in. This was almost immediately followed by "Aaah!" when he crawled under the car to pick up the exhaust and discovered that it was hot, and "bang" again, as he hit his head on the underside of the car, and "Shit!" when he realised that we were all watching.

And if that wasn't bad enough, when he finally did crawl back out me and my friends gave him a round of applause, and Davina, the one he fancied the most – even though he ended up marrying Claire – said: "That was great! Do it again!"

* * *

Most of the weekend I spent chatting with Claire – we did the usual thing when we got together, which was talk about our schooldays and speculate on what had happened to everyone – but on Sunday evening, while Claire was putting the kids to bed, Killian came into the sitting-room and settled himself down. He asked me how the job was working out, which redecorating task I was currently undertaking, if there was any news, and that seemed to exhaust all the safe topics of conversation.

Claire joined us and Killian moved onto the unsafe topics . . . he asked me how Des was getting on.

"He's fine. Working like crazy these days, but you know him, he's only happy when he's got lots to do."

Killian nodded. "Yeah . . . Listen, I hate to bring this up . . ."

I knew what he was going to say: a couple of years before, Des had managed to persuade Killian to invest quite heavily in the new shopping centre. Or to be more accurate, to invest in the land on which the shopping centre would be built. "Land," Des had said, "is *always* going to increase in value. Stocks and shares rise and fall, companies come and go, but people will always need land."

Des had organised a consortium of investors, Killian included, to buy up the land from the farmer who originally owned it. After a few months, the land was sold on to a single investor, some old woman who was apparently rolling in money. All the investors made a nice little profit and were very happy with themselves.

This was before the plans for the shopping centre were unveiled; as soon as they were, the value of the land more than doubled overnight. This did not make the original consortium of investors very happy, since Des had known about the plans all along. They maintained that he should have told them what he was up to; they'd have been willing to hold out longer if they'd known that they could have made an even bigger profit.

Des tried to explain to them that they'd known from the start that this was a short-term investment. But if they wanted to invest in the shopping centre itself, he could organise that.

This was how Killian invested the money I'd given him for his half of our parents' house.

After a few months, Killian started to get anxious about all his money being tied up in something on which construction hadn't even started yet. He phoned Des and said, "I've had second thoughts. I'd like to withdraw my investment."

Des had told him, "You can't. If you pull out, we won't be able to go ahead until we can find someone to replace you. And besides, the other investors might get edgy. Then where would we be?" He assured Killian that it would all work out fine in the end; he just had to be patient.

Killian had insisted, but Des was a lot better at this sort of thing and easily out-insisted him. "Killian, you signed the contract, you knew this was a long-term outlay. Trust me, okay?" So Killian contacted a few of the other investors and claimed that Des was just sitting on their money, collecting the interest and not bothering to actually do anything about it.

This of course led to some animosity between them, with me stuck in the middle.

And here we were, once again having that same conversation. "You want to know when you can expect to get your money back?" I asked Killian.

"Yeah."

"I don't know. You'd have to ask Des. But the contracts are being finalised this weekend, so it shouldn't be too long now."

"Look, the fact is I don't trust him. He's already screwed us over once before."

"Oh, give it a rest, Killian! He did *not* screw you over!"

"He knew we could have made a lot more money if we'd held onto the land, but he sold it to someone else. I don't know what *you* call that, but I call it 'screwing us over'."

I turned away from him and stared at the television. "I'm not talking about this."

"Well, Des never bothers to return my phone calls! Who else am I supposed to talk to about it?"

"He never returns your phone calls because you only ever call when you get into a panic about your money."

Killian said nothing for a while; he just stared at me. Out of the corner of my eye, I could see Claire biting her lip; it seemed to me that she didn't know whether to step in and take someone's side, or to leave the room and let us get on with the fight.

Then Killian sighed, and said, "Orla, I just don't trust him."

"So you keep saying."

"I mean it. One day it's all going to blow up in your face and don't think you can come running to me for help."

"When have I ever come to you for *anything*?"

"I don't know what you see in that lad, I really don't. What about Justin? He was mad about you, but you never gave him the time of day."

"You don't know anything! Justin was *not* mad about me!"

"He was, you know. He was totally in love with you, that's why he was always hanging around. But did you even notice? No, of course you didn't! There you were, spending loads of time with him and thinking, 'Wow, I'm so grown up! I have a friend who's a boy and there's nothing going on between us!' Well, you were fooling yourself."

I said nothing for a few seconds: Killian was right about how I'd felt about Justin when we were growing up – there *had* been something cool about having a male friend with no pressure or sexual tension – but he was wrong about Justin being in love with me. Justin only saw me as a friend. I knew that because a long time ago I'd asked *him* out and he'd declined.

I finally looked back at Killian. "So . . . that's out of the way. Now you have to go on to phase three."

"Phase three?"

"Go on. First you pick on Des, then you tell me your theories about Justin. Next you have to tell me that it's about time I got a *real* job again and did something with my life. After that, you have to complain that I'm tearing the house apart and destroying its character, and that Mam and Dad would be ashamed of the way I'm treating the place if they were still alive. And *then* you have to bring up Des again, and tell me that if Dad was alive he'd never have tolerated Des in the house in the first place."

Killian gritted his teeth and turned away from me.

"That's the way the conversation usually goes, Killian. Ever since me and Des started going out, that's how it's been with you. Nothing I do is *ever* good enough, is it? For God's sake, I'm twenty-seven – today! – and you still treat me like I'm twelve."

He put on his calming, understanding voice, which he knew infuriated me, and said, "Orla, it's not that. You had a really great job and you just walked away from it, and now what are you doing? Teaching night classes to OAPs and waiting on tables. I just don't think you're making the most of your life."

"That doesn't mean you have to try to organise it for me! It's not like your own life is that much better, is it?"

As soon as the words were out, I went, "uh oh" to myself, and had a little panic attack.

Okay, so I'm not the world's foremost authority on social graces, but if there's one thing I know, it's that you don't insult someone's life when you're sitting on their sofa, in their house, next to their wife, with their kids upstairs in bed.

"What do you mean by that?"

"I *mean*," I said, drawing the word out as long as possible to give me time to think of something, "that nobody's life is perfect. So okay, it *was* a mistake to leave the job and set up my own company, but at least I took the chance."

"Oh, there it is! See what I was telling you about, Claire?

31

The famous Orla back-pedalling! You never believed me, but there you are! She says the wrong thing and desperately tries to cover it up!"

"Just keep me out of this," Claire said, in a tone that very much suggested we'd both better shut up soon or there'd be hell to pay. I knew that this sort of thing was hard on her; it wasn't fair to expect her to choose sides between her husband and her oldest friend.

Killian said, "Look, Orla . . . I'm only saying that I don't trust Des, and I don't think you should either."

We more or less left it at that, but neither of us would look at the other for the rest of the evening. It was just like being a kid again.

* * *

After Claire brought the kids to school the next morning, she gave me a lift to the station. "Let me know how the attic turns out," she said as she pulled up just past an empty parking spot, "and the rest of it, whatever he's been up to."

"I just hope he hasn't done anything too drastic."

Claire craned her neck so she could see behind as she reversed into the spot. "I'm sure he hasn't. He has pretty good taste, doesn't he?"

"I suppose."

"And he said that he was going to stick closely to your designs."

She walked me in to the station, and waited with me until it was time to get on the train. "Look, I wouldn't worry too much about the things Killian was saying last night. He's just very protective of you, you know? He always has been."

"I know. But sometimes I wish he'd be supportive instead of protective. He's not like that with Sean and Niamh, is he? Finding fault with everything they do?"

"No, not at all," she said, but I got the feeling that she wasn't as sure about that as she sounded. "Anyway, it was a good weekend apart from that, right?"

I nodded. "It was."

"Give me a call when you get home, okay?"

I promised I would. I lugged my bag onto the train, found a seat, and settled down.

* * *

The taxi driver dropped me outside the gate. He'd been chatty and friendly all the way from the station, so I gave him a generous tip that I later very much regretted.

The first thing I noticed that was different about the house was that there were no curtains in the upstairs windows. And then I spotted that there were no curtains in the downstairs windows either.

I was a bit disappointed: whatever Des had been up to, it wasn't quite finished yet.

Then I saw that the front door was slightly open. I dumped my bag in the empty hall and called out, "Hello?"

There was no answer.

I had a look around the hall. The carpet had been taken up, and the little table and the coat rack were gone. The door to the sitting-room had been taken off its hinges, so I could see right into the room . . . The carpet had been taken up there, too. All of the furniture was missing, and the room seemed absolutely enormous. Even the pictures on the walls were gone, leaving behind their rectangular ghosts on the old wallpaper.

The wallpaper. That was my first real clue. The old wallpaper was intact. Why would someone take all the pictures off the wall if they weren't going to redecorate? I went into the room, my footsteps echoing on the bare boards.

Everything had been taken out of the room, but no actual decorating had been done, or even started.

The rational part of my brain tried to tell me that they'd just run out of time, and that the rest of the work would be finished soon enough.

But there was no smell of paint, no smell of fresh timber.

I went back out to the hall, and called, "Hello?" again. And again, no reply, except a faint echo of my voice.

The carpet was gone from the stairs, so my shoes made loud clunking noises as I went up. No carpet or pictures in the landing, no doors on most of the rooms. And there were no decorator's ladders, or paint buckets, or rolls of wallpaper. No sawdust or little slivers of timber, no discarded nails or used-up sheets of sandpaper.

The trapdoor to the attic was closed over – I'd been expecting a brand-new narrow staircase leading up. But at least someone had been in the attic: the dust and cobwebs were gone. I went into the smallest bedroom, the one we used as a junk room, to get the chair so that I could check out the attic. But there was no chair in the room. There was no *junk* in it either. There was also no light fitting or light switch.

My bedroom . . . no curtains, no wardrobes, no chests of drawers, no bookcase, no bed.

The other bedroom. On Friday it had contained my filing cabinet, a desk and chair, my easel, and hundreds of drawings and paintings. Now, it was empty.

With growing fear, I checked the rest of the house.

Everything – and I mean *everything*, from the cutlery to the curtains, from the television to the toaster, from the linoleum to the light bulbs – everything I owned was gone.

Chapter 3

My mind went into overdrive . . .

There's a perfectly reasonable explanation. There has to be.

The builders and decorators ran out of time.

All the stuff has been taken out so that it won't get splashed with paint and covered with sawdust.

All my clothes have been taken to the dry-cleaner's.

Everything's been put into the garage – but I knew instantly that that one couldn't be true: the garage had been packed with junk for years. You'd have had a hard time squeezing an empty envelope in there, let alone a houseful of furniture.

But I checked anyway, and the garage was as empty as the rest of the house, as was the ancient shed in the back garden.

For a few seconds I even got as far as wondering whether I was in the *right* house.

I went back to the hall to phone Des, but the phone wasn't there. Even the socket had been removed.

Then – rather later than it should – the thought occurred to me that the house had been burgled. My stomach suddenly felt as though I'd swallowed ten pounds of ball-bearings. My skin became cold and clammy, and an involuntary shudder ran up between my shoulder blades.

Someone had been in my house. Going through my things. Someone had broken in and taken everything they could see.

But then that didn't seem right. Who ever heard of burglars taking the entire contents of a house? The telly and DVD player I could understand, but the carpets? The toaster? The pile of junk mail that had been building up on the hall table?

My clothes were gone. Most of them I didn't care that much about, but what about the Miu Miu dress that I'd spent months saving up for? I hadn't even had a chance to wear it yet – I'd been saving it for the Big Night Out that Des had promised me when all the contracts had been signed.

And the gorgeous Ermanno Scervino corset top that a client had given me as a thank-you present, my second-hand-but-don't-let-on Versace boots, tops by La Perla and Temperley and Pelicos, a winter coat by Mills & Wagner, a genuine SolarWind clutch purse – very collectible and worth a small fortune – my Linea coat and top, which weren't very expensive but I loved them.

But worst of all . . . my one-of-a-kind hand-made Piefjé shoes! Okay, so they were a nightmare to wear and more suited to an Italian catwalk than the streets of Dublin, and they didn't go with anything, but they were gorgeous and delicate and perfect. And absolutely irreplaceable; not only did Geraldo Piefjé never make two pairs the same, but he'd actually retired from the fashion scene.

Not to mention all my underwear! I didn't want to think about where all that might have ended up.

And now all I owned was one pair of ordinary summer shoes, two pairs of jeans, two tops, a T-shirt, two sets of underwear, and my ultra-light summer jacket. Most of which needed to be washed.

As I stood in the kitchen looking at the spot where the washing machine used to be, I heard a strange banging sound, and my first thought was that the burglars were still somewhere inside the house.

Then I realised that the banging was coming from the front door.

I went out to the hall and opened the door, to see my next-door neighbour, known to everyone in the area as Old Mr Farley, looking at me with a disappointed expression.

Before I could say anything, he said, "After all these years, the *least* you could have done was let me know you were moving!"

"But –"

He interrupted me. "I come home on Friday evening to see that bloody great removals van outside."

"Mr Farley . . . what happened here?"

"Pardon?"

I stepped aside and ushered him into the hall. "Look," I said. "Everything is gone. You're saying that there was a *removals van*?"

"Yes. Huge great big white thing. They loaded it up and came back on Saturday morning for the rest of it, and again in the afternoon. Three trips it took them. And where were you?"

"I was staying with my brother and his family. Look, all I knew was that Des had organised to have some work done while I was away. I wasn't supposed to know about that, though. This was meant to be a surprise."

Mr Farley went into the sitting-room, and stood there looking around. "My God, they got *everything*!"

"I *know* . . . Who were they?"

"You really didn't know about this?"

"No!"

He scratched at his white beard. "Orla, I think you'd better phone the police."

I took my mobile phone out of my jeans pocket. "I'd better phone Des first."

Mr Farley looked at me. "It probably won't do any good. He was with them. I mean, he was here when the removals men were carrying the stuff out on Friday." He looked around again. "What about upstairs?"

I swallowed. "Apart from the bathroom fittings, it's all gone."

"Phone the gardaí, Orla. And don't touch anything."

I phoned Des. There was no answer on his mobile, so I left a message asking him to call me back as soon as he could. Then I phoned his office, but there was no answer there either. That wasn't unusual, though, because he was rarely there.

"I'm telling you, phone the gardaí," Mr Farley said.

"No, there has to be a reasonable explanation."

"Such as?"

I paused. "I don't know."

* * *

Two members of the gardaí arrived about fifteen minutes later. They wandered through every room of the house and agreed that everything was, indeed, missing.

"So what am I going to do?" I asked as we stood in the kitchen. Mr Farley had offered to wait with me, but I'd told him I'd be fine, which was more blind optimism than it was a lie.

They looked blankly at me, then one of them shrugged. "Have you tried to get in touch with your boyfriend?"

"Yes. There's no answer."

"I'm sure he'll be able to explain everything."

The other one said, "Look, Miss Adare . . . I wouldn't worry if I was you. Just sit down and have a cup of tea and before you know it he'll be back."

I stared at him. "Okay. Pass me the kettle."

He turned around, and then around again. "Ah."

"No kettle," I said. "And even if there was, there's no tea, no cups, no milk. And where am I supposed to sit down? On the toilet? Every single thing I own is gone. Now, maybe I'm wrong, but isn't that unusual?"

"I suppose you're right there."

They looked at me with expressions that were even blanker than before.

"What should I do?" I asked. Then, when no answer was forthcoming, I said, "You don't know, do you?"

"Er, no." said the first one. "Never seen anything like this before."

"Look," said the other one, "you have to try and get hold of your boyfriend and see if he has anything to say for himself."

"And suppose I can't find him?"

"Then . . ." He faltered, and glanced at his colleague. "Insurance?"

"Oh, yeah! You're insured, right?"

"Yes," I said. "Now if only I could find the insurance forms, I'd know the procedure to follow, and who to call. I keep all that sort of thing in a drawer in the desk that used to be upstairs." I could feel myself starting to get hysterical. "But even if I can't find the forms, then I could ask Des who to call, couldn't I? He's the one who organised it all. But, no, I can't do that, because he's gone too, isn't he?"

Again, they exchanged awkward glances.

"So what are the chances that he was the one behind all this?" I asked. "That's what you're thinking about, isn't it? That I've been completely ripped off by Des and that the insurance money probably never got any further than his own bank account, right?" Then I paused. "Oh shit. the bank account . . . we have a joint account. All our money is in there."

The first garda looked at me with an expression that seemed to me to be saying: "You mean, all your money *was* in there."

"You'd want to check with your bank, then," his colleague said. "It's a joint account?"

"Yeah. It's . . . No, it should be okay, because we arranged it so that if we wanted to withdraw more than a couple of hundred they had to have both our signatures."

41

"I'd check with them anyway," he said. "Just in case."

* * *

After the gardaí left, I spent a few minutes going through the house, wondering what I was going to do.

Part of me was convinced that this was some sort of horrible dream. There was no way this could really have happened. I'd wake up in bed with Des snoring next to me, and everything would be fine. I'd tell him about my dream, and he'd laugh, the way he always did when I related my nightmares, and I'd get a little annoyed at him because he never seemed to be bothered by bad dreams so he couldn't understand how powerful they could be.

But this *wasn't* a dream. Everything was gone.

I had to find Des, that was the right thing to do. Find him – he'll be down at the site, arguing with the architects or someone – and he'll be as surprised about all this as I am, and he'll take me in his arms and tell me that everything would turn out all right.

Even as I was thinking that, I knew the truth; Des would not be at the site. I wouldn't be able to find him. No one would know where he was.

Before I closed the front door behind me, I looked down at my bag, and wondered if that too would be gone when I got back.

That was the most horrible thing about the situation: everything I now owned was in a small blue sports bag. Aside from the house, of course, but I wouldn't really own that until I'd paid off the mortgage.

The sun was shining and the sky was a deep azure, speckled with white fluffy clouds, as I walked into town.

That annoyed the hell out of me; how *dare* the weather be nice on a day like this? It was like some meteorological conspiracy, as though the world didn't want anyone else to be miserable, only me.

Des had rented a small office in town, over the butcher shop. There was no answer when I rang the buzzer, but that wasn't surprising because he rarely spent much time there. Still, I decided I'd go in and check it out anyway.

I didn't have a key, so I went into the butcher's and up to the counter.

"Afternoon, Orla," said Mrs O'Toole, the octogenarian butcher. She was a pleasant, smiling woman with white hair, huge forearms and a permanently blood-stained apron. "The usual?" she asked, reaching for the sausages.

"No . . . Listen, have you seen Des at all today?"

She had a little think. "No, not today."

"You couldn't lend us the key for upstairs, could you?"

"Hold on, pet," she said, then opened the till and rooted through the change until she found the key. She'd once told Des that she kept the spare keys in with the coins because no burglar would ever think of looking for a key there. "There you are now."

I went back outside, unlocked the door and went up to the office, half expecting to find it completely empty.

It wasn't *completely* empty, but the expensive stuff was gone: the computer, printer and photocopier.

There was no doubt in my mind any more that Des had, to use an old phrase, "done a runner". If the office had been intact, I could have convinced myself that maybe Des really had planned to convert the attic and do a bit of redecorating in the house, that he'd taken everything out for safe-keeping, and then something had happened, like he'd been run over by a truck or had a heart attack.

I checked his desk drawer, and wasn't surprised to see that the cheque books were gone.

At least the phone was still there – though that seemed to be because it was a huge, clunky, old-fashioned thing that he wouldn't easily have been able to sell to someone else. I picked it up and phoned the gardaí again. When I explained who I was, the desk sergeant put me on to one of the policemen who'd been at the house earlier.

"Miss Adare, . . . any luck finding your boyfriend?"

"No," I said. "I'm at his office now, and I'm pretty sure he's gone for good. There's a lot of stuff missing from here too."

"I see."

"So where do I go from here?"

He paused. "Look, right now it's still early days. I mean, as for what happened in your own house, well, there's no signs of forced entry, so we can't treat it as a burglary."

"All my stuff is gone! If that's not a burglary, I don't know what is!"

"Well now, you see, the thing is, okay, Mr Mills was living in your house, so he had full access to everything. And you were saying that he'd planned to do some work, right? So right now we can't be sure that a crime has actually been committed."

I took a deep breath and counted to ten, in order that I wouldn't completely lose my temper and swear at him. "All right . . . but supposing that he *has* disappeared. There's every reason to suspect that he's also taken all the money that was invested for the shopping-centre project."

He paused again. "I see. Well, that would be a different matter, then. That would be grand larceny."

"Oh, so you'll do something if he'd committed *grand* larceny, but you won't do anything if it's just . . . just . . ." I tried to think of the opposite of "grand" but somehow I got a mental image of a piano and the only opposite I could come up with was "upright" ". . . if it's just *ordinary* larceny? You're more interested in protecting the interests of rich businessmen than normal people, is that it?"

"Now, there's no need to take that sort of tone, Miss Adare. We can only operate within the bounds of the law."

"Then he's one step ahead of you there, isn't he?"

He ignored that. "What you have to do now is wait. If he's missing for forty-eight hours, we can start to treat it as suspicious. Then we'll see if anything happens from there. You've tried his mobile phone, right?"

"Of course." I had an idea. "You people can track that, can't you? I mean, I saw it on a documentary, how you can find someone by using their mobile phone."

"Well, to a degree, yes, it can be done. But again it's only in extreme situations. I wouldn't be sure that this calls for it. And if he *has* left, then it's very likely he'll have thrown away his phone."

"Should I get myself a solicitor or something?"

"That might help."

I raised my eyes. This guy was so casual about everything that I couldn't believe it. "How am I supposed to live in the meantime? I can't stay at the house, because there's no bed. I don't even have a chair I can sit in."

"Surely you have friends that you can stay with?"

"Yeah, but I shouldn't *have* to."

45

The garda didn't seem to have any further opinions, but he did promise to let me know "if anything turned up". Whatever that meant. It didn't seem likely that Des would realise the error of his ways and come back with all my stuff.

I sat down in his swivel-chair and had a good think . . .

Supposing that Des really has absconded with all my money as well as all my stuff . . .what do I have to do?

Cancel the credit cards, that's for starters. And check with the bank, see if the account is intact. If it isn't, then I'm really screwed.

The money for the mortgage was automatically taken out of my account every month, and it had just been paid, so that meant I was okay on that front for at least a couple of weeks. But I was going to have to get some more money from somewhere.

I'd already lodged the money from the night classes, so if the account was empty, that was gone too. That meant I still had to teach twelve weeks of classes for no money.

And all the supplies for the classes were in the spare room, I said to myself. How am I supposed to tell the students that they're not going to have the supplies they've paid for?

I could ask Mr Flanagan at the bistro for more work. Technically I was only working part-time – nine hours a night on Fridays, Saturdays and Sundays – but I almost always did a few extra hours a week during lunch-times. There really wasn't that much more work available.

Thinking about work made me realise that my uniform – white top, black skirt – had been in the now-missing wardrobe at home, along with all the rest of my clothes.

"Shit!" I said out loud, "The bastard even took all the stuff belonging to Mam and Dad!"

I started to mentally go through the house, the way it had been on the previous Friday, and figure out exactly what was missing, but I stopped after a couple of minutes, because it was too depressing.

Instead, I locked up the office, snuck past the butcher's shop so I wouldn't have to hand back the key just yet, and went down the street and across the road to the bank. They were just about to close as I arrived.

The young man on the Customer Inquiries desk tried to get me to queue up for a cashier, but I wasn't having any of it, so he took my details and checked the account. "There's nothing in it."

I swore. "I *knew* it. I'm going to rip that bastard's heart out through his arse!"

The young man looked up. "I'm sorry?"

"Nothing. Okay, I need to speak to your branch manager."

"I'm afraid she's not in today."

"Well, the manager on duty, then."

He considered this. "I'm afraid that the manager on duty isn't here at the moment."

"God, give me strength!" I muttered. "Okay then . . . is there anything you *can* do?"

"I'm afraid I can't do much without authorisation."

"Scare easily, don't you?"

"I'm sorry?"

"And you apologise a lot . . . never mind. I want to make an appointment to speak with whichever manager is on duty tomorrow morning, can you arrange that?"

"You'd be better off phoning first, make sure she's available."

I gave in. "Okay, okay. I'll do that."

* * *

I went back to Des's office, not because I wanted to be there particularly, but because apart from the stairs and the toilet at home it was the only place I had to sit down.

There was something I had to do, aside from track down Des and make him regret everything he'd done. And aside from figure out where I was going to sleep tonight, or how I was ever going to get my life back on track.

I looked at the phone . . . I knew I had no choice but to get it over with.

I phoned my brother.

Chapter 4

After about ten rings, Claire answered the phone. "Hello?"

"Hi, it's me," I said.

"Hi! So? Tell me everything! What's the place look like?"

"Oh, you wouldn't recognise it," I said.

"So you're pleased with it?"

"That's not the word I'd use, no."

She could tell that something was up. "Oh. Is everything all right?"

"Not really. Is Killian there?"

"Yeah, hold on."

After a couple of seconds, Killian came to the phone. "What's up?"

I swallowed. "You were right. About Des, I mean."

"Shit. What happened?"

I started to tell him, but I just couldn't get the words out.

"Orla?"

"He's gone."

"How do you mean, gone? You broke up?"

"In a way, yeah . . . Look, what happened was that I came home and the house was empty. And I mean *empty*. The bastard even took some of the internal doors. There's absolutely nothing left. And I just checked with the bank, and he's cleaned out our account as well."

He swore. A lot. When he'd calmed down a little, he asked, "Did you go to the police?"

"Yeah, but there's not much they can do right now. Not until they're sure he's missing."

"And you're certain that this isn't some stupid joke he's playing on you?"

I hadn't thought of that at all. "I don't think so, but if it is, I'll kill him for this."

"Look, tell me again. You got home . . . ?"

"I got home and the first thing I noticed was that the curtains were gone. Then I went in, and . . . Killian, there's nothing left. *Nothing*. Not even the carpets. He's even taken some of the light fittings out. The whole place has been stripped bare."

"What about all your clothes and stuff?"

"Didn't you hear me? It's all gone."

He paused. "This is a wind-up, right?"

"No, I'm serious. And it's my bet he's stolen all the money invested in the shopping centre too. Or as much of it as he could get his hands on. So that means that you're probably not going to see *your* money again."

"Bastard! I'm going to murder that fucker!"

"Join the club."

50

"Shit! *Shit*!" There was a lot more like this. I let him rant and rave, until he said, "I bloody *told* you he was no good, didn't I?"

I gritted my teeth. "Yes. You told me. You might recall that the first thing I said to you when you came to the phone was that you were right."

"That lousy rat-bastard! I *knew* he was no good! But you wouldn't listen to me, would you? If you had, this would never have happened."

I did my best to remain calm. "That's perfect, Killian. That's just exactly the attitude I need right now. I've been betrayed by the man I thought loved me, I've had everything I own stolen, but what was really missing from my life was the feeling that this was all *my* fault."

He paused for a long time, presumably while he was trying to make up his mind whether to apologise. "What are you going to do?"

"I have no idea. If I can't find somewhere to sleep tonight, I'm just going to have to stay here. I'm calling from his office."

"What do you mean, if you can't find somewhere to sleep? You'll be safe enough in the house. It's not like he's going to come back."

"Thanks," I said.

"I didn't mean it like that."

"I know . . . Look, I can't stay in the house because there's no bed. There's not even any chairs."

"What about Dad's armchair? That's gone too?"

"Yeah."

"How about the old furniture in the garage?"

51

"Listen, let's save a bit of time, okay? I'll list out everything that's left." I paused for about a second. "Want to hear it again?"

"Fuck! All the stuff we grew up with!"

"I know."

"I mean, all the ornaments and everything. Sure, they were crap and we hated them, but even so, they're part of our childhood."

"I *know*."

Then, very quietly, he said, "They were all we had left of Mam and Dad."

"Apart from the house itself, yeah. You're right."

"Jesus, if I ever get hold of that bastard I'm going to hit the fucker so hard his *ancestors* will feel it!" Another pause. "For Christ's sake, Orla! How could you not *know* he was like that? What the hell were you thinking? How could you let this happen?"

"As a matter of fact, you stupid bastard, it's mostly *your* fault."

His voice rose another octave. "How do you mean? How could it be *my* fault?"

"It isn't. I just wanted you to know how it felt to be blamed for something you had no control over."

He sighed. "Okay. Point taken. I'm sorry."

I almost said, "You're *what*?": an apology from Killian wasn't something I could ever remember experiencing before.

"Do you want me to drive up? I can be there in about four hours."

"Thanks, but there's no point. And there's nowhere for you to sleep, anyway."

52

"You can come back here with me, stay with us until we get this sorted out."

"I don't think it's going to *be* sorted out," I said. "No, I'd better stay here, at least until the gardaí have started their investigation. I suppose it's possible that they'll find him. Or maybe they'll find some of my stuff. Anyway, I've got a class starting tomorrow night. Look, I'll phone Justin and Mags, see if they can put me up in the spare room. I suppose I could ask Pauline at the restaurant, but I know she doesn't have much room. Listen, you remember when you were about, I don't know, eighteen or nineteen, and Mam's car got broken into?"

"Yeah."

"Well, you were really pissed off about it, and you said something along the lines of: 'If the cops can't find who did it, I know someone who can.' Remember that? I know that Claire was around at the time so you were probably just trying to impress her by letting on you knew some hard cases, but still . . . did you really know someone, or was that just bullshit?"

"Sorry. That was just bullshit. I wouldn't even know where to start." He sighed again. "I can't figure it out. I mean, a lot of the stuff he could probably sell, but the *carpets*? Most of them were like twenty years old and all faded. What's the point of that? Who in their right mind would want to buy old carpets?"

"I don't know. I haven't been able to figure out that one myself."

"Maybe he thought that there was money hidden under the floorboards, or something. Did any of the boards seem loose?"

"Not that I noticed."

After another long pause, he said, "Look, you could just sell the place. A house that size is probably worth about three hundred grand these days, right? Maybe more, because of the work you've already done. So you sell it and buy a smaller place. There's no point in hanging on to it if all our stuff isn't there any more."

"Yeah, but in the meantime how am I supposed to live?"

"You've still got your job at the restaurant, right?"

"True, but my uniform is gone, and I can't afford to replace it. I have twenty-two euro and a handful of change. That's got to last me until after Sunday night's shift when I get paid. That's a week. And you know what makes it even worse? I got a taxi home from the station because I couldn't be arsed to wait for a bus, and I gave the taxi driver a tenner as a tip, because he was so nice."

"Okay, first thing in the morning I'll go to the bank and transfer some money into your account."

"Thanks, but don't do that just yet. I want to close the account first, just in case."

"All right . . . I'll tell you what. If you can't find someone to stay with tonight, find a B&B that takes credit cards, then phone me and I'll give them my card number."

"I hope it won't come to that, but thanks."

We both paused, then I said, "Killian, I am so sorry about this. I know it was a lot of money."

"It wasn't your fault. There wasn't any way you could have known. Give me a call later on and let me know your plans, okay? Or I'll phone you."

I gave him the number of Des's office. "There's probably

no point in phoning my mobile," I said. "I'm going to turn it off. It needs to be recharged soon, and, well, I don't have a charger any more."

"What about, like, toothpaste and stuff?"

"I've got my toothbrush and toothpaste, because I brought them with me. But that's pretty much all I do have. There isn't even any toilet paper. The house is completely bare. It's like a kleptomaniac tornado swept through the place."

* * *

Once I said good-bye to Killian, I phoned Justin's house. He and I had been great friends when we were growing up, and still met up every couple of weeks. Justin was married to Mags; I didn't know her quite as well as Justin, but we'd always got on pretty well. She was a teacher at the local primary school, and when I was forced to shut down my company it was Mags who came up with the idea of me teaching evening classes.

The phone was answered on the eighth ring, just as I was about to give up.

"Hello?" Mags said.

"Hi, Mags. It's Orla."

"Oh, hi."

"Listen, is Justin there?"

"No, he's off on his travels again." Justin was a rep for a chain of shoe shops; he and I used to have many long and interesting discussions about shoes, until Mags told us to stop it because she found it a little disconcerting. "He probably won't be back until Thursday."

"Okay, never mind. Will you just let him know I called?"

She said she would, and we exchanged good-byes, and hung up.

I didn't know what to do. I didn't have that many close friends, certainly very few with whom I felt comfortable enough to beg for a room for the night. Claire had married my brother and moved to Tipperary, my other best friend Davina had long since moved to France, so that really only left Justin and Pauline, and Pauline lived in a one-roomed "studio" apartment that was so small there wasn't enough room to swing a kitten.

So I had no choice but to phone Mags again. This time she answered after the fifth ring. "It's me again," I said. "Listen, I hate to ask this, but . . . I'm kind of in a bit of trouble, and I need somewhere to stay for the night."

Mags hesitated just long enough to let me know that this was going to be awkward. "Sure. Anything the matter?"

"It's going to take way too long to explain on the phone. It's not a problem for me to stay?"

"No, not at all."

"I'm not interrupting anything important, am I?"

"No, I was just going to spend the night in front of the telly. Come on over whenever you feel like it."

"Well, I'll be there in about an hour, is that okay?"

She said that it was. Again, we said goodbye and hung up.

I left Des's office and headed back to the house to pick up my bag. I was not looking forward to it.

* * *

Old Mr Farley must have been on the lookout for me, because he darted out of his house even before I'd reached

56

the front door. I say "darted", but actually he ambled out at a speed that was only slightly faster than the average old person can travel.

"So any news?" he asked.

I shook my head. "Nothing good. I went to his office, and it looks pretty clear that he's not going to be coming back. And I went to the bank – he's cleared out the joint account."

He peered closely at me. "I have to say, you're in remarkably good spirits, considering."

"This isn't good spirits, this is just shock."

"What are you going to do?"

"Well, I'm just here to pick up my bag. Tonight I'm going to stay in a friend's place. After that . . . I have no idea."

"Look, I have a spare bed you can borrow if it's any use to you."

"That would be great, thanks. But I don't think I'll be staying here until I can get a few more things. I mean, I've no bedclothes, no cooker, nowhere to sit but the stairs."

Mr Farley was silent for a few seconds, then he said, very deliberately, "If I ever see him again, he's a dead man."

This was quite a surprise, coming from him; Mr Farley was one of those incredibly neat and polite old people. He always wore a shirt and tie, his beard was always neatly trimmed, and he had little wire-framed bifocals hung on a length of string around his neck. In all the years I'd known him – which was all my life – I'd never heard him say anything bad about someone else.

When I didn't reply, he said, "Of course, I wouldn't

dream of murdering him without letting you have the first go." Then he smiled.

I couldn't help smiling back. "I'd appreciate that."

"Well, I'll leave you to it . . . but if there's anything I can do for you, just ask."

"Thanks."

He paused, as if he was about to add something, then nodded and went back into his house.

I took my key out of my pocket and unlocked the front door.

It would be nice to be able to say that everything was as it should have been: all my furniture was back in its place, the pictures were on the walls, the television was chatting to itself in the corner of the sitting-room, and there was the welcoming smell of cooking food coming from the kitchen . . .

But the house was cold, and empty, and dark.

Chapter 5

Mags was my age, twenty-seven, but she didn't look it. She looked about twenty-one, which is one of those extremely annoying things that you're not really supposed to hold against someone. She had straight, shoulder-length brown hair that she insisted was "auburn" and big brown eyes that were usually hidden behind unfashionably large glasses. The first time I met her she put me in mind of one of those cheapo spy movies where the female scientist – who is secretly in love with the hero – takes off her glasses and lets down her hair and suddenly becomes gorgeous. Except that I'd seen Mags without her glasses and she didn't look all that much different.

She looked me up and down when she opened the door, then stepped aside to let me in. "So what happened?"

"God, where do I *begin*?"

Mags showed me into the kitchen. "Tea?"

"Yeah, that'd be great, thanks. I haven't had anything since this morning."

While Mags was filling the kettle, she said, "Begin at the beginning."

So I told her about Des's alleged plan to do the attic conversion as a birthday surprise for me, and what I'd found when I got home.

She sat and listened without making any comment, watching me over the rim of her cup of tea, while I poured everything out. That is, she said nothing until I got to the part about my theory that Des had absconded with the money from the shopping-centre project.

"How sure are you about that?" she said warily.

"Pretty sure. I mean, the company cheque books are gone. I suppose that one of the investors will have to check."

Then she said, "Oh, don't worry. I will."

I paused. "I didn't know. I mean, Des never said that you and Justin had invested. And Justin never mentioned it either . . . But I suppose he's always been like that. Never mentions anything to do with money."

Mags swallowed, her face pale, her hands shaking a little. "Just over twenty-five thousand euro, Orla. It's pretty much everything we have."

We looked at each other for a couple of seconds.

"Oh shit. I'm so sorry."

"Why should *you* be sorry? You didn't know about any of this, did you?"

"Well, no, of course not." I put down my cup and buried my face in my hands. "Jesus, what are we going to do?"

"File charges against him, for a start." She got to her feet. "Look, give me a minute. I'm just going to phone Justin. See what he has to say."

So Mags left me alone in her spotless kitchen. I could

hear her in the hall, mumbling into the phone, but I couldn't make out her words.

I thought she was taking it all very calmly, and then I remembered that that was what Mr Farley had said about me.

Why *am* I being so calm? I wondered. That bastard stole everything I own, and here I am just treating it as though it's the sort of thing that happens every day.

Then I realised that I wasn't really taking things that calmly: there'd been a knot in my stomach ever since I arrived back at the empty house, and the more I thought about it, the tighter the knot became.

Little chains of thought kept bobbing to the surface in my mind; when I thought about all my clothes, that reminded me that apart from what I was wearing, all I had left were the clothes in my bag, which needed to be washed. And that made me think about my washing-machine, or rather the space in the kitchen where the washing-machine used to be. That, in turn, made me think of the other spaces, the former homes of the cooker and the fridge. And what about all the food in the fridge? What sort of scumbag steals a fridge with the food still in it? The answer was obvious: the same sort of scumbag who also steals all the other food from the presses, the cutlery from the drawers, and not only the handful of change in the jar next to my bed, but the jar itself.

I looked around Mags' kitchen. It was always much, much tidier than mine. Well, tidier than mine used to be, I realised. I no longer owned enough things to make the house look *un*tidy.

I understood then why I hadn't had a completely

hysterical panic attack: my brain wasn't letting me get that far. It was as though this whole thing was way too big to take in at once, so my brain was only allowing me to process the information in little bits.

But the trouble was, those little bits kept on coming . . .

In the bottom of the wardrobe that used to be in the spare bedroom I'd kept an old suitcase which contained a bunch of things from my schooldays. Nothing important, really, just a couple of my school books, some of my art projects, a pile of homework books, that sort of thing. In the big scheme of things, they weren't important at all. I hadn't looked at them in years, hadn't even thought about them . . . But now that I knew they were gone, I missed them.

What about the stuff in the attic? I asked myself. There could be some old bits and pieces up there.

Then I answered myself. Yeah, sure! Even if there is anything left up there, what use would it be? A bunch of mouldy boxes containing Dad's old seventy-eight-speed records, or Mam's huge collection of knitting patterns from the fifties.

This train of thought suddenly encountered leaves on the line: Mags came back into the kitchen.

"How is he?" I asked.

"He's not happy, I'll tell you that." She sat down again. "Orla, that was all the money we had in the world! We were saving like mad so that we could pay off the mortgage, and then Des offered us what we thought was a chance in a lifetime. He said that once the shopping centre was on the way to being built, some large corporation would come along and buy up the whole thing, and there was a very good chance we'd double our money. Maybe even triple it. And now . . ." she bit her lip, "now everything is gone."

"Look, it might still be okay. I mean, we don't know for certain yet that Des really has run off with the money."

She glared at me. "Don't, Orla. Just don't. This is bad enough without you giving me false hope." She stared at her hands for a couple of seconds, then said, "Justin's going to phone some of the other investors. I imagine that you're going to find yourself at the centre of a real shitstorm for the next few weeks."

"You're probably right," I said.

"I *am* right. You know, there are going to be people who won't believe that you didn't have anything to do with this. They're going to think that you *must* have known . . . I mean, how could you *not* know? You were living with him, for God's sake! There must have been some indication that he was planning to abscond with all our money!"

For a second, I thought she was still talking about the way other people were going to react, but then I realised that she really was asking me. "Mags, if I *had* known, I would have stopped it, wouldn't I? And don't forget I'm a victim here too. In fact, I've lost more than everyone else. At least you and the other investors still have the contents of your homes! He's taken all that from me, as well as clearing out our bank account!" I pointed to just inside the kitchen door, where my bag was resting. "See that? That's all I have left in the world, apart from a big old empty house. And the clothes in there need to be washed, but I haven't got a washing-machine any more. I don't even have enough money to go to the laundrette." I

63

reached into the pocket of my jeans and pulled out my cash, and placed it on the table. "That's all the money I have in the world, and it has to last me until I get paid on Sunday night. But I can't even go to work, because my uniform is gone."

Then I had another, more disturbing thought. "And my boss was also an investor in Des's project. What if he decides to take it out on me? Suppose he fires me? Then where will I be?"

"You could always sign on."

"I'd have to," I said, "but I doubt I'd get enough from the dole to cover the mortgage. And even if I did, there certainly wouldn't be enough money left over for me to buy any furniture, or pay any of the bills." Despite the way I was feeling, I suddenly laughed. "You know, I can see myself spending the next few months sitting on the stairs eating cold beans out of a tin!"

Mags laughed too, then I laughed harder. "That is, if someone's kind enough to lend me a spoon and a tin-opener!"

I laughed, and laughed, and laughed, until tears were running down my cheeks.

And pretty soon the laughter stopped, but the tears kept coming.

* * *

Mags and I talked long into the night. We invented several interesting and highly profane new names for Des, and discussed elaborate and painful revenge scenarios that we knew we'd never get the chance to try out.

We only stopped when Mags realised that it was way

past midnight and she had to get up for work the next morning. "I suppose I could phone in sick," she said, "but considering what's happened, I don't want to do *anything* that might jeopardise the job."

She showed me to the guest bedroom, and said, "Listen, I'll be leaving at half-past eight in the morning, and I'll be back about three. I don't have a spare key, but if you want to take mine, just make sure you're back before I get home."

"Thanks, but I really don't want to impose any more than I already have."

"Then you'll have to leave when I do," she said. "You can't lock the door without the key. No, I'll tell you what . . . you take the key and you lock up when you leave, then drop it into the school, how's that sound?"

I thanked her again, then said, "Would it be okay for me to have a shower in the morning?"

"Sure. And if you want to put your stuff into the wash, feel free."

"I'm – I'm glad that you're here. There's not really many people I know well enough to put out like this."

"It's no problem," she said, and as she turned to leave she added, "Shout if you need anything."

I got undressed and slipped under the duvet. The spare bedroom was kept for Justin's eight-year-old nephew, who came to visit occasionally, so it was decorated appropriately; it felt a little odd lying under a *Daredevil* duvet and looking up at a huge poster of The Rock and a bunch of other wrestlers, but considering the alternative, I wasn't about to complain.

* * *

It was the longest night of my life.

My mind kept playing the highlights of the day over and over, no matter what I did to avoid them. It was sort of like the way TV stations have in recent years taken to sneaking in trailers of upcoming shows in every available slot; just when you think it's safe, another one pops up.

I knew it was going to be a long sleepless night as soon as my brain decided that I really needed a good dose of the if-onlys . . .

If only I hadn't agreed to spend the weekend in Killian's. If only I'd figured out what Des was up to sooner. If only I hadn't been so much in love with him that I automatically believed him when he said he loved *me*. If only I'd decided to come home earlier, like on Sunday morning, then maybe he'd have been still around and I would have caught him.

Why did he do it? I asked myself. How long had he been planning it? Was this a spur-of-the-moment thing, or had he been thinking about ripping me off all along? How the hell could someone be so cold as to steal everything someone owned and then just disappear?

On top of all those questions was one I didn't really want to – or know how to – answer: Why didn't I see this coming?

I stared at The Rock, and he stared back, his only reaction to my questions being his permanently arched eyebrow. Lot of help *he* was.

Des liked wrestling. He knew that it was all fake, but he still thought it was fun.

"You're not seriously watching this rubbish, are you?"

I'd asked him. It was the second night after he'd moved in.

"Sure. You're not a fan?"

"No. Anyway, there's a movie I want to see on Channel 4."

But somehow we ended up watching the wrestling, even though it was *my* television set.

Thinking about it, I realised that maybe I should have taken that as a clue; Des always seemed to get his own way. Conversations would go along these lines;

Me: What do you want for dinner?

Des: I don't mind. What do you want?

Me: I'm easy.

Des: What do we have, then?

Me: Pasta, chips, rice, frozen veg, ham, carrots, potatoes, chicken sausages, frozen pizzas . . . That's about it, I think. Or we could get a take-away from the Chinese.

Des: I don't feel like a Chinese tonight. Will I phone for a couple of pizzas?

Me: But we have pizzas in the freezer.

Des: Yeah, but I'd rather have one from Four Star.

So we'd end up ordering a pizza, regardless of whether I'd wanted one.

It's not that I was a complete doormat and let him walk all over me. It's more that Des liked things his way, and I was more flexible than he was, so we tended to do things the way he wanted them. Not all the time, but certainly more than half the time.

I wondered if Des had been on the lookout for someone like me: someone who was easy-going enough for him to take advantage of.

How does someone get like that? I asked myself. What sort of upbringing did Des have that made him think it was okay to ruin someone else's life?

I'd never met his parents, or any of his family, but he'd always said that it was no big deal; none of them were close and they didn't keep in touch.

Then I began to wonder whether Desmond Mills was even his real name . . . For all I knew, he could have a number of different aliases and he could have done this same thing more than once. I never thought to check him out before he moved in with me, but then why would I? There was no way I could have known.

I turned on my side to avoid The Rock's accusing gaze, and tried to force myself to sleep. This is not an easy thing to do, and generally doesn't work.

I tried the old "blank wall" trick: what you have to do is picture a completely blank wall and mentally just keep staring at it. It's supposed to help you clear your mind so that you'll drift off to sleep, but it didn't work for me. I just kept seeing four blank walls, a floor with no carpet, and the light-fitting missing from the ceiling.

At one stage I almost drifted off to sleep, but then some part of my mind noticed and said, "Hey! It's working! I'm falling asleep! I'm not even *thinking* about Des and all the different ways I let him take advantage of me!"

That was all it took to keep me awake for most of the night.

* * *

There was a gentle knock on the door. "Orla?"

"I'm awake."

Mags opened the door a little. "I'm off to work. Do you want to lock the door after me?"

"Sure. I'll be down in a second."

When I heard her going downstairs I got out of bed and pulled on my jeans and T-shirt, then padded barefoot down the stairs.

"The kettle's boiled if you want to make a cup of tea," Mags said.

"Thanks."

"I've left the number of the school on the kitchen table, in case you need to get in touch. And I also put down my cousin's number. She's a solicitor."

"I don't think I'll be able to afford a solicitor," I said.

"Well, talk to her anyway. I'm sure she won't mind giving you a bit of advice." Mags looked at me. "Did you sleep at all?"

"Not really. And I can't even really go back to bed. I have to go to the bank, sort out some stuff there, then I need to have a think about what I'm going to do at the class tonight."

"Okay. Well, Justin said you're to call him as soon as you know for certain what's happened with the money from the project."

"I will. Listen, thanks for putting me up. And for putting up with me."

"It's no bother. Will you need to stay tonight too?"

I shrugged. "I don't know. Old Mr Farley next door told me that he's got a spare bed I can have. I might have to borrow some bedclothes from you, if that's okay."

"Sure. Just let me know what you need. Anyway, I'll be

home a little after three, so if you're not going to be here, just drop the key into the school."

I thanked her again. She nodded, then unlocked the door and stepped out. I locked the door after her, and stood there in the hall for a couple of minutes, wondering what I was going to do with the rest of my life.

Chapter 6

After I made myself something to eat – spaghetti on toast – I phoned Mags' cousin. She didn't answer her mobile phone, so I just left a brief message saying who I was and that I thought I might be in need of a solicitor.

It was only after I hung up that I realised that there had been no point in me giving her my mobile phone number; my phone had died some time during the night and, without a charger, I couldn't see how I was going to get it back up and running. So I left another message giving her my address and home phone number, even though phoning me at home wasn't really an option right now.

At half-past nine, I phoned the bank and asked to speak to the manager. I was very politely told that the manager was busy and that I should really make an appointment first. I explained that that was what I was trying to do, but the poor girl on the other end of the phone didn't seem to understand. "Look, just tell her that

Orla Adare needs to see her as soon as possible, okay?" I gave her Mags' phone number, and went back into the kitchen, where I sat nursing a cup of tea and hoping that it wouldn't be too long before they called me back.

The phone rang a little under an hour later. "Is that Ms Adare?"

"It is," I said.

"I'm Dearbhla McKenna, the branch manager. Is there any possibility you can come in and see us this morning?"

"There's every possibility," I said. "What time?"

"As soon as you can make it."

* * *

Half an hour later I was being ushered into Dearbhla McKenna's tiny windowless office. She was in her forties, average height and build, with a deeply tanned face that highlighted her wrinkles, and she was dressed exactly like you'd imagine a female bank manager to dress: immaculate skirt and blouse, thick tights, expensive flat shoes.

I was wearing the same clothes I'd put on the previous morning, so I felt a bit stinky. When meeting with someone from the bank I'd normally have worn something a bit more formal, but not too showy; something to give the impression that I was a serious business-person who was used to dealing with banks. Now, I felt like a serf who's been brought before the queen to beg for the return of grazing rights.

"Can I get you anything? Tea? Coffee? Water?" she asked.

"How about all my money back?"

She sat down opposite me. "This is a pretty bad situation."

"I know."

"We've been absolutely inundated with calls, as you can imagine. We haven't been this busy since the last time the stock market took a drop. We've even had to call in one of the temps to help on the switchboard."

"Well, my heart goes out to you, it really does, but I'm sure you'll forgive me if I'd rather get down to business."

"Of course . . ." She tapped away at her computer for a couple of seconds. "Now . . . your name was mentioned by quite a few of our customers, in relation to Mr Mills." She looked up, her fingers poised over the keyboard. "Some of them seem to think that you'll have more of a notion as to what's going on than they do."

"I had a feeling that they might," I said, "but I'm as much in the dark as anyone else. So, you're saying that Des really *did* take all of their money?"

She shrugged. "We don't know for certain, yet. He was always in here, moving the money from one account to another, trying to build up the interest. Last week he moved it out of our bank entirely."

"One of those untraceable Swiss bank accounts?"

"That sort of thing, yes, but it was a bank in the Cayman Islands."

"So all their money is gone forever?"

She paused before answering. "It's possible. We have people who investigate these things, but I wouldn't hold out much hope if I was you. Mr Mills had everyone give him sole authority over the account. Well, *almost* sole authority."

She looked at me in a way that was probably meaningful, but I didn't know what it meant.

"How do you mean?"

"You were a co-signatory on the account."

"No, I wasn't."

"Yes, you were."

I shook my head. "No. I really wasn't. I'd have remembered. And not only that, I wouldn't have done it in the first place."

"We have all the forms on file. I checked this morning. Your signature is there."

"Then he forged it," I said. "I never signed anything like that."

Dearbhla drummed her fingers on the edge of the desk. "I had a feeling you were going to say that."

"So what now?"

"Right now, we can't be absolutely certain that Mr Mills has absconded with the money. If we were certain . . . well, we've already called in the authorities, and they'll probably want to talk to you."

"Look, I'm not in on this! I'm as much a victim as everyone else, you know!"

She didn't seem inclined to believe me. "How so? You aren't one of the investors."

"Ah," I said. "I see . . . you don't know what's happened to me, do you? I was away for the weekend, and when I got back yesterday I found that the entire house had been stripped bare. And then I checked the joint account that me and Des had, and it's been cleared out."

She thought about this for a bit, then said, "Ms Adare, regardless of that, people are going to think that it's suspicious that you were away on the weekend that your partner disappeared."

"Yeah, but that was the reason he suggested I go away! He was supposed to be getting some work done at the house as a surprise for me."

She went "Hmmm . . ." which didn't go a long way towards convincing me she believed my side of the story.

"If you don't believe me, come over to the house and look for yourself."

"Some people might think that you're still involved, and that – for some reason – you've either backed down, or you were left behind."

"Yes, and *some* people think that it's wrong to judge someone without any evidence. Look, if I'd been involved, I wouldn't still be here. Even if everything went wrong and I did get left behind, I'd make a run for it or something."

"You seem to have given this an awful lot of thought."

I couldn't help myself: "Well, fuck you!"

She stared at me without speaking for so long that I got the horrible feeling that she'd gone into a sort of profanity-induced coma. Then, finally, she said, "There is no call for language like that."

"Sorry. But you're implying that I'm involved in whatever Des is up to. Well, I'm not. I would never do that sort of thing. You can ask anyone who knows me." Well, anyone except Des, I said to myself. I was pretty sure that he wouldn't give me a glowing reference.

"Ms Adare, *officially* you're a co-signatory on the account. Unless you can prove that you never signed the forms, we're going to have to assume that you're as responsible for the account as Mr Mills was."

"Look, this is absolute bullsh – er, rubbish. It's *not* my signature on those forms. You could check it with a handwriting expert, and I bet they'd be able to tell you. I'd have to have been here to sign, right? So check your security tapes for the day the account was opened, and you'll see that I wasn't in here that day."

"You wouldn't both necessarily have to be here. Mr Mills could have brought in the forms already signed."

"So he forges my signature and hands it in, and you just believe it? You already have my signature on lots of other things. Did you compare them when he brought the forms in? Did you even think of comparing them this morning?"

She hesitated. "Well . . ."

"You didn't, did you? Go ahead and check. I'll wait."

"It could take some time."

"I think it'll be time well spent, don't you?"

Dearbhla excused herself from the office, and was back within a minute. "Someone's going to check our records. Like I said, it could take a while."

"Well, in the meantime, maybe you can tell me what happened to *my* account." I explained about my discovery the previous day of the vast lack of money in the account.

I gave her the account details, and again she tapped away at her computer. "You cleared out the account on Friday," she said.

"No, *Des* cleared out the account. I knew nothing about it until yesterday."

"Nevertheless, it's empty."

"This much I know. But don't you need both of us to withdraw any large amounts of money from the account? Or is this the same thing again, Des forging my signature?"

"I suppose it *could* be . . ."

Well, finally! I said to myself. She was beginning to believe me.

"So," I said, watching carefully for her reaction, "if your people allowed him to clear out the account using a forged signature, wouldn't that mean that the bank is at fault? And wouldn't *that* mean that you have to pay me back?"

She was clearly a good negotiator; she kept very still so as not to give anything away. "That would depend on the exact nature of the situation."

"Look, I only had about eight thousand euro in the account. Surely it'll cost the bank more than that in legal fees if we have to go to court over it?"

"It would be foolish to start thinking in those terms until we know for certain what's happened." A very careful, diplomatic answer. I was nearly impressed. I couldn't help thinking that it'd be interesting to play poker with her, if only I'd had enough money to play even a single hand.

"I *do* know for certain what's happened. You people allowed him to steal my money. At the very least, that's gross incompetence."

Dearbhla didn't like that at all. "Perhaps we'd better take a break. At least until we can compare the signatures."

"Fine," I said.

She pushed herself away from her desk, and got to her feet. "If you could come back in, say, two hours?"

I was about to agree, until the rational part of my brain kicked in, and reminded me that it was the bank who had allowed Des to take my money, so therefore it should be me calling the shots, not them. "A couple of hours?" I asked. "No, that's not acceptable. It certainly shouldn't take that long for you to check a couple of signatures."

She sighed, and said, "I'll see what I can do," then left the office again.

And then it hit me . . . They were going to do everything in their power to maintain that either the forged signatures were really mine, or that I'd somehow given Des permission to have full access to the account. They were going to fight me on this every step of the way, and unless I had some sort of incontrovertible proof of my innocence, I was going to lose the fight.

The reason they were going to fight wasn't just because of the eight thousand euro missing from my account; it was because if they admitted that they'd screwed up with my account, then they'd have to admit that they'd also screwed up with the account Des had held for the shopping-centre project.

And that was a hell of a lot more than eight thousand euro.

* * *

It wasn't my signature on the forms, but it was damn close. Close enough, I feared, that it might even hold up in court, if it should ever come to that.

As I left the bank – filled with Dearbhla McKenna's promises that she'd do her "utmost to sort things out," – I had a mini panic attack; if I couldn't get my money back, what the hell was I going to do?

It wouldn't have been so bad if Des had just taken the money and left the contents of the house alone, or had at least left me enough furniture to get by. But as it was, I was starting completely from scratch.

Or maybe not from scratch, I reminded myself. After

all, the house itself was worth something. As Killian had suggested, I might be able to sell it and buy a smaller place. That triggered another attack of the "if onlys": if only I'd finished some more of the redecorating, then the house would have been able to fetch a much bigger price.

But I didn't want to have to sell. Not only had I lived my entire life in that house, but it was all I had left. If I was to sell it and start over in a new house, then Des would have taken *everything* from me.

I was wandering aimlessly, or at least I thought my wanderings were aimless, but soon enough I found myself heading back home. I wasn't sure I wanted to go there, and was about to change direction when a car pulled up on the other side of the road and someone shouted, "Orla!"

I turned to see Killian getting out of the car.

"I've been driving around for ages looking for you. I didn't know *where* you were."

"God, don't tell me you came all the way here this morning?"

"Yeah. Well, Claire insisted. Look, I called to the house . . ." He shrugged. "I've never seen anything like it. I swear on all that's holy, if I ever see Des again I'm going to murder him."

"There's a waiting list for that."

"So where did you stay the night?"

"Justin's. He wasn't there himself, but Mags was."

We got into the car, and on the way to the house I told Killian about the situation with the bank.

"But that's mad," he said. "There's no way they can hold you accountable for all that!"

"They're going to do their best."

"How much money was it, anyway?"

"I honestly don't know. Maybe a million. Maybe even more."

"And that's not enough for the bastard! He still has to rip you off as well!"

Killian pulled the car up onto the kerb outside the house.

"Look, I'm not sure I want to go in."

He ignored me, and got out of the car. Reluctantly, I followed him.

Killian unlocked the front door, and went in. "Do you want to hear something mad? When I got here this morning the first thing I did was ring the bell."

"So you had a good look, then?"

"Yeah. C'mon, I want to see if there's anything left in the attic."

We went up to the landing, and looked up at the trapdoor. "It would have been nice," I said, "having a little room up there."

Killian pulled a small torch out of his pocket, handed it to me, then laced his fingers together and put his hands in front of him. "I'll give you a boost."

"*I'm* not getting up there!"

"Well, either I help you up or you help me up, and considering that I'm probably twice your weight, why don't we do it the clever way around, and not the stupid way?"

"All right, all right!" I kicked off my shoes, put my foot in his hands, my hands on his shoulders, and he effortlessly lifted me up.

I slid the trapdoor aside, half expecting a tidal wave of

spiders to come scuttling out, then Killian lifted me higher, until I was standing on his shoulders.

"What's up there?"

"Dark."

"Well, use the torch and see what the dark looks like when it's all lit up."

I switched on the torch; even with its feeble light I could see that there wasn't much left. "There's a few cardboard boxes in the corner near the water tank."

"Any idea what's in them?"

"Stuff, probably."

"Jesus, you're a lot of use. Here, I'll lift you the rest of the way."

And he did; he took a foot in each hand and lifted me straight into the attic. I knelt on the boards and looked down at him. "I didn't know you were that strong."

"I didn't know you were that *light*. You're not anorexic or anything, are you?"

"No!"

"Just check the boxes."

I stood up and looked around. "There's a *lot* of footprints up here," I said. "Maybe we should leave it. I mean, the police will want to check for things like that, won't they?"

"I wouldn't worry about it. It'd be easier for them to check for fingerprints."

Keeping a close watch for low-flying beams and spindly things with eight legs, I walked over to the boxes. There were four of them; the first two contained nothing but air and dust, but the others were full. I opened the larger of the two. "There's a pile of old newspapers in this one . . . I think that's all."

Killian called up, "Oh yeah. Dad used to keep newspapers after important things happened. I forgot all about that."

The next box contained a very old glass lampshade that was also very ugly and very broken. "Just a lampshade in this one . . . That's the lot."

"Damn. Well, pass them down anyway."

* * *

Killian and I spent the next half an hour sitting cross-legged on the landing, going through Dad's collection of old newspapers. Almost all of them were dated the day after something big had happened, presumably because that was the first day the events were reported in the papers.

Killian picked up a paper and glanced at the front page. "Nothing important here . . . fifth of April 1968. Mean anything to you?"

"Wasn't Martin Luther King assassinated on the fourth?"

"You're right. Why did he keep this one, then, if there's nothing about that in it?"

"I don't know. Maybe he wasn't so much keeping the news about the events as the rest of the news, if you see what I mean. So that whoever found the papers would have a better idea of the way the world was then."

"That'd be you and me, I suppose."

We looked at each other. "Do you still miss him?" I asked.

"Sure. All the time. And Mam, too."

"You know, I bet that even *they* never saw the house looking like this."

Killian laughed. "At least it's tidy."

There was a knock on the door. "That'll be Mr Farley," I said.

"I know," Killian said, and went down to let him in. For some reason, Old Mr Farley always knocked on the door instead of using the bell. Maybe he thought that the bell wasted electricity.

I got to my feet and stretched, then clumped my way down the bare wooden stairs.

"I had a feeling that was your car, all right," Mr Farley was saying.

Killian turned to me. "Mr Farley says he has a bed for you."

"Oh, great. Thanks!"

"It's really just a base and a mattress, I'm afraid. I found some old blankets but I really don't think you want them. They're in pretty bad condition."

"I'll give you a hand carrying the bed," Killian said to him.

We went out and into Mr Farley's house. I hadn't been inside since shortly after his wife died, about five years before; the place hadn't changed at all. It still smelled faintly of cabbage and soap.

Mr Farley led us up to the spare bedroom, and introduced me to my new bed. It was a monstrosity; I'd expected a fairly old wooden single bed, but this was a huge metal-framed king-size, with an ornate headboard. I couldn't help thinking how it was exactly the sort of bed I'd spent ages looking for when I was decorating my bedroom.

"We'll have to take it apart first," he said. "I started to do it myself, but all the nuts and bolts are stuck fast."

Killian and I both knew that was an old person's euphemism for "I'm not as strong as I used to be".

"No problem," Killian said. "I've got some tools in the car."

He was about to disappear down the stairs again when I stopped him. "Let's get the mattress down first," I said. "It's going to be in the way otherwise, and we have to bring it down anyway."

Mr Farley said, "Good thinking, Orla," and started to haul the mattress off the bed. Killian grabbed hold of the other end.

It took them about five minutes just to manoeuvre the enormous thing down the stairs. I'd offered to help, but according to Killian moving mattresses was "man's work", as was taking apart an old bed frame and reassembling it in my bedroom.

However, making tea was a job that was more suitable for women, so I was despatched to Mr Farley's kitchen.

I was silently fuming as I waited for the kettle to boil, wondering when Killian had become so chauvinistic, until I realised that he'd said those things as a cover-up for allowing Mr Farley to feel useful. At least, that was what I hoped he meant; I decided not to ask him, just in case.

It took over an hour to get the bed disassembled, moved and reassembled, and it was with some relief that we settled in Mr Farley's kitchen for a cup of tea and a few plain biscuits.

"There's a spare armchair in the living-room," Mr Farley told me. "You're welcome to that, too."

"Thanks," I said, "but you'll have to allow me to pay

you something for it." When I was making the tea, I'd had a good snoop through his kitchen, and it was pretty clear that Mr Farley was by no means a wealthy man.

"Not at all. It's not like I need more than one armchair, now, is it?"

* * *

When I was about fifteen, I was in town one day with some friends and I bumped into Mr Farley. At that time his wife was still alive, though she was more or less bedridden and had been for as long as I could remember. Anyway, there we were walking along George's Street, and I heard someone calling me. I turned to see Mr Farley grinning at me.

I was of course utterly mortified: a fifteen-year-old girl with her friends does not want to acknowledge old people, especially not old people with whom the only regular contact she has is knocking on their door to ask for her tennis balls back. That was only when I knew they were in, of course; when I knew they weren't in, I just shinned over the wall and retrieved them myself.

Mr Farley proceeded to ask me how I was, how my family was, and what I'd been up to. He almost demanded to be introduced to my friends, who looked at him like he was carrying the Black Death. Then he told us that it was too nice a day for five lovely young ladies to be stuck talking to an old codger, and he tipped his hat and bade us farewell.

I remember I was blushing like mad, and desperately wondering how I was going to get the others to pretend that this had never happened, when Davina suddenly said, "He's dead nice. I never spoke to him before."

"Yeah, I suppose he's okay," I said.

"He kinda reminds me of me granddad," Claire said.

"Me too," said Davina.

Claire said, "I suppose all the kids call him 'Rusk' or something."

"How do you mean?" Davina asked.

"Because of his name. *You* know. Farley's Rusks."

I shook my head, and said, "Actually, no. But when we were kids he used to be a lot fatter, and he only had a grey moustache then, not the beard, so Killian used to call him The Elder Lemon."

Claire thought that this was great, and laughed her head off. And somehow she got it into her head that that would be a good nickname for Killian. He never understood why for a long time she called him "Lemmy", and he believed that it was something to do with Motorhead.

* * *

I left Killian and Mr Farley lugging the huge old armchair from one house to the other, and walked to the local primary school, where Mags worked.

It was the same school I'd gone to, though it had changed quite a bit. When I was there, there had been eight classrooms; now there was almost twice that number. And they'd managed to do that without building on – they'd just divided most of the rooms in two.

I arrived at lunch-time, which was not a wise move on my part, because within seconds of my passing through the gate I was surrounded by inquisitive ten-year-olds who wanted to know who I was, who I'd come to see, if I was a teacher, what my favourite colour was, where I lived, and how old I was.

Then one tiny little boy said, "Hey! I know her! She works in the rescheront!" and that was that; my entourage lost interest and quietly – well, noisily – drifted away.

I found Mags on playground duty. Around her neck she was wearing a length of blue wool with a whistle dangling from it. Mags taught fourth class, and from what I'd heard she was considered to be a pretty good teacher.

I walked up to her and said, "Miss! Miss!"

She gave me that "what is it *now*?" look that teachers are trained to do. "Miss Adare. I hope you're not here to tell on someone pushing you in the line."

I laughed, and handed her the key. "It's been a while since I last visited *this* place."

"I wish I could say the same."

I peered in through one of the classroom windows. "God, I'd forgotten how small the desks and chairs are." I taught my night classes in a secondary school, where everything was adult-sized.

"So how did it go at the bank?"

"Not great. I've got a feeling that they're going to try and hold me responsible for everything Des did." I told her a condensed version, which was interrupted every couple of minutes by Mags blowing her whistle or roaring at someone.

Soon enough, lunch-time was over. As Mags supervised the kids lining up, I said, "Listen, thanks for everything," I said. "I left my bag in your house, if that's okay. I'll call over later to pick it up."

"Well, where are you going to stay tonight?"

"My next-door neighbour has given me his spare bed, so I should be okay staying in the house."

"Do you still need bedclothes?"

"Eh, well, yeah, actually."

"Okay. If you call around this evening I'll sort something out for you."

* * *

I was most of the way back home when I realised that I'd forgotten to put my clothes in for a wash in Mags' machine. I hoped that she wouldn't mind me doing it later on, because otherwise it meant me spending *another* day in the same clothes.

Back at the house, I found Killian in the sitting-room, sitting on Mr Farley's donated armchair – a huge old thing covered in cracked leather and looking like it was stuffed with horsehair and pebbles – and going through Dad's collection of newspapers.

"Y'know, there's nothing more interesting than a really old newspaper," he said. "Especially this lot. Look . . ." He began to hold up the papers one by one. "Moon landing, Elvis Presley's death, JFK assassinated, and here's his brother." He flicked through the pile. "Here's a good one . . . the introduction of decimal currency!"

"I'm overjoyed for you."

He put the newspapers aside, and stood up. "Look, Orla, it could be worse, right?"

"I suppose it could. But it could be better too. And there's a lot more better it could be than worse."

"I was talking to Mrs Johnson, told her everything. She

said she has a kitchen table and a couple of chairs that you can have."

The Johnsons were an older couple who lived across the road. When Killian and I were kids their children were our mortal enemies; they used to call us names and throw pine cones over the hedge when we were in the front garden. It seems hilariously trivial now, but when you're eight years old that sort of thing really gets to you.

"That's good of her . . ." I swallowed. "I hate this. I hate having to get by on other peoples' cast-offs. I thought I'd hit the bottom when I was forced to shut down my company, but that was nothing compared to this mess."

"Yeah, but all this is only temporary. I mean, the insurance will cover the cost of replacing a lot of your stuff, right?"

"I don't know. Des was looking after that."

Killian stared at me with a "please tell me you're kidding" expression. "I see."

"He had a friend in the insurance business. At least, he *said* he did."

"And this friend's name . . .?" He shook his head. "No, stupid of me to ask, isn't it? You don't know his name, or the name of the insurance company, do you?"

"No."

"Shite."

"You got that right." I sat down in the armchair. It was more comfortable than it looked, but not much. "Maybe we can track down the people who actually stripped the place."

"I was talking to Mr Farley about that, but he can't remember anything other than it was a big white truck and that it made three trips."

"Yeah, he said that it was here on Friday evening, and twice on Saturday." I thought about that for a couple of seconds. "I wonder how long it was between the trips on Saturday? I mean, if it went off and came back pretty quick, then that would mean that they didn't go far, right?"

"I already thought of that," Killian said. "He told me that it was about three hours between when the truck left and came back. So that's not much use, really." He looked at his watch. "Listen, I'd really better get moving if I'm going to make it home at all today."

"Okay. Thanks for coming." I pushed myself up out of the armchair and followed him to the front door.

"Are you all right for money?"

"All donations gratefully received."

Killian pulled out his wallet and took out all his cash. "There's three hundred here. I can go to the bank and get more if you like."

"No, this is plenty. Thanks. I feel bad about taking it, though, after what happened to your investment."

Killian's shoulders sagged at the memory. "We had been thinking about moving, you know? Once the investment paid off, we were going to buy a bigger house, somewhere a bit nicer."

"It's possible that someone will find Des, get the money back."

"It's possible, yeah, but it's not likely."

I gave him an awkward hug. That was the first time I'd done that since the day he and Claire got married. "Thanks for everything."

"Just phone if you need me, okay?"

For a second, I felt like grabbing hold of him again and begging him not to leave, or begging him to take me with him. But I knew I couldn't do either; we both had our own lives to lead, and even though mine was in a complete shambles right now, I knew it wasn't fair to impose on him more than I already had.

I watched as he got into his car, did a three-point turn at the end of the cul-de-sac, and drove past the house once more. And just as I was feeling really, really low, he beeped the horn to say goodbye, and waved. That cheered me up a little, which was odd because if there's one thing I hate, it's visitors who beep the horn to say good-bye. It's as though they think we're so stupid we don't understand that them getting into the car and driving away pretty much means that they're leaving.

I don't know why it cheered me up; maybe it was because it was such a normal thing to do. The sort of thing that people do when they're in a good mood and everything is all right.

Of course, everything *wasn't* all right. And it didn't seem like things were going to be all right for a very long time.

Chapter 7

Ten minutes after Killian left a car pulled up outside. I was in the sitting-room, reading about the war in Vietnam, and – unhindered by curtains on the window – I could see that it was a police car. One of the gardaí from the day before got out, accompanied by a man in a charcoal-grey suit. He looked a little familiar, but I couldn't recall where I'd seen him before.

I ran for the door and opened it just as a horrible thought occurred: what if they've come to arrest me? But it was too late for me to run and hide; the door was open and here they were.

The man in the suit said, "Miss Adare? Detective Mason. We'd like to have a few words with you, if that's convenient." He was in his mid-thirties, good-looking in an angular sort of way: tall, quite thin but with broad shoulders, a narrow face with a slightly pointy nose, and short-cropped black hair with a prominent widow's peak.

He made me think of Sherlock Holmes, though that was probably mostly because he'd just said he was a detective.

"Are you going to haul me downtown and put me under a spotlight until I crack?"

He smiled, revealing straight, even teeth with quite long incisors: *now* he reminded me a little of Dracula. "No, nothing like that." He stepped closer. "May we . . .?"

"Sure." I led them into the sitting-room. "Sorry there's nowhere for you to sit."

Detective Mason looked round the room, started to speak, then changed his mind, took another look, then went back out to the hall and had a look around there. Then he came back in and said to the garda, "Get on to the station. I want this whole house dusted from top to bottom ASAP." As the garda went back out to the car, Mason said to me, "I need to know which rooms you've been in, anything you've touched."

"I've been all over the house. Probably touched almost everything."

"Damn . . ." He looked round again, and settled his gaze on the doorframe. "Might get some prints off this. With a bit of luck they weren't clever enough to wipe everything down."

"Any ideas why they'd take the doors? There can't be much of a market in second-hand doors, can there?"

He paused, a vertical frown-line appearing between his eyebrows. "If I had to make a guess . . . they knew they weren't going to be able to sell *all* of your property. They'd planned to dump some of it. And for that, they'd really need a skip."

"Ah. They took the doors off so that they could put

93

them in the sides of the skip so that they could get more in?"

He nodded. "Exactly. Which leads us to a very important question: if they knew they were going to have to dump some of your stuff, why did they take it in the first place?"

An answer came immediately to mind, and I didn't like it one bit. "Because he didn't just want to take my money; he wanted to hurt me as much as possible, by taking things that were worthless to anyone else but important to me."

For a second, I thought that I was going to burst into tears again, but after a few sniffs, a couple of dry swallows and a deep breath, I got control of myself. "Okay. Right." Another deep breath. "All right, then." I took a long, slow look about the room, then turned back to the detective. "Aren't you going to tell me that you've never seen anything like this before?"

"Matter of fact, I have, once. Place in Kilkenny. The owner came back from two weeks in Lisbon and found that the whole house had been stripped. It was worse than this, actually. At least you still have your armchair."

"This belongs to my next-door neighbour," I said. "He gave it to me this morning."

"Ah."

"Could it be the same people?"

"No, we caught them."

"So there's a chance you'll catch this lot too?"

He nodded. "I'd say it's a pretty good chance. That's mainly because they've taken so much. They won't be able to sell all of it, so whatever's left will be dumped somewhere. Now, about this other business . . ."

* * *

The detective was in the house for over half an hour, asking the same questions over and over: How well did I know Mr Mills? How did I first meet him? How, exactly, would I characterise my relationship with him? Was there ever any indication that he'd planned to abscond with the money? And so on.

You'd think that one advantage with being innocent is that all your answers will be true, therefore they'll be consistent, but as I found out there's more than one version of the truth, depending on how you look at things.

This was highlighted to me when Detective Mason asked me when it was that I first became aware that something was out of the ordinary . . .

"When I got in yesterday morning and everything was gone. Like I said."

"I see." He scribbled another note in his pad, which was resting on his knee. He was sitting cross-legged on the floor – I wasn't about to give up my armchair – and he shifted about a little. "Then why did you say earlier that it was unusual for Mr Mills to phone your brother? Didn't you find that a little odd?"

"Well, yeah. But that was because Des was planning to get the attic converted. Or at least that's what he told me."

"What he told *you*? I thought you weren't supposed to know anything about it?"

"Sorry, I mean, that's what he told Claire, my sister-in-law. She's the one who let it slip to me."

"And that's why you spent the weekend with her and your brother?"

"Right."

"But you wouldn't have gone otherwise?"

"Probably not."

"So was *that* the first time you noticed something unusual?"

I sighed. "Look, it was unusual, but that in itself is not unusual, if you see what I mean."

"No, I'm afraid I don't."

"People do things all the time that only seem unusual when you look back at them."

I was satisfied with this answer, until he went, "Hmm . . ." and said, "Give me an example."

"I've just given you one!"

"*Another* example."

"Okay . . ." I couldn't think of anything. "I can't. Look, I'm tired and hungry and extremely pissed off. I've answered all your questions more than once. How much longer is this going to take?"

"It'll take as long as it takes."

"Will it *really*?"

Detective Mason got to his feet and stretched, his pointy knees cracking loudly. As he brushed the dust off the bottom of his trousers, he said, "Miss Adare, I understand that you're upset – God knows *I* would be – but we're not going to get anywhere with sarcasm."

"We're not getting anywhere as it is," I said. "We might as well give sarcasm a go."

"Actually, we are getting somewhere."

I was surprised at that. "We are?"

"Certainly. We've established that you're innocent."

"Oh. Well, great. When did you reach that conclusion?"

"Shortly after I arrived."

"Then why the hell are we still doing this?"

"Because I need to know as much as possible about Mr Mills in order to try and find him, and you know him better than anyone. Do you have any idea where he might have gone?"

"None whatsoever."

"Any friends he's mentioned lately?"

I thought about this. "There's Peter Harney. You know, he owns the hardware shop in town? We've known him for years. That's where I get my decorating supplies. Well, some of them. Des mentioned him on Friday, said he was going to take the coffee table and the big chest of drawers down to Pete's place, get him to do some restoration on them. I thought that it was just an excuse to get everything out of the house so that he could get a start on the decorating."

"Decorating? I thought you said that he was converting the attic?"

"Yeah . . . but Claire said that as far as she knew Des was also planning do some other stuff as well. She didn't know any of the details, though. She just said that Des was going to get the decorators to follow my designs."

He gave me a quizzical look, urging me to elaborate.

"I'm a designer. Well, I used to be. I've been remodelling the house room by room."

That seemed to satisfy him. "We'll have a word with Mr Harney, then." He took a business card out of his pocket and handed it to me. All it had was "Detective Mason" and a couple of phone numbers. "Call me if you think of anything else."

"How? They took the phone, and my mobile needs to be charged, and they took the charger as well."

"What make is your mobile phone?"

"Nokia 3310."

"All right. I'll have someone drop over this afternoon with a charger."

"Wow. I didn't realise the police did that sort of thing."

"Officially, we don't. It's *my* charger, so I'll want it back tomorrow.".

"Oh, right. Thanks." I considered asking him whether he had a cooker and a fridge that he wasn't using at the moment, but decided not to push my luck. "So, what should I do now? Do I need to contact a solicitor?"

"You probably should, yes. Or at least the Citizen's Advice Bureau. They might be able to help you out."

Detective Mason moved towards the door. "Get in touch if you think of anything that might be relevant. Even if it doesn't seem that important to you, it might be important to us."

I followed him out to the hall. "Say we can't find Des and get my stuff back, what'll I do?"

He shrugged. "Start over."

"Well, that's a lot of use to me."

"And be more careful in future. Next time you meet some lad who tries to sweep you off your feet, make sure that he's not just trying to steal your shoes."

* * *

The previous evening, Mags had mentioned that I was going find myself "at the centre of a real shitstorm". Well, the brown clouds began to gather overhead that afternoon.

The first caller was a fierce-looking middle-aged woman I vaguely recognised from seeing her around the town. The second I opened the door, she pushed her face right into mine and shouted, *"Where is he?"*

"I wish I knew," I said, backing away a little.

"I've been trying to phone him at his office all morning! Half the time the phone is engaged, the rest of the time it just keeps ringing!"

She bobbed about, trying to peer past me. "He's here, isn't he? You're hiding him, aren't you?"

"He's not here, and I'm certainly not hiding him."

"There's all sorts of talk going round the town. They're saying that he's stolen our money and gone to Barbados."

"Barbados? Where did you hear that?"

"A-ha! So it's true!"

"No, I mean, I don't know how anyone got the idea that he's gone to Barbados. No one knows where he is."

"You know what's going on, don't you?"

"Look, the only thing I know is that he's stolen everything I own and disappeared." I opened the door wider and stepped aside to let her see. "I came home yesterday morning to find that he'd stripped the entire house bare."

This seemed to calm the woman down a little. "When you see him, tell him that Maura Kearney was looking for him."

"I doubt I'll be seeing him again," I said.

"Then tell me this: if he really *has* disappeared, then how come his phone was engaged earlier?"

"I imagine it was probably because there were lots of other people trying to get in touch with him."

"He took everything you had?"

"Yeah. And cleaned out my bank account too."

She seemed happy enough with the idea that other

people besides her had been hurt, which was a bit disturbing, then gave me her number and made me promise to get in touch with her as soon as I heard anything.

Just as I was closing the front door, a glistening white hatchback screeched to a stop outside the gate. It had a large *"No Fear"* sticker across the windscreen, extra-wide tyres, all sorts of dangly things hanging from the rear-view mirror, a ridiculously large spoiler on the back, the works. Two young men got out and marched up to me. One of them was wearing a thick, gaudy jumper and jeans, the other was a walking advert for Reebok: hooded tracksuit top, runners, cap, the works. I had the feeling that they were going to try and intimidate me somehow. I decided that wasn't going to happen.

"We're lookin' for Des Mills," said Jumper Man.

"Yeah, you and me and the woman who just left and probably half the damn town are looking for him."

"We've been hearin' a lot of stuff about him all mornin'," said Reebok. "They're sayin' he's done a runner."

"That's the way it looks. I presume you've invested money with him too?"

They both nodded simultaneously. "An' he was promisin' to sort us out with jobs when the shopping centre was built," said Reebok. "You don't know where he is, then?"

"No, and if I did, I'd murder the bastard."

"He screwed you as well?"

"In more ways than one," I said, and only realised the implications of that when Jumper Man sniggered.

Reebok said, "Lissen, if I find out that you're in on this . . ." He left the remainder of the sentence unsaid, as a sort of threat.

I gave him a good glaring. "What'll you do? Have me beaten up or something? Look, if I was in on this, would I still be here?"

"Prob'ly not," Reebok said. "But still . . . he owes me nearly two grand."

I was about to say, "Is that all?" but thought better of it; for all I knew, that could be this guy's life savings. Especially if his entire wardrobe was made by Reebok. "Give me your name and number, then. If I hear anything, I'll let you know. But I wouldn't hold out much hope if I was you."

"Shit."

"I couldn't have put it better myself," I said, which was a lie.

They looked at me a little awkwardly, as though they'd realised I wasn't impressed with their toughness and they didn't know what else to do. Then Jumper Man decided to give the hard act one more go. He leaned close and, in a low, menacing voice, said, "Did you talk to the cops about this?"

"Yep."

A pause. "Well, if you talk to them again, you better not mention us."

"Why not?"

"It'll be bad for you."

I laughed. "Oh, get a grip, for God's sake! You don't scare me. *Real* thugs don't wear jumpers their mammy bought them, or dress like they've just raided a sports shop! And they certainly don't drive around in a souped-up Micra that's covered in so much crap it'd be spotted a mile away. You're supposed to be able to *blend in* with the crowd, you know? That's much scarier."

They really didn't know how to react to this.

"So you just talk tough, is that it?" I asked. "Well, I imagine that before the week is out I'll be visited by people who make you two look as dangerous as bloody Tellytubbies. Now, just give me your names and numbers and if I hear anything useful, I'll call you, okay?"

Reebok meekly scribbled his name and phone number on a scrap of paper and handed it to me. "Uh . . . well, thanks anyway."

As they walked back towards their car, I said, "And keep the speed down in that damn thing, or you'll end up killing someone. How cool is *that* going to look to your mates?"

They didn't look back.

* * *

My next caller was a casually dressed middle-aged man who was carrying a large, square leather case. He produced an ID card, and announced that he'd come to check the place for fingerprints.

As I showed him through the house, I found myself telling him what had happened, but he didn't seem interested in the crime itself, just in getting the fingerprints.

He stopped in the kitchen. "Have you used the back door since it happened?"

"Yeah."

"How about the garage?"

"Yeah."

"Is there anywhere that you're certain you haven't touched?"

I thought about this. "Well, Detective Mason said that the doorframes might be a good place to get prints."

He nodded, walked up to where the kitchen door used to be, and looked at it without moving for about ten seconds. "Perfect."

I had a look. "I can't see anything."

He knelt, opened his case, and took out something that looked like a small airbrush. There was a hissing sound as he wafted the airbrush over the doorframe. "There's at least two sets of prints here . . . By the look of things, one of them was left-handed."

"How can you tell that?"

A set of black fingerprints appeared on the frame, as if by magic. "Because this is a right hand, here, and he was holding on pretty tightly, which he probably wouldn't do from this angle if he was right-handed. Not unless he was extremely tall, in which case his hand would be larger."

"Wow."

He paused, and peered at the frame. "So there was at least three of them taking this door off. One of them was wearing gloves."

Before I could ask him how he knew *that*, he added, "Some of the prints have been partly smeared by someone else." He turned to me. "If it's okay with you, I want to go over the whole house. The one with the gloves is the one we're going to want to catch."

"Why him?"

"Because he knew what he was doing. Removals men often wear builder's gloves to protect their hands. This lad was wearing latex gloves, like a dentist or a doctor would use; there's still traces of the lining powder. That means he was concerned about leaving his prints behind."

"Which means that he knows you already have his prints on file?"

"Exactly. The chances are he put on the gloves before he came in and didn't remove them until he was gone, but we might get lucky. Anyway, if you don't mind, I'll get to work. Please don't touch anything until I'm done." He picked up his bag and reached inside. "Detective Mason asked me to give you this." He handed me a phone charger.

"Oh, great!" I rushed off to find my phone, and plugged it in.

A few minutes later, my phone went *Beep! Beep!* to let me know that I'd received a text message, and then did it again before I had a chance to read it, and then it did it a third time.

The first message had been sent that morning; "Orla – I'm on my way. Should get to the house about ten. Phone me if you get this. Killian."

The next message was from Justin, who was a graduate of the school of thought that text messages didn't require spelling; "O – HRD ABT DES. CMNG HM THRDY – TLK 2 U THEN. DNT WRY 2 MCH WELL GET IT SRTD. CHRS JSTN." It took me a couple of goes to translate this into English, but it seemed to be saying that he'd be home on Thursday, that I shouldn't worry too much and that we'd get it all sorted out.

The third message was also from Justin; "O – HVNT HRD FRM U – EVTNG OK? MGS SEZ U STYD NITE. FL FRE 2 STY LNG S U WNT. HOP UR NT 2 DPRSD N UR KPNG UR SPRTS UP. CHRS JSTN."

I really was going to have to have a talk with him about how it wasn't rude to send comprehensible messages. Once, after a particularly obscure message from Justin, I replied with, "GW OPD R U FFT TCASU N WTPPNG TKD KL!" I don't know what he interpreted my message to mean, but the next time I met him he gave me a really funny look.

* * *

The fingerprinting guy was moving about upstairs when there was another ring on the doorbell.

I opened the door to see a good-looking man of about thirty years old. He was dressed in expensive-looking jeans, with a tan jacket – I'm no expert on male fashion, but it looked like Dolce & Gabbana to me – over a plain white T-shirt, very much the "80s casual" style. He had clear hazel eyes, perfect hair and dazzling symmetrical teeth; this man had money.

"Miss Adare?"

"That's me."

"Hi, my name's Thomas Kennedy. I've been working with Desmond Mills on the Nine Acres project."

"Nine Acres?" I asked, wondering whether this was some scheme of Des's that I hadn't even heard about.

"That's one of the names we've chosen for it. The site is actually a little larger than nine acres, but I like the sound of it so I've been trying to push that as a good name for the shopping centre."

"Oh, right. I suppose you're here looking for Des like everyone else?"

He nodded. "That's right. He was supposed to meet me at the site yesterday morning, but he didn't show and he hasn't returned my calls. He's not at his office, either."

"I see . . . So you haven't been hearing things about him throughout the town?"

He seemed a little puzzled. "No . . . I came straight here from the office. Can you tell him I'm here?"

"I can tell him, but he won't hear me. He's missing."

"Missing?"

"Yeah. Look, I hate to be the one to break this to you, Mr Kennedy, but Des has disappeared. He's cleared out the accounts and, well, it doesn't seem likely that he's coming back."

Mr Kennedy swallowed. "Oh God no."

"I'm afraid so. He sent me away for the weekend, then he stripped the house and cleared out my account too. He's taken everything." I felt like getting that printed onto a plaque and putting it on the front door, to save time.

"But . . ." he shook his head, "there must be some mistake. I mean, I had my people check him out. He seemed perfectly legitimate! Everything was above board."

"Maybe so, but he's still gone. Can I ask how much you've invested with him?"

"Well, we were committed to investing a little over nine million euro."

"Nine *million*!"

"Yes, but you see we haven't handed it all over yet. The original plan was that we'd meet on Saturday to finalise the contracts and pay the second instalment, but I had to cancel. So we rescheduled for Monday – yesterday – instead."

"So how much *does* he have?"

"Three hundred thousand."

I couldn't help laughing. "I'm sorry, but that's the first good news I've heard in the past two days. So you're saying that if the meeting on Saturday had happened as planned, he'd have a lot more than that?"

"Well, yes."

"Good. I hope he's feeling sick about all the money he's lost out on." Even as I said that, the thought occurred to me that if Des *had* managed to get all the money he was expecting from Kennedy's company, then maybe he wouldn't have felt the need to rip me off too.

"So no one knows where he is?"

I shook my head. "No. The police are investigating it, though. There was a detective here earlier who said that there was a good chance they'd be able to find the guys who took my stuff. And there's one here now, taking fingerprints."

He seemed to want to know more about it, so I explained everything to him. By the time I was done, he was looking very pale and nervous.

"What kind of man would do something like that?"

"The worst kind. Look, Mr . . ."

"Kennedy."

"Mr Kennedy, if you leave me your number I'll let you know as soon as I hear anything."

He handed me an embossed business card to add to my collection. "Call me any time, day or night." He started to turn away, then stopped. "I might have to ask you to explain this to my colleagues. Would you be okay with that?"

107

"Sure. When?"

"I'm not sure. Certainly before the end of the week. Do you have a number where I can contact you?"

I gave him my mobile-phone number, then said, "Listen, there's been quite a few people looking for Des today. Do you have any idea how many investors were involved in the project?"

"Not off-hand. That information should be in our files, though. We dealt only with Desmond's company. That's what led me to you."

"How do you mean?"

"Well, a company needs at least two people to act as directors. You're the other one."

I froze. "You have got to be bloody kidding me!"

He seemed as surprised as I was. "No, your name is on the stationery. You're down as 'Consulting Director'. Of course, we knew that you weren't involved any further than that."

"I wasn't involved at all. This is the first I've even heard about it." I took a deep breath. "Okay. Tell me everything."

"Certainly . . ." He shifted from one foot to the other. "Maybe we'd be more comfortable inside?"

I laughed again. "Have a look for yourself and see what you think."

Mr Kennedy walked into the hall and looked around. "This is *not* a good sign."

At that moment, the fingerprint guy came downstairs, stuffing things in his bag. "All done here, Miss Adare."

"Did you get any good prints?"

"At least five different sets, possibly six. One of them is probably Mr Mills."

"How long will it take before you can identify someone?"

"Not long . . . but there's one more step to take. I need to know who else has been in the house since the burglary."

"Well, apart from the gardaí, it's just me, my brother and the man next door. You need to take our fingerprints too?"

"Not yours, but your brother and neighbour, yes."

"Why don't you need to take *my* prints?"

Thomas Kennedy suddenly said, "Because you have smaller hands."

"That's right," the fingerprint guy said. "Where's your brother now, Miss Adare?"

"He's on his way home. He lives in Tipperary."

"All right. If you can ask him to contact his local station, tell them to get in touch with Detective Mason, they'll be able to sort it out. Unless of course we already have his fingerprints on file."

"That's not likely," I said, "but I'll tell him."

"Good, thanks. Well, I'm done here. Do you think your neighbour will be home now?"

"Probably."

I followed him out to the door, and watched as he walked around to Mr Farley's front door, and knocked on it. A minute later, Mr Farley appeared. The fingerprint guy explained who he was, gestured towards me, and then asked to see Mr Farley's hands. He looked at them for a second, then nodded. "That's fine. Your prints are only in the bedroom, living-room and stairs."

"You don't have to take my prints?" He sounded a little disappointed.

"No, I only need to know which ones to ignore." With that, he nodded good-bye to both of us, got into his car, and drove away.

Mr Farley came over to me. "How is everything going?"

"It's awful . . . but thanks for the armchair. Even if I don't manage to get any bedclothes I can sleep there tonight. I probably won't though."

He gave me a brave smile. "I'm sure everything will work out fine, Orla. I know it seems bad now, but sometimes you just have to say to yourself, 'Well, it's happened and I can't change that. I'll learn to live with it and go on.'"

"You're right, but I think it's going to be a while before I get to that stage. I mean, in some ways the bad stuff hasn't even really started yet. As you've probably seen I've had a few callers looking for Des, and I'm certain that there's going to be a lot more over the next couple of weeks."

"And you still have a caller at the moment," he said.

"Damn! I nearly forgot about him!" As I headed back inside, I turned and said to Mr Farley, "I'll talk to you later, okay?"

He nodded, and went about the business of pretending to be doing something in the garden as an excuse for seeing what the neighbours were up to.

Back inside, Thomas Kennedy was sitting on the arm of my armchair and reading one of Dad's old newspapers. He jumped to his feet when I came in.

"Sorry," I said. "As you can see, it's been a bit crazy here today."

"Indeed. Where were we?"

"You were about to tell me the whole story."

"Of course . . . Look, if you're not busy here we should go back to my office. At least there we can both sit down at the same time."

"Thanks, but I'd rather stay here. If any more people call I want to be here for them."

"But you're not responsible for what happened," he said that in a way that made me wonder if he was silently adding, 'are you?'.

"I know, but a lot of people have no idea what's going on. At least if I'm here I might be able to help stop the rumours."

"All right . . . in that case, maybe the best thing would be to get a list of all the people involved and organise a meeting of some kind." He paused for a second, then said, "I'll assign one of the clerks the task of organising it. Someone to act as a sort of nexus for the information."

I nodded, then said, "What's a nexus?" I knew that it wasn't what it sounded like: a car.

"Someone or something that ties everything together."

"Okay."

"In the meantime, it would be helpful if you could keep a list of all the people who approach you. Names, phone numbers, and so on."

"Sure . . . But tell me this . . . assuming for the moment that Des has taken the money and is never coming back, then what happens to the land?"

"The land?"

"Yeah, the nine acres."

"As I see it, Mr Mills arranged a small consortium to buy the land from the original farmer, and it was then sold on to a new owner, and the investors were paid back. But Mr Mills had struck a deal with this owner to build the shopping centre on the land, and that's where my company comes in. Our investment is – *was* – to cover the costs of the building of the centre. When it was completed, the new owner of the land would have sold it to us."

"God, that's way too complicated for me!"

He raised an eyebrow. "Really? But that's the simplified version! The complex version covers years of wrangling with various authorities to obtain the required permits. You see, there are several stages one has to go through . . ."

I put up my hands. "Stop right there! God, it's bad enough that Des has turned out to be a crook, now you're telling me he was a bureaucrat too? Just tell me this: how bad is it for your company?"

He considered this. "Well, we've been working on this project for two years, and we expected to be reaping the benefits for decades to come. It's about as bad as anything *can* be."

"But . . . can't you just write off the three hundred thousand as a bad move, and get on with something else? Surely that's not so much for a big company?"

"It's not that simple. The three hundred thousand was just the money we gave to Mr Mills."

"Listen, considering everything he's done, you can probably skip the formalities now. No need to call him

'Mr'. Just call him what everyone else does: 'that lousy bastard'."

He ignored me and continued: "Aside from that money, there's salaries and expenses to consider, not to mention the good will involved. All the investors we've been courting will have to be informed, and they won't be happy. They've put their faith in us. Many of them are small companies that will now either have to find another investment, or, eventually, they'll be forced to close, or at least radically change the way they work. For some, that will mean laying people off."

"So that lousy bastard has screwed a lot more people than just you and me and his other investors?"

"That's right."

"I suppose he didn't realise that."

"I'd say he did. He always struck me as extremely intelligent. Do you know, once when he'd called to my office we got to chatting about things, and somehow the subject of intelligence came up. I mentioned that I'd found a website that allowed you to check your IQ. Mr Mills was intrigued, and we had a look at it. His IQ was registered at one hundred and seventy-three."

I didn't know much about that sort of thing. "Is that high?"

"Exceptionally high. My own IQ is a hundred and fifty-five, and I was top of my year in college."

"Wow. I wonder how high mine is?" I thought about how I'd somehow managed to let Des con me out of everything I owned. "Probably not more than twelve."

Kennedy smiled. "I doubt that." He glanced at his

watch. "I'd better be on my way. You'll let me know if you hear anything?"

"Of course."

* * *

Once Mr Kennedy had left, I had a look through the house and wasn't impressed to see that the fingerprint guy hadn't bothered to clean up after himself. The whole house was covered in black fingerprints and handprints. It was then that I realised I didn't have an easy way to wipe them off – all of my cleaning stuff was gone.

I didn't even have a roll of toilet paper, something that would certainly be required sooner rather than later for the more usual purposes. There was no doubt about it: I'd have to make a trip to the shops.

Besides, I was getting hungry. That in turn led me to another chain of thought: I could buy food, but nothing that needed to be refrigerated or cooked, because I didn't have a fridge or a cooker. Nor could I buy anything in tins – no tin-opener – or anything liquid that couldn't be drunk out of the bottle. On top of that, it would be tricky to buy anything that required cutlery, since I didn't have any. That meant I'd have to buy a fork, a knife and a spoon, plus at least one plate and a mug. And I couldn't really buy anything that came with a lot of packaging, because my pedal-bin was gone. I didn't even have any bin-bags.

And this led to *another* realisation, a minor one, but annoying nevertheless: ever since the government finally concluded that plastic shopping bags were bad for the environment and were to be outlawed, we were required to bring our own bags with us to the shops, or buy some of those big reusable bags. Until the previous Friday, I'd had half a dozen of those bags. Now, I had nothing that could be used to carry groceries. Except for my holdall, which was still in Mags' house. Still sitting there in the spare bedroom, with my few remaining clothes unwashed and probably starting to stink up the place.

I went back downstairs and dropped into my borrowed armchair. This was getting depressing. I looked out at the houses across the street – all of which came fully equipped with curtains and blinds.

I'd never expected that one day I'd be jealous of the neighbours because they had curtains.

For a moment – but just a moment – I thought I was going to crack. It would be so easy to just burst into tears and hope that someone came along to make everything better. But I knew that wasn't going to happen. I was just going to have to face up to things and somehow kick my life back into shape.

Besides, I kind of liked the idea that one day – in the far future – people would be marvelling at how well I'd coped and how successful I'd become . . . "She started from nothing," the people presenting the documentary would say. "After her boyfriend stole everything she had, she rebuilt her life from the ground up, all on her own. And now she's a multi-billionaire and the first Emperor of Earth."

Right! I said to myself. I got to my feet, checked my phone and concluded that it was charged enough to make a call.

Killian answered on the second ring. I could hear that he was still in the car. "It's me," I said.

"Any developments?"

"Not really, but the gardaí were all over the place and the fingerprint guy has just left. He needs to know which fingerprints are yours to eliminate them from the enquiries."

"Okay," he said, slowly. "But I'm almost home. I don't fancy driving all the way back again."

"No, he said that if you go into your local garda station they should be able to do it for you. Unless there's some reason you don't want to be fingerprinted?"

"None that I can think of. I'll do it after tea. Garda stations open late, don't they?"

"I think they're open twenty-four hours a day, Killian. Something to do with crime never sleeping, and all that."

"Very funny. Okay. Let me know if anything happens, all right?"

After I hung up, I decided on a plan of action: since I had to go out to – somehow – teach the first art class of the course, I'd leave a note on the front door telling potential callers that Des had gone missing so there was no point in knocking and asking for him. Then I'd go to Mags' house and hint like mad that I'd like to stay another night, and I'd worry about everything else in the morning.

Unfortunately, the first part of this plan failed when I realised I didn't have a pen to write the note, and nothing to write on anyway, not counting my dad's collection of old newspapers, which I wasn't going to use for notepaper because they were pretty much all I had left of him.

So I decided to ignore that part of the plan. I gathered up my phone and Detective Mason's charger, and set off.

I did wonder for a few seconds whether it was even worth the trouble of locking the door, but I locked it anyway. The last thing I needed was squatters moving in.

Then again, you never know; maybe the squatters would bring their own furniture.

Chapter 8

Mags and I were sitting at her kitchen table, eating our way through a pasta, broccoli and sausage casserole that was made even more delicious because I hadn't eaten anything since my spaghetti on toast for breakfast.

"So how was school today?"

"Fine," she said. "The usual fights and crying and kids forgetting their lunch."

"It must be great," I said. "You're shaping these kids' minds. Preparing them for the big bad world."

"Sometimes it feels like that, but most of the time I just see it as a job. I just go in and do my best to get through the day with as little trouble as possible. But yeah . . . there are times when I sort of get this flash, and I realise that the things I'm teaching them will stay with them for the rest of their lives. Hopefully."

"So you could tell them all sorts of lies and really screw them up if you wanted to."

Mags didn't find that idea nearly as funny as I did, so I back-tracked a little. "Do you ever get tempted to tell them stuff that's a bit beyond the syllabus? Like, the truth about Santa Claus?"

"No, stuff like that we try to steer well clear of. We can't take the risk of upsetting the parents too much. Apparently a few years back one of the teachers was asked about sex by a class of eleven-year-olds, and he told them everything. I'm told he got so much trouble from the parents that he had to leave."

"I can imagine . . . So, you enjoy it, then?"

"Most of the time, yeah. What about *your* job? The restaurant, I mean. Wouldn't you rather be back in nine-to-five employment?"

I shrugged. "I miss the money, but that's about *all* I miss from the job. Okay, so my own company didn't work out, but I certainly don't miss working my arse off to make someone else rich."

In truth, the job hadn't been as bad as I let on. Most of the time I spent dealing with clients: measuring things up, refining sketches, arguing with suppliers and other designers, that kind of thing.

My friend Davina had once likened my job to working in an animation studio: the chief animators decide exactly how each shot should look, and it's up to the lower-paid slaves to make it all happen. They're hired for their creative skills and then not really allowed to use them.

Davina had hit the nail on the head with that one. After years of studying art and design I found myself in a job where at times I could spend three days trying to track down the precise shade of sienna dye the designer had requested – no, *demanded* – for the chair covers in a room that the client only used once a year.

"But the restaurant? It's okay. I got used to it pretty quickly . . . Actually, that reminds me, I have to get myself a black skirt and a white top before Friday. But yeah, it's all right. I hated it for the first week, but that was mainly because it was the week all the kids made their Holy Communion and we were packed."

"You're not *tremendously* fond of children, are you?"

"Not especially. I mean, I don't dislike them – I suppose I don't really know any, apart from my niece and nephew. When I was a kid I couldn't wait to grow up, but kids today seem a lot more childish than we ever were."

Mags laughed. "That's just your different perspective. I think that they're much more grown up than we were. I mean, most of the children in my class know a lot more about the world than I did. And they're not just better informed, I think they're smarter, too. Well, *some* of them are. After lunch today a couple of them were asking me about you. They said they'd seen you in the restaurant and seemed to be amazed that you existed outside of the place. The same thing happens to me, if I'm out shopping or something and I bump into them. It's like they have everyone categorised by their job; if you're a teacher, you teach. If you're a waitress, you . . . uh . . . what's the word?"

"Serve people?"

"I suppose. I was going to say, 'you wait' but that doesn't sound right." Mags chased the last pasta shell around her plate with her fork. "Does it pay well?"

"No, but now and again I get decent tips, so that

helps." I put down my fork, and sat back. "Flanagan used to keep asking me to work full-time, but I wasn't interested. Between the money I earn at the restaurant and the money I get from the evening classes, I'm doing okay. Or I was, until yesterday morning."

"What are you going to do now?"

I shook my head. "I don't know, I really don't." I glanced at the clock. "In two hours I've got to be at the school for the first class, and I don't have any of the supplies that they paid for. I don't know how I'm supposed to teach them about art if we don't have anything to draw on."

"You're in the school's art room, though, right? You could just use their stuff."

"I don't know . . . I asked about that last year, and they made it pretty clear that we had to keep our stuff separate from theirs. You wouldn't be able to put in a good word for me, would you?"

She shook her head. "I don't think so. Your school and mine are run by two different boards. But look . . . the principal will be there tonight, right? Just explain to her what happened and ask to borrow some of their art supplies. Tell her you'll replace them when you get your money back."

"*If* I get my money back, which doesn't seem likely. You know, I keep thinking that if I *had* been working full-time these past few years, I'd have a lot more money and I wouldn't be so broke now."

"But that only means that you'd have had more money for Des to steal, so you'd still have nothing." Mags started mopping up the remains of the pasta sauce with a slice of brown bread.

"This is true. Still, I might have no choice but to work full-time now, to get enough money to start buying furniture and clothes. God, my clothes!" I almost felt like crying again. "I know it's stupid to worry more about my clothes than, say, the cooker, but . . . I had some really nice stuff, you know?"

"I know."

"And *now* look at me! I don't have enough clothes left to fill a single drawer! All my stuff's going to end up in a dump, or a charity shop!"

Mags didn't seem to be quite so moved by this particular problem; when it came to clothes, she was a lot more down-to-earth than I was. "Don't knock charity shops, Orla. If you're willing to hunt around, you can pick up some great stuff. Or you can if you're not too much of a snob to wear second-hand clothes."

I wasn't sure if that was intended as a jibe or not. "No, that doesn't bother me. But it does bother me that someone would steal my stuff and then just throw it away. Stealing things because you want them, or to sell them for money is bad enough, but stealing things just to hurt someone is absolutely reprehensible. They even took the bloody bathroom cabinet!"

"Well, if you want to look at the positive side, at least you managed to get some of your redecoration done."

"True. But now the rest of my plans are screwed. I've been buying bits and pieces for the house over the past couple of years. I've already got all the tiles and wallpaper, and most of the paint. I've got all the flooring for the kitchen and the carpets for the bedrooms, and I've got . . ." I almost felt like crying again. "At least, I *did* have it all, until last weekend. God, to think that I spent over two hundred and forty euro on a pair of bedside lamps and now I'm never even going to see them working! And all my sketches are gone. There were hundreds of them, and now they're probably sitting in the bottom of a landfill somewhere. All my notes were taken too. As well as all the receipts, and the colour charts, all that sort of thing. And I had a big box stuffed with carpet samples and scraps of cloth. *And* the material for the curtains is gone! I was going to make them myself. It was a sort of Prussian Blue with little gold flecks in it. It cost me a fortune, and I just *know* I'll never be able to find the same pattern again! *And* my sewing machine is gone. I mean, it wasn't great, but it's still another thing I have to replace."

Mags started to say something, but I was on a roll . . . "They took my ladders as well, and one of them was *brand new*! I only got it last week and I never even got a chance to take the bloody plastic off it! God, they even took the planks!"

"Planks?"

"You know, you put them between two chairs when you're painting the ceiling! Not that I have any chairs any more. My drop cloths are also gone. And I'd bought a whole box of cheapo rolls of kitchen towels for wiping up any splashes, that's gone too."

I could tell from the way Mags sat back in her chair, thin-lipped and silent, that she wasn't all that interested in me listing the former contents of my house.

"Sorry," I said. "I'm getting carried away again."

She pushed her chair back and got to her feet. "Tea?"

"Yeah, please." Mags and Justin were those strange

sort of people who didn't drink tea with their meals, only after.

As she was filling the kettle, she said, "How about Des? Did he do much of the redecoration?"

"Not really, but that was because I wanted to do as much as possible myself. You know? I liked the idea that one day, when I became a famous designer, I'd put the house on the market and it'd go for a fortune, because everyone would go mad for a whole house designed by the legendary award-winning Orla Adare." I laughed. "And now it looks like I am going to be famous, but not in a good way. Now I'm the failed designer who allowed herself to get completely screwed over by the man she thought she was going to marry. God, I can't believe how much I trusted that bastard!"

Mags looked at me with a curious expression. "Did he ever give *any* hint that he couldn't be trusted?"

"No, nothing. As far as I knew, he was as honest as anyone else."

"Never any hint of indiscretion?"

"How do you mean?"

"Did either of you ever, you know, see anyone else?"

"Not that I know of. I mean, *I* didn't, but I can't be sure about him. I suppose it's possible, but I never had any reason to suspect him." Then I looked at her. "Why? You haven't heard anything, have you?"

She shook her head. "No, nothing. I was just wondering. I mean, he's a good-looking man."

"Yeah . . . but look what good that did in the end. No, next time I'd rather have someone I can trust. That'll be my first priority, coming way before great looks and loads of money. But they'll be important too, of course."

She grinned. "Of course."

We sat in silence for a while, waiting for the kettle to boil, and the silence dragged out so long that I couldn't think of anything to say.

Eventually, as Mags was pouring out the tea, she said, "So you're not sworn off men forever?"

"No. But if the next one screws me over, then I'll give that serious consideration."

"How about that guy you were going out with before Des? You never really said what happened to him."

"You mean Keith? Oh, that was just a short-term thing, really, For the first couple of weeks we couldn't get enough of each other, but then we sort of lost interest and only met up about once every two weeks. I don't think that either of us really cared much about the other."

"How did it all end?"

I thought about this as I put a carefully measured quarter-teaspoon of sugar into my tea – I'd wait until she wasn't looking before I added another spoonful. "You know, it never really ended officially. We just stopped calling each other. One day I suddenly realised I hadn't seen him in ages. I probably wouldn't even have thought about him again except that I was tidying up the bedroom and I found a paperback he'd left behind. I still have it somewhere. Actually, no, I don't. But I did until a few days ago."

"God, you're probably going to spend the rest of your life remembering things you used to have."

"Yeah, I know. I still can't believe that they took *everything*. If I hadn't brought my toothbrush with me to Tipperary, they'd have taken that too."

"Even your little black Zac Posen dress? Remember that? You wore it that night when you and Des were here for dinner and it was so short you couldn't sit down?"

I laughed. "I'd forgotten about that! God, Des couldn't keep his hands off me that night!"

"You know, despite everything he did, I suppose at least if he fancied you then that meant he hadn't been planning to steal from you all along."

"You could be right there." I took a deep breath and let it out slowly. "Why didn't I see it coming?"

"How *could* you have?"

"I don't know . . . but when you live with someone you think you know them well enough that you'd be able to tell when they're planning something like that."

"Orla, no matter how well you know someone, you still don't know them well enough to be able to see everything coming."

I said, "I suppose," and then I noticed her expression: she had something important on her mind, and desperately wanted to tell me. "So how about you and Justin?" I asked. "How well do you really know each other?"

"Well enough."

"It must be tough, with him being away so much."

"At times it is. But he phones every day when he's on the road."

We sat in silence for a little while, and I tried to keep my expression neutral.

Oh my God! I said to myself. She thinks that Justin is having an affair or something! But he couldn't be – that's not like him.

I'd known Justin for fifteen years; I knew he wasn't the

126

sort to cheat on someone. When he first met Mags, he fell in love with her on the spot, but he didn't do anything about it because he was already seeing someone else. And even after he broke it off with her, he waited a respectable amount of time before asking Mags out.

But maybe I didn't really know him *that* well. After all, I thought I knew Des too, and look what happened there.

Maybe this is one of the reasons Mags and I have never really been that close, I said to myself. Maybe she thought that me and Justin were sleeping together, and it's only now that she's realised it's not me.

I didn't know how to approach this. I could ask her right out, but then if I was wrong and she'd never even thought about it, I might be putting the seeds of doubt in her mind.

So I decided to go at it from a different angle: I'd ask her if *she'd* ever considered having an affair, and then I could lead that into asking her whether she thought Justin ever had.

"Let me ask you this," I said, "and of course you don't have to answer if you don't want to . . . have you ever, you know, thought about it? I mean, since you and Justin got together, have you seen anyone else?"

Mags paused. "Yes. I have."

This nearly floored me. "Oh. Really?"

She nodded. "Justin doesn't know, of course."

"Well, no. I can't imagine that you'd ever tell him. Nor should you. These things are better left in the past."

"That's true. Except . . . it's not in the past."

This one not only floored me, it paved over me and built a shopping centre.

When I didn't say anything, Mags added, "But you can't tell him."

"No, I won't." My voice was small and weak.

How the hell could she *do* this? He's one of my best friends – one of my only friends, a part of my brain reminded me – and she's sleeping around on him!

"I suppose you want to know all about it?"

"Not really."

Mags looked down at her hands. "I have to tell someone . . . it's like this thing is eating away inside me."

"Okay," I said. "Tell me. I promise not to judge. Well, I promise to *try* not to judge."

"It's stupid, really. It started about four years ago. I was convinced that Justin was seeing someone else. I won't say who – it doesn't matter. But anyway, I didn't know what to do about it. I tried to mention it a few times, but I wasn't able to get the words out. And as time went on, I got really, really bitter about it. So I decided that if he was having an affair, I would too."

"Just like that?" I blurted. "You just *decided*?"

"Well, yeah. At one of the parent-teacher meetings I was chatting with this guy, and he started flirting like mad. Then he started to make excuses to see me. Like, he'd call in to the school early to take his son to the dentist or the barber, that kind of thing. And well, it was about this time that I was half-convinced Justin was sleeping with someone, so one thing sort of led to another."

"And you're still seeing him?"

"About twice a week, when Justin's away."

"God. Do you love him?"

She didn't answer.

"Well, do you love him more than you love Justin?"

Again, no answer.

"Shit. What are you going to do?"

"What *can* I do?"

"Well, you can't really go on like this, can you? I mean, if Justin finds out he'll be devastated."

Mags reached across the table and grabbed my hand. "Please swear that you won't say anything to him!"

"I won't, I promise. But . . . God, Mags! You're either going to have to stop, or you'll have to tell him. Otherwise it'll tear you apart! Who else knows about this?"

"You're the only one."

"What about the kid?"

"God, no! If he found out he'd tell someone else in the class, and that'd be that. No, we never meet at his house."

"Here?"

"Sometimes, if there's an excuse for him to be here."

"Wait, Justin *knows* him?"

"He does. Peter's a cabinetmaker by trade, so when we were getting the kitchen done he had a lot of reasons to turn up here. And then he built us a bed, and put in the fitted wardrobes."

"You mean, you're sleeping with *Pete Harney*? The same Pete Harney from the hardware store?"

She nodded. "Yeah."

I almost said, "But he's not even good-looking!" but I realised that wasn't going to help her feel any better about things. Peter was a thin man with a pot-belly and skinny arms and absolutely *huge* hands. All he needed was a pair of white gloves and couple of black saucers strapped to his head and he'd have been a dead ringer for Mickey Mouse. "Mags, he's *married*!"

"I know that."

"Well, now I don't know *what* to say."

"I can imagine."

"Look . . . why did you tell me? I mean, we don't even know each other all that well."

She shrugged. "I suppose that's the thing about having a secret. If you haven't got anyone to share it with, it grows and grows. God, the number of times I almost told the priest in confession!"

"Why didn't you?"

"Because, well, I know it's a sin, but if I told him, then he'd tell me things I didn't want to hear."

"So you're ashamed of it?"

"What do *you* think?" She sounded hurt and angry. "It's like an addiction. I know it's wrong, I want to stop, but I can't. And . . . well, there's another problem."

Oh great! I said to myself. What now? Please don't tell me you're pregnant!

She continued: "I'm afraid that if I break it off with Peter, he'll tell Justin."

"Why do you think that?"

"About a year ago I started to tell him that I thought we should stop seeing each other, or at least cool things down a bit, and he said, 'Are you sure that's the way you want to do things?' But it was the *way* he said it, like he was implying that there would be consequences."

"Jesus. And this is the man you love more than Justin?"

"I never said that."

"I know, you just didn't answer me. So *do* you?"

"I don't know. He's . . . exciting, you know? He's very attentive, very kind. He knows what I want in bed."

"And Justin doesn't?"

"Oh, he does, but he's not as . . . how can I put it? He's not as adventurous. With Justin, sex is more like a duty he has to perform than an act of passion. Sometimes he's away for more than a week, but when he gets back it's not like he's raring to go, not like he's been driving all the way home with a massive hard-on and just dying to get me into bed."

That kind of caught me off-guard; it was weird to think of Justin in that way. That said, when I was about fourteen I had a dream that me and Justin were walking along a beach and I turned around and saw that he was naked and erect. He said to me, "Orla, will you let me put it in you?" Thankfully, I woke up then, but I wasn't able to look him in the eye for weeks afterwards. I kept getting the feeling that somehow he knew he'd starred in one of my sex dreams.

"So how do you keep all this covered up?" I said to Mags. "Surely there isn't enough work in the house for you to pretend that Pete has a reason to be here all the time?"

"I told Justin that Pete's a nice guy, but he's a bit slow, and he's paranoid about his own lack of education. The official story is that Pete can't read too well."

"You're pretending that you're teaching him to read?"

"Yeah."

"So that's just one lie on top of another."

"I thought you said you weren't going to judge?"

"I'm not judging, I'm just observing . . . Mags, you have to break it off with him. Either that, or you have to leave Justin. It's not fair to either of you."

Mags said nothing, just got to her feet and started clearing away the dishes.

"Let me do that," I said. "It's the least I can do after you feeding me." I took the dishes from her and carried them to the sink. "Where do you keep your washing-up stuff?"

* * *

Mrs Darcy, the principal of the secondary school, had listened with great patience to my tale of woe, and reluctantly agreed to let me use some of the school's supplies. "Just keep a note of everything you use," she'd told me. "I expect it to be fully replaced sooner rather than later."

So now I was standing inside the door of the art room for the purpose of greeting my students as they arrived. There were nineteen of them due, I remembered from my enrolment sheet. Unfortunately, that was about all I could remember from it – the sheet was stolen along with everything else – so I didn't know most of their names.

The class was due to start at eight. I knew from experience that this was not going to happen . . .

Eight o'clock: the classroom held me and two students, a retired married couple who had decided that it might be nice to spend a couple of evenings each week *not* in front of the television.

Eight-fifteen: five students arrived together, all post-menopausal women, all a little on the tipsy side.

132

Eight-thirty: only four people missing, time to get started.

The students had settled themselves around the classroom, most huddled in little bunches with a few stragglers looking uncomfortable. The huge desks had been spread with old newspapers and one old guy had found a crossword and was busy filling it in.

I cleared my throat, and said, "Well, we're still a few people short, but we should get started."

An elderly woman said, "Can we just hold on for a few minutes more? My friend Betty said she'd definitely be here."

"She did know that we were supposed to start at eight?" I asked, trying to keep any hint of sarcasm out of my voice.

"She's running late on account of she's having trouble with her budgie."

I didn't want to know. "Let's just get started and I can fill her in later, okay?" I wrote my name in big letters on the blackboard. "I'm Orla Adare, but you don't need to call me Miss or anything, just call me Orla."

A really old man put up his hand. "Do we need to put up our hands if we want to ask you something?"

"No, not at all. What did you want to ask me?"

"Er . . . just that. Thanks."

Someone else put up his hand. "What about if we need to go to the bathroom?"

"The bathrooms are down the hall, to your left."

"No, I mean do we need to ask you if we have to go?"

"No, just go." I smiled to myself, remembering a similar situation at the start of the previous term's course.

Most of these people hadn't been in school in over forty years. In their minds, "school" still meant Latin, canings and teachers with short fuses and hard fists. "You'll be pleased to know that this isn't like when *you* were in school. You can come and go as you want, you can chat with each other when you're drawing or painting – within reason, of course. There's no exams, and no homework if you don't want to do it. The main point of all this is to learn a little about art and to have a good time."

The first old man raised his hand again, then realised that he didn't need to and put it down. "Will there be life studies?"

"Sorry? Life studies?"

"You know. People to draw."

"Probably not in this class, no. But next term, if there's enough interest, I might take an advanced class."

He looked a little disappointed – perhaps he'd been hoping he'd get a chance to draw some naked young women.

I picked up a ream of A3 sheets from my desk, and passed them out, three or four sheets to each person. "We're going to start off simply," I said. "A pencil sketch of . . ." I looked around for something they could draw. "A chair."

I lifted my chair off the floor and placed it on the desk. "This should be easy enough. Straight lines, only a few curves." I passed out the pencils and erasers, then asked them all to gather around one of the desks while I demonstrated. "Now, there are two tricks that you really need to master right at the start, but they're pretty straight-forward. First off, you really need to *look* at what you're drawing. Draw what you see, not what you *think* you see. It doesn't matter if your chair looks a little out of shape; you can't expect to get it right first go. And that leads me to the second trick: rough out the shape using very light pencil lines, like this. That makes them easier to erase later on."

Someone said, "So we draw lots and lots of lines and only keep the ones we need?"

"Exactly."

I watched from the head of the class as they began scribbling. At the back of the room, the five women who had arrived together were whispering about something. I decided that if they kept it up for the whole class I'd have to have a word with them.

Some of the students showed real talent. The old man who'd asked whether he needed to put up his hand to ask a question was actually very good. Using deft, light strokes, he quickly blocked out the chair, shaded it, and even added the desk underneath. This man had been drawing all his life, I could tell.

Most of the students made the mistake of thinking that their sketch needed to fill the whole page, but one or two copped on rather quickly and produced a sketch that was no bigger than their hands. This was not only faster than doing a full-page drawing, it was a lot easier to be accurate.

I stopped them after ten minutes, then went to each student in turn and talked about what they'd done wrong, and suggested possible ways to improve it. In every class, there's always at least one person who has no artistic talent whatsoever, and this class had two of them: the couple who'd arrived first.

My God, their drawings were bad! Even though the chair was at an oblique angle to them, they'd both elected to draw it from the side, completely missing my "draw what you see" hint. I sat down between them and took a blank sheet of paper. "Now . . . here's the way *I* see it, okay?" I dashed out another sketch of the chair. "See?"

They went "Ohhhh!" and "*Now* I get it!" a lot, but I could tell that they were going to require a lot of supervision over the coming weeks. I got the feeling that neither of them had *ever* drawn anything before.

The quintet at the back had produced five rough sketches ranging in quality from quite good to average, but when I approached them their whispers hushed and they kept giving me furtive glances. As I talked about their drawings with them, one of them said, "You wouldn't by any chance be the *same* Orla Adare, would you?"

I knew what was coming, but even so I said, "The same Orla Adare as who?"

"*Whom*," the woman corrected, automatically. "Desmond Mills' partner."

"That's me," I said. "I suppose you've heard what happened?"

She went, "Hmmm . . . there's been some talk."

"I don't know who's saying what, but you know how these things are. Most of what's being said is probably not true. Look, we're short on time so if you don't mind I'd rather discuss that outside the classroom."

She put her hand on my arm in a manner that I imagine she meant to be supportive. "Of course, dear."

I quickly finished up with them and move on to the

next desk, where – ignoring the fervent whispers breaking out behind me – I tried to explain to a middle-aged man that "light pencil lines" didn't mean leaning as hard on the pencil as possible. "This is a pencil, not a chisel," I explained.

He nodded, grinning. "I know, I know . . . I'm just used to filling out forms in the office all day. You have to press real hard with the pen because it has to make five copies."

Once I was done assessing their abilities, I asked them to all write their names on their sketches and pass them up to me. "I want you to draw the chair again," I said, "and then we'll see how we're doing."

The second time things were a lot better. Okay, so the artless couple managed to produce sketches of chairs that even Picasso would have thought looked wonky, and the heavy leaner broke the point of his pencil twice, but on the whole the drawings showed improvements.

Next, we went on to sketching with charcoal, which produced an incredible mess and the students ended up looking like it was Ash Wednesday down a coalmine.

But I was generally impressed with how quickly they were all taking to it. In the past I'd had students who took weeks just to learn how to *hold* a pencil; if this lot kept it up, we might be able to progress on to watercolours before the month was out.

At a quarter to ten, I started wrapping it up. "Tomorrow night, we'll go a little further and start adding shade and depth to the drawings. Now, if you get a chance, I'd like you to do a couple of sketches of things around the home. You don't need to have them done by tomorrow night; next week will be fine."

Someone asked, "Do we have to?"

"No, it's not mandatory. But the more you draw the quicker you'll learn."

The errant Betty – she of the troublesome budgie – showed up at five minutes to ten. Without a word she wandered in and sat down next to her friend.

I stared at her. "And *you* are?"

"Late, I know," she said. "Sorry, dear."

"I mean, what's your name?"

"This is Betty," said Betty's friend.

"Em . . . you do know that we were due to start at eight?"

She nodded.

"And you know that it's almost ten now?"

She nodded again. "Better late than never. Can you just quickly run through everything I've missed?"

* * *

I ushered them out all of the classroom a few minutes later, then set about tidying up the room.

Before I'd left for the school, Mags has asked me if I wanted to spent the night again, and I'd gratefully accepted, even though I was pretty sure that her offer was more because she wanted to continue our discussion about her affair than out of sympathy for my plight.

I was thinking about this as I straightened the chairs and gathered up pencils and sticks of charcoal, when someone knocked on the door and came in. I almost dropped everything: it was Peter Harney.

"Hey, Orla. How'd it go?"

"Okay. You?" I couldn't help picturing him and Mags in bed together, shagging each other's brains out.

"Not bad. All fifteen showed up. How about your lot?"

"Three no-shows. Well, there was a fourth, but she only turned up about ten minutes ago."

He nodded in that "I'm not really listening, I'm just waiting for you to stop" fashion. Then he said, "I heard about Des."

I looked up at him. "So what have you heard exactly?"

"He's absconded with all the money from the shopping-centre project."

"And the entire contents of my house, plus my bank account."

Peter bit his lip. "Jesus. That's bad. And you didn't see it coming?"

"What do *you* think?"

"Sorry. So what are you going to do?"

I shrugged. "Right now, I'm just happy enough to be able to keep going from one minute to the next."

"Look, do you need a lift home?"

"Thanks, but I'm not going home. I don't have a bed any more. You don't happen to have any old furniture knocking about in your shop that you can let me have for free, do you?"

"Nothing's come in for weeks. But I'll keep an eye out. So where are you staying?"

I watched him carefully as I answered. "I'm staying with my friend Justin and his wife. I think you know them, don't you?"

He batted not an eyelid. "I do indeed. I've done some work for them over the years. Come on, I'll give you a lift."

While we drove back through town towards Justin

Jaye Carroll

and Mags' house, I found myself explaining everything that had happened in great detail.

When we reached the house, Pete said, "What are you going to do now?"

"The next step is to try and earn some more money. I'm going to have to see Mr Flanagan tomorrow and see if he'll let me work more hours."

"Do you think he will?"

"I can't see why not," I said. "He's asked me enough times in the past. I can't see any reason why he might change his mind. I know that he'd invested money with Des, but he's not going to blame *me* for that."

I was wrong about that.

"I mean, Mr Flanagan's always been very good to me. He's one of the nice guys."

As it turned out, I was wrong about that, too.

Chapter 9

I arrived at the bistro next morning to see my co-servers Steve and Pauline setting the tables for the lunchtime shift.

Pauline came over to me. She was about twenty-one, short, a little overweight, and with what the shampoo ads called "dull, lifeless hair". She wasn't classically good-looking, but somehow she always seemed to have a string of men following her. Steve was completely in love with her; he'd once told me that the only reason he was still working in the restaurant was because he knew that he didn't stand a chance against any of Pauline's other male friends, and this was the only way he'd be able to spend time with her.

"He's in the back," Pauline said, referring to Mr Flanagan. "Listen, I heard about everything. The whole town's talking about it. Are you okay?"

"Not really. But I'm getting better. What sort of things have people been saying?"

"That Des ran off with all the money from the shopping-centre thing, and that he cleared you out as well. A few people seem to be of the opinion that you were involved and that Des double-crossed you and left you behind."

"Shit."

Pauline nodded towards the back room. "He hasn't said anything about it to us, but if I was you I'd go in prepared for a fight."

"All right. Thanks for the heads-up." I left them to it and went into the back room.

The "back room" wasn't much more than a large pantry off the kitchen that doubled as Flanagan's office. He stood in front of me with his arms folded and stared at me without blinking.

Mr Flanagan was a stick-thin old man with cauliflower ears, a beetroot-red nose and – in keeping with the food theme – liver-spotted skin. He bore a red toupee that wouldn't have looked out of place in a book of carpet samples. Apparently way back at the dawn of time he'd been a prominent head chef, and this restaurant was his retirement. Or at least it would have been if he hadn't been there all day every day. As a boss, he was more or less ideal; he was pretty generous about time off, didn't push too hard or expect too much, and generally had a cheery disposition that today he was keeping very well hidden.

"Orla, what's this I've been hearing about your boyfriend? There's a lot of people saying a lot of things. Is it true?"

"Depends on what they're saying. If they're saying that he's disappeared with the money for the shopping-centre project, that's true. And it's also true if they're saying that he's cleaned out my bank account and taken everything I own."

"What are the chances of getting the money back?"

"They're not good."

He studied me for a long time, then said, "I invested almost seventy thousand euros with his company. You're telling me that it's all gone?"

"I can't be sure but . . . it looks like that, yeah."

"Then I'm in trouble. I might not be able to keep the restaurant open."

I said "Oh," because I couldn't think of anything else.

"You . . ." He took a deep breath – well, as deep as he was able – and said, "Orla, do you remember the day you told me about the shopping centre? And do you remember saying that it was going to revitalise the area? And do you remember telling me that it would be a great investment?"

"Actually, no. The way I remember it is that you heard about it from someone else and you asked me for Des's number so you could talk to him about it. It wasn't me who gave you the idea."

"Well, it was. I certainly didn't hear about it from anyone else."

He was either lying or mistaken, but I didn't think that arguing that point was a priority right now. "I don't remember that at all, but if it was me, I'm sorry."

He bit the inside of his cheek with his false teeth. "I'm probably going to have to close the restaurant because I borrowed money to invest with Desmond. If I sell the restaurant and pay back the loan in one lump sum at least I won't have to keep paying the interest. So thanks to you, I'm back to where I was ten years ago."

I stepped back from him. "Now, look! It's not my fault! It's got nothing to do with me."

"Really? Well, you were living with him. You're a director of his company. You have to accept at least *some* responsibility for all this."

"But that's crazy!"

He hesitated before going on, and I could see that this was what he'd been building up to. "There might be a way I can keep the restaurant open."

"Well, that's good."

"You'll have to work more hours and take a pay-cut. And any tips you get, you give them to me. I realise it's going to take you a long time to pay me back that way, but the alternative is for you to sell your house, and I'm sure you don't want to do that."

"Now hold on a second! *I* don't owe you that money, Des does! I'm *not* responsible for his actions!"

"Orla, the only other alternative is for me to get my solicitor to start drawing up a lawsuit against you, and you'll only end up having to pay the court costs as well." He gave me a sympathetic look. "I'm only looking out for your best interests. I mean, anyone else wouldn't even give you the option of staying on. They'd fire you *and* sue you."

"Well, aren't you Mr Fucking Considerate!"

"All right, now there's no call for that sort of language!"

"No, you listen to *me*, Mr Flanagan! If you try and sue me *you* will lose, and then I'll hit you with a counter-suit so big you'll lose the restaurant *and* your house! How's that sound? And don't think that I won't win, because I will! The police are already satisfied that I had nothing to do with it. The bank records will show that I wasn't involved in the company in any way – that bastard forged my signature on the forms – and how sympathetic do you think the judge is going to be to you after he hears about the way you're trying to intimidate me?" I stopped myself before I could add, 'So there!'

He looked at me for a long time, then said, "You're fired."

"You can't fire me without a reason."

"Insubordination."

"You're supposed to give me written warnings."

"All right, then, you're not fired. But considering the dire financial situation in which I find myself, I have no choice but to let you go."

"You can't make me redundant without giving me some sort of severance pay."

"If that's the way you want it, I won't make you redundant, or fire you."

"Well . . . good."

"Oh, before I forget, it looks like this weekend is going to be pretty slack, so there's no need for you to come in."

"I see. And next weekend?"

"I imagine we're going to be slack then, too."

"Mr Flanagan . . . you can't do that."

"Yes, I can. It's up to me to decide who's needed and who isn't. And I say you're not needed."

"So I have no choice but to resign?"

"You *do* have a choice. Sit at home waiting for me to phone you and let you know when I want you to come in."

I laughed. "You know, that would sound a lot more

sinister if Des hadn't stolen my phone. So why don't you die and go to hell and we'll see how accurate your self-righteous attitude is then?"

* * *

By the time I got back to the house I was absolutely furious with Mr Flanagan, with Des, with myself, with Mags for cheating on Justin, with the woman who worked in the drapery shop because she gave me a funny look, with a motorist who had passed by with his radio too loud. I was pissed off with the birds because they were chirping in an annoying way, with the sun because it was too hot, with one of my neighbours who hadn't cleaned up all his hedge-clippings from the path.

I opened the front door and wasn't at all astonished to see that my furniture hadn't mysteriously reappeared. Still, there was one difference: the postman had been.

I put down my bags and scooped up the mail; phone bill, bank statement, free tiny sample box of washing powder, four flyers for local businesses.

The bank statement showed the amount Des had withdrawn from my account, which was the same amount as the balance for the previous entry. He'd cleaned me out down to the cent.

And the bank statement had another withdrawal listed . . . Bank charges: fifteen euro and thirty cent. Marvellous.

So now I was not only broke, I was overdrawn.

I threw the statement aside and gathered up my bags, then went upstairs.

In the drapery shop I'd bought curtains – horrible, but cheap – a pillow, and a set of bed sheets, and a trip to the charity shop had resulted in two thick blankets. At least now I'd be able to sleep in my own house.

I'd also bought a pair of jeans and two T-shirts in the charity shop – total cost, fifteen euro – so at least I had another change of clothes. Though I couldn't really see myself going outside wearing the T-shirt which said: *Golfers Do It In The Rough!!!*

My burglars had thoughtfully not taken the curtain pole along with the rest of my stuff, so that saved me some money, and some time: it took only five seconds for me to attempt to hang the curtains and then realise that I didn't have any hooks. Still, the curtains were way longer than I needed – because I'd planned to cut them in half and use them on one of the other windows – so I just hung them over the poles and decided to worry about fixing them properly some other time.

I stood back and looked at my curtains.

Well, I said to myself, that's all the housework done.

As I was going back downstairs for a good sit in my armchair, the doorbell rang.

I opened the door to see two familiar spotty faces: Jumper Man and Reebok from the day before.

"Any word?" Jumper Man asked.

"Nothing," I said. "I don't suppose you've heard anything yourself?"

They glanced at each other, then Jumper Man said, "Lotta people've been sayin' you were in on it."

"I know. But a lot of people say a lot of things. That doesn't make them true."

Reebok stepped closer. "Lissen, we don't want to cause any trouble."

"Good. I don't want you to either."

"It's just that . . ." He paused, and I got the impression that he was trying to remember his lines. "It's just that you have certain obligations to us."

"No, I don't."

"Yes, you do, actually," Jumper Man said.

"How so?"

"Because you just do."

"Well, you've got me there." From their blank expressions, it was clear that the appreciation of sarcasm was a dying art. "Look . . . Des stole two grand from you, right?"

Reebok nodded, the peak of his baseball cap bobbing up and down.

"Okay. So if you can find Des and get *my* money back – and all my stuff – as well as the money he owes you, I'll pay you another two grand. How's that sound?"

"You're just tryin' to put us off," said Reebok.

"That's true. But you can't blame me for that. Look at it this way, lads. Say I kept coming knocking on your door and bothering you about it, would you think that was fair?" Before they could answer, I continued: "No, of course you wouldn't. But I've lost way more than you have, so why are you bothering me? Are you going around to everyone else Des ripped off and threatening them?"

"We never threatened you," said Jumper Man, in what he probably believed was a menacing tone.

"Yes, you did," I said. "Yesterday you told me that if I mentioned you to the gardaí it would be bad for me. That's a threat if ever there was one."

The fight went out of Reebok then. His shoulders sagged and for a second he looked as though he was about to cry. "What're we goin' to do? I *need* that money!"

"I'm sure you do. And I'm sorry for you, I really am, but there's nothing I can do about it. I've lost all my savings, everything in the house, the man I thought I loved, and today I lost my job. So you'll understand if I'm not more concerned about your situation than I am about mine."

And then Jumper Man said, "Lissen, can we come in and talk about this?"

Normally I would have said no, but there was something in his eyes, something in his tone of voice, that made me realise that these young men weren't really bad sorts, just rather pathetic. "You can come in," I said, "but there's only one chair and I can't offer you coffee or anything."

But they came in anyway, and – like everyone else – spent a couple of seconds looking around the bare sitting-room in surprise. Reebok turned to me and said, "He took *everything*?"

"Yeah. My neighbour gave me that armchair and a bed. They even cleaned out the attic – those newspapers were all that was left up there."

"Fuck."

"That's putting it mildly."

Jumper Man said, "Sometimes you hear stuff down the pub, you know, lads bullshittin' about breaking into someone's house and all that. But this . . . I never heard of anythin' like this before. What would they *do* with it all?"

"Beats me," I said.

"No, I mean, there's no way they can sell everythin'. Like, who'd *buy* it? Who in their right mind would buy second-hand carpets? So all that stuff will end up dumped somewhere. They musta known that when they were takin' it, so why'd they do it? It musta taken *hours*. It can'ta been worth their while doin' it."

"Believe me, I've thought of that."

Reebok took off his cap and scratched his head as he looked around. I was behind him, and I could see why he wore that cap; even though he was only in his early twenties, he was starting to go bald. "Then he did it just to hurt you." He turned back to me. "That's the only thing that makes sense."

"I thought of that, too. But I can't see why. I never gave him any reason."

And then, amazingly, Reebok said, "Well, I've got a spare telly and video you can borrow, if you want."

"Hold on . . . a few minutes ago you were acting the hard man, and now you're willing to lend me your stuff?"

He nodded. "Yeah. Sorry. It's just . . ." he shook his head, "there are some things you just don't do, you know? I mean, even the lads we know who really do nick stuff, well, they'd never do anythin' like this. Not even the real psychos. Not unless they wanted to get back at someone and *really* wanted to hurt them."

"Yeah," Jumper Man said, "and even then they'd just set fire to the house."

I didn't know quite how to react to that.

"Lissen, I've got stuff you can borrow too. I was in a flat last year, but I had to give it up, so I've got a fridge and a microwave that're just sittin' out in the shed. You can have them for a while. But I'm goin' to want them back at some stage."

So that was how I came into possession of a noisy fridge that smelled a bit, a microwave oven that needed to be cleaned, a set of fairly new steak knives, a television, video recorder and a ridiculously large ghetto-blaster. Reebok even brought along a big box of videos. They were mostly kung fu movies, but I wasn't complaining.

I also had a medium-sized rickety kitchen table and two mismatched chairs, courtesy of the Johnsons who lived across the road; old Mrs Johnson had seen Jumper Man and Reebok carrying in the fridge, and called me over.

Mrs Johnson was one of those tiny old women who look like they've been made at the Generic Old Woman factory, sole proprietors of Grannys 'R' Us. She had the rosy cheeks, the beaming Steradent smile, the support stockings, the black handbag – the works.

We stood on opposite sides of her gate, which had been carefully tied with one of those red plastic strips that turf briquettes come wrapped in. "Your brother was telling me about what happened with Desmond," she'd said. "I told him to let you know that we have a table and two chairs you can have."

"That's very good of you, thanks."

"You can ask them young lads to give you a hand."

So she untied the plastic strip from the gate, and me, Jumper Man and Reebok – I really was going to have to try and remember their real names – spent a good ten minutes in her garage clearing away all the debris between the table and the door.

And I even had a bed of my own to sleep in. It didn't look like it was the most comfortable thing in the world, but for the first time in nearly a week I would be able to sleep in my own house.

* * *

Everyone turned up for Wednesday evening's class. That was the first time – ever! – that I had a full class of students. It would have been nice to think that they all showed up because they knew I was a great teacher, but I was pretty sure that the truth was they'd all heard about Des and they wanted to see what a world-class victim looked like.

It went pretty well. As there were a few who hadn't been there the previous night, I quickly covered the same ground, then started to tell them how to shade a sketch to give it the appearance of three dimensions.

I pinned a large sheet of paper to the blackboard, drew a circle and was in the process of turning it into a ball by adding a shadow and some shading when a woman interrupted me. "Sorry, Orla . . . I was just wondering when we get our books? You said at the enrolment last week that the course fee covers the cost of a couple of books."

"Ah. Well, there's a bit of a delay . . ."

Someone else said, "You're not going to tell us that they were nicked along with everything else from your house, are you?"

I heard someone whisper to the person beside him, "Oh . . . you mean *she's* the one yer man ripped off?"

Honesty, is the best policy, I decided. "Unfortunately, yes, that's exactly what happened to the books. But I promise that I'm doing my best to replace them. With luck we'll have them for next week." This was a complete fabrication; I had absolutely no idea where I was going to be able to get the money for the books.

Most of them were satisfied with that, but I did hear a couple of low grumbles.

* * *

That night, as I lay on my borrowed bed under my second-hand blankets, I dreamed that I was back in my old bed, and I could sense that Des was there with me. As usual, he was lying right on the edge of the bed, and I reached out to touch him, but he was too far away. No matter how much I stretched, he was always out of reach.

Then, in the dream, I sat up and saw that he wasn't in bed at all; he was standing in front of the mirror, wearing only his socks, underpants and a red shirt. He was putting on a white tie.

"Morning," I said to him.

He stared at my reflection in the mirror, and nodded.

"What're you up to today?"

"Got to go down to the site. They're going to start laying the pipes."

"How are you going to get all those pipes into your removals truck?"

"We'll find a way. After that, I have to go to the bank, and then I need to buy tickets to Rio."

"Tickets? Plural? You mean you're taking me with you?"

"No, I'm taking someone else."

I was shocked. "Oh. Who?"

"Orla."

"But . . . *I'm* Orla!"

He frowned at me. "No, you're not." And then he stepped aside, and angled the mirror so that I could see my reflection. It wasn't me.

Chapter 10

I sat up suddenly, wide awake, my heart pounding like crazy, making a deep, low booming sound.

It took me a few seconds to realise that the booming sound wasn't my heartbeat, but someone knocking on the front door.

Then I heard a man's voice calling, "Miss Adare? I know you're in there!"

I swung my legs out of bed, pulled on my new jeans and one of my two T-shirts, and went down to the front door. It was Detective Mason.

"Afternoon," he said.

There was an envelope dangling by one corner from the inside of the letterbox and I pulled it out and stuffed it in the back pocket of my jeans. "Afternoon? What time is it?"

"Lunchtime," he said. "Just about."

"Okay . . . and what *day* is it?"

"Thursday. I've come to collect my phone charger."

I pulled the door open wider. "Sure . . . come in. Hold on a second while I get it." Halfway up the stairs I stopped and turned back to him. "Any word?"

"Nothing, yet. It's still early days, though."

"And the fingerprints?"

He shook his head. "No luck there. There aren't any matches on file. I'm guessing that whoever your boyfriend hired for this, they weren't criminals. They were just normal movers. And we got your brother's prints, too. You'll be pleased to know that he's not wanted for anything."

"So what's next?"

"Next we're going to have to ask your neighbour to give us descriptions of the men he saw. If he can remember anything useful, we'll ask him to come to the station to go through some photos."

"If they were normal movers, then surely they'll know where they brought my stuff?"

He nodded. "That's what we're hoping. And maybe they'll have a better clue as to what happened to Mr Mills."

I went upstairs to unplug the charger – and to change out of my *Golfers Do It In The Rough!!!* T-shirt – and came back down to find Detective Mason going through Jumper Man's box of videos.

"Here you go," I said. "Thanks. I'm going to have to buy my own charger eventually, but at least now I'll get a couple more days out of the phone."

"I have a few more questions for you . . . if that's okay."

"Don't tell me you've changed your mind about me being not guilty?"

"No, not at all. But your situation here is pretty much

all anyone has been talking about for the past couple of days. We've had a *lot* of people complaining about Mr Mills, and most of them seem to think that, even if you weren't directly involved, then you should at least have known something was up. I have to ask: have you had any people calling about it?"

"Yeah, a few."

"Has anyone threatened you at all?"

"Not really. A couple of them hinted that they wouldn't want to find out that I was involved. The thing is, I think that once they realise I'm just as much a victim as they are, they know I didn't have anything to do with it."

He considered this. "Miss Adare, I feel obliged to warn you that *we* have heard some threats made against you."

"How do you mean?"

"More than one complainant has intimated that you will be – as one of them put it – 'up shit creek without a paddle *or* a boat' if they find out that you and Mr Mills were in collusion. So far, all such comments have been made in anger – we doubt that any of them are serious. And we have of course made it clear to them that as far as we're concerned, you're completely innocent."

"Well, good. Thanks for that."

"But to be on the safe side, I think that you'd probably be better off moving away, at least until everything dies down a little."

"I can't do that," I said. "First, I really don't have anywhere to go. Not unless I go to a hotel or something, and I can't afford that because I lost my job yesterday. And second, as long as I'm here, most people won't think I was

Jaye Carroll

involved. Plus I've got to be here on Tuesday and Wednesday nights for my classes. And anyway, this house is all I have left! I'm not going to give it up."

He nodded, and it seemed to me that he had known I wasn't going to move anyway. "I understand. How did you lose your job?"

"My boss was one of Des's investors. He wanted me to take responsibility for the money he invested. We had a fight about it."

"So he fired you?"

"No, but he made it clear that I wasn't welcome there any more."

The Detective considered this for a few seconds. "I see. You worked in Flanagan's Bistro, right?"

"Yeah."

"That's not on at all. I actually know Mr Flanagan quite well. We all do, down at the station. We have our Christmas parties in the Bistro."

"Ah! *That's* where I know you from! Last Christmas you climbed onto the table and sang 'Love me Tender'. Well, most of it. And then you dragged Pauline up and more or less forced her to join you in a duet of 'Summer Nights'."

This quiet, dignified police detective suddenly looked absolutely mortified. "I did?"

"Oh yeah. You were up there belting out the song, giving it loads. The woman you came with was giving you really filthy looks, too. You were pretty drunk. At one stage you were wearing your tie around your head like Rambo. And later on, you went around to the other tables and gathered up the forks and knives, and you stuffed

158

them up the sleeve of your jacket. I don't know what *that* was all about, though."

He cringed. "Harpo Marx," he said. "There was one of the movies where they were at an exclusive hotel and Harpo kept stealing the silverware. He stuffed them up his sleeves, and at the end he shook hands with someone and all the knives and forks came spilling out."

I couldn't help laughing. "Not the sort of thing you want to be remembered for, I'm guessing."

"God, I can't believe I did that! None of the others have ever mentioned it."

"That's because you were *not* the drunkest one there. Not by a long way."

By way of changing the subject, the detective gestured towards the equipment Jumper Man had lent me. "I see you've acquired a few things."

"Yeah, someone was kind enough to lend them to me. And wait until you see the kitchen. I even have furniture in there too. *And* appliances."

He smiled. "It's good to see you're keeping your spirits up."

"Well, I'll be a lot happier when you track down my own stuff. What do you think the chances are?"

"They're better than they were, I can tell you that."

"And how about the chances of finding Des?"

He hesitated. "If you want my honest opinion, off the record, as it were . . ."

"Go on."

"He's gone."

"But how hard can it be to find him? He must have left some kind of trail! He's not exactly Keyser Söze!"

159

Jaye Carroll

"You won't be seeing him again. Not unless he's completely stupid and comes back to Ireland."

"So you think he's gone abroad?"

"I'm certain of it. We've checked with the airlines, but there's no record of him buying a ticket. However, that's not significant in itself. He could easily have used a fake passport, flown to London, and gone from there to his final destination. Or he could simply have driven up to the North and taken the ferry over to the mainland UK."

"But if he does show up, he'll be arrested?"

"Right now, we don't have a warrant out for his arrest, no. But he'll certainly be brought in for questioning."

"If that happens, how likely is it that he'll accidentally fall down the stairs at the station? Everyone knows that sort of thing happens all the time."

He wasn't amused at that. "Just like everyone knows that people who work in restaurants spit in the soup of customers they don't like."

"Point taken," I said. "Sorry."

He moved towards the door. "Anyway, back to the reason I'm here . . . If you have any reason to believe you're under threat, call me immediately. You have my card, right?"

I checked my pocket. "Yep."

"It doesn't matter what time of the day or night. Phone that number and I'll have someone here within five minutes."

I said, "Thanks, but are you sure it'll come to that?"

"No, it probably won't, but it's best to be safe."

"You're not just being over-protective of me because I'm the only possible link with Des, are you?"

160

He gave me a wry smile. "We're protective of everyone, Miss Adare. That's our job."

* * *

After Detective Mason left, I took the letter out of my back pocket and looked at it. There was no return address, but the French postmark and the familiar handwriting were all I needed to know: it was from Davina. Inside was a single sheet of ultra-thin writing paper with a cute cartoon of a puppy in the corner, and three crisp fifty-euro notes.

"Dear Orla,

"Just got a phone call from my mother telling me about Des. What a prick! It sounds like you're up to your neck in it over there! I tried to phone you at home, but no luck. I suppose he took your phone as well.

"Hope this little contribution helps a bit. I'd send more only my stockbroker and my accountant have advised me that they don't exist and that I am actually a bit strapped for cash myself!

"Anyway, just wanted to say that if you need to get away from it all, feel free to visit any time you like.

"Love, Davina.

"P.S. I'm on the look-out for Des just in case he turns up anywhere near here. I'm going to invest in a stun-gun and a pair of rusty pliers."

My first thought was to phone Davina and thank her, but common sense kicked in and reminded me that a call to France on my mobile was going to eat rather quickly into my new-found hundred and fifty euro.

My next thought, I'm ashamed to say, was, "Is that all? Surely Davina can afford a lot more than a hundred and fifty!" Even as I was thinking it, I knew how ungrateful I was being. After all, I had no idea what her life was like in Nice. From her occasional letters and phone calls it always sounded like she was a high-ranking member of the jet-set society, but I was sure that was mostly exaggeration on her part.

* * *

After a quick breakfast, I went down to the local social welfare office, which thankfully was fairly quiet. This meant that I didn't have to wait long at all to be told that I wasn't entitled to any money there and then.

"You didn't work up enough hours in the last year to qualify for unemployment benefit," said the guy behind the reinforced glass. "Now, if you'd been made redundant from the restaurant it might be different, but you resigned."

"Well, he didn't really give me any choice."

"I understand that, but even so . . . If you're qualified for UA – that's unemployment assistance – then it'll be about six weeks before your first payment."

"Six weeks! I'll have starved to death by then!"

"Look, one thing you can do is go to the health board and explain your situation to them. They might be able to provide you with emergency money until you get back on your feet. It'll be means-tested. Do you understand what that is?"

"They're going to check me out and make sure I'm not a millionaire trying to pull a fast one?"

"More or less. They'll probably want to make a home visit too."

"Thanks. I'll go and see them first thing in the morning. But I should still start looking for a job, right?"

"Definitely. If you do get one, come back and let us know."

* * *

On the way back home, I decided what my next step would have to be. I wasn't happy about it, but I didn't really have any choice.

I sat down in my armchair, took out my phone and dialled a number that I never expected to be phoning again.

A woman's voice said, "Hello, Desire and Design, how may I help you?"

"Hi . . . can I speak with Mark Ennis, please?"

There was a brief pause. "I'm afraid Mr Ennis is no longer with the company."

"Oh . . . then how about Brian Dunbar?"

"May I ask who's calling?"

"Orla Adare."

"Of?"

"It's more of a personal call," I said.

"One moment, I'll see if he's available."

The phone went "Boop" and then I could hear something that sounded like a version of 'Money's Too Tight to Mention' played on a xylophone by someone wearing boxing gloves. In the dark.

After a couple of minutes, the phone went "Boop" again, and a man's voice said, "Well, well, well . . . Orla Adare!"

"Brian?"

"The one and only. How are you doing?"

"Okay. Well, no, not really. That's what I wanted to talk to you about."

"Let me guess . . . you want your old job back, right?"

My heart was suddenly bouncing about like crazy; this was even harder than I'd expected it to be. "Is that possible?"

"Orla, you walked out on us two years ago right in the middle of our most important project. You might recall that particular incident."

I cringed. "I do."

"And you might also recall that you refused to work out your notice and that you insulted myself and the other directors in front of the whole company. Or am I wrong?"

"No . . . no, you're not wrong."

"I imagine that you thought it was funny at the time."

"I'm sorry about that."

Brian sighed. "Look, you know me, Orla. I don't bear grudges. I wouldn't have got where I am today if I did. I know you were upset because you felt that you were being continually passed over for project leader, and I can understand how frustrating that might have been. But you should have come to me or Mark or Suzanne, and not just stormed out and set up your own company. I mean, you didn't even have any clients to take with you! I'm amazed you lasted as long as you did."

I didn't know how to respond to that.

He continued: "I'll be straight with you, Orla. We can't give you a job here, because we can't trust you not to walk out again. And on top of that . . . you want to know why you were never put in charge of any projects? Well, I'll tell you. It wasn't politics or bureaucracy or anything like that. You just aren't that good a designer."

I swallowed. "I see. That's what you think, is it?"

"Be honest with yourself," he said. "If you were that good, how come your own firm didn't work out?"

"Because you guys went around bad-mouthing me to everyone."

"No, we didn't. I promise you, we did no such thing."

"Well, *someone* did!"

"If you'd even come to us straight after you shut down your own company, we might have been able to come to some arrangement, but not now. I mean, that was a year ago!"

"Look, just forget it! I only called you because I had nowhere left to turn! I'd hoped that all the years I worked for you would mean something!"

Not unkindly, he said, "They *did* mean something, Orla, but then you abandoned us when we needed you most. You can't burn your bridges behind you and then expect us to come and rescue you."

Again, I didn't know what to say. He was right, of course. I'd left the company with my head full of grand dreams and big plans, and they'd all come to nothing. On absolutely no evidence, I'd managed to convince myself that I was better than the others.

"So what happened to Mark?"

"He quit a few months back. Sold off his shares and is now, I believe, living the good life on some island in the Caribbean."

"Really?"

"So I've heard."

"And how have you been?"

"Not bad," he said. "So are you still going out with that guy . . . what was his name? Desmond Mills?"

I hadn't planned on saying anything about what had happened, but I decided that it probably wouldn't be long before everyone found out, so I might as well tell him now. I took a deep breath, and launched into a short but intense version of recent events.

Brian paused for a long time after I was done, then said, "Jesus. I'd no idea . . . I mean, we worked really closely with him when he was with that shop-fitting crowd!"

"I know. That's how I got to know him." All of a sudden, I saw an angle that – if I was unscrupulous – I might be able to exploit: I wouldn't have met Des if I hadn't been assigned to help out on his project. If, say, I'd been given my own project to run – like I'd spent months practically begging for – then Des and I would never have started going out. Which could be taken to mean that everything that happened to me because of Des was really the company's fault.

Brian must have been thinking along the same lines too, because he suddenly said, "Still, you're better off single than with someone like that. Trust me, I should know."

"Don't tell me you split up with . . ." My mind went blank: I couldn't remember his girlfriend's name, even though I'd met her a dozen times.

"Cheryl? Yeah. I got home one day to find a note on the table saying that she'd been seeing someone else and that it was all over."

"But you were together for *years*!"

"Eleven years and five months," he said. "Good thing I never got around to asking her to marry me, eh?" He took a deep breath. "Anyway . . . Look, Orla. It's nice to hear from you, but I'm sorry about the job thing. Right now, we've got more people than we have work. And . . . I'm sorry about saying that you weren't a good designer; that was unfair. You *were* good. Just not the best."

I wasn't certain how I should take that. "Well, thanks anyway."

"And don't leave it so long before calling next time, okay? Just because you resigned from the company doesn't mean we don't want to see you down the pub every now and again."

* * *

From my time with Desire and Design and the year I spent working for myself, I knew a lot of design firms and architects, and I was fairly sure that at least one of them would have a job for me. Unfortunately, without my address book, I was kind of stuck: I could remember a few names of companies and individuals, but no contact numbers. I didn't even have a phone book in which I could look them up. On top of that, my phone was running out of power.

This was a depressing situation. Even if I could have wangled an interview, I didn't have my portfolios any more. I didn't even have anything to *wear* to an interview!

I decided that, for the short term, any old job would do. Once I got my life up and running again, I'd be in a stronger position to find a better-paying job.

So I spent the rest of the afternoon wandering through the town keeping an eye out for "Help Wanted" signs in shop windows. I wasn't successful, not even in the local Burger Hut, where there was a sign in the window that had been there so long the ink had faded to a muddy brown.

The owner's son – a lad of about eighteen, who had a squeaky voice, masses of spots and blackheads and a really prominent Adam's Apple – sat me down at one of the empty tables. He seemed keen, especially in light of my experience as a waitress, until I gave him my address. "Wait . . . isn't that Dessie Mills' address?"

That was the first time I'd heard him called Dessie in years. "Yeah. He used to live with me."

"Oh." He looked down at the form he'd been filling in, and without looking up, he said, "Any idea where he is?"

"No."

"Only, well . . ."

I finished his sentence for him. "Your company has invested lots of money with him. Am I right?"

"Not with him, but we put in a down-payment on a tender for the franchise, because we're going to open another restaurant in the shopping centre. Or we *were*." He finally looked up. "I'm afraid that we don't really have a position available at the moment. Not for someone with your experience," he quickly added.

"I don't mind. I'll do anything. I'll sweep the floors and wash the dishes if that's what it takes."

"Those positions are already filled. I'm sorry."

"Well, which positions *aren't* filled?"

"Right now, everything's taken." He stared at me, as if daring me to contradict him.

"But the sign in the window . . ."

After a long pause, he said, "I'm sorry."

"Look at it like this," I said, trying not to sound too desperate, "a lot of people will want to talk to me about Des, so if I'm working here then they'll have to come here to see me and we can tell them they're not allowed to talk to the staff unless they're customers."

He carefully tucked my not-quite-completed application form into a manila folder, and stood up. "I'm sorry, but we don't have any positions here for you."

I remained seated. "For me? Or for anyone?"

"I'll have to ask you to leave now."

I gave him a damn good glaring, and got to my feet. "I *see*." I turned towards the door, then turned back. "You know, I've a couple of things to tell you. First, your burgers are crap. Second, I'm glad you don't want me to work here because this place has the worst reputation in town. And third – soap and water."

"Pardon?"

"Your face. Soap and water. Wash your face every morning and every evening. And stop eating greasy food. There. Free advice."

By now he'd turned so red that his spots were almost camouflaged. "Please leave the premises," he squeaked.

So I left. I wanted to slam the door after me, but it had one of those springy door-closer things and that didn't allow it to move at much more than a snail's pace.

* * *

I also asked for a job at the laundrette – which would have been a handy place to work because I still didn't have a washing machine – the second-hand bookshop, all three of the town's cafés, but without success.

I walked all the way to the old hotel and asked them. The manager recognised me on sight even though I couldn't remember ever meeting her before, and told me that she'd love to be able to give me a job, but right now there were no openings. I went through the now-familiar "I'll do anything" speech, but it didn't work.

Everywhere I applied, it seemed, my reputation had preceded me. Or rather, *Des's* reputation had preceded me.

I wasn't sure if I was just being paranoid, but on the walk home I was sure that there was more than the usual number of neighbours who just happened to be in their gardens as I passed.

Certainly, quite a few of them looked away when I caught their gaze.

I wondered if that was the way things were going to be for the rest of my life: people muttering to each other about me as I passed by. "That's the one I was telling you about. Her boyfriend stole everything she had and ran off with her best friend" – I figured that the story would undoubtedly grow in the telling, so I might as well embellish it myself. "Way I heard it, she murdered him and he's buried under the patio." "But she doesn't *have* a patio." "That's to make sure no one suspects."

When I got back to the house there was a car waiting across the street. The driver – an overweight forty-year-old man – had watched me carefully all the way up the road, and as soon as I opened the gate he jumped out of his car. "Miss Adare?"

I stopped and turned. "Yes?"

He ran towards me with his right hand extended. I had to shift my shopping to my other hand to shake.

"I'm glad I caught you," he said. He had thick glasses, greasy grey hair, really large teeth and thick lips. He stood there grinning like the Cheshire Cow.

I pulled my hand away from his. "What can I do for you?"

"Nothing!" he said, gleefully. "It's not what you can do for me, it's what *I* can do for *you*!"

"I'm sorry, *who* are you?"

"My name's Nathan Fowler. I'm a solicitor."

"Really? And exactly what are you soliciting today?"

This didn't slow him down at all. "I've heard about your case, and I'm willing to take it on *pro bono publico*!"

"Is that right?"

He nodded.

"And that means . . .?"

"It's Latin."

"This much I guessed."

"It means 'For the public good'."

"You mean, I won't have to pay you?"

"Not one cent. My services come completely free of charge."

"And why would you do something like that?"

"My wife told me about your case. She overheard it in the hairdresser's. *Shocking* case. Absolutely shocking. I intend that Mr Mills will be punished to the very extent of the law." He looked up at the house. "And this is the scene of the crime, is that right?"

"Yes. But . . . I'm sorry, *what* did you say your name was again?"

"Nathan. Nathan Fowler." If he'd been wearing a hat he'd have doffed it. "I've extensive experience in tracking down absconded thieves, and I'm certain that we can find Mr Mills, take him to justice for his *odious* crime." He pulled off his glasses, blinked at them a little, then put them back on. "Believe you me, there's nothing that makes my blood boil more than to see a helpless victim like yourself reduced to abject poverty at the hands of a criminal mastermind. But we'll get him for this, trust me. I have contacts all over the globe, and I'm certain that within two months we'll have Mr Mills before a high-court judge. He may try to run, to cover his tracks, but he'll soon learn that there is nowhere on this earth that he is safe. No matter how devious he may be, all criminals leave a trace. We'll find him *and* we'll find your possessions and make sure that they are returned to their rightful owner, you in other words, and of course we'll also make certain that all the investors in his shopping-centre project are fully reimbursed. All I require is of course the usual finder's fee of ten per cent, plus daily expenses which are, I assure you, extremely meagre and the bare minimum. *Less* than the bare minimum, in fact, and that's because I'm so outraged by Mr Mills's *heinous* actions. I have three daughters of my own, so as you can imagine I don't take kindly to sinister men preying on the gullibility of young women."

There was a lot more like this. God, he has to stop to breathe *sometime*, I said to myself.

"Furthermore, may I say that it is an *honour* to meet someone like yourself. Why, here you are, devastated, barely able to make ends meet, and yet you're not letting this situation get the better of you. Well, bravo, I say! Or rather, brava, because you're female. We'll find Mr Mills, you mark my words. We'll leave no stone unturned, no avenue of possibility unexplored. We won't rest or sleep until justice is done, and *seen* to be done."

I waited for more, but that seemed to be it. "Well, thanks, but I'm not interested."

He was ready for that. "Of course, of course. I completely understand. At a time like this, the last thing on one's mind is retribution. But I should warn you that the longer Mr Mills goes unchecked, the harder it will be to track him down."

"I'm sorry, are you a solicitor or a private detective?"

"A solicitor, as I said. But every good solicitor has certain skills of a detective nature. At the risk of dislocating my shoulder by patting myself on the back, I have to say that my own skills in that area are highly developed."

"And how do I know you're not a shyster just chancing your arm?"

"Such a thing could not be further from the truth. I can produce many references attesting to my honesty and abilities."

"I'm sure you can. But like I said, I'm not interested."

"Well, please do me the favour of hearing me out before you decide."

"I thought that's what I *have* been doing. Look, I'm sorry, but I've already got the gardaí and the people at the bank looking for him. Now, if you don't mind, I'd like to go inside and put my milk in the fridge before it reaches its best-before date."

But he wasn't going to give up that easily. He went on and on, and I found myself shifting from one foot to the other, trying to edge towards the front door.

He asked me a lot of questions, and answered them himself without giving me a chance to tell him to get lost.

After about five minutes I began to daydream. I could picture this man tracking Des down and *talking* him into submission.

"Have you got a pen?" I asked, interrupting his flow.

"Yes, certainly." He took a fancy fountain pen from his inside jacket pocket and resumed waffling.

I found the receipt from the supermarket in my bag and wrote "Go Away" in nice big letters on the back, then handed it and his pen back to him.

Nathan Fowler nodded, tucked his pen away, stuffed the receipt into his wallet without looking at it, and still didn't stop talking.

"Listen —" I said, but that didn't work either.

"There are only so many places he could have gone," he was saying, "and certainly he's left a big clue behind, as of course you've undoubtedly realised yourself. And that big clue is, as you know, the contents of your house. Once we track down the people he hired to move your possessions, we'll have a *much* better idea as to his overall game plan."

"Listen very carefully: *I'm not interested.*"

"I understand, I understand; why would you need to know the exact details of the investigation, when all you're interested in is the outcome? No, I won't bother you with the specifics. Now that I have your go-ahead, I'll begin the investigation. That is, I'll officially begin the investigation. I'm sure you'll pleased to know that unofficially – on my own time, as it were – I've already begun. I've eliminated several possibilities . . ."

I decided I'd given this fool enough opportunities to get the hint. I turned and walked up to the door – he followed me, his voice box still going at full speed, presumably thinking that I was inviting him in – and then I unlocked the door, stepped inside and closed the door in his face.

Amazingly, that only halted him for a second. "Miss Adare? The door seems to have slammed shut! Anyway, where was I?"

As I was putting away my groceries, I wondered how long he'd have to stand out there before he finally twigged that I wasn't interested.

* * *

Nathan Fowler gave up ringing the doorbell and knocking and shouting through the letterbox in the middle of *Countdown*. I noticed this somewhere between Richard Whitely reciting a sweet little anecdote about his childhood and one of the contestants asking Carol Vorderman for a vowel.

I went out to the hall to see that he'd stuffed half a dozen business cards through the letterbox. On one of them he'd written, *"Please give me a call if you change your mind. Best, N. Fowler."*

It cheered me up to see that the business cards were not professionally printed: they'd been done on one of those machines you get in arcades. It cheered me up even more when I saw that he'd managed to mis-type his own name: each of the cards had "Nathan Flower" with a hasty correction made in pencil.

* * *

At about six in the evening, I got a call from Mags, who told me that Justin had phoned to say he was on the way home and they wanted to know if I'd like to call over for dinner.

Mags didn't mention anything about what we'd talked about on Tuesday night, but there was something in the *way* she didn't mention it that let me know I wasn't to give Justin any clue about her and Peter Harney.

It was as I was changing to go out that I found possibly the only advantage to having all my stuff stolen: I didn't have to spend ages in front of the mirror trying on outfits. Not that I had a mirror.

I laid all my clean clothes out on the bed – it was a little distressing to be able to do that without anything touching anything else – and decided on my new second-hand jeans and the non-Golfer T-shirt. I just hoped it wasn't going to rain on the way over.

I had a quick shower and washed my hair, shaved my legs with the single disposable razor that I'd taken with me to Tipperary, then luxuriated in the process of drying myself with my fluffy new towel. I'd bought it that afternoon, along with shampoo and body wash. I kept thinking to myself, "If only I'd brought more stuff with me when I went to Killian's, then I'd still have it." That, of course, led to the more obvious thought; "If only this had never happened in the first place."

But chains of thoughts don't always lead to comfortable places . . . After a few wonderings along the lines of "If I'd taken more of an interest in Des's project then maybe he'd have panicked and changed his mind" and "Maybe I should have broken up with him after the first month, like I was thinking about doing," I finally reached "If I'd never gone to work in Desire and Design in the first place, I'd never have met Des and I'd be fine right now."

* * *

I'd been going out with Des for about three weeks when I began to wonder exactly what I was doing. He was charming, good-natured, not especially unattractive, quite well-off, but there wasn't really any spark there.

Not that there'd always been a spark with any of my previous boyfriends, but by that stage I was reaching my mid-twenties and all my friends were getting married and moving away, and I hadn't ever progressed much past the "going out for a few months and then breaking up" stage.

So it wasn't like I'd fallen in love with Des immediately. That had happened to me a couple of times, so I knew what it was like. But with Des, my feelings went from "He's actually not bad" to "I love this man" over the course of about eight months.

And when I finally was in love with him, it wasn't like I realised I'd been in love with him all along, but just didn't know it; it was more like "Okay, *now* I'm in love".

But *why* did I love him? That question had been bothering me a lot since I came home and discovered that he'd ripped me off. What was it about him that I'd been in love with?

I'd been prepared to marry this man – we'd never set the date, but we were more or less engaged – but why? I thought about this as I walked over to Justin's house, and the conclusion I reached was almost as disturbing as realising that I'd been played for a fool.

Maybe I'd loved Des because he was there.

Was that all it was? It was an unsettling thought. He was there, I was lonely – most of my friends were gone, my parents were dead, my brother had moved away – and being with someone was better than *not* being with someone.

Chapter 11

Justin, as always, looked just like he did the first day I met him, about fifteen years earlier: still disturbingly tall and lanky, with the same bright red hair that went curly if he let it grow, the same oversized nose, the same crooked front teeth, the same large ears and pointy chin.

Actually, put like that, it doesn't sound like Justin was particularly good-looking, but he wasn't bad. All of his features worked pretty well together.

He gave me a big hug and practically carried me in from the doorstep, bombarding me with questions. He was careful to avoid any direct questions like "Where the hell is my money?", but I could tell that was on his mind.

This is the sort of thing that was running through my own mind: for God's sake don't mention anything about affairs, or Peter Harney, or sex, or furniture, or anything at all. As far as you're concerned, Mags never said anything and it never happened and oh God he's looking at me funny! Did I just make a guilty expression or something?

Suppose I accidentally let it slip and give Mags a nasty look and Justin guesses what's happened?

"Still a bit down in the dumps?" Justin asked.

"I'm so far down in the dumps that even Stig is referring to me as The Hermit."

In the kitchen, Mags was taking a dish of vegetables out of the oven. She gave me a pleasant smile that in my mind meant 'Don't you say a bloody *word* about Pete!', and asked, "How've you been?"

"Okay, considering. Lost my job yesterday, though."

"How'd that happen?" Justin asked.

"A consequence of me being involved with Des. Flanagan wanted me to pay him back the money Des owed him."

Justin said, "Bastard!" and opened the fridge. "Drink?"

"Yeah, please."

He opened a couple of bottles of Carlsberg and ushered me towards the table. "Sit down, sit down . . . so, tell me *everything*."

"But you know everything already."

"Tell me anyway."

We were mostly finished dinner by the time I was done.

Mags said, "Orla, some of the other teachers and a few of the parents have been talking about you . . . there could be a hundred people who invested with Des. And they all seem to think that you're going to know more about what's happened than they do."

"Yeah. Well, this guy Tom Kennedy says that there should be some sort of big meeting with all the investors, to let them know the story. Actually, that reminds me, he said that he wanted that to happen before the end of the week. It's getting a bit late now."

"How are you going to even know who the investors were?" Justin asked. "You might get a lot of people turning up just on the off-chance."

"I'm sure Des kept books," Mags said.

I said, "He might have, I don't know. There's still some stuff in his office. I suppose I should check it out."

"Here's a thought," Justin said. "You should get everything you can out of that place and keep it. After all, Des took your stuff, so you're entitled to his."

"Well, yeah, but I think he only leased the furniture."

"So?"

"So I wouldn't be stealing it from him, I'd be stealing it from the leasing company."

Again, he said, "So?"

"Two wrongs don't make a right."

Justin gave me a sly grin. "Look, if you don't take the stuff someone else will. At least you'd have a desk and a chair. I'll tell you what, tomorrow morning I'll pick you up and we'll go and clear out whatever we can carry."

"Oh yeah, sure!" Mags said. "How's *that* going to look? People will see Orla going in and out of Des's office and it'll only reinforce the idea that they were working together on his scam."

By the end of the night, Justin had drunk far too much to drive, so he walked me home. Mags had thoughtfully gone through some of her clothes and picked out some stuff that she thought might fit me. She'd also thrown in a quilt and some basic essentials; cutlery, a couple of plates and cups, a small saucepan, and a packet of cream crackers.

That last one was almost too much for me; when you have to accept second-hand cream crackers from someone, you know you've *really* hit rock bottom.

I wasn't sure whether Mags had donated her stuff from kindness or from guilt, but either way I wasn't complaining. Stuff was better than no stuff.

Mags had packed everything into two large bags, which Justin insisted on carrying. That was just as well, because I was fairly drunk myself and I didn't think I'd have been able to manage them.

Once we got to the house, Justin decided he was going to have a look around. Naturally, he had to comment on how everything was gone.

When he pointed out that the carpets had been taken, I said, "Yeah, I did notice that myself."

"Still, it's good to see that people are rallying around. I mean, at least now you have a bed and everything. *And* a telly and video." He turned to me. "Where do you go from here?"

I shrugged. "I suppose I'll have to start over. Get a job, buy clothes and furniture."

"You know what you should do? Get a lodger. I mean, you've got plenty of space here, and the money would help you get back on your feet."

"Yeah, but before I can get a lodger, I'll need to get another bed, do the place up a bit. And I'll definitely need a cooker. Still, it's not a bad idea."

* * *

On Friday morning I went to the local health board. After taking a number and then daydreaming so much that I didn't hear my number being called and then having to take *another* number, I found myself in a second-floor office with bars on the windows, talking to a woman who was not much older than me.

For once, things seemed to be going my way: the woman took down all my details, asked a lot of questions about my bank account and my house, then went away for a few minutes for some unspecified reason – I figured she was going to phone the bank to check – and then she came back with a big smile and a fairly big cheque, which she handed over to me.

I stared at the cheque; it was for five hundred euro. "Just like that? Aren't you going to send someone out to the house to check up on me?"

"Miss Adare, everyone in town knows about your situation. I don't think there'd be any point in us sending someone out, do you?"

"Not really."

"Now . . . normally you'd have to specify exactly what your Emergency Needs payment is for, but in your case I think it's obvious."

"Thanks. I really appreciate this. I was getting a bit worried, you know? Especially yesterday, when no one would give me a job."

The woman told me that there was no need for me to panic, and that things would sort themselves out in time. I didn't believe her, but I thanked her anyway.

* * *

I brought my cheque straight to the bank, and I was barely in the queue when one of the junior tellers came over to me. "Miss Adare? Miss McKenna would like to see you if you have a few minutes."

Very much aware of all the other customers turning to look at me, I said, "Sure," and followed the girl into Dearbhla McKenna's office.

Dearbhla stood up from her desk as I walked in. She shook my hand and gestured for me to sit down, all in one swift and efficient movement. I wondered how long it had taken her to learn that.

"So," she said, "I don't suppose you've heard anything from Mr Mills?"

"Nothing. Have you?"

"No . . ." She pursed her lips. "Orla, we have a difficult situation here."

"Yes, so you said last time."

"You see, from the bank's point of view, no wrongdoing has taken place. People open and close accounts every day, money gets transferred from one account to another, that's what banks are for. Do you see where I'm going with this?"

"Not really."

"Then I'll put it simply: Mr Mills had a business account with us, and shared a joint account with you. He closed the business account, and withdrew some money from your joint account."

I waited for her to continue. When she didn't, I prompted her: "Okay . . ."

"And that's the extent of our involvement."

A sick feeling began to form in the lower regions of my intestines. "You're trying to cover your backs, you mean."

"Not at all. We'll be the first to admit to any mistakes

we've made. But in this case we haven't made any. Everything we've done has been in accordance with standard banking practices and is, I assure you, completely without reproach."

"Except that you allowed Des to take all my money out of my account without my signature."

"As I showed you on Tuesday, we do have a withdrawal slip with both of your signatures."

"But he *forged* my signature!"

She spread her arms in a "nothing to do with me" gesture. "It looks genuine enough to us."

Right, I said to myself, that's it! "Now, you listen to me . . . That bastard robbed me of everything I had and stripped my house bare! That's bad enough, but now you're not taking responsibility for your part in this! Your people allowed him to clear out a joint account and you didn't even phone me to check first. As far as I'm concerned that's gross incompetence!"

"I'm not going to respond to such inflammatory remarks, Miss Adare."

"Look, you *know* that the bank is in the wrong, don't you? And you're not going to admit liability in my case, because then you'd have to admit liability for Des's business account."

She didn't respond, just stared at me.

I went on. "I spent ages yesterday going over the situation with my solicitor," I lied. At least, I thought it was a lie when I was saying it, but then I realised I *had* spent a long time trying to get away from Nathan Fowler. "And it's pretty clear to us that unless you can prove those signatures are mine, and prove that I was knowingly connected with

Des's company, then the bank is at fault. So, prove it to me. If you can."

"We have your signatures. That's all the proof we need."

"Well, *we* need more than that. How about your security cameras? If I was in here with Des signing forms, then wouldn't we be able to see that on your security videos?"

"Unless there's special circumstances, we only keep the tapes for about six months." She hesitated a second, then added, "I think."

"Well, then you'll certainly have tapes of last Friday, when I allegedly came in here with Des and cleared out the joint account."

Her normally passive expression wavered, but just a little. "As I've said, you wouldn't necessarily need to be here yourself to make a withdrawal. We *do* have your signature."

"Nevertheless, I'd like to see the tapes."

"I'm afraid that's not possible."

"You're allowed to film us, but you won't allow us to see the tapes?"

"That's our policy. We have to protect the privacy of our other customers."

Good answer, I said to myself. "Then we'll see what my solicitors have to say about that. I'm sure they can persuade you. In the meantime . . . why has your bank charged me fifteen euro and thirty cent?" I showed her my bank statement.

After a tiny pause, she said, "In light of what's happened, I think we can waive that charge."

"I'd appreciate it." I took out my cheque from the health board. "Now, I'd like to open a new account. And believe me, I wouldn't be coming here if there was another bank in the area."

She picked up the cheque and looked at it as though she'd never seen one before. "Certainly . . . it'll take five to six working days for the cheque to clear."

"How can that be? It's from the health board! Why does it need to clear? You think that *they* might suddenly run out of money?"

"That's standard policy."

"Well, I'd like to cash it, then."

"Considering your situation, that's not really possible. You see, for us to cash a cheque like this, you'd need to have sufficient funds in your current account to cover it."

I raised my eyes. "You're making this up, right?"

"No."

"So you're telling me that you allowed my boyfriend to steal all the money from my account, and now you won't honour the emergency payment from the health board because I don't have any money in my account?"

She sighed, and sat back in her chair. "Miss Adare, please don't try and trick me into admitting that we're liable for Mr Mills' actions."

"I wasn't," I said, "but it's a good idea. So there's no other way I can get access to this money, apart from opening a new account and waiting for five to six working days?"

"None. Not unless you have an account in the post office."

"Well, I don't. Okay then. I'll open a new account."

She swivelled around in her chair and found some forms in her filing cabinet, and we went through the painful process of the bank allowing me to give them more of my money.

* * *

On the way home I called into the supermarket. Being Friday it was pretty busy; shoppers meandered through the aisles, temporarily abandoning their trolleys to go in search of bran flakes or whatever. They dithered over the pasta sauces, trying to mentally calculate whether the more expensive sauce that had twenty per cent extra free was better value than the cheaper sauce that didn't.

In the bread aisle, I spotted a woman I vaguely knew and nodded hello to her. She looked at me as though I was something she'd discovered at the bottom of the bin, and then turned her back on me.

That did not make me feel good, but I cheered up when I spotted Pauline from the restaurant. She was pushing a full trolley and had a young man fetching stuff off the shelves for her. When she spotted me, she said to him, "David, go and wait in the next aisle, I need to talk to my friend here."

We watched him go. "How do you *do* that?" I asked Pauline.

"I dunno. They just seem to want to please me. How are you doing?"

"Not too bad."

"I suppose everyone you meet keeps asking you if there's any news about Des, so I won't."

"Thanks. You're right, though. You wouldn't believe the shite I've been going through. How are things at Flanagan's?"

"We've been rushed off our feet. The old bastard won't hire anyone to replace you."

"So there's just you and Steve serving?"

"Most of the time, though if it gets busy Kalim helps out." Kalim was our kitchen technician, an absolute whiz with the old Fairy Liquid and scrubbing brush; Flanagan maintained that he didn't trust mechanical dishwashers. "So when are you coming back?"

"I'm not," I said. "He fired me. Well, as good as. He made it clear that I'm not welcome there. Has he said anything about me?"

"Nothing positive. I tried to tell him that none of it was your fault, but he won't listen. All the customers keep asking about you, though."

"In a good way or a bad way?"

She gave me a look. "What do you think? We even had a few people coming in and demanding to see you, then acting like *we've* done the dirty on them because you're not there for them to them to blame instead of Des, if you take my meaning. It's like they need to have someone to take it out on."

"Sorry about that. God, this whole thing just isn't going to get any easier, is it?"

"It will eventually," Pauline said. "Anyway, I'd better go and find this lad before he has a panic attack. I'll see you around, okay? I hope it all works out for you, Orla. You don't deserve anything like this."

I carried my basket around the supermarket, looking at things I'd normally be able to afford, but since I was now on the world's tightest budget I had to pass them by.

Before, when I had money and at least some dignity, I

never took that much notice of prices, but suddenly it had become extremely important. I loaded my basket with the cheapest stuff I could find, and even then it was only the bare essentials: milk, bread, a few vegetables, the shop's own-brand beans and cereals. I was appalled to see how expensive meat was, so I decided that I'd be a vegetarian until I could afford otherwise.

I also picked up a two-kilo bag of flour, which I carried halfway around the shop before I realised that I didn't have a cooker so my idea of baking my own bread to save money wasn't really an option.

And in the soup aisle I bumped into Mrs Diggle, who'd been one of my mother's oldest friends.

"Hello, Orla," she said, and looked me up and down a bit.

"Hello, Mrs Diggle. How've you been? I haven't seen you in ages!"

Her lips went thin and barely moved as she spoke. "Your Desmond is in a *lot* of trouble."

"I know," I said. "He's . . . oh. Don't tell me you're one of his investors?"

"I am. I trusted him with a great deal of my money – I won't say *how* much, but it was a lot – and now I hear he's run away with it."

"God, I'm so sorry."

"So you *should* be, Orla. This is partly your fault."

"No, it's not! I didn't know anything about it until . . ."

She interrupted me. "I hate to think of what your mother would say if she was alive to see how you've turned out! Associating with common criminals! You should be ashamed of yourself!"

"Mrs Diggle, it wasn't like that. He stole from me too, you know."

"Be that as it may, Orla, you still have to accept responsibility. I'd never have met him if it wasn't for you. And I'd certainly never have trusted him if he hadn't been going out with you. And now I've lost practically everything I had, thanks to you!"

I wanted to just turn and walk away from her, but I'd known this woman all my life. "How was I to know what he was planning? I just came home on Monday and discovered that he'd cleaned out the house. Until then I thought he was all right."

"Nevertheless, you *should* have known. I find it hard to believe that you can live with someone and not know them that well!"

And then she did something that Killian and I had always found amusing when we were kids; she completely changed the topic: "I remember when I was growing up. We had nothing then, but we still stuck by each other. You didn't get people stealing cars to buy drugs. You could leave your door unlocked all night and nothing would happen. And we didn't have television blaring all night long next door and children screaming their heads off and running up and down the stairs."

I let her go on a little, in the hope that – as she sometimes did – she'd eventually get back to the main topic and these little asides would all tie in and make sense.

My dad once said that Mrs Diggle's problem was that, "she thinks that everyone else can tell what's going through her mind – she thinks she has a glass head".

191

After a couple of minutes, when she reached the point of complaining about how difficult it was to get used to the *new* new money – apparently she was still thinking in pounds, shillings and pence, and had only just got the hang of decimal currency when the euro was introduced – I stopped her. "Mrs Diggle, I'm sorry about what happened with Des, I really am. But I promise you I didn't know anything about it. If I had known, I certainly wouldn't have let it happen."

"That's all very well to *say*, Orla, but it doesn't change things, does it?"

I sighed. "No, it doesn't."

"There you are, then."

"But blaming me for Des's actions won't change things either, will it?"

She had a think about that. "I suppose not."

"Well, there *you* are, then," I said, playing her at her own game. I continued: "I like to think that if Mam was alive today, she'd at least try and see things from *my* point of view. She'd understand that I knew nothing about Des's plans and that I've been hurt more than anyone. And she certainly wouldn't put up with other people blaming me for what he's done. I mean, I could just as easily blame *you*, and all the other investors, because if you hadn't given Des your money, he might never have been tempted, and then he wouldn't have stolen from me."

Mrs Diggle gave me a nasty look. "So now it's *my* fault? Now you're blaming me?"

"No, I'm not. I'm just making a point."

She decided to be offended: "*I* see. You're blaming

everyone but yourself. First it's Desmond's fault, now it's my fault. Orla, you're far too old to be blaming other people. You have to take responsibility for your own actions."

To myself, I said, Damn, she's good at this! Aloud, I said, "So tell me, then . . . what were my actions in this case?"

"For a start, you were living in sin with Desmond. Now that's something I know your mother would never have approved of. And I knew her a lot longer than you did, Orla, so you can trust me on that."

I almost said, 'God, there's just no talking to you, is there?', but just in time I realised that wasn't going to help matters one bit. "Mrs Diggle, I promise you that I had nothing to do with it, and I promise you that if I'd known what he was planning, I would've done anything to stop him. And if you can't see that, well, I'm sorry about that, too. But I can't change things."

Her lips went thin again. She raised her head and said, "Well, if *that's* the way you're going to be . . .", and she picked up her basket and walked away.

I was tempted to go after her, but I knew it wouldn't have helped. There was nothing I could do or say to make her understand.

* * *

After I paid for my groceries I went up to the information kiosk and asked to speak to the manager. The girl at the counter – who looked about fourteen years old and about fourteen months pregnant – said, "Hold on a minute" and roared into the PA thingy: "Mr Waters to the information kiosk, please!"

Within a minute, Mr Waters approached. He was huge, about six-foot-six, and looked as though he'd been loaded into his suit by the shovelful. He had caterpillar eyebrows and a comb-over that was so severe his parting was only half an inch over his right ear.

"This lady would like to speak to you," said the girl.

Mr Waters said, "How can I help you?"

"Actually, I'm looking for a job, if you have one."

He nodded as he spoke, but carefully so as not to dislodge his hair. "Uh huh, uh huh, and, eh, do you have any experience?"

"Well, I've worked in supermarkets before, though it's been a few years."

"I see, I see. Well, we do have a couple of positions open at the moment. Entry-level only, I'm afraid. As long as you wouldn't mind working checkouts?"

"No, not at all."

He smiled, showing of his impressive collection of multi-coloured teeth. "Well, great, that's great! We've been having some trouble getting people. Or rather, keeping them. That's the problem with teenagers these days. They don't want to start at the bottom. They all want to be managers. And you can't have all managers and no staff, right? Am I right?"

"You certainly are. That'd be like an army with one soldier and ten thousand generals. They might have a lot of great ideas on how to fight a war, but they wouldn't be a very effective fighting force."

"Hah! Brilliant! I like that! You don't mind if I use that, do you? Actually, we just hired a new assistant manager last week, and he said something similar at his interview.

It was about a boat with a dozen captains and one crewman, I think. I don't know much about boats myself. Okay . . . well, we'll need to see a reference from your last employer, but apart from that, when can you start?"

I was chuffed. "As soon as you need me."

"Fantastic! Okay, come along to the office and I'll take your details." He walked ahead of me, constantly turning his head to check that I was still there. "I don't mind telling you, it's been a tough time recently. What with the budget and everything. And of course, like everyone else in the area, we've all lost a lot of money to that bastard Des Mills. You heard about that, right? Of course you have, everyone's heard about it. We were going to open a new store in the shopping centre. I mean, we've been here so long . . . just look at the state of that!" He pointed towards the ceiling tiles. "See?"

I didn't see. "Er, yes. But listen, Mr Waters. I have to tell you, I'm Orla Adare."

He stopped walking, turned to me. When he frowned, it looked like the caterpillars on his forehead were sizing each other up in preparation for a fight. "Where do I know that name from?"

"I'm – I *was* – Des Mills' girlfriend."

"Ah."

"This is the part where you tell me that you can't give me a job, right?"

"I don't suppose you've any idea where he is?"

"No." I went through the now-common ritual of denying any involvement in Des's scam, and explaining how I'd been ripped off as much as anyone else.

Mr Waters was a little more sympathetic than most of

the other prospective employers had been. "I'm really sorry, Miss Adare, but . . . well, you know how it is. A lot people are suggesting that you must have known when was going on. And of course some people are hearing that and saying, 'There's no smoke without fire' and the like. I can only imagine what they'd be saying if I hired you. They'd be saying, 'You're just throwing good money after bad,' most likely. At the very least, I know that quite a few of our customers and suppliers would get it into their heads that had them."

"So you're not going to give me a job?"

"No, I'm afraid it's not really practical. In the future, certainly, but not right now." He started to move away from me. "Look, perhaps your part in all this will be cleared up tomorrow at the meeting, okay? If that happens, we'll talk then."

"Wait, which meeting is this?"

"You haven't heard? Oh, well maybe I wasn't supposed to mention it." He considered this. "No, can't see why not. You've as much right to be there as anyone else. More, probably, considering everything you're going through. No, he never said *not* to mention it to you. But then why would he? I didn't know you before today."

"*Who* never said not to mention it to me? And exactly what is this meeting?"

"Can't think of the lad's name . . . hold on . . ." He poked about in his ear while he thought, and it looked to me like he was trying to find a reset button for his brain. "Well-dressed man. Represents some big financial bunch . . . Kennedy, that's it. Thomas Kennedy. He's trying to arrange a meeting with everyone that invested their money with

Mills, try and get it all sorted out to some degree. It's happening tomorrow afternoon down in the hotel. Didn't you see the notice in the local paper this morning?"

"No."

"Oh. So you haven't seen the article either, then?"

"Article?"

"Yes . . . about you and Mills. Mainly about him." He backed away even further. "Look, Orla, I'm sorry about the job. We'll talk tomorrow after the meeting, if it all goes well, okay? Okay."

And with that, he was gone.

* * *

Despite fact that the local paper was free, I hadn't looked at a copy in years. Officially it was called *The Sentinel*, but everyone referred to it as *The Sentimental*, because of a regular feature on how great things used to be in the old days. It was a bi-weekly sixteen-page tabloid with about eight square inches of space on the front page devoted to actual news, and most of the rest of the page taken up by ads for the local funeral home, florist and TV repair shop.

Luckily, the under-twelves football team had just won some important match, so their story took up the front page and mine was relegated to page two:

CON MAN FLEES COUNTRY

When Orla Adare, 32, of [here the bastards gave my full address], *returned home on Monday from a weekend away she thought she was coming home to a house that would be redecorated and have its attic converted. Instead, she got more than she bargained for. Her con man boyfriend, Desmond Miles,*

197

had stripped the house bare and cleared their joint bank account.

Miles is a freelance accountant who had arranged for many local businesses to invest in the proposed new shopping centre on land purchased from farmer Paddy Kane. But Miles has been missing since Monday, and many investors are now seriously concerned as to the whereabouts of where their money is.

"He was always charming and friendly," said one investor who did not want to be named. "We trusted him with all our savings, and now they're gone."

Hysterical

"Ms Adare is extremely upset and has been unable to work," said her boss Kenneth Flanagan, who owns Flanagan's Bistro, where she works as a waitress. "Some people have suggested that Orla was involved," said Mr Flanagan to The Sentinel. "I don't know if she is, but she lived with him for years."

According to a close friend, Ms Adare has no known income apart from her part-time waitressing job. "I don't know how she's able to afford to live in such a big, expensive house," says her friend.

Broke

The Sentinel has been unable to get in touch with Mr Miles, but according to sources in the Gardaí, it is believed that he has fled the country, taking his ill-gotten gains with him, leaving up to over a hundred investors seriously out of pocket. "We're going to have to sell the house unless we get our money back," said one investor.

It was bad enough that they wrote an article about me without bothering to ask for my opinion, and worse that they gave the impression that I was involved, laughable that they got Des's last name wrong, pathetic that they used the phrases "the whereabouts of where their money is" and "up to over a hundred", but the most annoying thing was that they made me out to be five years older than I really was.

* * *

When I got home, I found a note stuffed into the letterbox. It was from Thomas Kennedy, informing me about the meeting the next day.

It wasn't something I was looking forward to, but I knew I had to go. Otherwise God only knew the sort of things people would be accusing me of.

Chapter 12

I almost didn't make it to the meeting at all . . .

I was woken up at about eight the next morning, Saturday, by a loud hammering on the door. I pulled on my clothes and started to go downstairs, but there was a *lot* of noise outside – so much noise that I didn't feel comfortable about opening the door.

So instead I went across the landing and looked out of the spare-room window. There were about a dozen people gathered outside. Some in the garden, some outside the gate. I didn't recognise any of them, but they all looked like normal people, only extremely angry.

I opened the window and leaned out. "Hello?"

A dozen faces looked around in confusion for a couple of seconds, then one man spotted me and shouted "*There she is!*" and pointed. He looked very pleased with himself, as though he'd just discovered a new continent.

The man who must have been the one knocking on the door stepped back and looked up at me. "Come down, we want to talk to you!" The way he stood – all defiant and arrogant – made it pretty clear to me that he was the leader. He looked about thirty, prematurely grey but still kind of handsome.

"What about?"

"You *know* what it's about!"

"Well, I'm not coming down. I suppose you're looking for Des?"

"You know where he is, don't you? The both of you are in this together!"

"Yes, that's right. I organised for him to steal all my stuff and take all my money."

One of them, a middle-aged man who had apparently left his sarcasm-detector at home, said, "She admitted it!"

"Come down right this minute!" said the leader.

"Or?"

"Or we'll *make* you come down!"

I pretended to think about this for a second. "Get lost."

"We're not going away until you come down and talk to us!"

"Tell me this. Suppose *you* woke up to find an angry mob on your doorstep. Would you go down to them?"

"This isn't about me!"

"Then why are you here?"

"Look, we only want to talk."

"Okay. Just give me a couple of minutes to get changed." I pulled my head back in and closed the window.

Then I went into my bedroom, found my phone, and made a call.

"Hello?" a woman's voice said, sleepily.

"I'm looking for Detective Mason?"

"Hold on . . ."

A couple of seconds later, the detective said, "Yeah?"

"This is Orla Adare. I'm in trouble, I think. Can you send someone over to the house?"

He was suddenly more awake. "Hang on a minute."

The mob were hammering on the door again by the time he came back to the phone. "All right. What's going on? Are you in any danger?"

"I think I am, yeah. There's a bunch of people beating up my front door at the moment. I don't recognise any of them, but it's pretty clear that they're pissed off with me because of Des. So, can you send someone over?"

"There's a car already on the way – I just made the call. If you can keep them there for about five minutes . . .?"

"They don't look like they're going to leave any time soon."

"All right. I'm on my way too. In the meantime, do *not* open the front door. Can you lock yourself in your bedroom?"

"No. There's no door."

"Oh shit, yeah. I forgot about that. Any rooms upstairs that still do have a door?"

"The bathroom."

"All right. Go into the bathroom and lock it. I'll phone you as soon as I get there."

* * *

The mob outside grew more and more angry. They shouted through the letterbox and pounded on the door.

Somehow, just hearing them was worse than seeing them. If I could have seen them, then I'd have known exactly what they were up to. As it was, I could imagine them walking around the house checking to see if any of the windows were unlocked.

By the time I heard the sirens I was pretty scared, but at least I was in the right place for that.

I jumped when my phone rang again. "It's me," said Detective Mason. "We're outside. It's safe for you to come out now."

"Are they gone?"

"No. As soon as they saw us coming they left your garden and were waiting on the path."

So I unlocked the bathroom door, went downstairs and opened the front door.

Detective Mason was at the door, looking dishevelled, unshaven and a little hung over. Perhaps it was only because he had come to my rescue, but somehow he seemed much better-looking this time than he had on our previous meeting. Beyond him I could see four members of the gardaí taking names and addresses from the mob.

The detective said, "There's always a ringleader with this sort of thing. Which one is he?"

I pointed to the grey-haired man. "That one. He did most of the talking."

"Did he threaten you?"

"Well, he said that if I didn't come down they'd *make* me come down."

He considered this. "All right. That's good enough for me. We can take him in on threatening behaviour and trespassing."

"And don't forget disturbing the peace," I said.

He smiled. "Are you trying to tell me my job?"

"Look, I don't want them to be arrested. I'm pretty sure they're just venting their frustrations."

"Well, they can vent them down the station."

"No, seriously. If you arrest them all then it'll only make things worse for me. Why don't I invite the leader in so that I can talk to him and he'll see that I'm as innocent as everyone else?"

"I'm not sure about that."

"You can stay. He won't do anything when you're here."

"All right." He gestured towards the grey-haired man and said to one of the gardaí, "Dave, tell that gentleman that I'd like a quiet word with him."

The ringleader didn't seem nearly as scary when I saw him face-to-face without his mates to back him up; a real sheep in wolf's clothing. He was only a little taller than me; Detective Mason loomed over him.

"Right," said Detective Mason as we all stood in the hall. "What's your name and why are you harassing this woman?"

The man swallowed and the colour drained from his face. "I'm Ron Byrne, and . . . Look, we were just looking for Des Mills."

"And that's why you threatened Ms Adare?"

"We never threatened her!"

"You told her that if she didn't come down and answer the door then you'd make her come down. That's a threat."

"Mr Byrne," I said. "I know how you feel about what Des did. I feel the same way, believe me. Look around."

He looked. "Yes, but . . ."

"But nothing," I said. "How about we all sit down in the

204

kitchen and have a cup of tea and talk about everything?"

"All right," he said, and he followed me into the kitchen, with the detective close behind.

"Oh!" I said, faking surprise. "There's only two chairs, so we can't all sit down. And there's no kettle, so I can't make tea. Which is probably just as well, because I only have two cups and I don't even have any tea bags." I looked at him. "Do you see what I'm getting at?"

He looked blank, which was probably easy enough for him.

"Desmond Mills stole everything I have. Everything you see here was donated by friends. Don't you think that if any of us knew where he was we'd already have had him arrested?"

"I suppose."

"How much did he sting you for?"

At that, Ron Byrne looked even more sheepish. "Me? Well, he didn't get anything off *me*, but my mates . . ."

The detective said, "So you yourself have actually got no connection with Mr Mills?"

"No, not really, but you see, the thing is, he . . ." He trailed off again.

"You're just here to fill out the numbers, is that it?" I asked. "Who are you, the mob's henchman or something? And there you were, hammering on my door and threatening me. God, that's absolutely pathetic!"

"Do you want to press charges, Ms Adare?" asked Detective Mason.

"I probably should. I mean, what's to stop them coming back after you're gone?"

"We won't come back," Mr Byrne said. "I'm sorry. We didn't know. I mean, last night in the pub everyone was *saying* that you were involved. And there was the article in the paper, that made it seem like you had something to hide."

"But the paper couldn't even get Des's last name right! If they can't get that right, why would you think that they were right about anything else?"

Detective Mason said, "So you thought you'd take the law into your own hands, is that it? Let me tell you something, Mr Byrne, the courts do not look kindly on this sort of misguided vigilantism. Didn't it occur to you that if Ms Adare was involved we'd have found out about it? This *is* what we do for a living after all, and we're actually pretty good at it." He leaned his faced close to Byrne's, and added, "We're going to be watching out for Ms Adare. If anything happens to her, *you* will be the first person we call on. Do you understand me?"

Byrne nodded.

"So it's in your best interests to look after Ms Adare too. If you and your friends want to form a mob, you can use it to protect her, not intimidate her. Understand?"

Again, a nod, this time accompanied by a nervous swallow.

The detective stepped back. "Now . . . do you want to go and tell your friends what I've just said, or would you prefer me to tell them?"

"No, no. I'll do it." He looked at me. "I'm sorry. We really didn't know the whole story. We won't bother you again." He turned back to the detective. "Is it okay for me to go now?"

"Wait," I said. "Tell your friends that there's a meeting in the hotel today at two o'clock. It's to let all the people who invested with Des know what the situation is."

"All right."

"And it's only for the people who invested with him," I said. "So I don't suppose I'll be seeing you there, will I?"

He shook his head. "No. Again, I'm sorry."

* * *

When we went back out to the door to see him off, the detective gave a nod to the other gardaí, and they allowed the rest of the mob to go. By now, pretty much all of the upstairs windows on the road had faces in them.

My next-door neighbour Old Mr Farley was standing at the hedge that separated our gardens. "What's going on, Orla?"

"The angry villagers came to storm the castle," I said. "I hope they didn't wake you up."

"No, but the other lot did, charging around first thing in the morning with the sirens blaring."

"Oh, sorry."

He looked at me with one eyebrow raised. "Sorry? Orla, there's no need to be sorry! If I have to be woken up by sirens, I'd rather they were from squad cars than from ambulances!"

I smiled. "That's a good point."

"How are things otherwise?"

"Okay. Well, no, they're not okay. But they're getting better. Except that I lost my job."

"Because of Des?"

"Yep."

"Is there anything I can do?"

"I don't think so, but thanks."

"Now don't be too embarrassed to ask for help," he said. "I'd ask you if I needed anything, wouldn't I?"

Detective Mason came up to us. "I think we're all done here, Ms Adare. Do you want me to have a couple of the lads wait here in case they come back?"

"No, I don't think that's necessary. Byrne seemed to get the message."

"All right . . . But I'll have a car at the hotel this afternoon, just in case. In fact, I'll have them pick you up and drive you there. How's that sound?"

A ride in a police car? I told him that it sounded great.

* * *

There were only two more callers that morning: a couple who had been away for most of the week and had come home late the previous night to find a dozen panicky phone messages from other prospective investors. They told me they'd sat up all night worrying and waiting for a suitable time to call over that wouldn't be *too* early. I explained about the meeting in the hotel, and they said they'd definitely go along.

Of all the people I'd met who'd been ripped off by Des, I felt the most sympathy for them, though that was probably because they seemed so confused by everything. And it helped that they weren't automatically blaming me like most of the others were.

At a quarter to two, the gardaí arrived to pick me up. I have to admit that it felt pretty cool to be driven around in the back of a police car – I was half hoping that as we went through the town someone I knew would see me and wonder if I was being arrested.

The gardaí accompanied me into the hotel, where there must have been a couple of hundred people milling about in the lobby.

I spotted Justin and Mags in one corner, and went over to them. "So, did you hear about what happened to *me* this morning?"

"Yeah," Justin said. "It sounds pretty bad."

"Well, I don't think it's going to happen again. At least, I hope it won't."

Mags started to say something, but stopped as someone approached. I turned to see Thomas Kennedy standing behind me. He was wearing an immaculate three-piece suit, complete with cufflinks and a college tie – I didn't know which college – and he carried himself like he owned the room. In my T-shirt and jeans I felt positively scruffy next to him.

"Orla . . . I heard about this morning's events." He shook his head. "Terrible situation, just terrible. I hope that this meeting will help to clear things up a little."

"So do I." I gestured towards the rest of the crowd. "How do you know that these people are all legitimate?"

"We have a list – it's not up-to-date but it's close – and most of them have some sort of paperwork given to them by Mr Mills. I only hope that they don't think that my company is going to be able to honour Mills' commitments."

Mags said, "Then in that case exactly why *are* we here?"

"We really just want to clarify everything, get some

209

clearer idea of the extent of this problem." He shook his sleeve back and glanced at his watch. "Okay, let's get started . . ."

* * *

Thomas Kennedy had done a pretty good job of organising the meeting; there were at least a dozen people there from his company, all with name badges, and it was their job to gather as much information as possible from the investors.

Once that was mostly done – I say "mostly" because there were a lot of late arrivals – everyone was led into the largest conference room. Thomas asked me to sit somewhere near the front, because I'd almost certainly have to answer some questions.

"Look, I'm not too keen on speaking in public."

He put his hand on my arm and said, "Don't worry, it'll be fine. Just tell the truth."

"Suppose it gets out of control?"

"It won't. Trust me."

At the front of the room there was a screen and a projector, connected to a video recorder. The image on screen showed an artist's rendition of the shopping centre with the words *"Nine Acres"* across the top.

Thomas went up to the front of the room and said, very loudly, "Can I have everyone's attention, please?"

When they'd all settled down, he began.

"Okay. Good afternoon everyone. My name is Thomas Kennedy, and I'm an associate with Wagner, Kennedy and Parker. Though I should point out I'm *not* the same Kennedy from the company name." The way he said that,

I think he was expecting a laugh. Instead, he got silence, which threw him off-balance a little. "Em . . . all right . . . you all know why we're here, but I want to go over the facts as my company is aware of them. This won't take too long, and I'll answer any questions you might have afterwards. Now, we first heard about Desmond Mills' project almost three years ago, but it was only about two years ago that we became involved. Mr Mills approached us with an impressive proposal for the Nine Acres retail complex. He wanted us to invest in the project. We naturally checked out everything, and it all seemed to be in order. He'd done a tremendous amount of ground work, and that was one of the main reasons we were interested. All too often someone will approach us and they've only done the bare minimum, and want our company to flesh out the details. But Mr Mills had covered almost all of the details. Now, that's something I'd like you to keep in mind, because I think that later on you'll find it's pertinent."

He continued for about five minutes, detailing his company's involvement. It seemed to me that they really had done their homework on the project. Thomas produced copies of in-house reports, charts, details of accounts, and so on, all illustrating that they'd been very seriously committed to the project. He also showed a short computer-generated video of the shopping centre, and told us that his company had put it together to show other potential business investors. It didn't have any real relevance to the meeting, but it looked cool.

Then he got to the previous Saturday, and explained how his meeting with Des – during which a large chunk of money would have been handed over – had been

211

cancelled. This seemed to cheer people up a bit; they liked the idea that if things had gone slightly differently Des would have had a lot more money.

Wrapping up, he said, "We're convinced that it was not Mr Mills' plan from the beginning to defraud any of us. As I said earlier, he did a *lot* of work on the project, and much of that work was done before he received any outside investment. He commissioned artists, designers, surveyors, and architects. We are of course going to continue investigating, but so far it appears that, at the beginning, he genuinely believed in the project, and was one hundred per cent committed to it. But at some stage, presumably shortly before he formed the company that named Orla Adare as a co-director, Mills became aware that he would be in charge of a lot of money. I think that he saw an opportunity and decided to go for it." Thomas paused for effect. "He wasn't evil. He was just weak."

And then it was time for the questions.

As I'd feared, one of the very first questions was about me. A woman stood up and demanded to know why I hadn't been arrested, on the grounds that it was common knowledge that I was involved.

Thomas looked at me. "Orla? Do you want to answer that?"

"Not really," I said, "but I suppose I should." So I stood up and turned around to face the woman, and the rest of the crowd. "It might be common knowledge that I was involved, but that particular piece of common knowledge is wrong. I was away last weekend and only found out about all this when I got home on Monday."

A man called out, "Oh yeah, *sure!*"

That pissed me off. I looked around to see who had spoken, but whoever it was didn't seem willing to make himself known.

"Who said that?" I asked.

There was no response.

"Well, whoever you are, if you want to accuse me of lying, you should at least have the courage and the courtesy to do it to my face." Again, there was no response. "Anyone else got anything to accuse me of?" I waited for a few seconds, but no one said anything else. "Good. So everyone understands that I'm innocent. This means, I hope, that I won't have another mob turning up on my doorstep like I did this morning."

I sat down again.

The next dozen or so questions were directed towards Thomas Kennedy, and were all along the same lines: "Are we going to get our money back?"

To his credit, Thomas kept his calm and answered each question in full, even when a man stood up and asked the exact same question – word for word – as the person before him.

And then a man with a familiar voice spoke up: "I want to know who's going to be held accountable for all this!"

I turned to see my former boss, Mr Flanagan, at the far side of the room.

Thomas Kennedy said, "Unfortunately, the only person we can hold accountable is Mr Mills himself. There was no one else involved in his plans."

"But Orla Adare was named as a director of his company!"

"Yes, that's true. But the fact remains that she didn't know anything about it. Mr Mills forged her signature. Just as he did when he was withdrawing all the money from the bank account he and Orla shared."

At that, a woman a few seats away raised her hand. I turned to see Dearbhla McKenna, the bank manager, getting to her feet. "With respect, Mr Kennedy, that's incorrect! Our experts have checked the signatures and have pronounced them to be indistinguishable from Ms Adare's signature."

"That's complete rubbish," I said.

She ignored me, and sat down again.

And then Thomas Kennedy said, "Yes, so you said at our meeting yesterday. But, as I told you then, *our* experts are not convinced. Now . . ." He walked over to the video recorder and ejected the tape, then inserted another one. "Ms McKenna has kindly given us a copy of the bank's security tapes of the day Mr Mills closed his account." He looked up at the audience. "The quality isn't great, but Mr Mills is definitely recognisable . . ." He picked up the remote control, and hit the "Play" button.

The image was pretty grainy, and the colours were a little off, making everyone look like they had jaundice, but there, on screen, was my ex-boyfriend.

We watched as he entered the bank, and nodded hello to the security guard. He went up to one of the side counters, filled out a withdrawal slip, then joined the queue.

At that point, Thomas said, "He's in the queue for a

little over seven minutes . . ." He hit the fast-forward button, and the customers shuffled forward like penguins. "Here we go."

On screen, Des reached the end of the queue and handed the withdrawal slip to the cashier.

Thomas stopped the video, and turned to the crowd again. "As you can see, Ms Adare wasn't with Mr Mills at the time."

Dearbhla McKenna said, "Yes, but that doesn't mean she wasn't involved! Besides, that was only when he was withdrawing from their joint account. He dealt with his company account *after* that. Either way, it's irrelevant."

Thomas nodded. "Perhaps . . . but surely you can't have missed the *most* important thing about that video?"

And then a voice from the back said, very softly but clearly, "Des didn't bring the withdrawal slip with him." I turned to see that the speaker was Justin. "We saw him taking it out of the rack. That means that Orla couldn't have signed it herself."

"Exactly," Thomas said. He gave me a wink, and said, "Ms McKenna, can you explain that?"

Her face cold and impassive, she said, "I'll have my people look into it."

"Good," said Thomas. "And while they're doing that, perhaps you can have them look into the possibility that Mr Mills also forged Orla's signature on the forms for the business account. And I suspect you'll find that the reason your handwriting expert declared that Orla's signature on the forms was a perfect match for the signature on record is that you were actually comparing two forgeries. Check

215

them against Orla's *real* signature and you'll see there's a marked difference."

I don't think I'd ever been as happy as I was then; it proved that the bank was at fault. That meant, I hoped, that they might pay me back for all the money they'd let Des steal. I knew that they'd do everything they could to avoid that, but at the very least it showed that there was room for doubt.

There was some speculation from the die-hards that the video was of such low quality that we couldn't see exactly what Des was signing, therefore the slip he handed over might not have been the one he signed, but none of them were able to come up with a good explanation as to *why* Des would do that, so the matter was dropped.

I expected that the meeting would break up then, but it went on for another hour and a half – which only went to show that most of the people there were more concerned with their own situation than mine.

Afterwards, Justin, Mags and I hung around in the lobby. Quite a few people came over to me and apologised for assuming that I'd been in cahoots with Des, though there were a few notable exceptions; old Mrs Diggle, for one, went out of her way to walk past me so that she could completely ignore me.

And Mr Flanagan . . . while he did apologise for assuming that I was involved, he kept saying how much I'd be missed at work. It didn't take me long to figure out that I wasn't welcome back.

Dearbhla McKenna told me that we'd "talk about this early next week" and went on her way.

Then I spotted Jumper Man and Reebok in the corner, looking uncomfortable. I excused myself from the others and went over to them.

Reebok said, "That was a waste of a Saturday. I was hopin' we'd get our money back."

"Well, you heard what Mr Kennedy said. Unless the police can find Des, that's probably not going to happen," I said. "Listen, thanks for the loan of the stuff. It's come in handy."

"No problem. Is that video workin' out all right?" Reebok asked.

"Yeah, it's fine."

"Only, the thing is, I forgot I promised someone I'd make a copy of a tape for them."

"So you want it back?"

"Nah, but if you don't mind me bringin' me other video over tomorrow, I can do it there and then. It'll only take about an hour."

"No problem," I said. "Give me a ring before you come over, though. You never know, I might have a job or something by then."

"You don't want a lend of a sandwich toaster, do you? Me sister just got married and she got two of them and she has one already. In fact, I'll ask her to sell it to you cheap, if you want."

"God, toasted sandwiches! I miss them! Yeah, that'd be great, thanks. But I don't want to put her out."

"Ah no, it's no trouble. She got tons of stuff. Her boyfriend – well, her husband now – he's mad into gadgets and appliances, so people bought them all that sort of stuff for the weddin'. So now they've got two of nearly everythin'. Three of some things. I'll have a word with her, see if she has anythin' else that would be useful to you."

"She wouldn't have a spare bed, by any chance, would she? I was thinking about getting a lodger."

Reebok shook his head. "A bed? No, I don't think so. But I'll keep me eye out for one."

I thanked them, and wandered back to Justin and Mags.

"So what now?" Justin asked. He checked his watch. "Fancy heading over to the restaurant here?"

"It'll be mad busy," Mags said. "We could go home and order a pizza. What do you think, Orla? Unless you have other plans?"

"No, the only thing I have to do is phone Killian and let him know the outcome of the meeting. He . . ." I paused.

A man had walked up and was standing right in front of me.

I had no idea who he was, but he didn't look to be in a good mood.

"I hope you're bloody happy now!" he said.

"I'm sorry?"

"You . . ." Words failed him. He glared at me for a couple of seconds, then said, "Fuck!"

Justin said, "If you don't have anything positive to say, get lost, okay?"

"The both of them were behind this! That wanker Mills and this bitch! You *heard* what they said!"

Justin stepped in between us. "Listen, you stupid bastard, you call her a bitch again and it'll be the last coherent thing you ever say! If you'd been paying attention in there, it was made very clear that Orla was *not* involved."

"Don't you play the fuckin' hard man with me, boy!" He placed his hand on Justin's chest and shoved him backwards, hard. Justin staggered, caught the back of his legs on a small coffee table, and fell backwards over it.

I barely had time to register this: the man had whirled about to face me again. "And *you*, bitch, you owe me ten thousand quid!"

I was vaguely aware of the people around turning to see what was going on, but I was more concerned with the man in front of me. "Look, I had nothing to do with it!"

He pressed his face close to mine. Bizarrely, I couldn't help noticing how he wore the same aftershave as my father used to. "I'm gonna give you a week to come up with the money. If you don't, you're gonna regret it."

"Just calm down, all right? I've lost more than anyone else . . ."

And then he made a serious mistake: he reached out and grabbed hold of my arm.

* * *

A few seconds later two members of the gardaí were pushing their way through the crowd.

"What happened here?"

"He attacked me," I said. "So I defended myself."

They looked down at the man, who was lying on the floor, clutching his groin and moaning in agony.

"I kneed him in the balls," I explained, even though it was pretty obvious.

219

I looked around for Justin, and saw that he was on the ground too. Mags was helping him to his feet. "Is he okay?" I asked.

"He hit his head when he fell, but I think he's all right."

Justin gingerly touched the back of his head. "Is there any blood?"

"No," Mags said. "You're fine. Orla?"

"I'm going to have bruises on my arm, and I feel like I'm going to throw up."

One of the gardaí was crouched in front of the man, trying to get some sense out of him. The other one, who was about fifty and looked kind of like Mike Baldwin from *Coronation Street*, said to me, "Tell me exactly what happened." He took out a biro and a tiny notebook, licked the tip of the biro for no reason, and stood there poised to write down the events.

So I explained it all as well as I could.

When I was done, he said, "And everyone else just stood around watching this?"

"Yeah. Apart from Justin."

"They didn't jump in to save you, or anything? God, what's the world coming to? Look, Miss Adare, I know this man. He's a bit of a troublemaker."

"You're not kidding."

"But I don't think he'd really have hurt you. He's all mouth and no trousers, as the saying goes."

"It's not his mouth or his trousers that worry me. It's his fists."

The man on the floor seemed to be recovering. He'd

stopped moaning and the colour was slowly returning to his face.

The garda said, "He definitely grabbed hold of you first, right?"

"That's right."

"Okay, so you only fought back in self-defence. I'll take some names and addresses of witnesses, just in case."

Then I saw Thomas Kennedy excusing his way through the crowd. "Orla . . . what happened?"

So once again I explained the events. By the time I was done he looked particularly worried. "I thought I made it very clear that you're innocent."

"Some people only hear what they want to hear."

"That's true, unfortunately."

We watched as the man was helped up. He seemed a lot less angry now. He hobbled over to me, and said, "Look, I'm sorry."

"You should be."

"It's just . . . I borrowed money to invest with Mills."

"Are you all right there, Miss Adare?" asked the older of the gardaí.

"I'm fine, thanks," I said.

My attacker lowered his voice so that no one but me could hear, and said, "The people I borrowed if off . . . they're going to want their money back. I mean, they lent it to me on the understanding that I'd pay them back with twenty per cent on top when Mills paid us."

"You've *got* to be kidding. You borrowed money off a loan shark?"

"It seemed like a sure thing. Now what am I going to do?"

"I don't know."

"If I can't pay them back, they're going to do a lot worse to me than you did."

I said, "Well, if you're stupid enough to go to a loan shark for something like this, then you deserve what's coming to you."

The expression on his face hardened for a second, and then his shoulders sagged. He looked lost, desperate, and I almost felt sorry for him.

When the man apologised again, and painfully wandered away, I turned to Thomas. "How many more of these people am I going to have to fight?"

"I wish I could tell you that."

* * *

Reebok – whose real name was Noel – arrived at noon the next day, carrying a video recorder and a bundle of cables.

"I should never've separated these two," he said to me as he was connecting the cables between the videos.

"They get lonely?"

"It's just that it takes forever to get everything set up right." After ten minutes of fiddling with it, he gave up. "I don't think it's goin' to work. I'll have to check with Wayne, he's the expert."

Wayne, I remembered, was Jumper Man.

"All right if I leave this one here until I get it sorted?"

"Sure."

222

After he left, I made toasted sandwiches. They were delicious, even though I only had cheese to put in them.

Reebok wouldn't accept any more than ten euro for the sandwich toaster, even though I was sure it cost at least twice that in the shops. "Look, me sister's loaded," he'd explained. "And like I said yesterday, they've got two of them, so this one was just sittin' in the box."

I spent the rest of the afternoon watching television, then I had a nice long bath and tried, with more success than I'd expected, to stop feeling sorry for myself.

Sure, I'd lost a lot of stuff. And, okay, so I still didn't have a job, but at least now I'd been officially vindicated, and there was a possibility that the bank would refund my money.

I even had some furniture now, and a few appliances.

I was definitely in an "up" mood by the time I got out of the bath, until I realised that the only towel I had was still damp from the day before.

My positive feelings evaporated as I sat on the edge of the bath, attempting to dry myself with a wet towel and very much aware that the remainder of the money Killian and Davina had lent me was *not* going to last long enough for the health board's cheque to clear.

When I felt I was dry enough, I climbed into my borrowed bed, under my second-hand blankets, and tried not to think about the future.

On the whole, it had not been a good week.

Chapter 13

When I woke up on Monday morning, the first thought on my mind was Justin's idea about getting a lodger. It certainly seemed like the right thing to do. Not only would it bring in some money, but it also meant that there'd be someone else around.

It wasn't that I didn't feel safe in the house – despite all the hostile callers – it was more that the house felt cold and empty.

When Des was around, he was generally coming and going all day. Plus I always had something to do: stripping wallpaper, sanding down a window frame, or filling in the gaps at the tops of the skirting boards, that sort of thing.

As I was getting dressed I decided that I wasn't going to let things get me down. I'd find the positive in every situation and become one of those "Go for it!" people. What had happened to me wasn't a set-back; it was an opportunity. How many other people get the chance to start over?

I got up, got dressed, and had a quick breakfast of a microwaved cheese sandwich. I could have used the sandwich toaster, but I was curious to find out what a microwaved sandwich tasted like. It was horrible.

My first step, I decided, would be to pay another visit to the supermarket and talk to Mr Waters again. He'd said he'd speak to me after the meeting, but either he hadn't turned up, or he'd changed his mind about hiring me. The latter possibility didn't fit well with the new, positive me, so I dismissed it. If Waters wouldn't give me a job, then someone else would.

Probably.

* * *

The girl at the information kiosk told me that the caterpillar-browed Mr Waters wasn't in.

"Well, who's in charge at the moment, then?"

"That'd be our new assistant manager, Mr Sheridan. D'you want me to get him for you?"

"Yes, please."

So she grabbed the microphone and roared out, "Mr Sheridan to the information kiosk, please!"

While we waited, I noticed that the girl glanced at me a couple of times, looking away when I caught her eye.

After the fourth time, I said, "Yes?"

She said, "It's you, isn't it?"

"No, I'm not me, I'm someone else. But I get that all the time."

"Oh. All right then." That seemed to satisfy her, so she returned her attention to her copy of *Bella*.

The new assistant manager was about thirty. He had

dark brown hair that was close-cropped in a not very flattering style – probably because he was starting to go bald – with a lot of grey at the temples. He had brown eyes, well-tanned skin, and shaggy eyebrows, though they weren't nearly as bad as Mr Waters'.

His badge identified him as Barry Sheridan. "What can I do for you, madam?"

Madam? I said to myself. God, how old do I look? "Well, I was hoping to talk to Mr Waters. I spoke to him on Friday about a job. He said that he'd talk to me on Saturday, but . . ." I wasn't quite sure how to finish that without telling him the whole story, so I just let the sentence trail off.

"You must be Mrs Adare, right?"

"*Miss*," I corrected.

"Miss, sorry. Yeah, he mentioned to me about you yesterday. Look, he said that you might call in, and I was to tell you that he's sorry, but he doesn't think it would be a good move to hire you. He said that he has to think of the customers first."

"Damn. I suppose he told you everything?"

"Not really, but everyone *else* did." Then he gave me a friendly smile and added, "Let me tell you, it's not every day you move to a new town and come across a situation like yours. I mean, yesterday was my first day, and the very first thing that happened to me was a customer complaining about you."

"Who was it?"

"Ah, some mad old bat. She said that she'd heard about you looking for a job here and that if we hired you she'd take her business elsewhere. So there I am thinking that I don't want to screw up on my first day and lose a valuable customer, and then she wandered off and the only thing she bought was a small tin of dog food. And not even the good stuff. I feel sorry for her dog. If she even *has* one."

"Well, I'm sorry about that."

He looked surprised. "There's no need for you to apologise, Ms Adare. From what I hear, you're not to blame for anything that happened."

"That's true, but you might feel differently if you were one of the people who got their money stolen."

He scratched his chin. It was only ten o'clock in the morning and he already had five-o'clock shadow, as though his face belonged to a different time zone. "In a way, I suppose I have. The plan was for me to take over here as manager when the new store opened."

"So what's going to happen now?"

He shrugged. "Who knows? According to Mr Waters, they're looking for another location. But that could take years."

"God, this is a right mess, isn't it?"

"You have to look on the bright side." He paused. "At the moment I haven't figured out what the bright side *is*, but I'm sure it'll come to me. Anyway – unless there's anything else I can do for you, I'd better get back to work."

"Okay. Well, tell Mr Waters I said thanks anyway."

* * *

As I wandered through the town that morning, I was amazed at how different it seemed to the previous week.

People I'd never set eyes on nodded hello to me, some I vaguely knew stopped to ask me how I was, and – unfortunately – some people I knew quite well completely blanked me.

I could understand that; even if they didn't blame me for what Des had done, it was always going to be awkward for them to talk to me. At the very least, they probably felt embarrassed for me. I wondered if I was going to be known as "that poor woman" for the rest of my life.

On the way home I stopped into one of the town's many mobile-phone shops. There was one on every corner, and they were always packed. You'd think that once everyone had a mobile phone the novelty would wear off and it wouldn't be long before the shops started to close down, but there was no sign of that happening yet.

This early in the day, thankfully, the shop wasn't too busy. There was only one "retail engineer" on, and he quickly and efficiently dealt with the other customers, then turned to me. "How can I help you?"

I showed him my phone. "I'm having a bit of trouble with this," I said.

He turned the phone over in his hands. He didn't seem particularly impressed with the Winnie-The-Pooh cover. "What sort of trouble?"

"Well, it won't charge properly."

"It could be your charger. Did you happen to bring it with you?"

"No, but I know it's not the charger, because my friend has the same phone and her charger won't work on my phone, but my charger will work on her phone."

228

"Well, let's have a look, then." He rummaged under the counter and eventually produced a charger, plugged it in and attached the phone.

He dealt with another couple of customers before coming back to me. "It seems to be charging okay."

"Yeah, that's how it always looks, but I bet it's *not* charging."

"How old is the battery? On these models you'd be lucky to get more than a year and a half out of them."

"I got a new one only a couple of months ago."

Sensing a possible sale, he said to me, "Have you considered replacing the phone?"

"I'm not sure I can afford that."

"These days it's often cheaper to get a new phone than to get yours fixed."

"Well, which models do you have?"

So I spent some time pretending to go through a bunch of glossy brochures, occasionally asking him questions in the hope that he wouldn't catch on to what I was really up to. After about fifteen minutes, it began to dawn on the young man that he wasn't going to make a sale. "Look, there doesn't seem to be *anything* in your price range that has the features you want."

"Are you sure you don't have anything stashed away? Any new models that just came in?"

"You've already seen everything we have."

He seemed to be only one step away from asking me to vacate the premises, so I said, "Okay. Look, thanks for your help. I'll have a think about it, and see how much I'm able to afford. Can I hold onto these brochures?"

"Sure." He unplugged my phone and handed it over.

"This one does appear to have charged up a bit, though."

"Oh. Well, I'll have a look and I'll get back to you. Thanks anyway."

As I walked home I felt a little bit guilty about stealing the shop's electricity and wasting the assistant's time, but I consoled myself by making a silent promise that when this mess was all sorted out, I'd go back in there and really buy a new phone. Probably.

* * *

There was a letter from the bank waiting for me when I got home. There was no stamp or address on it, so it must have been delivered by hand.

The letter said: *"Dear Ms Adare, in light of the unfortunate situation regarding the joint account you held with Mr Desmond Mills, we have decided that in order to maintain the good will between us, we would like to offer you a compensatory settlement of one thousand euro, which has been credited to your account."*

Then there was a whole bunch of paragraphs explaining how this wasn't an admission of error on their part, and that a "thorough investigation" had revealed that the bank was not in any way at fault.

It was signed: *Dearbhla McKenna, Branch Manager.*

I wasn't sure what to do about that; it was great to think that I now had a thousand euro more than I thought I did, but still . . . Because of their incompetence, I was still down about seven thousand.

Did accepting this money mean that I'd lose out any claim I might have to the rest of my money?

I needed to talk to someone who knew about such things, but unfortunately I only knew one expert in financial matters, and that was Des.

I needed the advice of someone I could trust, so I went next door to see Mr Farley.

* * *

We sat at his kitchen table, drinking tea and eating sandwiches of sliced ham and iceberg lettuce, while he read over the letter.

In the far corner, Mr Farley's washing-machine was grumbling away to itself, sounding like it was complaining about having to wash my clothes; he had kindly offered the use of it.

"I don't know about this kind of thing, Orla. You really need to speak to a solicitor."

"That's what I was thinking. My friend Mags gave me her cousin's number last week. She's a solicitor. I left a message, but she never got back to me."

"I mean, if you accept the money, then there's a good chance the bank will be able to argue that you've also accepted that they're not to blame for letting Des steal your money."

"But they've already lodged the money into my account."

"So what you have to do is write back, and say thanks for the money, but you can't accept it because you feel you're entitled to *all* of your money back. And you never know, they might double it to two grand."

"That still wouldn't be enough."

231

"True. But let me tell you a little story . . . About ten years back an old friend of mine was walking along, minding his own business, and he was passing by a shop that was being refitted. As he was passing, a carpenter or someone came out, carrying a large plank over his shoulder. He was being pretty careful, but just as he got outside, someone called to him and he turned around, and the plank swung out and hit my friend in the face. Broke his nose and his glasses, and knocked out a few of his teeth. Not that he had many left. But the thing is, the building foreman gave him a couple of hundred pounds there and then, and when my friend went to get legal advice, he was told that because he'd already accepted the money, there wasn't really much he could do."

"I see."

"So you should write back to the bank, like I said, and tell them that you can't accept the money. And you should try and get in touch with your friend's cousin again."

I agreed that seemed like the best approach, so we spent the next hour drafting a polite but firm letter. After that, I phoned Mags' cousin – Mr Farley insisted that I use his phone – and this time, she answered.

After I explained who I was, she said, "Of course, Ms Adare. I'm sorry I didn't get back to you. Mags was only talking to me yesterday about your case."

I told her about the latest development, and she offered to meet me. "Can you come and see me in the office this afternoon, say about three?"

"Sure." I wrote down the address. "Listen, I don't know how much this is going to cost, and I don't actually have any money. That's the whole problem."

"Don't worry about that," she told me. "For now, don't post your letter – that sort of thing is much more effective if it comes from a solicitor."

* * *

It was only later, as I was on the bus heading towards the solicitor's office, that a nasty thought occurred to me; she hadn't bothered to get in touch with me because she thought I didn't have a chance, but after the meeting on Saturday – which Mags had almost certainly told her about – she realised that since the bank's security video had proved I wasn't to blame, then it was probably worth her while taking on the case.

Her name was Nora Collins, and she was only a couple of years older than me. Her office was in a huge, dark old building that smelled of old books and leather. There was also a faint smell of vinegar from the chip shop downstairs, which immediately made me hungry.

After I gave her my version of events, she said, "And you haven't talked to any other solicitors? I need to know in case there's a conflict of interest."

"Well, there was one guy who turned up at the door and wouldn't go away. Nathan Fowler, his name is."

"Nathan Fowler . . . I don't think I've ever heard of him. But why didn't you deal with him?"

"Well, like I said, he turned up out of the blue. That kind of bothered me. It made me think of him as an ambulance chaser."

"And you specifically told him you didn't want to work with him?"

I nodded. "Yeah, several times. He didn't seem to

understand, though. Or at least, he didn't *want* to understand."

"Well, it shouldn't be a problem. Now . . ." She tapped a well-manicured finger on the bank's letter. "How about this? I can write to your bank and make it clear to them that you're pleased that they've given you some of the money they owe you, and that you want to know when you can expect to receive the rest of it. I'll make it clear that we're well aware that the bank is at fault, and that we'd like the rest of your money and a written apology. I'll also suggest that they compensate you for all the trouble they've caused. How does that sound?"

I grinned. "Great! I thought I was just going to have to completely refuse the money."

"No, I wouldn't do that just yet. In fact, you should try to avoid any further direct contact with the bank. At least, not on this matter. Allow me to deal with them."

"Okay. Now the awkward part: how much will this cost me?"

She considered this. "Normally, we have set charges for this sort of thing, but since you're Mags' friend . . . How about thirty per cent of whatever you get above the original amount in your account?"

I wasn't sure whether I was supposed to haggle, so I agreed. "But suppose I only get my money back and nothing else?"

"In that case, you get my services for free. It's not likely that'll happen, but it's a chance I'm willing to take."

"So if they give me a million euro . . ."

"Then I'll get three hundred thousand."

We both grinned at each other.

"Not that we'll get *that* much, but you never know. I'll argue that everything that happened to you is a direct consequence of their incompetence."

"Even me losing my job?"

She nodded. "That's right. It's conceivable that if they hadn't been so lax as to allow Mr Mills to clear your account, or to forge your signature on the business forms, then he might never have been tempted, and you wouldn't be going through all this."

* * *

On the bus on the way home, I had a good time fantasising about the things I was going to spend my millions on. New furniture, for a start. And a flash car. And if I got enough, I might be able to pay back Killian and Justin. I decided that I wouldn't bother paying anyone else.

By the time I got home I'd worked out a whole scenario where I opened my own restaurant directly opposite Flanagan's, and the old bastard was forced to close. Then I'd hire Pauline and Steve and Kalim away from him, and I'd offer Flanagan a job as a chef, but only for the same salary that he'd paid me to wait on tables.

Nora Collins had told me that it probably wouldn't be wise to spend any of the money from the bank yet. I'd been a bit disappointed about that, because I'd been thinking about buying a bed for my potential lodger. When I mentioned that to Nora, she looked at me as though I was being remarkably stupid. "Look," she said, "you already *have* a bed, right? So you give that bed to your lodger and you just need to buy a mattress for

235

yourself. It's not that uncomfortable. When I moved into my house I couldn't afford a real bed for years."

So that was my new plan. First thing in the morning I'd to hunting for a reasonably cheap mattress, and if I couldn't afford one, I'd ask Justin and Mags if I could borrow the one from their spare bedroom. Then once that was sorted out, I'd have a think about how to go about finding a lodger.

* * *

There's something very undignified about two twenty-something women carrying a single mattress right through the town at four o'clock in the afternoon.

Mags had the back end, because she was so embarrassed that she wanted to be able to hide her face if she saw any of the kids from school.

This meant, of course, that I had the front end. Lots of people stopped and stared and no one offered to help.

The mattress wasn't heavy, but it was awkward. The weather had turned colder that morning, and dark grey clouds were gathering overhead to see what we were up to, wondering whether they should rain on us just to make things harder.

At one stage we were crossing the main road when the wind suddenly picked up and almost knocked the two of us over. Mags screamed, and we ran for the far side.

"I thought we were goners there," Mags said, as we wobbled past the shoe shop. "I could see the headlines: 'Disturbed Women Killed in Freak Mattress Accident.'"

I laughed. "You have to admit, it's pretty funny."

"Oh, it's hilarious!"

"Well, it was your idea to carry it. *I* wanted to get a taxi!"

A voice from behind me said, "Orla?" and I turned to see Pauline from the restaurant coming up. She looked at me, at Mags, and at the mattress, and said, "Just out taking your mattress for a walk?"

"You know how it is," I said. "If we don't take him for a walk now, he'll be scratching at the door all night. So how are things?"

"Pretty good. You?"

I patted the mattress. "Getting better. How's what's-his-name?"

"Who?"

"The guy you were with in the supermarket that day."

"Oh, him . . . fine, I suppose. He's not my boyfriend or anything, we're just friends."

"Well, from the way he was obeying your every command I think he wants to be *more* than friends."

"Don't they all? So what's the story with the mattress?"

"I'm getting a lodger," I said. "Well, I'm hoping to. I borrowed a bed from the man next door, and Mags is lending me her spare mattress until I can get a bed for myself." I had a thought. "Actually, you're not looking for somewhere else to live, are you? I know you don't have much space in the flat. I've got *tons* of space. Nothing in it, unfortunately."

"No, I'm all right where I am, thanks. But I'll ask around if you like."

I told her that would be great, and then – because of the expression on Mags' face – told her that we'd better get moving.

* * *

When Mags and I got back to the house, we carried the mattress up the stairs and into one of the empty bedrooms, and propped it against the wall.

"So this'll be your room now?" Mags asked.

"Yeah. Well, the lodger deserves the bigger bedroom. Besides, this was my room when I was a kid."

She looked down at the floor. "You'd want to give this place a bloody good hoovering before you put the mattress down."

"I'll borrow Mr Farley's hoover in the morning."

Mags looked out the window. "Damn. It's starting to rain. I'll get soaked on the way home."

"Well, stick around for a while, it might ease off. Justin's away again this week, right? So you're not in any rush to get home."

"I've got homework to mark," she said.

I wasn't convinced. "Don't tell me *he's* coming over?"

She nodded. "He is."

"God, Mags, you're playing with fire, you know that?"

"I know."

"Justin is going to go absolutely nuts when he finds out."

Mags bit her lip. "On Saturday when he stood up to that guy – the one in the hotel?"

"Right, the soprano."

She laughed. "I've never seen him do anything like that before. I mean, I think he'd have flattened that man if he hadn't been knocked back over the furniture. It was like . . ." She paused, and looked as though she was searching for the right words. "You know how Justin is.

He's always so placid. He never loses his cool. But on Saturday it was like there was real fire in him."

I looked at her. "You're having me on, aren't you?"

"No. It was like he's been half asleep all his life, and suddenly he woke up. Did you see his *eyes*?"

"How do you mean?"

"They were filled with . . . I don't know. Rage. Anger." She paused. "Passion. I've never seen him react that way to protect *me*."

"Don't tell me you're another one of those people who think that he's secretly been in love with me all this time?"

"No, of course not. But, well, you have to admit it was a bit out of character for him."

"And did that make you see him in a different light?"

"Not in the way you mean, but it did make me think."

"About?"

"About me and Peter, mainly. You see, Justin had the same kind of look that Peter gets when he's with me."

I didn't know how to react to that. Not for the first time, I wished Mags had never told me about her affair with Peter Harney.

It wasn't a nice situation to be in; loyalty to my friend meant that I really should tell him, but I'd already promised Mags I'd keep quiet.

But even if I was to break the promise, how would I do it? I couldn't really take Justin aside and say, "Listen, you know when you have sex with your wife? Well, you're not the only one." Nor could I sit him down and say something like, "I heard a rumour from a friend of a friend that, someone – I won't say who, but you're married to her –

has been having an affair with Pete Harney for the past few years."

The question I had to ask myself was this: if I'd been in Justin's position, would I want to know about it?

Yes, I told myself. Of course I would.

Even if it destroyed my marriage?

That was a tougher one to answer, but in the end I came to the same conclusion: I'd want to know.

Mags was staring at me. "What are you thinking?"

I hesitated a little before answering, trying to think of the best way to say it. "Mags, suppose Justin was the one having the affair . . ."

She raised her hand to stop me. "Don't! I know what you're going to say!"

"Well?"

"I don't want to talk about that."

"Do you mean you don't want to *talk* about it, or to *think* about it?"

"Orla, you don't know what it's like."

"I realise that. Look, Mags, I'm not going to say anything to him, as much as I think I probably should. But suppose he finds out by himself and he asks me about it? What should I tell him? If I tell him that I already knew, then he'd feel even worse. He'll know I betrayed him."

"Then if that happens, you'll just have to lie."

"It just doesn't seem fair."

She shrugged. "I know." She looked out at the rain again. "God, it's never going to stop."

"Look, let's go downstairs and have a cup of tea and talk about everything."

Mags laughed. "I thought you didn't have a kettle?"

"Oh shite, yeah, you're right. Well, we'll heat up two cups of water in the microwave."

"And do you have any tea bags?"

It was my turn to laugh. "Damn it!"

We went downstairs anyway, and sat in the kitchen.

"God, it's getting cold," I said. "And that's another problem. If the weather turns worse, how am I going to heat the house? All my convector heaters are gone, and I can't afford coal for the fire. I'm not even sure I can afford matches."

"That's going to be difficult if you get a lodger."

"Yeah . . . I suppose I'll have to ask her to pay in advance."

"How much are you going to charge per week?"

That made me pause. "I have no idea. I never even thought about that."

"Well, what's the going rate?"

I shrugged.

"That's the first thing you should try and find out. They sometimes have ads for lodgers on the notice-board in the supermarket. Next time you're there have a look and see how much other people are charging. Any particular sort of person you're looking for?"

"Someone who's incredibly rich. And quiet. And has her own cooker and washing machine."

"Yeah, but younger or older or what?"

"I'm not bothered, as long as she's got a steady job to pay the rent."

* * *

The next morning, I walked up to the supermarket and

examined their notice-board. There were no ads for lodgers, which was both good and bad: good, because I wasn't going to be facing any competition, but bad because I had no idea how much to charge.

After dithering for a few minutes, I decided that a hundred and fifty euros per week sounded about right. That was six hundred a month, which was enough to cover my mortgage and help pay some of the bills.

I filled out a card with all the relevant details, pinned it to the notice board, then walked down the road to the charity shop, where I bought some blankets for my mattress.

When I got home I borrowed Mr Farley's vacuum cleaner and spent a couple of hours cleaning the house. Then I made up my bed, and had a good look around.

The house was not, to be brutally honest, in a fit state to receive a lodger. It was barely in a fit state to receive a burglar.

Still, there was nothing more I could do about that at the moment.

I returned Mr Farley's vacuum cleaner, then went back to my own kitchen to have some lunch.

Five minutes later I was on my way back to the supermarket, mentally kicking myself for not thinking about buying food the first time I was there.

With my rapidly dwindling finances I bought bread, milk, vegetables and cheese. I was idly wandering around, wondering if it would be possible to plant vegetables in the back garden to save money, when I passed the notice-board. I stopped and stared.

My notice was gone.

I stormed up to the information kiosk, interrupted the

girl in the middle of her jumbo crossword, and demanded to know why it had been taken down.

"I dunno," she said. "When did you put it up?"

"This morning! God, it's bad enough that all my money was stolen and that no one will give me a job, but now the people of this damn town won't even let me get a lodger! I thought that after Saturday everyone would know I was innocent, but that would have been too convenient, wouldn't it? No, they still have to bloody persecute me!"

The girl watched me all through my tirade, and didn't seem moved to offer any sympathy. "I'm sorry, but we can't control what happens to the notice-board. Why don't you just put up another one?"

"So that they can take that one down too? What's the point? I've just about taken all I can, you know that? I mean, I come here looking for a job, and first your boss is all over me, and then he finds out who I am, and he has to change his mind. And now it's like no one's going to let me get on with my life!"

The girl said, "I'm sorry, Mrs Adare, but it's really got nothing to do with us."

"It's *Miss* Adare! I'm not married! Do I look married to you? Do you see a wedding ring? Of course, even if I had one, I'd have had to sell it, wouldn't I? All because that bastard saw me as an easy mark and destroyed my entire life!"

She sighed. "Do you want me to call the manager?"

I wasn't sure whether she asked that as a sort of warning that I was getting out of control, or because she thought that the manager might be able to help. "Yes! Please do!"

So she roared into the PA system for Mr Sheridan.

He arrived a minute later. "Ah, Ms Adare!" He had his hand extended. I didn't shake it.

"Look, you! I put a notice up on your board, looking for a lodger, and some bastard came and took it down! Now, you know what I've been going through lately, and I have to tell you I don't *need* this sort of shit! Things are bad enough as they are. I've got half the people in the town blaming me for what Des did, and the other half ignoring me because they're embarrassed that they *did* blame me!"

"Yes, but –"

"No, I'm not going to let anyone push me around any more! Now, I'm going to fill out another card and put it on your notice-board, and you'd damn well better make sure that it stays there! I'll be coming back to check, and if the card is missing then I'm going to hold you personally responsible!"

"Yes, but –"

"Is that clear?"

He nodded. "Perfectly. But if someone takes down the card –"

"They'd better not."

"No, I mean, what if they take down the card because they're looking for a place to stay and they don't want anyone else to get it?"

I froze. "Oh."

Barry Sheridan reached into his back pocket and took out my card. "At the moment I'm staying in a bed and breakfast, but it's not ideal. I was going to call over this evening. So how about it? I've got a regular income and I can pay you the first month in advance. In fact, I can pay you right now, in cash."

"But . . . you haven't even seen the place yet!"

"Well, I'll call over this evening, then, and you can give me the grand tour. Now, if you want I'll put your notice back up . . .?"

"No, that's okay." I hoped I didn't look as embarrassed as I felt. "I'm sorry about losing my temper."

"No worries," Sheridan said.

The girl behind the kiosk said "Ahem!" in a very loud voice.

"I'm sorry to you, too," I said. "I've been under a lot of pressure. I didn't mean to take it out on you."

"Oh, it's no bother," she lied, and returned to her crossword.

"So what do you think?" Sheridan asked. "I'll call over at about six, how's that sound?"

Chapter 14

Barry Sheridan arrived at the house half an hour late, but it didn't help; I was still cringing every time I thought about my little outburst at the supermarket.

My dad, who was wise in the ways of the world, had always told me and Killian how important it was to find out the facts before you did anything rash. This was highlighted for us when Killian was about fourteen. He came home one winter's evening with a black eye and a bloody nose. Tears, blood and snot mixed together as he stammered out what had happened . . .

Killian and a couple of his friends had been making their way home when a man jumped out from behind his hedge and grabbed hold of Killian and one of the others. The other one managed to break free, but Killian was held fast. Then the man – for absolutely no reason – punched Killian in the face.

As my mother was doing her best to clean up Killian's

face, Dad asked him who his attacker was, where he lived, and so on.

I guess that most fathers would go berserk or phone the police or something, but Dad just got up, put on his jacket, and said to Killian, "Right. Let's go and have a few words with him."

So they went over to this guy's house, but Killian dragged his feet the whole way. "Dad, I don't think we should."

That only made Dad more determined. He practically pushed Killian up to the front door, rang the bell, and waited. There was no answer, but they could hear someone moving around inside. So Dad knocked and shouted "Hello?" through the letterbox, until finally the door was opened by a rather shaky-looking man in his mid-thirties.

Dad just said to him, "My son says you grabbed him and punched him in the face. Is that right?"

The man nodded nervously. "Eh, yeah, I did."

"You're twice his size, twice his age. Give me one good reason why I shouldn't do the same to you."

The man said, "Look, I know I shouldn't have done it. I just lost control."

"Why did you do it?"

The man looked from Dad to Killian and back, and said, "Him and his friends . . . every night for the past year they've been ringing the bell and running away. Usually two or three times a night. It's been getting to the stage where we hardly answer the door at all. It was only about a week ago that I actually saw who they were. I was waiting behind the door and opened it as soon as they

Jaye Carroll

rang, but I wasn't able to catch them. I thought that might be the end of it, but it got worse. Last night they did it about eight times. I decided I'd wait for them tonight."

"And you think that justifies hitting him?"

The man swallowed and said, "No. I'm sorry. But they've been driving us mad. Last night I tried to talk to them. I thought that if I got to know them they'd stop, but they just thought it was funny. I couldn't think of any other way to make them stop."

Then Dad said, "Well, I don't blame you," and he reached out and belted Killian across the back of his head.

Killian yelped and jumped back, and Dad said to him, "You or your friends *ever* bother this man again and I'll make sure you regret it." Then he turned back to the man. "I'm sorry about this, I really am. We had to put up with the same thing for years, about the time Killian was born, and I never managed to catch the little bastards."

Killian said, "Look, I'm sorry. We were just havin' a laugh."

The man said, "Do you see *me* fucking laughing?" To Dad, he said, "My wife's mother died three weeks ago. We came home from the hospital and we were pretty upset, as you can imagine, and about ten minutes later the doorbell rings, and I go out and answer it, and what do I see? There's no one there, but I can see your son and his friends running like mad down the road. I swear to God, if my wife hadn't calmed me down I'd have gone and found them and quite probably killed them."

"I can understand that," Dad said, and belted Killian again.

"It wasn't always *me*!" Killian said.

248

"Who was it, then?" Dad asked.

But Killian refused to name the friends involved, though Dad was pretty sure he knew who they were. He said, "Killian, I respect that you're loyal to your friends, but since you're not going to name them, you'll have to receive their punishment as well."

A week later, Killian had his worst ever Christmas: he got a card.

Dad took him aside on Christmas morning and said, "You know why this is, don't you?"

"Yeah, but Dad –"

"But nothing! You tormented that man and his wife for a year, and God only knows who else you've been doing it to."

"Jesus! This is so unfair!"

"Killian, when you're grown up and you have a house of your own, and this starts happening to you, you'll realise that it's not unfair at all. Look at it like this . . . when you go back to school the week after next and your friends ask you what you got for Christmas, and you have to tell them you didn't get anything, some of them are going to think it's pretty funny, aren't they?"

"Yeah."

"But *you* don't think it's funny, do you?"

"Of course I don't!"

"There you go," Dad said. "Just like you thought it was funny to ring that man's doorbell and run away."

"Yeah, but that's completely different!"

"God, I'm not getting through to you at all, am I? *Why* is it different?"

"It just is."

Then Dad reached down behind the sofa and took out a large box wrapped in Christmas paper. Killian thought that it was for him, but Dad said, "You are going to take this box of sweets over to that man's house and give it to him. And you are going to apologise for all the trouble you caused."

"Well, he might not be in."

"Then you wait until he *is* in."

"But it's raining out!"

"And?"

"I'll be soaked! They don't have a proper porch!"

"Well, you should know. And don't go thinking that you can just ditch this somewhere and pretend that you delivered it, because I'm going to go over to his house tomorrow and check."

Killian left the house at one o'clock, and wasn't back until after four. He was freezing, soaked to the skin, and very hungry, having missed his Christmas dinner.

"Well?" Dad asked.

"They were out all day and just came home."

"Embarrassing, was it, standing there waiting for them?"

"Yeah."

"So have you learned your lesson?"

Killian didn't understand what Dad meant.

"The lesson," Dad explained, "is that you can never know what's going on in someone else's life. Just because something is funny to you doesn't mean it's funny to them."

"Look, I've said I'm sorry about a million times. How much more am I going to have to put up with?"

And then my mother said, "You've *said* you're sorry,

Killian, but it sounds to me like you're just sorry you got caught, not sorry you did it." That was how Mam was; she was quiet, but every now and then she'd come out with something like that, an observation that summed everything up in just a few words.

But even so, nothing my parents said could make Killian really understand, and it wasn't until about two years later that he finally realised what he'd put that couple through: one of his classmates at school had decided he didn't like Killian, and every day for about three months the boy found a way to put a sticker reading "I'm a Bastard!" on Killian's back. Killian had no idea who was even doing it, until the boy was caught by one of the teachers.

* * *

I showed Barry Sheridan around the house, which didn't take long. He went "Hmm . . ." a lot.

"I know what you're thinking," I said.

"And that is . . .?"

"You're thinking that there's no way in a million years that you're going to stay here."

He shrugged. "No, I'm not. I can see you've done a great job on the bathroom and the bedroom. It's just a pity you don't have . . . well, much of anything, but there's a bed, a bath and a toilet. That'll do me for now. Pity about the bedroom door, though. You wouldn't mind if I replaced it with one of the other doors, would you?"

"Not at all. So you're going to take it?"

"If you'll have me."

"You're not one of those mad party people who'll be coming and going all night long, are you?"

251

"Nope. You'll hardly know I'm here. Besides, I'm probably going to be working twelve hours a day, six or seven days a week for the foreseeable future. Have to make sure that they know I'm indispensable. So, what's included in the price?"

"Well, just what you see. We don't have a washing machine at the moment, though. Or a cooker. But once I get back on my feet they're the first things I'm going to get."

We had another little wander through the house.

Barry said, "About the television privileges . . . I mean, if I want to watch something and you're already watching something else, what do we do?"

"I suppose we'll just have to record one of them."

"Fair enough. So what do you think?"

"I'm happy if you are."

"Great! How soon can I move in?"

"Whenever you want. Though I've got to go out this evening. I'll be back about half ten."

"Well, when are you leaving?"

"About half seven."

"I could get to the B&B and pack everything up and be back here before then."

That meant that he'd be in the house alone while I was at the school . . . I wasn't comfortable with that, until he said, "And I'll stop by the ATM on the way, of course. I'll be able to pay you four weeks' rent in advance."

* * *

So Barry went off to the bed and breakfast and came back about an hour later with a car full of stuff. I helped him carry it all up to his room.

252

"I'll have to get myself a wardrobe or a chest of drawers," he said as he put the last of the boxes on the floor. He'd hung his work shirts from the curtain pole. "I don't suppose you have an iron and an ironing board?"

"No, sorry."

"Ah, they'll be all right for a couple of days." He reached into his pocket and took out his wallet. "So, four weeks in advance, right?" He handed over twelve fifty-euro notes.

I had to restrain myself from grabbing the money and running around in excited little circles. "Thanks!"

"Great! So, I'm starving. What are you making me for dinner?"

"Hold on . . . this doesn't include meals, you know!"

He grinned at me. "I know, I'm just having you on. Do you have the number for a local pizza place or something? It's on me."

I checked my watch. "Thanks, but I've got to go in a few minutes."

"Oh, right. You're teaching your classes down at the school, yeah? I heard about that. Well, I'll give you a lift if you like. I can get myself a pizza on the way back."

* * *

The previous Tuesday – the first class – there had been three no-shows; this time there were six who failed to turn up. The old man who'd been the best in the class was one of them.

At the end of the first lesson I'd asked them to do a few sketches during the week. Naturally, most of them hadn't bothered, but one or two were proudly showing off their drawings of cars, chairs, fridges – for some unfathomable reason it's always fridges, never cookers or washing machines.

Betty, the woman who'd arrived at the very end of the first lesson, was only an hour late this time. She had, however, done her homework: she'd brought in a dozen sketches of various household items. They weren't great, but showed a good deal of enthusiasm.

"So how am I doing?" she asked.

"Not bad . . . you're certainly getting the hang of the shading. But I can see you're a bit heavy with the pencil. You should use light, easy strokes to define the shape. You're using a 2B, right?"

She looked up at me. "A 2B?"

"A 2B pencil. It's a very soft, dark lead. A 2H would be better."

"You mean there's different kinds of pencils?"

At that, an old man raised his hand. "Orla? How come some pencils are round and some are hexagonal?"

The woman sitting next to him said, "Isn't it obvious? Because round pencils are more likely to roll off the desk, you daft old git!"

"What do you mean 'old'? I'm two years younger than you are!"

"Get out of it! I'm only sixty-one!"

"And the *rest*," he said. "If you're only sixty-one, then how come your daughter is forty-five?"

"She's never forty-five! She's only forty! I should know – I was there when she was born."

He sneered at her. "Look, I happen to know that she's forty-five because she only just told me the other day."

"What!?" The woman pushed her chair back and stared at him, and for a second I thought she was going to belt him. "And you were in Belfast, were you? Because that's where she lives and she hasn't been back home in two months!"

He looked baffled. "Oh. Really? Then who was I talking to?"

I said, "Listen, you two. There's no fighting in this class! Do you want me to have to separate the two of you?"

"Throw a bucket of water over them," someone suggested.

* * *

When I got home, I found that Barry had settled himself in nicely. He'd taken the door off the linen cupboard and attached it to the doorframe of his new bedroom.

He probably should have measured the door first; it was about an inch too narrow for the frame. "Sorry about that," he said to me, opening and closing the door and looking at it a lot. "I forgot that about old houses; the guys who built these things tended to use measuring tapes made out of elastic. Well, it'll have to do for now."

"So that's *two* bedroom doors I'll have to get," I said. "Any idea how much a door costs?"

"Not a clue. I suppose all we really need for the moment are a couple of sheets of plywood and some hinges. There's a hardware store in town, right? I'll check it out tomorrow, if you like."

"No, I'll do it. I'm going there anyway, to get the key copied for you."

We tromped back downstairs to the sitting-room. "So how did your class go?" he asked.

"Not bad. We're only in early days, though. By the time we get to the last lesson we'll probably be down to about seven or eight students."

Barry settled himself in the armchair – on the arm of which was perched his empty pizza box – then he realised that I had nowhere to sit. "Sorry! Here, you take the good chair. I'll get one from the kitchen. Are you hungry?"

"A bit, yeah."

"Great, because they had a two-for-one special at the pizza place, so there's a spare one going if you want it."

"What's on it?"

"Just cheese. And it's only a tiny little one. They called it a two-for-one offer, but you know how it is with these places. You'd never get two *proper* pizzas for the price of one."

Barry heated the pizza up in the microwave and brought it in to me.

"Thanks," I said. "But you really shouldn't have to run around for me."

"It's no bother. I'm just happy to be out of the B&B."

"So what's your story?" I asked between mouthfuls.

"How do you mean?"

"Well, where were you before you moved here?"

"Oh, all over the place. You wouldn't believe some of the jobs I've had."

"Such as?"

"Well, after I left school I spent a summer in Berlin, then I spent six months in France."

"My friend Davina emigrated to France," I told him, rather pointlessly. "So what did you do there?"

"I working in an abattoir. Well, actually I was only working there for about three weeks. I just couldn't take it any more."

"Did *you* have to, you know, kill the cows?"

"No, it was a very humane place," he said. "They just played country music all day long, and sooner or later the cows just shot themselves."

"Oh, very funny!"

"But no, I was just there to clean up. I won't go into any details while we're eating."

"What else have you done?"

"I used to build sheds for a living. You know the ones that come in big flat sections and you put them together? That was a good job, I liked that. But I had to leave after getting into an argument with one of the customers. I spent an hour erecting a shed in this guy's garden, and he stood there watching me, and only when it was done did he notice that it wasn't the model he'd ordered. I'd showed him the plans before I started, and he'd said it was the right one."

"And that's what the argument was about?"

"That's where it started. I had to dismantle the whole thing and go back and get the right one, and this time I was about halfway through putting it together and he says, 'Actually, I think it'd be better over by the other wall.' I'd already put down the base and to dismantle and move the whole lot would take another couple of hours, so I refused. Then he decided he wasn't going to pay."

"So what did you do?"

"I told him exactly what I thought of him and I left. When I got back to the garden centre I found out that he'd called my boss, and it turned out they knew each other from years ago. So my boss told me that I had to go out and move the shed, and I was to apologise. I told him where he could stick his sheds."

I couldn't help laughing. "God, and I thought it was bad when a customer complained about the soup being cold!"

"You work in a restaurant?"

"Used to."

"Me too. Did you ever get one of those couples where they're obviously on a first date and the guy is trying to impress the girl by being a complete prick?"

"Oh yeah, loads of times. We even had one guy do the same thing three times with different girls, all in the space of a month, and Pauline served him each time, the poor thing. First he'd spend ages and ages examining the menu, then he'd finally order something and keep changing his mind when she was writing it down, then he'd complain about each course. He'd complain that the food was undercooked, or overcooked, or that the wine was corked. He turned up again about a week after the third time, with *another* girl, and Pauline told him that we were fully booked, even though the place was completely empty. So he kept going on and on, demanding that we give them a table, and Pauline said to the girl, 'Get out while you can, he's *always* like this.' The guy went mad, of course, and then Mr Flanagan came out – that's the boss – and he recognised the guy immediately and told him he was barred forever."

Barry reached over and helped himself to the second-last slice of pizza. "Yeah, we had a guy who tried that trick twice too. Maybe it's the same lad. But I found the worst thing about the job was around Christmas, the party season. It didn't bother me that I had to work when everyone else was having a great time, but it did bother me that they seemed to think I was having as much fun as they were."

I nodded. "It was the same for me. If you're not going around with a huge grin on your face, someone's bound to stop you and say, 'Cheer up! It's Christmas!'"

Barry rubbed his arms. "It's getting a bit nippy. Any chance of putting the heating on?"

"Ah." I said. "The thing is, all my heaters were taken. And I can't light the fire because I don't have any coal or briquettes."

"They stole your coal as well? Jesus, that's low." He pushed himself out of the armchair. "Well, we'll have to improvise. What do you have that's flammable?"

All I could think of was Dad's collection of newspapers, and there was no way I was going to burn them. "Nothing. Apart from the pizza boxes."

"No old bits of wood out in the garage?"

"Not any more."

"Damn. Well, it's too late for me to go up to the store now. Anything open at this hour?"

"The petrol station down by the bridge is probably the best bet."

Barry pulled on his jacket. "Okay . . . whereabouts exactly?"

"I'll come with you, if you don't mind," I said.

So we got into Barry's rather ancient Toyota Corolla and drove to the petrol station, where I bought a large sack of coal and a box of firelighters, as well as a bag of logs. I also took the opportunity to – finally – remember to buy tea bags.

On the way back, I asked Barry to make a short detour.

"Where are we going?"

"I'll show you the site where the shopping centre would have been. Take the next right."

It was too dark to see much, but we got out of the car anyway and stood looking at the empty field. "It would have been *huge*," I said.

"I know. I saw the plans."

I pointed. "Your store would have been over that way. God, looking at this now, I can't see how Des could ever have managed to get it built."

Barry leaned on the roof of the car and watched me. "So what was he like?"

"He was okay. Or at least I thought he was. We had some good times."

"I heard you were engaged."

"Well, it was never really official. We didn't get around to getting a ring or anything. And we never set the date. But, yeah, we did talk about getting married. How about you? Ever been engaged?"

He gave me a strange look. "Oh yeah. Very definitely."

"How did it turn out?"

"We got married. That was where it all went wrong. We didn't see eye to eye on anything. We had a fight pretty much every day, and after two years we decided that things weren't going to get any better. Well, I say *we* decided, but the honest truth is that I left her. She didn't want me to go, but there was no point in me staying."

"Did you love her?"

He nodded. "Yeah. Definitely. Even when we were fighting, even when it was at the worst, I loved her. And I still do. If I thought we could make it work, I'd go back in a second. But I've seen her three or four times since I left, and each time we get on great for about half an hour, and then a fight will break out. It's always over something really trivial, but, I don't know . . . I suppose she just rubs me up the wrong way. And I do the same to her, of course."

"How long ago did all this happen?"

"Tomorrow it'll be six months since I left."

* * *

When I woke the next morning I was startled to hear someone moving around in the kitchen, and it took me a few seconds to remember that I now had a lodger. I waited until Barry had left for work before I slid myself out of bed and ventured downstairs.

I was beginning to wonder whether it had been wise to accept the first lodger who came along. Barry seemed like a nice enough guy, but how clever was it to let someone move in the day after you met them?

And it wasn't as though I had a spot-free record when it came to choosing men, was it?

Then I remembered the six hundred quid in my pocket. Along with the cheque for five hundred I'd received from the health board, I had enough money to buy some more essentials, pay a couple of bills, and buy the books for the art class.

So I sat down and made a list of everything I needed,

261

starting with the top priorities: two bedroom doors, a kettle, a cooker, pots and pans and other essential cookware, a washing machine, a carpet or a rug for Barry's room, a couple of chests of drawers, wardrobes . . . The list went on, and on, until I actually thought that I might run out of paper.

And on top of all that, I needed stuff for myself: clothes, underwear, shoes, cosmetics, and the like. At least shoes wouldn't be too much of a problem; with Justin being a rep for a shoe company, he should be able to get me a few pairs at a good discount. They wouldn't be anything great, though; certainly nothing even remotely approaching my Geraldo Piefjé masterpieces, which by now were probably in a dump somewhere, providing a family of mice with a swanky new home.

But first things first, I said to myself as I stood in the porch looking out at the pouring rain: top priority is an umbrella.

* * *

At the ESB shop I ordered a cooker and a washing machine that I could pay for in instalments with my electricity bill. The guy behind the counter wasn't able to give me an exact delivery time: "Sometime between the day after tomorrow and the end of next week, or if not then definitely early the week after. That's as long as we have the right models in stock. If we don't, it could take longer. Though sometimes we don't have something in stock, but we know one's on the way in, so we ship it straight to the customer."

"So you're saying I should sit at home and wait until the cooker and washing machine arrive?"

"Well, yeah."

"Will you at least be able to give me some warning?"

"Oh, absolutely! We always phone in advance to let the customers know the item is on the way. And then if they're not there we'll leave it with a neighbour."

After that, I needed to get a copy of the front-door key made for Barry, so I went to the hardware store. I was a little worried about that, because the store was owned by Peter Harney, Mags' lover-boy. I hoped he wouldn't be in. He was.

Peter Harney, supplier of assorted bits and pieces to the gentry, was in front of his key-cutting machine, sparks going everywhere. He looked up as I approached. "Hi, Orla . . . what can I do you for?"

I handed him the key. "Can you make a copy of this for me?"

"Sure. It'll be ready in about an hour." He attached a little label to the key and scribbled "Orla" on it in pencil. "So . . . any word from himself?"

I shook my head. "Nothing."

"I still can't believe it, you know?" Harney pushed a finger through a gap between his shirt buttons and scratched his pot-belly. "The gardaí were here last week, said that Des had told you he was going to bring some stuff in. That was the first I heard about it. Let me tell you, if Des ever comes back to this town he's going to be lynched."

"How about you? Did you lose any money to him?"

"Not as such, but I was hoping to get some work out of him when the shopping centre was being built. But no, I didn't invest anything with him. Just as well, really. God, what a bastard! Lemme tell you, I never saw that one coming. Never would have expected it of *him*."

"Me either. Listen, when my place was stripped they even took some of the internal doors. You wouldn't have any in stock, would you?"

"Nothing good . . . but I can get hold of some for you. Any particular size and style you're after?"

"At this stage, I don't care about the style. As long as they're cheap, I'll be happy. The cheaper the better."

He lifted up the hinged bit of the counter. "Come on in the back and have a look at what I have in furniture, see if there's anything that takes your fancy. Dean!"

From somewhere far away came a muffled, disgruntled reply: "What?"

"You're on the counter!"

Peter led me through the back of the shop and into the storeroom. An overcoated young man approached from the opposite direction, and Peter handed him my key. "Make a copy of this while you're there, will you?"

The young man grunted a reply and wandered off to the counter.

"Have a look around," Peter said. "Seeing what's happened, I'll do you a good rate."

I looked: the storeroom wasn't nearly as big as I'd imagined, but it was packed. Stacks of timber, hundreds of storage boxes – most of which were marked with "Bits"– huge coils of cable and chains. Almost everything was covered in dust and cobwebs. But there didn't seem to be much in the way of furniture: two or three old tables, now dismantled, a few lamp standards, not much else.

"This is all you have?" I asked.

"What? God no! This is nothing! The rest of the stuff's out the back."

He led me through a paint-splashed door and into a very long narrow yard, at the back of which was an enormous shed. All along the walls were piles of furniture covered in tarpaulins and huge sheets of plastic.

"The really good stuff we keep in the shed, out of the damp," Peter explained. "Can't have someone dropping in something to be restored and them getting it back dripping wet and covered in mildew. There's not much in there at the moment, but feel free to browse through the rest of this. Anything that belongs to someone will have a tag on it."

I lifted up the end of one tarpaulin, and dropped it very quickly and stepped back. "Did you know that you have rats? Well, one anyway."

"Aw not again! I blame that bloody woman from two doors up! She keeps putting out food for the cat! I keep telling her, 'Don't feed the cat, we want him to be hungry enough to go after the rats!' I think she feels sorry for the rats or something." He looked around, then pointed to the top of the wall, where a fat black and white cat was sunning himself. "There he is, the lazy little bugger!"

As if the cat could tell that someone was talking about him, he twitched his tail a little.

We moved on to the next pile. I kept my distance, just in case the rat had brought a buddy, and let Peter lift up the tarpaulin.

"Hang on, what's all this?" he muttered. Then he flipped the tarpaulin all the way back. "One of the lads must have taken this in when I wasn't here."

Most of the furniture seemed to be quite old, but in fairly good condition. There was quite a lot of stuff there but towards the front I could see two almost-matching armchairs, a large sofa, three big wardrobes, two chests of drawers, a dismantled bed frame, some wooden chairs that were the same make as the chairs that used to be in my kitchen, a coffee table that needed to be revarnished, and a number of doors.

"Holy *shit*!"

Peter looked around. "What is it? Another rat?"

"No . . . This is *my* furniture! All of this is mine!"

Chapter 15

"Yeah, that's the stuff," Dean said, glancing at my furniture. "Yer man said he just wanted it appraised first."

"Well, when did it come in?" Peter asked.

Dean shrugged.

"What did he look like?" I asked.

Another shrug. "Can't remember."

"You must remember *something* about him! Was he tall? Short? Fat? Thin? Old? Young?"

"He was just a guy," Dean said.

"So it wasn't a regular, then?" Peter asked.

Dean shook his head. "No. No one I recognised. And he didn't ask for you, or anything. He just said that he had some furniture and could we have a look at it, and I said yeah, and he said okay, and I said where is it and he said it was in his truck, and I told him to bring it around the back but that he'd have to leave it here because you weren't in and we weren't allowed to appraise furniture without you being around."

"Did he leave a number or anything?"

"No, he said he'd come back. But he never did."

"Jesus, Dean! Haven't you been listening to the news? Orla here has had everything stolen from her house, and you never made the connection? And besides that, if someone came in with a load of stuff they wanted to us to appraise, why didn't you tell me?"

"I forgot."

"Look, you must have *some* idea of when this happened," I said.

Dean frowned, struggling to collect his thought. "A while ago," he concluded. "It might have been a Saturday. Or a Monday."

Peter let out a deep breath. "All right. Go on back to the counter."

After Dean had plodded away, Peter said to me, "He's not the brightest, that lad. I only gave him a job because I needed someone who was able to lift the heavy stuff. Look, you're sure this furniture is yours, Orla?"

I pointed to one of the chests of drawers. "That one, the second drawer down. There should be a sheet of wrapping paper lining the bottom of it. A couple of years ago I spilled a bottle of nail varnish and I couldn't clean it all up properly, so I put the paper down to soak it up and the paper stuck so I just left it there." I reached out to open the drawer, but Peter grabbed my arm.

"Don't touch it! There could still be fingerprints. Look, whenever this stuff arrived, it must have been *after* the gardaí were around. I told Dean and the others to keep an eye out, but . . . Shit. Still, at least you have it back now. Or you will have, as soon as they've finished checking it over."

"So you don't mind if I phone Detective Mason and let him know it's here?"

"Fire away."

* * *

The detective wasn't answering his phone, so I contacted the local garda station instead. They promised to send someone around as soon as possible.

"I'll look after it," Peter said to me, as we walked back to the shop. "I'll get the lads to deliver it once the gardaí give the all-clear."

"Thanks. Sorry if all this is putting you out."

"It's no problem," he said, then suddenly laughed. "Hey, is it true that you kneed Jimmy Bandon in the balls?"

"Is that who he was? I didn't know his name."

"Everyone was saying that you practically lifted him off the ground. I saw him yesterday morning – he's still walking funny."

"Good. He deserves it."

"Yeah, he's absolutely full of it, that guy. I kind of knew him when we were kids. He was always acting the hard man." Peter smiled at me. "He chose the wrong woman to pick on, I'm thinking."

"Him and Des both," I said.

"I wouldn't want to be in Des's shoes if you ever catch up with him."

* * *

Shortly after I got home the phone rang: it was Detective Mason. "I've just been down to Mr Harney's store," he said. "Spent ages talking to young Dean. He can't remember anything about the man who dropped the furniture in."

"So how long before I can expect it back? I mean, isn't it evidence now?"

"Not necessarily. We'll fingerprint everything and take some photos, catalogue the lot, but unless we find some specific evidence there'll be no need for us to keep it. So it shouldn't be more than a couple of days."

"Great! Listen, thanks for everything."

"I haven't actually done anything, Orla."

"Well, just knowing you're there helps."

"I heard about your little altercation on Saturday afternoon, at the hotel. Has anything else happened?"

"No, it's been fairly quiet on that front. But I did get myself a lodger."

"Oh? Who?"

"The new assistant manager at the supermarket. Barry Sheridan, his name is. Though now that I'm getting my furniture back I'm not sure I need a lodger. But I'll give it a couple of weeks and see how it works out. Oh, and the other news is that the bank offered to pay me some of my money back. It's not nearly enough, though. My solicitor's writing to them, asking when I can expect to receive the rest of it."

"So things are starting to work out, then? Well, that's good. I'm pleased for you."

* * *

Barry didn't get home until seven-thirty that evening. The first thing he said was, "Hey! We have a kettle!"

"And you'll be pleased to know I bought an iron and an ironing board too," I said. Then I explained about my discovery in Peter Harney's yard.

"That's great! We'll have a sofa and everything. *And* we won't have to buy new doors!"

"Yeah . . . Listen, I have to run. I've got another class tonight."

"Oh, right. What's all that about, anyway? I mean, is it like art class in school?"

I started to explain it, then said, "Actually, I don't have enough time to go through it now."

"Here's an idea," he said. "I'll drive you over and I'll sit in on the class. How's that sound?"

"Well, okay."

* * *

Barry sat at the front of the class, and it was a good thing he was there too, because this time ten people didn't show.

The first question, as I'd expected, was about the books that the students had already paid for. "I'll be getting them tomorrow or the day after," I said. "So they'll definitely be here by next week."

After a few more questions about the direction the class was taking, one of my younger students raised his hand. "Sorry, Orla . . . but this isn't really what I thought the class was going to be about."

"Well, what *were* you expecting, Kevin?"

"I thought we'd be shown how to use Photoshop or Adobe Illustrator or something like that. I mean, I thought that this was tied in with the computer classes."

"I don't know where you got that idea from. Besides, a computer is only a tool, just like a pencil or a paintbrush. Knowing how to use something like Illustrator won't

271

make you a better artist. The only thing that can do that is practice."

Kevin shrugged. "Okay."

I looked around the room. "Did anyone else think that we were going to be using computers?"

Three people raised their hands.

"Why did you think that?"

One of them pointed to Kevin. "Well . . . that's what *he* told us."

* * *

"That was funny," Barry said as we drove home. "It always amuses me the way some people are seemingly intelligent but they can still get something so completely wrong."

"I know . . . A few years ago, apparently, someone turned up for the crochet classes with a ball and a set of croquet mallets. So anyway, how was *your* day?" I asked. "Settling into the new job okay?"

"Mad busy. I was run off my feet. There were reps in and out all day, and of course they'd all heard about Des and wanted to ask about it. And you know how it is, you can't just tell them to get lost when you're busy. You have to keep on friendly terms with them."

"I always thought it was the other way around."

"Well, yeah, but you never know. One day I might find myself working for them. That's how it goes in this business. I mean, that's where I came from. I was a rep for years, that's how I got to know the business."

"Do you enjoy it?"

He had to think about that. "Yeah, I suppose I do. I'd prefer shorter hours, but it's all right."

Barry explained the intricacies of his job as we drove back home. It sounded a lot more complicated than I'd imagined.

When we got in, he set about making himself a sandwich. "Want one?"

"No, I'm fine, thanks."

"Fair enough." He buttered two thick slices of bread, spread on some salad cream, added slices of turkey, cheese and ham, and diced two tomatoes and half an onion. By the time he was done I was starving.

"Y'know," he said, "it's great to be living in a place that has a fridge. When I was in the flat if I bought anything I had to eat it the same day. God, that was a grotty little hole of a place! Before I got the job at the supermarket I was on the dole for just over ten weeks, and I'm still paying the mortgage on the house. There was one stage when I was so broke and so hungry that I almost went back to the missus, that's how desperate I was."

"You said last night that you still love her."

Barry thought about that. "Yeah . . . I *love* her, but I'm not *in* love with her any more. Do you see where I'm coming from? I swear to God, she used to drive me mad. And I suppose I did the same to her. I'll give you an example: about a year ago some friends of ours invited us for dinner, and she couldn't decide which top to wear, the red one or the white one. So she asked me, and I said, 'The red one.' And she says, 'Why? What's wrong with the white one?' So I said, 'There's nothing wrong with it, I just prefer the red one.' Then she goes, 'You never said anything about this before!' like I'd been keeping it a secret or something. 'How am I supposed to know which one you prefer?' she says,

'I'm not a bloody mind reader!' So I said, 'It doesn't matter which one I prefer, wear the one *you* prefer.' So she turns to me and says, 'You don't care what I look like, isn't that it?' Then I said, 'Look, don't start on me now. We don't want to be going over to Frank and Lorna's with both of us pissed off with each other.'" Barry finished the last of his sandwich and licked the crumbs off his fingers. "But I suppose every relationship is like that, to one degree or another."

"I suppose so."

"Anyway, we ended up not going at all, because she threw a wobbly when I asked her which jacket I should wear. I've got these two jackets, right? And if I put one on, she says, 'Don't wear that one, wear the other one.' But the thing is, she does that no matter which one I wear. So I ask her which one I should wear, and she goes mad and complains that I can't even make up my mind about something as simple as a jacket." Barry shrugged. "So, is it just me, or is she mental?"

"God, don't ask *me* about relationships."

He sat back in the chair, stretched his legs out under the table and crossed them at the ankles. "You know, everyone keeps wondering how come you never saw it coming."

"I've been wondering that myself, but it's not like there were loads of clues. I mean, I can't remember coming across something and going, 'Hmm . . . *that's* odd' and then dismissing it. And it's certainly not like I was so much in love with him that I was completely blinded to what he was doing."

"Yeah, but come on! The guy rips you off and practically destroys your life! That didn't come out of nowhere."

I shrugged. "Well, you can never know what someone else's life is really like. I mean, you see what's on the surface, the things they *let* you see, or the things you can uncover by accident. There's a guy I know whose wife is having an affair, okay? From his point of view, everything is fine. He's happily married."

"All right, but again there has to be some clues. No one can do something like that without leaving any traces."

"I suppose you're right, but if he doesn't suspect anything how is he supposed to *see* those traces?"

Barry said, "So, like, you know this guy well?"

"Yeah."

"And you haven't told him?"

"No."

"Well, you should."

"Why? It wouldn't do any good. Right now, he's happy because he doesn't know, his wife is happy – well, happy enough – because she's getting what she wants. The guy she's sleeping with is happy too, and *his* wife is happy because *she* doesn't know. So if I told my friend, then there'd be a big fight and all four of them would be miserable."

"That's mad! Look, imagine that Des had never left, but he still stole all your money, only you didn't know about it. And imagine that one of your friends finds out about that. Wouldn't you want her to tell you? Unless you're saying that having an affair isn't as bad as stealing money."

"Well, from some points of view maybe it's not."

"Orla, you're only saying that because Des stole from you. I bet you anything you like that if he cheated on you,

you'd be thinking that you'd have been better off if he'd only stolen your money."

"Did *you* ever cheat on your wife?"

"No."

"Did she ever cheat on you?"

"Not that I know of."

"But you can't be certain, right? If she did and you found out about it, you'd be pissed off, wouldn't you?"

"Well, yeah."

"So if you don't know about it, you're just as happy as you would be if she wasn't having one."

"Okay . . . so you're saying that ignorance is bliss?"

"What?! No wonder you used to fight with your wife over trivial things!"

"No, she used to fight with me. She always started it."

"Oh yeah, sure! And I suppose if I was to ask her, she'd tell me that you're the one who always started it."

"She might, but she'd be wrong. And then she'd demand to know who you are and how you know me. And next thing you know she'd be roaring and screaming and trying to pull your hair out because she'd think you were trying to seduce me or something. Let me show you something . . ." He loosened his tie and undid the top four buttons on his shirt, then pulled it open. "See that?"

A thin, three-inch-long scar ran from his right collarbone down in the direction of his right armpit. It was almost hidden under the hair on his chest.

"Your wife did that?"

"This? No, she never laid a hand on me. No, I got that when I was a teenager, cycled my bike into a parked car one night."

"How on earth did you cycle into a *parked* car?"

"I don't really know, to be honest. Actually, I had another pretty bad accident with the bike once, but that's a different story. Anyway, the only thing I can think of is that I must have fallen asleep. I remember going along and the road curved around way ahead of me, and I saw a car on the side of the road in the distance. Next thing I know I'm on my back skidding across the top of the car. When I got home I was a mess of scratches and bruises. This is the only one that hasn't faded." He buttoned his shirt up again.

"So what has that got to do with your wife?"

"The first time she saw me naked, she saw the scar and asked where it came from, and I told her about it, and she laughed. She said that I must have been pretty stupid to ride right into a parked car. So you see what I'm getting at?"

"She's got no tact?"

"No, I mean there we were, about to have sex for the very first time – the first time with *each other*, that is – and she managed to say exactly the wrong thing and put me off the mood. That's my point. She has no empathy. She can't see things from other people's points of view. Anyway, is there anything else to eat? I'm starving."

"But you just had a sandwich!"

"Yeah, but that wasn't dinner, that was a snack. I didn't get time for lunch today." Barry got to his feet, opened the fridge again, and crouched down in front of it. "Do we have any chicken?"

"No."

"Pity. If we had chicken we could have chicken fried rice. If we had rice."

"And if we had a frying pan. And a cooker."

* * *

Much later, as I lay in bed trying my best to ignore Barry's snoring and get to sleep, I thought about the day's events, and about our conversation, and I became more and more certain that having Barry as a lodger was not the best idea in the world.

He was nice enough in most respects, and he could be pretty funny, but – God! – he could be infuriating. I found myself sympathising with his wife; imagine having to put up with that for years and years.

Barry was a two-for-the-price-of-one arguer. Not only that, he had fifty per cent extra free as well. You got both sides of the argument, plus some stray bits and pieces from other arguments.

Several times during the course of the evening I'd had sudden flashes of *déjà vu*, the feeling that I'd had this sort of argument before, but it was only as I was about to drift off to sleep that it all became clear.

Talking to Barry was exactly like when I was about eight years old and Killian used to tease the hell out of me by disagreeing with everything I said.

Killian's trick had been to make some innocuous comment he knew I'd disagree with, and then twist the conversation round and round until I was convinced he was right, and then he'd twist it again. It was his way of proving to himself that he was smarter than I was. It took me years to realise that Killian suffered from pretty low self-esteem, but that still didn't excuse being mean to his little sister.

Is that what Barry's doing? I wondered. Maybe he doesn't have any faith in himself.

Then I heard a loud "Aaah!" followed by a thump and some swearing.

"Sorry!" Barry shouted, very loudly. "I fell out of bed! I hope I didn't wake you up!"

That's it, I said to myself. He's *got* to go.

Chapter 16

On Thursday morning I was woken by Barry slamming the front door shut behind him. When I say "slamming" I don't just mean that he closed the door rather loudly; I mean that he must have put all his strength into it, like he was practising for the Olympic door-slamming competition.

I groaned and rolled out of bed. I'm awake, I told myself, so I might as well head into town and get the books for the design course.

I had a quick breakfast, showered, changed into the least scabby of my clothes, and was just about to leave when I felt the urge to check out Barry's room to see what I could find.

Now, I'm not by nature a nosy person, but . . . this man, whom I barely knew, was living in my house. I'd lived with Des for years and not known what *he* was really like, so how could I be sure that Barry wasn't a homicidal maniac?

So I crept silently back up the stairs – why I was being silent, I don't know as there was no one around to hear me – and nudged open the door to his bedroom.

Everything was still in bags and boxes, except for a couple of shirts and a pair of underpants that was puddled on the floor.

I carefully poked through his boxes and along with the usual shirts, socks, underpants and so on, I found four electric shavers, two Mach 3 razors along with a dozen blades, and two dozen condoms.

There were no drugs, body parts or explosives, so at least that was something, but I did find a pornographic magazine that according to the cover date was thirteen years old. Maybe it's the very first porno mag he'd ever got, I said to myself, and he's kept it for sentimental reasons. It was pretty mild stuff: lots of photos of half-naked women staring seductively out of the page, ads for "neck massagers" and so on. Nothing more graphic than you'd find in the average lingerie catalogue.

I carefully put everything back where I found it, and returned to my own room to get dressed. It was only later, that I realised the extent of my actions: I'd invaded someone else's privacy, and violated their trust.

I tried to tell myself that I'd done it because I needed to be sure that he wasn't a psychopath or anything, but the truth was that I'd just been a nosey bitch.

I'd never even done anything like that to Des, though a small part of me said, "Maybe I should have. I might have found out what he was really like."

But there was no excuse. I felt incredibly guilty, and wondered if there was anything I could do to make it up to him.

Without him finding out what I'd done, of course.

I decided I'd cook him a nice meal, as soon as my cooker arrived.

* * *

I was still feeling guilty when Barry arrived home. I hoped it wouldn't show on my face.

He barged in through the door carrying two full shopping bags. "Got some stuff," he said, rather pointlessly. He dropped the bags on the kitchen table. "No sign of our furniture yet, I take it?"

"No, nothing. But it's still early days. But how do you mean '*our* furniture'?"

"I live here too, you know."

"I suppose."

He smiled. "You don't sound so sure. Having second thoughts?"

"Not as such, but I've been wondering if maybe I should have got to know you a bit better first."

"Sure I know people who got married in less time than that." Barry took off his jacket and hung it on the back of a chair. "To be honest, it's been a second-thought kind of day for me too." He began to unpack the shopping bags. "I had a good shot at getting a position as a buyer for Tesco's. But I thought – nah, been there, done that." He looked at me. "How do you fancy my famous extra-special fish and chips tonight?"

"What's extra-special about them?"

"There's no cooking involved, only a drive to the chipper."

"Sounds like a plan."

"Great!" Barry slapped his hands together and rubbed them briskly, making me think of an amateur actor playing the part of a greedy miser cackling over his chest of gold. "Or we could go out? Hey, we could go to the place you used to work! We could complain about everything and give them all a really hard time!"

"Better not," I said. "I know what they do to complainers."

"Any other good places in town?"

"The restaurant in the hotel is pretty good, but it's expensive."

"Anywhere else?"

"Nothing I'm in the mood for."

"How about the Burger Hut?"

"No way. Those bastards turned me down for a job last week."

"Then how about this: we do the same thing me and Jemima used to do – we'd drive about until we saw someone who looked like he knew where he was going, then we'd follow him until we found a decent pub or a restaurant. Are you up for it? Trust me, it's great crack! You get to go places you never even knew existed!" He saw me staring at him. "What?"

"You're kidding, right?"

"No, really. We used to do it a couple of times a month. Well, when we weren't fighting over something."

"That's not what I mean . . . *Jemima*? Like the doll from *Play School*?"

He grinned. "Yeah . . . God, she used to get some slagging from our friends."

"How on earth could anyone name their child Jemima?"

"She used to joke that she was supposed to have been called Gemma, but the priest at her baptism had a stutter. But the truth is that her parents just liked the name."

"But even so . . . they must have known that she'd be slagged about it."

He raised his eyes. "You know, talking to you is just like being married all over again. Jemima used to do this too, you know. I'd be talking about something and she'd pick on one barely relevant point and spend ages on it."

I laughed.

"What?"

"Jemima!"

He laughed too.

* * *

"There's one!" Barry said, pointing to a car ahead of us. "He'll do!"

"Look, I'm not playing this stupid game. Let's just find the nearest restaurant that doesn't look like you get a free order of salmonella with every meal."

"Aw!"

For the past ten minutes, Barry had been insisting that we try out his and Jemima's trick of just following a car at random to see where we ended up.

"Didn't you and Des ever do anything like this?"

"Not that I can think of, no."

"Not even when you first started seeing each other? Didn't you ever just get into the car and drive?"

"Oh yeah, we did that a lot, but we didn't make up daft rules. We'd just drive until we spotted somewhere we liked the look of. It was a lot easier."

"Ah, but if you do it *my* way, you end up discovering really out-of-the-way places. Tiny little pubs where they haven't seen an outsider in ten years, that sort of thing. It was pretty cool, sometimes. We'd go into these little country pubs and everyone would stop and stare, and the barman would ask us where we were trying to get to, as if he couldn't possibly imagine that anyone would *want* to go there."

"So how did you and Jemima meet?"

"Ah, now *there* lies a tale . . . Are you sitting comfortably?"

"Just about."

"We met in a nightclub. I asked her to dance, and she said yes."

"That's it?"

"Yep. Good story, isn't it?"

"Hans Christian Anderson would be jealous."

* * *

Half an hour later we were being seated in an average-looking restaurant that specialised in Cajun cuisine.

"Have you ever eaten Cajun before?" Barry asked.

Fearing that if I told the truth he'd probably end up giving me the entire history of Louisiana, I said, "Sure."

"Great! What's it like?"

God, you can't win with this man! I said to myself. "It's nice," I ventured. "Give it a go."

He peered at the menu. "Nope. Nope. Nope. Yes! Oh. Nope. Nope." After a few more Nopes he closed the menu over and put it down on his side-plate.

"Well?"

He shrugged. "I'm going to ask them to do me steak and chips."

"We're in a Cajun restaurant and all you want is steak and chips?"

"No, that's not all I want. I want a pizza, but I doubt they do pizzas here."

Halfway through the meal, Barry suddenly asked, "So what's your favourite colour?"

"Pardon?"

"Your favourite colour. I mean, you said you used to be a designer. You dealt with colours more than most people would, so you must have a favourite colour."

"I haven't been asked that question since I was about nine . . . I suppose my favourite colour is topaz." I could tell from his face that he didn't know what colour topaz was, so I added, "A kind of deep yellow. The same as the walls in your bedroom."

"Oh, right."

"And yours?"

"Don't have one."

"You don't have a favourite colour?"

He thought about this. "No. Colours are just colours. I suppose you have a favourite sound as well?"

"The laughter of innocent children."

"Gimme a break!"

We both laughed, then he said, "You want to know *my* favourite sound? It's the car starting up. And do you want to know why?" He didn't give me time to answer. "It's because when I was a rep, if the car didn't start in the mornings I was screwed for the day. Even now, I still hold my breath when I'm starting the car."

"That makes sense."

"And my second-favourite sound is the letterbox rattling. I know it's not always good news, but ever since I was a kid I've loved getting mail. That's because I once sent away loads of tokens from a comic so that I could get a free model airplane. Even though it said, 'Please allow at least twenty-eight days for delivery', I somehow got the idea into my head that mine would arrive sooner, so every morning I got up early and waited for the postman to arrive. In the end it took about six weeks. All my friends got theirs before I got mine, which was annoying. Especially when my supposed best friend Johnny decided to form a club for all the lads who had their model airplanes, and he wouldn't let me join. Bastard."

Barry looked so miserable telling his tale of woe that I had to bite the inside of my cheek to keep from laughing. "You're not still upset over something like that, are you?"

"No, but he was always like that, you know? His family were much better off than mine, and he loved to keep reminding me about it. Like when he got to see a movie before I did, or something like that."

I took another bite of my incredibly spicy blackened

chicken. "And this is what shaped you into the mature, well-balanced man you are today?"

He nodded. "Yeah. But I got my own back on him. I got pubes before he did."

I was in the middle of yet another sup of water to cool my mouth down, and almost choked. "Jesus! You can't say something like that in the middle of a respectable restaurant!"

Barry shrugged, and continued slicing his steak into little cubes.

I discreetly looked around, in case any of the other diners had overheard. If they had, they didn't seem bothered.

Then, as though we'd been talking about it all evening, Barry suddenly said, "So are you going to press charges against the furniture guy?"

"No. Why?"

"Well, it's pretty obvious that him and Des were working together."

"How do you figure that?"

"He had all your stuff. I mean, he'd definitely heard about what happened, right? Don't tell me you seriously think that he'd have heard about all your stuff going missing and at the same time a huge pile of second-hand furniture has appeared in his stockroom and he didn't make the connection?"

"But he didn't know about it," I said. "I was there, remember? He was as surprised to see it as I was."

Barry gave me a look that made it clear he thought I was being conned.

"Besides, the police talked to him, and they're convinced

he's in the clear. He wasn't there the day all the furniture arrived, and he'd already told his staff to be on the look-out for my furniture. It's not Peter's fault that the guy who was there when it arrived was too thick to make the connection."

"I've been thinking, though . . . once you get all your bits and pieces back – and I realise that you won't get *everything* back, but certainly a lot of it – and if the bank gives in and pays you back the money they let Des steal from you, then does that mean you won't need a lodger any more? Or are you going to wait until you get another job before you tell me that I need to find somewhere else to live? I'm only asking because I don't want to get too settled and then have to move again. I hate moving." He lowered his fork and watched me carefully.

"I haven't thought about it. Anyway, even if the bank does pay me back, it's not going to be any time soon. It's going to take ages. They'll want to string it out for as long as possible, because as soon as they admit they're at fault with me, that makes it easier for all of Des's investors to claim that they're at fault in that case, too. And they certainly won't want that."

"So I'm safe enough for the time being?"

"Definitely. Assuming that you don't do anything to really piss me off. Besides, there are still some people in the town who are convinced that I was involved in Des's plans, so as long as you're here they're less likely to keep trying to intimidate me."

He seemed pleased with that.

Later, as we left the restaurant and headed towards the

car, Barry walked slightly behind me and to the right, and I couldn't help thinking that he now saw himself as a sort of bodyguard.

That was my first indication that he was starting to see me as something more than his landlady.

Chapter 17

On Friday afternoon, Peter Harney's truck stopped outside my house. Peter stood beside me in the hall, ticking the items off a list as Dean and one of his colleagues carried them in past us.

"So what's missing?" Peter asked.

"My dressing-table, a couple of kitchen chairs, my desk . . . and all the really old stuff from the garage and the shed, but I don't care about any of that. I've been meaning to get rid of it for ages. So anyway, what did the police say?" I asked.

"They interviewed Dean, but he couldn't give them much more than a basic description of the man who brought your stuff in. God, it was painful! 'What colour hair did he have?' 'I don't know.' 'What do you mean you don't know?' 'He was wearing a hat.' 'What kind of hat was it?' 'I can't remember.' 'Was it a baseball cap? A trilby? A woolly hat? A sombrero?' 'A baseball cap.' 'What colour was it?' 'I can't remember.'" Peter sighed. "Still, we

Jaye Carroll

know it wasn't Des, because Dean would have recognised him."

"And he's sure he didn't get a phone number or any other contact details?"

Peter shook his head. "The guy said that he'd be calling back. My guess is that this guy got the furniture from whoever stole it from you, then he heard about what happened to you and put two and two together, and decided that he didn't want to be involved."

"Listen . . . thanks for doing this."

"It's not a problem. But I'll tell you this for nothing: you've got powerful friends. That detective lad told me that if I didn't give this stuff back to you, they'd start to keep a very close eye on any other furniture I took in. Plus, if for some reason I ended up with a criminal record, or even if I was only, you know, *under suspicion*" – he waggled his fingers to make quotation marks around the phrase – "then they wouldn't be able to pass any more work my way."

"Oh. What sort of work?"

"Fixing locks or repairing broken windows after a burglary, that kind of thing."

"Do you get much of that?"

"A bit. About once a month, usually. Though in the past year burglaries around here have been on the increase, and it's nearly always in the middle of the night. There I am, in bed, and the phone rings and it's the desk sergeant. 'Can you go to such-and-such a place right now? There's been a break-in and the owner is going into a complete panic about the house not being secure.'" He looked at the front door. "See that lock you have there?"

"Yeah . . ." I said, a little uncertainly.

"Well, watch this." He stepped out through the door and closed it after him.

I could hear him fiddling with the lock a little, and then there was a small *click*! and the door opened and he came back in. "Less than fifteen seconds," he said, "and you don't even have an alarm. What's to stop someone breaking in here?"

I didn't know where to look. "Jesus. It's *that* simple?"

"For me, yeah, but then I'm a qualified locksmith. But there's no reason a burglar couldn't learn all the same tricks I know. I mean, all he'd have to do is go to the local library. All the books are there. Or he could do a correspondence course, like I did."

"But don't they check whether you have a criminal record before they let you do that?"

"If they do, all the potential burglar has to do is get someone else to apply for the course. I mean, it's not like he's going to be concerned with sitting for the exams. He just wants the knowledge."

We stepped into the sitting-room to let Peter's lads carry my wardrobe upstairs.

"Are there any locks that can't be picked?" I asked.

"There are, but they can be expensive. But your type can't be picked if you put the latch on at night. Another good trick that's fairly cheap is to get *two* Yale locks. You pretty much need both hands to pick them, so if you have two locks, the burglar will have to bring someone else along. Of course, that won't stop someone from just smashing the window."

"Yeah, but that makes noise."

He looked at me like I was five. "Orla, if you want me to show you how wrong that is, lock me out and go into the kitchen for a couple minutes. I'll come in through that window there, and I promise you won't hear a thing."

"No thanks. But how's it done?"

"Lots of ways, but Sellotape is probably the easiest. You know those wide rolls of brown tape that are used for taping up boxes? Well, you put tape all over the window, give it a good sharp belt with the hammer, and the tape keeps the bits of broken glass from going all over the floor. If you do it right, all you get is a muffled crack. Pulling the tape off the roll is actually louder."

I thought about this. "Okay, now you've got me worried. How can I prevent someone doing that?"

"Double-glazing would be a start. Or you could get a good alarm with shock-sensors on the windows. That wouldn't set you back more than a couple of grand, including installation. Though that depends on the other features you might want. I can give you a good quote."

"Ah! So *that's* it! You're just trying to drum up business!"

He spread his huge hands wide in a sort of "who, me?" gesture. "I'm just concerned for your personal security."

"Well, maybe sometime in the future, when I can afford it."

There was a loud *bang*! from upstairs, which was followed by, "Shite! Sorry!"

"What happened?" I called.

After a brief pause, Dean shouted down, "Er . . . nothing!"

I sighed and trudged up the stairs, where I saw that Dean and his friend had developed a clever plan that seemed to consist of having Dean – clearly the stronger of the two – at the light end of the wardrobe, and his weedy friend at the heavy end. They'd managed to bash the corner of the wardrobe into one of the walls, gouging a lovely new hole into the wallpaper.

"That was already there," Dean said, his face a picture of innocence, despite the ragged strip of wallpaper and plaster dust that was still on the corner of the wardrobe.

"Just be more careful," I said.

When I went back down, Peter had a stern look on his face. "We're not paying for that. Whatever it was."

I shook my head. "It's all right. I'm halfway through redecorating the place anyway." I had a think about that. "Actually, that's sort of how I got into this whole bloody mess in the first place."

Peter's lads were finished in a surprisingly short time. "That's the lot," Peter said as I followed him out to the front door. "Don't forget to tell Detective What's-his-name how cooperative we were."

"I won't. Thanks again."

As he walked backwards down the driveway, he said, "And you'll let me know when you decide to upgrade your security system, right?"

"Oh yeah, shout it out for *everyone* to hear."

* * *

I spent the early part of the evening moving the furniture around, then I happened to look out and saw Mrs Johnson across the road at her front door polishing the brasses. I went over to her and thanked her for the loan of the kitchen table and chairs. "I'll ask my lodger to give me a hand carrying them back over when he gets in from work."

"Take your time," she said. "We're not in any rush for them. I'm just happy that you got your own furniture back."

"Me too. I really thought I was going to have to replace everything."

She went tut-tut-tut for a few seconds, then said, "Let me tell you, Orla, I'm only glad your mother and father aren't here to see what this town is coming to. Imagine the man you loved doing something like that! There's no discipline these days, that's the trouble. You take those two lads who were with you the other week . . . I'd hate to be *their* mother."

I was puzzled. "Which two lads?"

"You know, they gave you a hand carrying over the table and chairs."

"Oh, right." Reebok and Jumper Man – I'd forgotten about them.

"You can tell just by looking at them that they're no good. Speeding around in that flash car, thinking they're God's gift. Your Killian was never like that. Always polite, he was. Had respect for the older folks."

The thought occurred to me that I should ask Mrs Johnson about *her* kids. "How are Lisa and Brian and Stephen getting on? I haven't seen them in a while."

That turned out to be a mistake: when Barry arrived

home almost an hour later, I was still standing there, shifting from one foot to the other, getting the low-down on her children, and – to my surprise – her two *grand*children, the offspring of her eldest son Brian, who was the same age as me. When I was seventeen he'd asked me to his debs. I'd turned him down, and he never spoke to me again.

I could see Barry desperately pretending not to notice us as he darted into the house. Mrs Johnson spotted that too, and went, "Hmph! Didn't even say hello!"

To cover up for his rudeness, I said, "He's probably dashing to the loo."

"What does he do, then?"

"He's the new assistant manager in the supermarket," I said.

"I *thought* I recognised him, all right. That's not a bad job. Maybe he can get *you* a job there?"

"Maybe," I said. "But I'm not sure I want another job working with the public. Not after everything that's happened. It's bad enough that I have to face two classes on Tuesday and Wednesday nights."

"Oh yes. I heard about that. I was thinking I might take it up myself next year. Do me good to get out of the house more. But the thing is, you'll have to face everyone sometime, Orla. You didn't do anything wrong. Most people know that already. The others will come around soon enough." She paused. "Well, most of them will. I bumped into your mother's old friend Mrs Diggle on Monday. She's not happy at all. I probably shouldn't tell you this . . ." She looked around in case anyone was watching, then leaned closer and lowered her voice. "She was hoping to sell up her house and move in with her sister."

I almost said, "So?" when Mrs Johnson continued: "And she was going to give up work and live off her savings, but now she can't because she'd invested everything with Desmond."

"How do you mean 'give up work'? I thought she retired *years* ago." Mrs Diggle had been a seamstress; she'd made my mother's wedding dress, and always said that when I got married she'd make my dress for me for free, as a wedding present.

"Not completely. She's not so able as she was, but she's still working a few hours a week."

"God. I didn't know that. No wonder she was so annoyed with me."

"Well, I think she understands now that it wasn't your fault, but she's still hurt."

"People are going to be talking about this for years, aren't they?"

She nodded vigorously, her white hair bobbing about all over the place. "They are. That's one of the reasons *you* should get out more, get to know everyone, so they can see that you've got nothing to hide. I mean, even before all this we barely saw you from one end of the year to the next."

"I know. Sorry about that." I tried briefly to think of a really good reason for being a recluse, but nothing occurred to me.

"Anyway," she said, and leaned over very slowly to pick up her cloth and tin of brass polish from the step, "I'd better get in. He'll be wanting his dinner. Don't be a stranger, Orla."

"I won't, thanks. And tell Brian and the others I was asking for them."

* * *

Barry was hiding in the kitchen when I went back in. "I see we got everything back." He was sitting at Mrs Johnson's kitchen table, using his mug to gesture towards my old table, which was still dismantled and resting against the wall.

"Most of it, yeah. You ran in in a hurry."

"I didn't want to talk to yer one. A couple of days ago she was in the store and started giving me a hard time."

"What about?"

"Ah, something about the signs. She said that the 'Ten items or less' should be 'Ten items or fewer', which is just plain mad. It means the exact same thing, right?"

"Not really," I said. "Less than ten items could be nine and a half. But 'fewer' means that there has to be a whole number."

"I suppose. And then she was going on about another of the signs that said there was a ten per cent discount off Fairy Liquid. I really don't know what she was getting at there." He shrugged. "I normally don't mind chatting to the old dears, but some of them just don't let up. Anyway . . ." He smiled. "Do you want your present now, or later?"

"Present?"

"Yeah . . . well, it's sort of a present." He swigged back the rest of his tea, then reached into his jacket pocket, took something out and placed it on the table. "This was in the lost and found box. It's the right one for your phone, yeah?"

I picked up the phone charger and examined it. "I think so, thanks."

"No problemo."

A few minutes later my phone went *Beep! Beep!* a few times, and I scrolled through a bunch of almost indecipherable messages from Justin.

The first few messages were all along the lines of "HP UR OK. PHN WN U GT A CHNC. CHRS JSTN", but the newest message – sent less than an hour earlier – was in English, so I knew that Mags had probably sent it: "HI ORLA. FANCY COMING OVER FOR DINNER TONIGHT? RING IF YOU CAN MAKE IT! JUSTIN."

I phoned the house, and Justin answered. "So how are you doing?"

"Okay. Not bad at all, in fact."

"So are you free tonight? I take it you're not back working at Flanagan's?"

"No. Still gainfully unemployed. But listen . . ." I glanced over at Barry – who was engrossed in a motorbike magazine – and lowered my voice, "I've got a lodger."

"That's great. Bring her along!"

"She's a him."

"Oh." He sounded a little disappointed. "Well, bring *him* along, then. It'll give us a chance to suss him out."

"If you're sure . . ."

"Sure I'm sure."

"You'd better check with Mags first."

"All right . . . hold on a second." There was a clunk as

Justin put the phone down, then a muffled conversation, and he was back: "Does he eat lamb?"

"Hang on . . . Barry!"

He looked up from his magazine.

"We're invited to dinner tonight. Interested?"

"Free food? Definitely!"

"Do you eat lamb?"

"I'll eat anything if it's free."

* * *

On the walk over to Justin and Mags' house, my mobile phone rang again. I didn't recognise the number.

"Hello?"

"Orla? It's Thomas Kennedy."

"Oh, hi. How are you?"

"Fine, fine. And yourself?"

"I'm not bad. Any news?"

"Not as such . . . but I was wondering if you were interested in meeting up tonight?"

"I'm actually on the way out at the moment. How about tomorrow afternoon?"

"Tomorrow evening would suit me better. How does seven sound? I can pick you up."

"That sounds great. Seven it is, so." I said goodbye and disconnected the call.

"Who was that?" Barry asked.

"Tom Kennedy. He's the guy I was telling you about who works for the finance company Des attempted to defraud."

"So there's been a development, then?"

I shook my head. "I don't *think* so, but he wanted to meet up tonight. Maybe he's got news but he can't talk about it over the phone. He wants me to meet him tomorrow instead."

"That doesn't sound like a business meeting to me. It sounds like he was asking you out."

"No, he wasn't," I said. "Anyway, a guy like him wouldn't be interested in someone like me. I don't even own my own yacht."

"Even so . . ."

We walked in silence for a while. I doubted that Barry's theory was true; what would Tom Kennedy possibly see in me? He must have any number of gorgeous, intelligent, sophisticated, successful women fawning over him. Compared to them, I was just a plain, ordinary, unsuccessful woman.

Then Barry said, "Anyway, what's the story with these friends of yours?"

I gave him a massively condensed version of my friendship with Justin, but I held back from telling him too much about Mags. I didn't want to say that she and I had never really got along, and that it was only in the past couple of weeks that we'd had much more than the most basic of conversations.

Just as we were crossing the road towards their gate, Barry whispered, "Don't worry, I won't say anything."

"About?"

"These *are* the people you were talking about the other night, right? The extra-marital relationship, and all that?"

I slowed down a little. "What makes you think that?"

"Because you haven't really mentioned any of your other friends, apart from the one who went to France and your brother's wife, so it has to be them. I'm right, aren't I?"

"No."

"Yes, I am."

"All right then, but you say *one word* . . ."

"Let me guess: I'll be out on the street before I know it. Don't worry, I'm not a *complete* moron."

* * *

Dinner went pretty well. Because Barry had been a sales rep in the past, he and Justin had a lot to talk about. They had a few mutual acquaintances that they didn't really like, they knew all the same bottlenecks on the roads, they talked about their least-favourite kinds of other motorists.

After dinner, when Barry and Justin started to enthusiastically compare cars they'd owned in the past, Mags raised her eyes and ordered them into the sitting-room. "We'll be along in a minute," she said.

Once we were alone, she said to me, "So you got all your furniture back?"

"Almost everything. Once I get the beds sorted out, I'll ask Barry to bring back your spare mattress. I don't think it'd be wise for you and me to try and carry it through the town again!"

She laughed. "Probably not. I've still got people asking me about that."

"So what's he like? Barry, I mean?"

"God . . . he's . . ." I paused, realising that I didn't even

303

know how to begin to describe him. "He talks. A *lot*. He talks about anything and everything, and he has an opinion on anything and everything. You say to him, 'Nice day, isn't it?' and next thing you know he's asking you why you think that. 'You can't judge the quality of the day just by the weather,' he said to me the other day. Then I said, 'Look, when people say that it's a nice day, they're *talking* about the weather, not the bloody world economy!' And then he started going on about the economy, and how everything would be so much better if he was running the world."

Mags said, "Yeah, but you like him, don't you?"

"Most of the time."

"No, I mean you *like* him . . ." She gave me a meaningful look.

"You mean, do I fancy him? Not even nearly."

We went into the sitting-room, just as the anecdote Barry was telling Justin increased in volume by a couple of notches: "And then, *Bang*! The whole car shudders, skids to a stop. And he gets out, thinking that it was a puncture or something, but all the tyres are fine, and then he walks around the front of the car and there's a hole" – Barry made an "o" with his thumb and index finger – "*this* big in the bonnet! So opens it up and has a look, and sees the same size hole right the way through the engine! Completely totalled it. And apparently the hole was perfectly round – no rough edges or anything."

"Jesus!" Justin said. "What caused it?"

Barry spread his hands wide. "No idea. He never figured out what it was. The guy from the AA said that it looked like a bullet hole, only it was too big. But they called the cops anyway, and they examined the car and they couldn't understand it. They said that if it was some kind of projectile, then it wouldn't have gone clear through the engine, it would have ricocheted around in there somewhere. And they even scoured the road, but they didn't find anything."

Justin looked astonished. "So did the insurance pay up?"

"No, they said it was an act of God."

"God's a good shot, in that case."

"The car was a total write-off."

"Sorry," I said, "*who* did this happen to?"

"A friend of mine," Barry said. "Well, a friend of a friend."

"Ah," said Mags. "So you don't actually know the person yourself?"

"Not personally."

"Urban myth," Mags said. "I bet you anything you like it never happened."

"Oh, it happened all right. Definitely."

Justin said, "Maybe it was the army testing their new stealth rail-gun?" I could see from the look on his face that he no longer believed the story.

"Could be," Barry said. "Either that, or it was a meteorite. There's no other explanation."

"Yes, there is," I said. "It could be a lie."

He grinned. "Oh, now *you're* ganging up on me too?"

* * *

We talked long into the night, and it was pretty good fun.

Just before we left – when Barry had gone to the bathroom – Justin said to me, "I like him."

"Don't look at me like that!" I said.

"Like what?"

"Like he's my new boyfriend or something! There's nothing going on between us."

"I know . . . but even so. You could do a lot worse."

"That's true," Mags said, "but I wouldn't rush into it if I was you, Orla."

"I'm not rushing into anything. I've no interest in him in that way."

Justin and Mags exchanged a glance. "If you say so," Justin said.

* * *

On the way home, Barry and I walked in silence for a while, then he said, "He has no idea, does he?"

He's doing it again; assuming that I know what he's thinking about, I said to myself. "Who, what, why and where?"

"Justin. He doesn't suspect a thing about Mags, does he?"

"No, I don't think so."

"So who's the guy she's been seeing?"

I shook my head. "Sorry, I can't tell you that. You're not even supposed to know about the affair in the first place."

"Well, how did *you* find out?"

"She told me."

"Just like that? She just told you?"

"In a way. I think she needed to let *someone* know, otherwise she'd go mad keeping it all bottled up inside."

Barry considered this. "Either that, or she wanted to tell someone because it's more exciting that way."

It was my turn to stop walking. "You're kidding, right?"

He looked back at me. "*You* know . . . the allure of forbidden fruit, and all that. Maybe she gets turned on by the whole idea of having an affair, and telling someone makes it more exciting. And she knows you can't tell Justin, so that could be exciting to her as well."

"You don't really think that's true, do you?"

"I dunno. It *could* be, that's all I'm saying. But didn't you ever have a secret that was made more interesting because you confided in someone else?"

"Not that I can think of. I don't think I've had any really juicy secrets. Have you?"

He nodded.

I looked at him expectantly. "Well? Go on, then!"

He tilted his head in the direction of the house. "Come on, we'll freeze to death out here."

I fell in step beside him. "Was it something sexual? Your secret, I mean?"

"I'm not sure I know you well enough to tell you."

"It was, wasn't it?"

"*Dum de dum de dum!* Can't hear you," he said, trying not to grin.

"You had an affair with someone?"

"*Tra la la la laaaa!* Here I am not paying any attention to you."

"You lost your virginity to your best friend's mother?"

307

Barry's grin suddenly faded. "Shit."

"I'm *right*? Oh my God! Really?"

"It was a long time ago, Orla."

"I guessed that. So tell me everything."

"No."

"Go on."

Neither of us said anything until we got to the house. "Cup of tea?" I offered.

"All right, then."

"You don't have to work in the morning, do you?"

"No, I'm on lates for the next week. I'm not in until two."

So we settled into the sitting-room, where I stretched out on my sofa for the first time in ages. At first, Barry refused to even discuss his secret, but I could tell from the way he wasn't – for a change – changing the subject that he really did want to tell me.

Eventually, I said, "So was she good-looking?" and that opened the floodgates.

Barry was sitting side-ways across Mr Farley's armchair, staring at the ceiling. "God, yeah. Stunning. All the lads were mad about her. She even starred in my first wet dream."

"So go on, tell me . . ."

"All right, then, but I still know this guy so you can't say anything to anyone. *Ever*."

"Okay."

"And I've never told anyone before."

"So what was all that you were saying about a secret being more exciting if you can share it with someone?"

"That was just a theory about why Mags told you. Anyway, do you want to hear this or not?"

"I do."

"Okay . . . I was fifteen. My best friend was . . . well, I won't say *what* his name was. Let's just call him Danny."

"Why don't we call him Johnny?" I asked, doing my best to look completely innocent.

Barry bit his lip. "I didn't think you'd remember. Okay, Johnny then. Anyway, his mother was about thirty-five. Incredibly good-looking. One of the reasons the rest of us put up with Johnny's bullshit was because we all fancied his mother. And one Saturday afternoon, I cycled over to his place. But just before I got there, I hit a pot-hole or something, and went flying off the bike. Landed on my side, skidded along the ground. I grazed my cheek on the tarmac pretty badly, but I was in shock and I didn't really notice. So I picked myself up, got back on the bike and wobbled the rest of the way to Johnny's house. When I got there, his mother answered the door and the first thing she said was, 'Barry! What happened?' 'Oh, I fell off my bike. A bit.' She took me inside and cleaned up the cut. She sat me down in the kitchen, and stood in front of me as she mopped up the blood with cotton wool. She was leaning forward, okay? And I could see a good bit of the way down her blouse. She was wearing a black lacy bra. 'Johnny's not here,' she said. 'He's gone out on the boat with his dad. They'll be gone all day.' So I said, 'Oh. Okay.' When she was done putting TCP on the cut, I said, 'Thanks. I'd better head on, so.' And she said, 'You're still in shock. You shouldn't be getting back on your bike just yet.' So I said okay, and she sat down opposite me, and said, 'So how are things? I haven't talked to you in a while.'"

"My God!" I said. "She *seduced* you?"

"Not really," Barry said. "Well, maybe she did. She started asking me whether I had a girlfriend, things like that. I was a bit embarrassed, because – like I said – she'd been the star of my first wet dream. And quite a few others since. In fact, even just the other night . . ."

I interrupted him. "I don't think I want to know *that* bit."

"Oh, okay. So anyway, we were talking for a while, and she could see the way I was trying not to stare at her breasts. And when I realised she'd noticed that, I did my best to keep my eyes focussed on the table. Then she said, 'Barry . . . you seem a little uncomfortable. Do you want to go?' And I said, 'No, I'm fine,' because right then I wasn't in a position to stand up, if you see what I mean."

"I do," I said. "Go on . . ."

"So she said, 'Are you shy around women, Barry?' I said that I wasn't, but we both knew I was lying. And she said, 'Well, there's nothing to be shy about. In fact, you're only making it more obvious because you won't look me in the eye.' So I tore my eyes away from the table and looked at her. The light was coming in through the kitchen window behind her, creating a sort of halo with her hair . . . Very, very beautiful. She said, 'Have you ever been with a woman, Barry?' And I sort of squeaked out, 'Er, no, Mrs Palmer.' And she said, 'Now, call me Maria. I mean, look at you: you're practically a full-grown man. We're two adults here, we can call each other by our first names.'"

"This is sick!" I said.

"Do you want me stop?" Barry asked.

"God no."

"Well, then she started talking about how there's a point in every boy's life when he becomes a man. And she made it clear that she wasn't just talking about puberty. So she said, 'Do you want me to help you become a man, Barry?' I nodded, because I wasn't able to speak, and she reached across the table and took hold of my hand. I almost came in my pants there and then. And she sort of pulled me forward, and placed my hand on her left breast. That was it; I went, 'Uhhhh!' because . . . well, you know. And she gave me a smile and said, 'Don't worry about that. That's perfectly natural. We'll give it a couple of minutes.' Then she led me up to her bedroom, and watched me carefully as she took off her blouse and her jeans. I was doing my best not to think about when Johnny and I were little kids and we used to play Tarzan in that room by jumping off the windowsill and onto the bed. Anyway, then she asked me to undress. I was really, really embarrassed, but that didn't stop me."

"Well, *I'll* stop you. I can figure out the rest of it by myself."

Barry smiled. "So now you know. It only happened the once, though. The next time I saw her, she just whispered, 'It never happened, understand?' So I nodded, and that was it. I never told anyone before. Not even Jemima."

"Wow . . . so why tell *me*?"

He shrugged. "I dunno. I trust you, I suppose."

"But you barely know me."

311

"So what about your first time?"

"No way. I'm not telling you that."

"Ah, go on."

"No. Anyway, there's nothing to tell, really. I certainly wasn't seduced by my best friend's father."

"Okay, then tell me some other great secret that you've never told anyone else."

"I can't think of anything."

Barry said, "Fair's fair, Orla. I told you one, now you have to tell me."

"But I already did tell you one. I told you about Mags' affair."

"Well, strictly speaking you didn't tell me the whole story. I figured most of it out for myself. So, go on . . . your turn."

I could see that he wasn't going to give up easily. "All right . . . when I was seventeen my geography teacher made a pass at me."

He sat up. "And . . .?"

"And nothing. I didn't even realise that was what had happened until years later."

"Tell me anyway."

"I had to stay back after school. I was in detention for passing notes. Anyway, that day I was the only one who had detention, and it was his turn to monitor."

"What was he like? Young? Old? Good-looking?"

"He was about thirty, I think. Not particularly good-looking. We were sitting there, him at the desk reading the paper, and me just staring at my maths book wishing for the time to pass, and he suddenly threw his paper aside and said, 'Sod this, Orla. There's only you and me here.

Let's just say we did it and go home. If anyone asks we can back each other up, how's that sound?' I said, 'Sounds fine to me.' 'All right,' he said. 'I'm heading your way if you want a lift home.'"

"Uh oh," Barry said.

"I didn't think anything of it. As far as I was concerned he was just another teacher. So he drove me most of the way home, and then he pulled the car in to the side of the road, and said, 'I've just had a thought. Did you let your folks know that you were getting detention? Because if you did, and they see you coming in early, they'll be wondering what's up.' I said that I hadn't told anyone. Then he said, 'Okay. It's just that I don't want to get you in trouble. Maybe we should just go somewhere else and I'll drop you back home at the right time?' I said, 'No, I'll be fine. But thanks anyway.' And that was that. He dropped me to the door and drove away. Neither of us ever mentioned it again."

Barry seemed disappointed. "That's your great secret? Your teacher may or may not have made a pass at you?"

"I'm pretty sure that he did. I just think that he didn't know how to go about it, and I was too inexperienced to notice it."

"Well, as juicy secrets go, I think I'm the winner here." Barry finished his tea, and clambered out of the chair. "All right, time for bed, said Zebedee." As he passed by the sofa, he paused for a second, and looked as though he was about to ask me something, then said, "Goodnight" and went on his way.

I lay there for a while, listening to the sounds of him

313

getting ready for bed upstairs: the flushing of the toilet, prolonged gargling, the creak as he sat down on the bed, the *thump, thump* of his shoes hitting the floor, then the sound of all the change rolling out of the pocket of his trousers, followed by much moving about as he presumably was on his hands and knees gathering up the coins.

If, as Mags and Justin seemed to think, Barry was interested in me, I wasn't sure what to do about it. I didn't fancy him. On a scale of one to ten, I might put him at five, on a good day. Des had been at least an eight.

And so is Detective Mason, a tiny part of my brain suddenly said, catching me out. Well, maybe not an eight, but definitely a seven. But you can't judge a man just by the way he looks. The way he carries himself is just as important, and in that respect the detective scored another couple of points. Tall, confident, calm . . . Unfortunately he was already spoken for, judging by the woman who'd answered the phone the morning I'd called him to rescue me from the mob.

But Barry . . .? On the positive side, he was a nice guy, he was . . . Well, I couldn't really think of anything else that was positive enough to be included on a list. But on the negative side, he suffered from extreme verbal diarrhoea and didn't seem to be equipped with even the most basic ability to know when to shut up.

Are Justin and Mags right? I wondered. Does Barry see me as a possible girlfriend?

It was kind of nice to think that someone was still interested in me, but I couldn't ever see it working out.

Aside from me not actually fancying Barry, there was the added complication that he was my lodger. If we did start to go out, how would we deal with that? In that sort of situation, how do you know when you've reached the point where you're not just going out, but are in fact living together?

And it would get *really* awkward if he was paying me rent; I had a sudden, disturbing vision of me and Barry waking up after a night of passion, and him saying, "Last night was great. Hold on a second and I'll get your money for you."

If, for some strange and currently unimaginable reason, we *did* get together, what would everyone think? That I was so desperate for someone after Des left that I latched onto the first man who came along?

Okay, so it didn't really bother me that much what other people thought; the past couple of weeks had clearly demonstrated that most people's opinions of me were pretty flexible.

Thinking along those lines reminded me of Thomas Kennedy. In many ways he was Barry's exact opposite. They were both about the same height and build, but Tom was fair where Barry was dark. Tom's teeth and skin were flawless, he didn't chew his nails like Barry did, and he had a clipped, reserved manner that I really liked. He kind of reminded me of Jude Law, though he wasn't quite as good-looking. But if I was to compare Barry to someone from television or movies, I'd probably have to choose Animal from *The Muppet Show*.

I came to the conclusion that I wasn't going to get

anywhere thinking like that. If, as Barry seemed to think, Tom Kennedy was interested in me, then I'd just sit back and let it happen. I wasn't going to ponder over it.

With that conclusion reached, I went up to bed.

As I passed by Barry's room, I heard him whisper, "Orla?"

"Yeah?"

"I had a good time tonight. Thanks."

"You're welcome."

"We should invite Mags and Justin over in return."

We? I said to myself. Where did you get 'we' from?

"Goodnight, Barry," I said, and went into my room.

Chapter 18

When Thomas Kennedy phoned on Saturday afternoon, my first thought was that he was going to cancel the seven o'clock meeting. But it turned out that Barry's guess had been right: Thomas hadn't been inviting me to a meeting, he'd been asking me out.

"The thought just occurred to me that I might not have made myself clear when I called yesterday," Thomas said. "You do realise that I wasn't asking you to meet me on official business, right?"

"I do now," I said.

"So . . . are you still interested?"

I pretended to think about it for a second. "Okay . . . but the thing is, I don't have anything nice to wear. Most of my clothes were stolen, remember?"

There was a slight pause, then Thomas said, "Of course. Um . . . well, that could be a bit awkward. I was thinking of asking you if you wanted to come along to a little function the company is hosting. It's black tie."

"Which means a cocktail dress for me?"

"Traditionally, yes. Is that going to be a problem?"

"Can I phone you back? I'll ask my friend if she has a dress I can borrow."

"Sure. You can reach me at this number any time, day or night."

So I hung up and wondered whether it would be even more of an imposition on Mags if I was to ask her if I could borrow one of her good dresses. *And* a decent pair of shoes.

The more I thought about it, the more uncomfortable I became: I didn't have a nice bag, I didn't have any jewellery, hardly any make-up.

Maybe it'd be best to just phone Thomas back and tell him that I wouldn't be able to make it . . . but then he might get the wrong idea and never call again.

Well, if he's really interested in me, he won't let something like that stop him, I decided. So I waited a respectable few minutes, then called him back.

"Thomas? I'm sorry, but there's no way I'll be able to get a dress. But thanks for the invite anyway."

"Never mind, it's not that important an event. I'm not obligated to be there. In fact, I really wasn't looking forward to it. Would you like to go out for dinner instead?"

"Sure, thanks. Only we can't go anywhere too posh. Not unless they're currently having a fancy-dress night."

He laughed politely. "Seven o'clock, then? I'll pick you up."

After we hung up, I checked the time. It was a little after four. That gave me three hours to get ready. Plenty of time, I said to myself. All I needed to do was have a bath, then go through the few clothes I had, and the ones Mags had lent me, and find something acceptable.

Of course, in this sort of situation time has a way of slipping away from you . . . Once I got into the bath I realised that my legs were long overdue for a shave. Unfortunately my only remaining disposable razor was no longer up to the task; it took a good five minutes to do the front of my left calf.

The first thing I'll do when I get my millions in compensation from the bank, I told myself, is get electrolysis done. No more bloody shaving or waxing or having to wear jeans because I don't have time to shave.

I'd only tried waxing once. Once was enough; not only had it hurt like hell, but I was left with red rectangular blotches that were itchy as hell and took about three weeks to fade, by which time the hair had mostly grown back.

I looked around the bathroom. Barry's razor and shaving foam were on the little glass shelf above the sink.

No way, I said to myself. I can't just use someone else's razor. Besides, it's not exactly hygienic.

The only other option was to remain stubbly and not wear a skirt or a dress, but I didn't have any trousers apart from jeans.

So, I felt it was best to shave. I leaned out of the bath and found my mobile phone in the pocket of my jeans – I always bring the phone into the bathroom on the theory that people always phone when I'm in the bath, even though that's never actually happened – and called Barry at work.

"Hello?"

"It's me," I said.

"Daddy?"

I laughed. "Listen, I'm in the bath . . ."

There was a tiny pause, which I guessed was him trying to picture how I looked in the bath. "Oh yeah?"

"And I have a favour to ask."

"Fire away."

"I need to shave my legs and my razor's too blunt. Can I borrow yours?"

"Sure. There should be a new packet of blades there on the shelf. Or if not, they're in the drawer beside my bed. So what's the occasion?"

This was a little awkward. "Remember when we were on the way over to Justin and Mags' place last night, and my phone rang?"

"Ah. That lad. So I was right about him asking you on a date?"

"You were."

"And you want me to lend you my razor so that you can shave your legs to impress another man?"

"Well . . . yeah."

"Okay then."

"Cheers, Barry. You're a star."

"I know . . . Enjoy yourself, Orla. But be careful. Sometimes those rich lads don't know how to treat women."

"I'm sure I'll be fine."

"All right. I won't wait up for you."

* * *

Thomas arrived at *exactly* seven o'clock. That was a little unexpected, because when I first started going out with Des he'd often arrive an hour or more late, muttering apologies about being held up with some deal or other.

In the end, I'd opted for a skirt and top that Mags had lent me. I'd had a minor panic attack when I spotted the beginnings of a ladder in my only pair of tights. Tights! On a first date! The fashion snob inside me was mortified; at the very least I should have had stockings.

Luckily, thanks to some very careful manipulation, I was able to adjust my tights so that the ladder didn't show. My shoes weren't ideal, but the only alternative was my runners. I wasn't exactly dressed up to the nines, maybe the four-and-a-halfs, but it was a bit more respectable than jeans and a T-shirt.

Thomas was wearing a tan sports jacket over a chunky jumper, slacks and light brown loafers. Very much the "casual but loaded" look.

"You look lovely," he said.

"Thanks. You too."

He held open the car door for me, and waited until I was settled before gently closing the door and walking around to the driver's side.

That was pretty much the whole tone for the evening; he held open doors, pulled out my chair for me in the restaurant, stood up when I got up to go to the loo, and all that. Chivalry was alive and well and personified in Thomas Kennedy.

He didn't seem to mind that I was dressed at least two social classes lower than everyone else in the restaurant, including the waiters. He treated me as though I was a princess.

Thomas didn't hog the conversation, either: he even allowed me to finish my own sentences. Barry could have learned a thing or two from him.

"So tell me a little about yourself," I asked, after we'd given the waiter our order.

"There's not much to tell," he said. "I'm thirty-two, an Aries. No brothers or sisters. I studied in Trinity and UCD. I've got a master's degree in business analysis." He shrugged, then smiled. "That's about it."

"You're not married or engaged or anything like that?"

"My wife said that if you asked I was to say no." He laughed. "No, I'm about as single as they come. I was engaged once, but it didn't work out. Luckily, we discovered how incompatible we were before it was too late."

"So tell me about your job, then. It must be tough."

"Not really. We do have some hard times – the situation with Desmond Mills didn't help matters – but generally things go pretty smoothly. Are you familiar at all with statistical analysis?"

"If by 'statistical analysis' you mean 'waiting on tables in a restaurant', then yes. Otherwise, I've no idea what the term even means."

Thomas explained it to me, and I was still no wiser. To me, it sounded like all they did was look at bunches of numbers and try and tweak them to make them fit the answer they wanted to get.

"It all sounds fascinating," I lied. "But the big question is, is it a satisfying vocation?"

Thomas considered this. "Yes . . . I think so. Especially when we're involved in a building project, like Nine Acres would have been. For a long time it only exists on paper, and then one day there's a grand opening and you see this building that wouldn't have existed if you hadn't been involved. Granted, it's probably not as satisfying as if you built the thing yourself, but there *is* a certain sense of accomplishment. I've always thought that if your job doesn't give you the feeling that you've achieved or created something, then there's not much point in doing it." At that, he seemed to realise that he'd been talking enough about himself, and that it was my turn to speak. "How about you? What's your grand plan?"

This caught me out. "Grand plan? I don't have one right now . . . not that I can think of."

"You don't want to scale Everest or learn to play concert piano? No dreams like that?"

"I did have, but I sort of screwed them up. I studied art and design, worked for a few years with Desire and Design."

"Oh, I know them! We were going to employ them to plan and outfit the offices at Nine Acres! Did you know Brian Dunbar?"

"Yeah, he was one of my bosses. God, that would have been weird: Des always said that he was going to put *my* name forward for designing the offices. I started my own company after I left Desire and Design, but it didn't really work out."

"Why not?"

"I bit off more than I could chew, I suppose. When I was with D&D, it was usually my job to run after the clients, making changes here and there, suggesting alternatives when something wasn't available, scheduling everything and making sure that all the work was done on time."

"Sounds like a lot of responsibility."

"It was, but it wasn't what I wanted to do. I wanted to *be* a designer, not just someone who cleans up after one. So I left and set up my own company. I'd managed to convince myself that if I was the lead designer on a project, I'd get everything right first time and there'd be no need for changes, and there'd be a lot less follow-up work. I was wrong about that! In the year I was in business, I only managed to complete two projects. I was expecting to do about one a month. So anyway . . . to answer your first question: until Des disappeared, my grand plan was to completely renovate the house so that it could be a showcase."

"And you were doing all the work yourself? I'm impressed. I don't think I'd know one end of a paintbrush from the other."

"Of course, that's all in the past . . . there's no way I'm going to be able to afford it now. The idea was that all the time and money I invested in doing up the house would pay off in the long run, because then I could sell the place, buy another old house, and do the same. If everything went according to plan, I'd have made enough money from selling the house to be able to quit the restaurant and devote all my time to renovating the next one."

"But surely that's a tremendous amount of work! It can't be cost-effective!"

I shrugged. "It would have worked out at more per hour than I was getting in the restaurant. It's like what you just said about job satisfaction. And I suppose the long-term plan was that I'd be able to retire early. That's the thing, you see . . . by nature I'm quite lazy, but I'm willing to work like mad now so that I can be lazy later on! I want to be able to sit around most of the time and not worry too much about work or anything like that. I was the same in college; I did the bare minimum I needed to do to get by and pass my exams. And after I left college, I never wanted to study again. And I never have," I added, proudly.

Thomas raised an eyebrow. "Interesting . . . Myself, I've never stopped studying. I've always got two or three things on the go at any given time. Right now, I'm in my second year of learning Japanese, and I spend at least four weeks a year on the slopes," Thomas said.

"Skiing?"

"Snow-boarding, mostly." He laughed. "Oh, I know what you're thinking: I'm far too old to be snow-boarding, but it's a lot of fun, and great exercise."

"I imagine it is."

"But you . . . well, in many ways you're quite lucky, Orla. You're a few years younger than me and you've already defined all your goals."

"Put like that, yes, I suppose I have. Or had, until Des stole the goalposts. Before, I didn't have much, but I was happy with it. Now, I have a lot less, and I'm certainly *not* happy."

"Any sign of a job?"

"Nothing yet. Though to be honest I haven't really had much of a chance to look. I've got my evening classes on Tuesdays and Wednesdays, and . . ." I stopped. "Well, I suppose I've got more time now that I've got most of my furniture back and things are a little more organised."

"If you like, I'll ask around. I'm sure that one of my friends will be able to find something for you."

"That'd be great. God, I suppose I'm pretty dull compared to most of the people you know. I'm sure they're all go-getters?"

"They are. Amongst my friends there's always a sort of unspoken competition as to who has the best car, the best job, the sexiest girlfriend, and so on. But, you know, it's all superficial. A person isn't what he or she owns or can lay claim to. It's who they are on the inside."

After a line like that, for a second I had the horrible feeling that he was about to burst into song, then he tilted his head to the left a little, and stared at me. "Can I be honest with you?"

"Sure."

"Okay . . . as soon as I saw you, that day I called looking for Desmond, I said to myself, 'She's not bad-looking'."

"Thanks," I said.

"Don't thank me yet! No, you see, I was automatically categorising you. I was judging you by how you looked. And not only that, but when I saw your house, I was also judging you by how you lived. Setting aside the fact that your house had been stripped, I could see that you didn't have much."

"That's true, but then you haven't seen the bathroom or the main bedroom. I think I did a pretty good job on them."

"A lot of men – most, probably – treat good-looking women in the same way, when they first meet them. We think, 'Is this someone I could get involved with?' And . . . well, I'm ashamed to say it, but after our first meeting I had you definitely locked into the 'No' box. Don't take this the wrong way, but you're not really, well, my sort of person. Do you know what I mean?"

I knew exactly what he meant, but I decided to make him sweat a little. If he even did sweat; I wasn't certain that he'd allow himself to do something so ordinary. "That I'm below you in the social order?"

That was supposed to just be a semi-sarcastic comment. He wasn't supposed to *agree* with me: "Exactly. I apologise for that, I really do."

"That's okay. You didn't see me at my best that day."

"Well, I'm thinking that perhaps I *did*."

"I'm sorry?"

"I'm thinking that maybe I saw you at your best, but I just wasn't able to grasp the fullness of the situation. Orla, if any of the other girls I know had been in a similar situation, they'd have gone to pieces. Either that, or they'd have been outraged. I saw you hurt, but coping. You didn't sit around wishing that it hadn't happened."

"Actually, I did."

"Well, perhaps. The point is that you coped anyway. But of course I didn't realise this at the time. No, what really clarified it for me was at the hotel, when that man threatened you, and you kneed him in the unmentionables. That itself showed courage, but more than that, you dealt with the matter afterwards in a very mature way: you spoke to him, you made him realise how wrong he was, and you didn't press the matter with the gardaí. Almost everyone else I know would have been straight on the phone to their solicitor. And they'd have sued my company and the hotel while they were at it."

I wondered where he was going with this. "So . . .?"

"So what I'm trying to say is that you're unique."

I couldn't help smiling at that. "I'm unique."

"Yes. After the incident at the hotel, one of the people I was working with made some comments about you. They weren't too bad, but they were along the lines of, 'She's the product of Eliza Doolittle crossed with The Terminator.'"

I laughed.

"It wasn't meant in jest, I'm sorry to say. But I saw then that there was more to you than met the eye. The more I learned about you – especially from people like Dearbhla McKenna at the bank – the more intrigued I became."

"I can't imagine that Dearbhla said anything nice about me."

"No, she didn't. And that's the point. She's used to her position of power; she expects the customers to roll over and say, 'Kick me again'. She didn't like it that you stood up for yourself. I also spoke to your former employer, Mr Flanagan. He was still adamant that you were involved with Desmond's plans, despite all the indications to the contrary. But when I pressed him for evidence, he had to admit that he realised that you weren't involved. In fact, I'm sure that he now feels very badly at how he treated you. Don't be surprised if he asks you to come back to work."

"You think he will?"

"Almost certainly. In that sort of situation there are two ways to assuage guilt: try and brush the incident under the carpet and pretend it never happened, or go to great lengths to make amends. I'm guessing that he can't do the former, because he'll always be reminded by one thing or another. So, yes, I'm pretty certain that he'll offer you your old job."

"Do you think I should take it?"

"Well, now . . . that's up to you. Would you be happy to work there again?"

"Not for the same money, no."

"He'll almost certainly offer you either a raise or a promotion. I've seen this sort of thing before. Well, perhaps not *exactly* this sort of thing, but similar enough. I'm guessing that he'll tell you that he's sorry, and that the place isn't the same without you, and that he'd like you to come back. He will, of course, also do something to reassert his position, because he can't be seen to be weak. That means he'll probably tighten some old rules. Dress codes and the like."

"And this is the sort of thing you learned for your master's degree?"

"No, not at all. This is the sort of thing you learn from spending ten years working with a huge number of small companies."

At that moment there was a sudden rush of air, and I looked to my left to see that a pair of waiters had materialised next to me. Without a word, they laid out the food with expert precision, then disappeared.

"Well," Thomas said, "*bon appetit!*"

* * *

Halfway through the meal, when Thomas was telling me about his rebellious teenage years – for one brief, mad summer he'd considered getting one of his ears pierced – my phone rang.

329

"Sorry," I said, "I should have shut it off."

"Not a problem. Feel free to answer it." Thomas folded his napkin and got up from the table.

I pulled the phone out of my bag. "Hello?"

"It's me," Barry said. "Sorry to bother you, but there's two lads at the door."

"And?"

"And they want to know whether you're interested in buying a blender. Hold on." I heard some muffled voices, then Barry said, "Forty quid."

"Can you ask them to come back during the week?"

"I already did. They said that they're not going to be around for a few weeks, and they won't get a chance to call again for ages. Hang on . . ." I heard Barry say, "Let's have a look at it, then," and there was some more muffles, which got louder and louder, until Barry eventually said, "Okay . . . look, this is awkward, but I'll deal with it, okay?"

"Are you talking to me now or to them?"

"To you. I'll see you when you get home."

"Okay. Thanks. But why is it awkward?"

"Never mind. You just enjoy yourself, okay?"

After I hung up, Thomas came back to the table. It was only then that I realised he hadn't got up to go to the bathroom; he'd left the table to give me some privacy while I was on the phone.

"Everything okay?" he asked as he sat down.

"My lodger had a minor problem, but it's all sorted."

He nodded. "Excellent. How is that working out for you?"

I hesitated before answering. "It's . . . strange. It reminds

LOOKING FOR MR WRONG

me a lot of when my brother was still living in the house. We don't seem to agree on much. Don't get me wrong; he's a nice enough guy, but there's been more than one occasion when I wished I hadn't chosen the first person who came along. But, well, I needed the money."

"I can understand that," Thomas said. "Still, at least things will be a little better when the bank reimburses you for the money they allowed Des to take."

"I suppose," I said. "But how long's *that* going to take?"

"Probably not more than another two or three days," he said. "A week at the most."

I stared at him. "Pardon?"

He stared back. "You haven't heard? No, of course, that's the way they work, isn't it? I imagine they're trying to think of a way to make it look as though they're doing you a favour."

"So you're saying that they're *definitely* going to pay me back?"

Thomas nodded. "I believe so, yes. At our meeting Ms McKenna seemed to be rather desperately looking for a way to disconnect your predicament from the situation with Desmond's business account."

I was chuffed. "That's great! God, that'll really make a difference, you know? It'll go a long way towards replacing my clothes and things. I mean, almost everything I'm wearing now is borrowed. She didn't happen to mention anything about compensation, did she?"

"No, but then we weren't directly discussing your details."

"What's happening with the money your company lost?"

"We've already written it off."

"Oh. Did you get into trouble?"

"Me? No, not at all. But then I'm sort of protected."

Thomas didn't look comfortable with admitting that, but I didn't let that stop me. "How do you mean?"

"Well, the name of the company *is* Wagner, Kennedy and Parker."

"But at the meeting at the hotel you said that you're not the same Kennedy from the company name."

"I'm not, but my father is."

"Ah," I said.

"I know that a lot of people think that I wouldn't even be there if I wasn't related to the old man, but the truth is that I *am* qualified for the position. My father's not the sort of man who'd hire someone just because he was related. He made that very clear to me when I was younger. 'In my world,' he said, 'you don't get anything handed to you. You have to earn it.' As you can imagine, this causes some friction in the family. Not between me and him, but I have a lot of first and second cousins and most of them seem to think that their rich uncle will give them a job solely on the grounds that they're related to him."

"And he doesn't?"

"Actually, he usually does, but he'll only ever offer them jobs that they're qualified for, and then only if there's an opening. I mean, I started off there answering phones and opening the mail. That was while I was still in college. I worked my way to where I am now. That's how it should be, I think. You wouldn't believe the number of senior executives in this country who only got where they are today because one of their parents was on the board of directors. In fact, a lot of my friends are in that position. They left college and automatically became an executive. It's like that old joke: How does an executive ask for the day off? 'See you tomorrow, Daddy.' But my father always said that if you're going to inherit the company, you're far better off knowing how it runs from the ground up. Of course, a lot has changed in the past couple of years, but I do my best to keep informed of what's happening on the lower decks. I mean, I know most of the staff by name. I have friends who think that the receptionists or whoever in their companies are nothing but slaves."

"But don't your friends know that all they're doing is widening the divide between the workers and the management?"

Thomas said, "Orla, most of them don't realise that there *is* a divide. I have one friend who doesn't even have a real job. When he left college his father created a high-level position especially for him. His job title is 'Executive Consultant'. He spends his time in meetings with people in similar positions in other companies, and as far as I can tell, they discuss wide-ranging plans that are never put into action, because any decisions they make are either ignored or passed on to a higher level for approval. And my friend genuinely believes that he's doing good work. Once, just for fun, we asked him what would happen if he didn't go into work for a month. He believed that the place would fall apart without him. I don't think he saw the point."

"Which was?"

"Well, the previous winter he'd taken *two* months off

without letting anyone know in advance, and when he came back nothing had changed. He attributed that to the stable situation he'd created before he left."

"That reminds me of a conversation I had with Barry the other night. He'd said, 'You can never be sure that you're not really locked up in a padded room somewhere imagining your life.' Maybe that's how it is for your friend, in a way. He thinks that his job is important because he's been told it is."

Thomas considered this. "Interesting . . . perhaps that's true for many of us. How can any of us know for certain that what we do is worthwhile?"

"Well, if you stopped doing your job and everyone else could get along without you, then maybe it's *not* worthwhile. Like, I'm sure that Flanagan's Bistro is doing fine without me. I didn't bring anything to the job that someone else couldn't have."

We both sat in silence for a while, then Thomas smiled and said, "Now that's a kind of depressing thought! You know, if I left tomorrow, they could fill my position very quickly."

"Ah, but you *do* bring something to your job that no one else could," I said.

"And what's that?"

"Well, your intelligence, for a start. I mean, you spotted that the bank's security video proved that Des was forging my signature."

"Your friend Justin spotted that too. What does he do for a living?"

"He sells shoes."

"Really?"

I nodded.

"But he struck me as very intelligent. Why is he selling shoes?"

"He enjoys it. Oh, I'm sure that if he applied himself he could be running a major company in no time, but that's not what he wants to do. He drives all over the country and sells shoes to department stores and shoe shops. He gets to meet all kinds of people." And on top of that, I said to myself, I'm fairly certain that Justin has a shoe fetish.

"Amazing," Justin said. "He's a lot like you, then? He doesn't have any driving ambition to better himself?"

I wasn't sure I liked the implication. "Now, wait a second! Why would having a better job make him a better person?"

"Well, that's not *quite* what I meant . . . I only meant that I'm sure he could be earning a lot more money in a different occupation."

"Perhaps he could, but money isn't everything."

"True, but surely more money couldn't hurt?"

"Let's say for the moment that you had ten million in the bank, okay? And then you get the chance to double it by doing a job that you won't enjoy as much. Would you do it?"

"Probably," he said. "I'm sure that most people would."

"Twenty million is twice ten million, but that doesn't mean that you'll be twice as well off."

"You've lost me there," he said, grinning.

"If you have more money than you can spend, it doesn't matter whether you have twice as much as you need, or a hundred times as much. That's something I've never understood about people who play the stock market. Surely they'd save a lot of time and stress if they just invested their money into a safer account and spent all the time they would have been playing the market by going for a nice walk on the beach instead?"

"Yes, but the quality of life –"

I interrupted him. "The quality of life should only be determined by how happy we are, not by how much we have."

"And if playing the stock market makes you happy?"

"Then that's fine, I've no problem with that. But it does bother me when I see people who are obviously wealthy and the only thing they use their money for is making more money. I met enough of them when I was working with Desire and Design. People who spend a hundred grand remodelling houses that they only lived in for a couple of weeks a year. Wouldn't they feel a lot better about themselves if they gave a big chunk of their money to a charity?"

"It's not that simple," Thomas said.

I could see that I was making him far too uncomfortable, so I decided to shift the topic to something safer. "Well, tell me how your average day in work goes."

Thomas seemed a lot happier to be talking about that. I learned more about hostile takeovers and such than I ever thought I'd need to know. Then he asked me about waitressing, and he learned a lot about how to tell which customers were likely to be the best tippers.

By the time we left the restaurant – Thomas had taken careful note of everything I'd said about working in a restaurant, and had left a very generous tip – I decided that I liked him well enough that if he asked me out again, I'd accept.

As before, he held the car door open for me. When he got into the driver's seat, he said, "So . . . it's still quite early. What would you like to do?"

"I'm easy," I said. "Do you have anything in mind?"

"Whatever you like."

Ah, I said to myself. This is the difficult part where neither of us wants to be seen to be too keen. "Why don't we find a late-night coffee shop and settle in for a few hours?" I suggested.

"So you're not anxious to get away from me as fast as you can?"

"Not at the moment."

"Well, that's good. You know what we could do? We could go for a drive up into the mountains. It's such a clear night – it'd be a shame to spend it sitting inside somewhere when we could be looking at the stars."

I almost said, "I've seen them" but decided that wouldn't be polite, so I agreed.

"In fact, I can even go one better than that."

"We're going to the moon?"

He laughed. "You'll see."

* * *

Half an hour later we were driving along a very quiet country road, when Thomas slowed the car down and pulled into a wide driveway that led up to a very impressive house. "This is my parents' place," he explained, as he held open the passenger door for me. "They're away at the moment."

We crunched our way up the gravel drive and Thomas unlocked the door and ushered me through the hall and into the sitting-room.

I'd half-expected a dark, panelled room with animal heads on the wall and a cabinet full of sports trophies, but the place was quite moderately furnished; subtle wall-mounted lamps, a couple of items of designer furniture that I happened to know were a lot more expensive than they looked, and a single framed print by Walter Richard Sickert over a large but reasonably modern fireplace.

"Very nice," I said. "Elegant. Underfloor heating?"

Thomas nodded. "Yes. How did you know?"

"No radiator, no vents."

"Come on through," he said, and led me into the kitchen – it was about the size of the ground floor of my house and absolutely packed with shiny appliances and shinier cookware – and through to the conservatory, which was about the same size and filled with huge-leafed plants in ceramic pots and wicker baskets.

Then Thomas opened the door to the garden and flipped on the outside lights. There was a small hut in the middle of the garden. "The observatory," he explained. "The roof rolls back."

A few minutes later we were huddled together in front of an expensive-looking telescope, taking turns to squint through the eyepiece and look at the stairs.

Thomas knew the names of all the constellations. When he asked me which was my favourite, I said, "Orion" because it was the only one I was able to recognise.

It should have been dead romantic, sitting side-by-side

with a gorgeous man, looking at the stars, but, well, it wasn't really. It was kind of cold and uncomfortable, and Thomas seemed to be much more interested in educating me than wooing me. "This one is stunning," he said more than a few times, before spending ages adjusting the telescope to point to the correct star.

By the time he dropped me home, at about two in the morning, I'd come to the conclusion that, yes, I liked Thomas. He was a lovely guy and I was sure that my mother would have approved.

He was definitely husband material, there was no doubt about that. And he seemed to be very keen on me.

Thomas walked me to the door.

"Thanks," I said. "I had a lovely evening."

"No, thank *you*. I haven't enjoyed myself so much in ages. You're remarkable, you know that?"

I shrugged.

"So . . . can I see you again?"

"Sure. That would be nice."

He leaned forward and kissed me, gently, on the lips, then stepped back. "I'll give you a call."

There was brief awkward moment when I realised that I was standing in the porch waiting for him to drive off, and he was sitting in the car waiting for me to go in, then I waved and opened the door.

I liked the idea of seeing him again, but there was a little nagging doubt in the back of my mind that, nice as he was, and considerate and wealthy and successful as he was, he wasn't really *that* much fun to be with.

And then suddenly Barry was in the hall in front of me, arms folded and with a very stern expression on his face.

"I thought you said you weren't going to wait up," I said.

"Yeah, but remember when I phoned you? I said I'd see you when you got home."

"Oh right. So you did."

"Well . . . you have a bit of a problem here, don't you?"

I was sure he wasn't referring to the problem of my lodger being jealous of the man I went out with. "How do you mean?"

He showed me into the sitting-room. Piled up in the centre of the room was my sandwich toaster and the video recorders, television and tapes that Reebok and Jumper Man had left, along with a brand-new blender, still in the box. "I'm pretty sure that the microwave oven and the fridge should be in with this lot too," he said.

"Look, what's going on?"

"The two guys who called over this evening to sell you a blender . . . you know what the official term for that is?"

"Being kind to someone who's had all her stuff nicked?"

"No, it's called receiving stolen goods."

Chapter 19

I stared at him. "Oh. Really?"

"I'm certain. What did they tell you? That they just happened to have a spare fridge, and a couple of spare VCRs? And you *believed* them?"

"Now wait a second! They didn't charge me for any of those! Only for the sandwich toaster! And that was because Reebok's sister got married and she already had one!"

He raised his eyes. "God, they saw *you* coming, didn't they? What are you, 'Gullible Woman of the Year'?"

"How do you know they're stolen?"

Barry picked up the box containing the blender, and turned it over. "See that? Price sticker. This was stolen from *my* store this afternoon! I know that because I saw four out on display just after I got in, and they were right near the door. I went to find someone to move them, and when I got back a minute later there was one missing.

And I know it wasn't bought, because I checked the registers when I was closing up."

"Shit. I didn't know. I just assumed that they were being kind."

He looked disgusted. "God, am I mad to expect that – after all that Des did to you – you'd be a lot more careful about who you trust?"

"Well, I trusted *you*, didn't I?"

"What's that got to do with it? No, look, we have to take this stuff down to the police station first thing in the morning and explain everything to them."

"No way!"

"Orla, you can't keep it."

"I know *that*, but I've had enough trouble involving the police lately."

"Look at those videos! *They* weren't taken from a shop – that's someone's collection! There's some poor guy out there who probably spent years buying them, then these two bastards break into their house and nick the lot!"

"It probably wasn't them who broke in," I said.

"What difference does that make? These things have to go back to their rightful owners."

"Well, in the morning I can phone Reebok and get him to take them away."

"So that he can just sell them to someone else? No. We have to phone the police."

"Oh great! As if things weren't bad enough! If I tell them where this stuff came from, Reebok and Jumper Man aren't going to be happy."

"Then don't tell them. Just say that someone left the

stuff outside the house and you came back and found it."

"That won't work. Detective Mason has seen most of it. He'll know I've had it for a while."

He shrugged. "In that case, you have to be honest." Then he said, "Why do you call them Reebok and Jumper Man?"

"Because that's the way they were dressed the first time I saw them. Their real names are Noel and Wayne. Noel was decked out completely in Reebok stuff, and Wayne had a jumper that looked like the sort of thing you get from your mother at Christmas."

"How old are they?"

"I don't know . . . nineteen, twenty, something like that. Why?"

"Then it wasn't the same two guys. These were a lot older. Late twenties at least."

I almost collapsed with relief. "Oh, well that's okay then."

"Why is that okay?"

"Because it might mean that the stuff I got from Reebok and Jumper Man wasn't stolen."

"Then in that case, phone them tomorrow and ask them to come over. But arrange it for before two, because that's when I'm due back in work, and I want to be here to meet them."

"No, wait . . . if it wasn't them tonight, then what reason would I have to talk to them?"

"Picture the scene," Barry said. "Wayne and Noel are sitting in the pub when two lads they know approach them. 'Do you want to buy a blender?' one of them says.

'Fell off the back of a lorry.' 'No,' says Noel, 'but I know someone who might want it.' So he gives them your name and address and suggests that they call over. Sure, they lent you this other stuff, but how long will it be before they tell you that they're short of cash, so they'll sell it to you at a really good price?"

I didn't like the sound of that at all. "Okay, okay. I'll phone them in the morning."

* * *

"I swear to God, Mr Sheridan, on me mammy's *life*, I have no clue what you're talkin' about! Honest!" Reebok lied.

He was sitting on my sofa and looking very, very worried.

Barry was standing in front of him, arms crossed. "You're telling me that these two guys showed up out of the blue, asked for Orla by name, and wanted to sell her a blender that was stolen from my store just yesterday afternoon, and you know nothing about it?"

Reebok nodded, the visor on his cap bobbing up and down. "Yeah. I don't know who they are. It's nothin' to do with me!"

"And you're also saying that this other stuff you've given Orla had not been stolen?"

"Yeah."

"So that box of videos you *lent* Orla . . . name them. *Without* looking at them. If they're yours, you'll know the names of them."

Reebok stared at him for a long time.

"Name *one* of them!"

344

Reebok continued staring at him.

"You can't, can you? Jesus, you stupid little bastard! Don't you think that Orla's been through enough without you selling her stolen property! What was the plan, leave the stuff here for a while and then tell her you got a new telly or whatever, and if she wants you'll sell her the stuff cheap? Was that it?"

Reebok looked at me. "I'm tellin' you, Orla, that's not the way it was."

I said nothing. I could see that he was lying, but Barry and I had agreed that he'd do all the talking. That way, if it all turned sour, I'd be able to claim that it wasn't my fault.

"So in that case," Barry said, "you were using Orla's house as a place to stash your stolen goods, right?"

"Jesus, you think I'm the Jammie Dodger or somethin'?"

We both stared at him, puzzled. "The who?" Barry asked.

"You know, from *Oliver Twist*."

"You mean the Artful Dodger. A Jammie Dodger is a biscuit."

"Whatever." Reebok stood up. He was taller than Barry, but only about half his weight. "I don't have to take this shit from you!"

"No, you don't," Barry said. "You can take it from the gardaí instead. How's that sound?"

For a second, Reebok looked like he was on the verge of saying something along the lines of, 'I know where you live,' but then he crumbled. "Fuck it!"

"So what are you going to do about it?"

"Look, the fridge and the microwave really *are* mine."

Jaye Carroll

"And the rest of it?"

"We didn't nick any of it ourselves."

"But you know who did?"

"No."

"Yes, you do. Look, here's how we're going to do this. You're going to walk away and never bother Orla again. You're giving her the microwave and the fridge as a present. In return, I'll talk to the cops and tell them what happened, but I won't mention any names. I'll just give them the stuff. I'm sure it'll have been reported missing, so they won't have any problems finding the real owners."

"Yeah, but –"

Barry interrupted. "Shut up. This way you don't get into trouble, understand? We won't say anything that implicates you or your friend."

After a few seconds, Reebok's shoulders sagged. "All right." He turned to me. "Sorry."

"You bloody *should* be," I said.

Barry showed Reebok to the door. I could hear them talking, but I couldn't make out the words. A few minutes later he came back into the sitting-room. "You okay?"

"I'm pissed off," I said. "But apart from that . . . I suppose it could have been worse. What were you saying to him at the door?"

"I just made sure that he won't be dealing in stolen goods again."

"How?"

"I reminded him that his fingerprints are all over everything. I said that if his prints aren't already on file,

346

they will be by the end of the day. So if he's ever caught for anything else, they'll be able to get him for this too."

"So now what do we do?"

"Well, now, we wipe it all down so that there *aren't* any fingerprints – because we really don't want these guys getting caught because of this and taking it out on us – and then we phone the gardaí."

* * *

At about four in the afternoon, I answered the door to see Detective Mason standing there. "Ms Adare," he said, nodding. "*Now* what trouble have you got yourself into?"

I brought him into the sitting-room.

"This is the alleged stolen property?" he asked, looking over the stuff.

"That's the lot."

"Mr Sheridan said you're not going to say who gave it to you?"

"No. Well, there's always the possibility that there'd be repercussions."

He nodded. "All right."

"I thought you were going to give me a lecture about how we have a responsibility to tell you everything we know."

The detective shook his head. "I understand the situation you're in. If you told us who these people are we *might* be able to get them for dealing with stolen goods, but they almost certainly wouldn't get jail time. With luck Mr Sheridan scared them straight. I admit that's not likely, but we live in hope."

"If you don't mind me asking, how come they sent you? I thought you only dealt with serious crimes."

"*All* crimes are serious, Ms Adare." Then he smiled. "No, when I heard that you were involved I decided to check it out for myself. Just in case there's a connection with your case." He crouched down and began to examine one of the video recorders.

"I don't suppose that there's any news about Des?"

"None, I'm afraid. But you'll be pleased to know that we haven't received any complaints about you in the past few days. Almost a week now, in fact."

"Well, that's good . . . So what are you going to do with this stuff? Take it all back to the station?"

"We'll check it against the stolen property lists." He stood up again. "You're sure that you don't want to say who it was?"

"Positive. I've had enough trouble with people blaming me for things. The last thing I want is another angry mob at the door."

"I have to tell you . . . that could be seen as obstructing the course of justice."

"I know that. But I like to think of it as protecting myself."

"Fair enough. How are things otherwise? Any sign of a job yet?"

"No, but I've been told that Mr Flanagan will probably offer me my old job. And apparently the bank are going to pay me back the money Des stole."

"And I see you have your furniture back too. You're lucky, you know. *Very* lucky."

"Well, I'll wait and see if I *do* get my job and my money back before I decide how lucky I am."

"How is Mr Sheridan working out as a lodger?"

"Pretty well. It was awkward at first, but it's getting better."

"Okay . . . I'll send someone over later to pick up these items, and catalogue everything. You'll be in for the rest of the day?"

"Yeah."

"All right." He walked out into the hall. "Nice seeing you again, Ms Adare."

"Please," I said. "Call me Orla."

"Orla, then." He opened the door.

"I don't know *your* first name," I said. "Or should I be calling you Detective Mason for the rest of my life?"

He paused in the porch. "You can call me Philip, if you like. That's my middle name. I usually go by that. I rarely tell anyone my first name."

"You mean like Inspector Morse?"

"In a way."

"Is that because of security reasons?"

"Not really."

I smiled. "Do you have an embarrassing first name like Hillary or Ashley something?"

"No, I've a perfectly ordinary first name."

"Ah, go on. Tell me."

"I'd rather not."

"Please?"

"Another time, perhaps. In the meantime, I'll take care of your stolen property problem . . ." He sighed. "You

349

Jaye Carroll

wouldn't consider giving the force a break and moving to another community, would you?"

"Sorry. This is where I grew up, and this is where I'll stay."

He nodded. "Oh well. Worth a go. At least you're helping us earn lots of extra overtime. I'm thinking about buying a boat with mine."

He left me laughing on the doorstep.

350

Chapter 20

Over the following four days, I went out with Thomas four times. That meant I'd been on five dates in a row, which was kind of a record for me. Even when Des and I had been at our most passionate, we hadn't gone out so much. On Tuesday and Wednesday evening, Thomas picked me up at five o'clock, because my evenings were taken up with the classes. He even picked me up after the classes and dropped me home.

Each night, Thomas and I went to a nice restaurant and had a nice meal, or to a nice pub for a nice drink, then went somewhere for a nice chat afterwards.

It was nice.

Because Barry was on lates that week, he hadn't yet met Thomas, but he didn't let that stop him from having an opinion about him.

Over breakfast on Thursday morning – Barry was having cereal, but I opted for sausages and eggs, which I was frying on my newly delivered cooker – Barry said, "So when am I going to get to meet this lad?"

"Why?"

"I'm just curious about him."

"In what way?"

Barry shrugged. "Well, you like him, right?"

"Yeah."

"And he doesn't mind that you pretty much wear the same clothes every time you go out?"

That one came out of the blue. "What difference should that make?"

"I'm only saying. You should buy yourself something new. If you're still strapped for cash, I'll lend you a few quid. You should make the effort, if you're really interested in him." Then he looked at me strangely. "Ah! So that's it! You're not that interested in him, are you? You're just going out with him to pass the time. Or is it because he's so completely devoid of personality that he's no threat whatsoever?"

"Given this a lot of thought, have you?"

"No," he lied.

"Anyway, he *does* have a personality. You think just because he's well-off and really polite that he's a wimp, don't you?"

"I never said that. But if he has such a great personality, how come you haven't mentioned anything about your dates other than where you went and what you had to eat? You haven't told me anything about him at all. At least, nothing that gives me a hint as to why you find him so attractive."

"Barry, why *should* I tell you? It's none of your business."

He looked a little hurt at that. "Well, we're friends, right? Friends tell each other things. If you remember, oh . . . way, way back about a week ago, we talked all the time. Now all you do is go out with Tom and have dinner and come back home and say nothing to me about it."

"It's not Tom, it's Thomas."

"Well, excuse *me*! In that case, I'm not Barry, I'm Bartholomew."

"Hah!"

"Hah what?"

"Just hah! You're just jealous because I'm going out with someone and you're not."

"As a matter of fact, I'm seeing someone tomorrow night." He stuck out his tongue like a four-year-old. "So there!"

"Oh really? Who?"

"None of your business."

"Well, where are you taking her?"

"Out."

"Where to?"

"A restaurant."

I grinned. "You're making it up, aren't you?"

Barry tilted his cereal bowl towards him to spoon up the last of the milk. "No, I'm serious. One of the girls in work. She was dropping hints like mad all last week, so I caved and asked her out."

"Is this the first date you'll have been on since you broke up with Jemima?"

"Yeah."

"Scared?"

"Not scared, no, but I'm a bit apprehensive. I mean,

she's only about twenty-two! That's nearly a whole generation younger than me! What'll I do if she starts talking about music or something? God, what if she wants to go to a nightclub?"

"You'll survive."

"No, seriously . . ." Barry got to his feet and began clearing the table. "I really shouldn't have asked her."

"What's she like?"

"She's funny. A bit mad, too. Right from day one she started giving me a hard time. We didn't get on at all at the beginning. She fought with me about absolutely everything. Then last week I overheard her talking to two of the other girls, complaining about me. She was saying, 'He's not here a wet day and he's changing things! It's like he owns the bloody place! Did you know he's already shacked up with yer one Orla Adare?' So later I called her into the office and said, 'Listen, Jennifer, I think we got off on the wrong foot.' And she looks at me in all innocence: 'How do you mean?' I said, 'You seem to have a few problems with me being here.'"

"So what did she say to that?"

"She just shrugged her shoulders – well, what else would she shrug? – and said, 'No, I've no problems. Except that . . .' And she started to go on and on about the changes I've made. Then the next day, just after I got in, she came right to the office and started up again. The day after that we ended up in a screaming match. I think that everyone in the place heard it. It ended when I shouted, 'You're fired!' at the exact same time as she shouted, 'I resign!' Then we glared at each other for nearly a minute, and we both burst out laughing. That sort of cleared the air, and since then we've been getting to know each other better. We take our breaks together."

I'd watched him carefully through all this. "Well, that sounds great. But how come you never mentioned her before?"

"You've had enough on your mind without me coming home and dumping all the stress of work on you."

"How are you getting along with the boss?"

"Mr Waters? Fine. He's not there that much. He's a nice guy, but he's not really suited to running a store, and I think he knows that himself. You have to be able to be a bit ruthless from time to time, especially when it comes to managing the staff. Otherwise, they'll walk all over you. I saw that myself the day I was interviewed. The car park was full, and all the trolleys were all over the place, and when I went in one of the lads who rounds up the trolleys was arguing with Waters. 'I'm on me break,' he was saying. 'I'll do it after.' And Waters just let him sit there in the cafeteria, smoking and reading his comic."

"You have to let people take their breaks," I said.

"True, but the impression I got was that this kid did as little as he could get away with. So on my first day I saw him doing the same thing, just arsing about and chatting up the girls on the checkouts, and I took him aside and introduced myself. I said, 'Colin, how about going outside and gathering up the trolleys?' He said, 'Yeah, sure. I'll do it in a few minutes.' So I said, 'Okay.' And I went off, and came back five minutes later, and he was still goofing off. I said, 'All right, Colin. Any plans to start rounding up the trolleys?' He said that he was just about to do it, so I said,

'Do you think that you might get around to it today?' And he gave me a dirty look."

"What kind of dirty look?"

"Just, you know, a dirty look. How many different kinds of dirty looks are there? Anyway, I said, 'Listen, do you have a friend who might be looking for a job?' And he said that he did. I told him, 'Great! Can you get in touch with him and ask him to come in as soon as possible? It's just that we're going to have an opening for a trolley boy real soon. Unless, of course, you'd like to hang on to the job yourself.' He got the message."

"That was a bit mean," I said. "You wouldn't really have fired him, would you?"

"Sure I would. What's the point in paying someone who won't do the job?"

"But won't things get awkward if you're going out with someone who works there?"

"I can't see why. I mean, I'm not going to let any relationship get in the way of work, am I? If this works out with Jennifer, and she starts to take advantage of me just because we're going out, well, I'll deal with it."

"What would you do? Fire her or break up with her? Because either way it wouldn't be pleasant."

"I don't know. I'll deal with it if it happens."

"Then suppose you break up with her for some other reason? Wouldn't that make things difficult when you still have to work together?"

Barry said, "Are you trying to tell me that you think it's a bad idea?"

"Well, yeah."

"Orla, it's been nearly seven months since I left

Jemima. I think I'm entitled to at least a *little* happiness, don't you?"

"It just seems a bit early. I know that seven months might seem like a long time to you, but you were married for *years*."

"Oh really? And how long after Des left did *you* wait before going out with someone?"

"Ah." He had a point there. I almost started to say, "That's completely different!", but I couldn't think of what the differences might be. "Okay, you're right."

"And you're seeing him again tonight, aren't you?"

"Yeah."

"Getting a bit serious, is it?"

"Actually, no, it's not."

We looked at each other for a few seconds. I wasn't sure what was going through *his* mind, but I was thinking: this has nothing to do with him. Nothing at all. It's none of his business and anyway I don't care if he's going out with someone else, because I don't fancy him in the slightest. Good luck to them. I hope that it all works out and they get married and then he'll move out and I'll have my own house back again and I won't have to listen to him thumping his way up and down the stairs and singing Bon Jovi songs when he's on the toilet.

I was snapped out of this by the ringing of my mobile phone. The number looked familiar, but as my phone wasn't displaying a name, it wasn't a number that I had stored on the phone. "Hello?"

"Orla?"

"Ah . . . Mr Flanagan."

"Listen . . . we're going to be pretty short-staffed tonight, and I was wondering if you wouldn't mind coming in. Steven needs to take the night off, I can't find anyone to fill in for him, and I can't really ask Pauline to be the only server. So it'd be just for tonight. Unless, of course, you've changed your mind and you'd like to come back." He added a friendly chuckle that didn't fool me in the least.

Thomas had told me that Flanagan would probably offer me my job back, so I'd been kind of expecting this. "I'm not sure, Mr Flanagan. Besides, it wasn't my decision to leave, remember?"

"Yes . . . well, we both said things we regretted that day."

"*I* didn't."

"Even so. What would it take for you to come back?"

"A raise and an apology would be a start."

There was the briefest of pauses, then he said, "All right. I'm sorry. And I'm not just saying that. I was wrong to blame you for something that you had no part in. But you have to see it from my point of view too . . . I lost a *lot* of money. I reacted without thinking."

"But, Mr Flanagan, that doesn't explain why you were so mean about me at the meeting in the hotel. Surely by then you'd had plenty of time to think? And even after it was proved that I wasn't involved with Des's plan, you still blamed me. How am I supposed to go back working for you with all that hanging over me?"

"I'll make you assistant manager."

"We've never had a manager before, assistant or otherwise."

"Well, in that case I'll make you a full manager. How's that sound? But only if you're going to work full-time.

And that means lunch-times five days a week, as well as the nights at the weekends."

"Let me think about it," I said. "I'll call you later today." I ended the call, and looked at Barry. "What do you think? He offered to make me the manager. Full-time."

"I think you should take it. You haven't had any other luck getting a job. Not that you've tried *that* hard. Sure, if it doesn't work out, all you have to do is leave. No one would hold that against you, not considering what's happened."

"Yeah, but if I'm working there, I won't have nearly as much time to spend with Thomas. Not if I'm still doing two nights a week at the school."

"My heart bleeds for you, it really does."

"He wants me to start tonight. That means I'd have to cancel the date."

"So? If Tommy's really that interested in you, he'll understand. And if he doesn't understand, then sod him. You can do better than him anyway."

"It's Thomas, not Tommy," I corrected. I had a little think. "All right. I'll do it."

* * *

Thomas's voice-mail very politely told me that he was in a meeting, but if I left a brief message with my name and number, he'd call back as soon as possible.

"It's me," I said. "Listen . . . remember what you said about Mr Flanagan offering me my old job back? Well, you were right! He just phoned a few minutes ago and he wants me to go in tonight. He even said that if I want to go back full-time then he'd make me the manager. Not that we really need a manager, but I'm not complaining because it'll mean more money."

The answering machine on the other end went *Beep!* and the line went dead.

So I phoned again: "It's me again. Sorry. The thingy cut me off. Anyway, where was I? Okay, so I didn't tell Flanagan yet that I'd do it, but I think I should. I mean, I think I'll go in tonight. I'm not saying that I'll go full-time. I'll wait and see how it works out tonight. So anyway, give me a call as soon as you can, because if I'm working tonight that means I'll have to –" *Beep!* "Damn it!"

Barry was washing up the breakfast things. "What if he doesn't get the message until it's too late?"

"Well, he always phones in the afternoon, so I can tell him then."

"He phones *every* afternoon?"

"Yeah."

Barry laughed.

"What's so funny about that?"

"He's a little lap-dog, isn't he? I bet that if you told him he could only phone every second day, and only between four and five-past four, then he would. You've got that lad eating out of your hand. I bet he pays every time you go out, too. I'm right, aren't I?"

"I paid the night before last," I said. "Anyway, he doesn't mind paying."

"I can imagine. So . . . what does he get out of it?"

I didn't like where this was going. "None of your business."

But Barry wasn't going to be stopped so easily. "Slept with him yet?"

"That's *definitely* none of your business!"

Barry stopped rinsing the frying pan and turned to me, suddenly quite serious. "Are you in love with him?"

"I refer you to the answer I gave earlier."

"So you're not. But is he in love with you?"

"I don't know. It's too early to say."

He returned his attention to the sink. "I bet he is. I bet he's thinking that he's never met anyone like you before. And he probably hasn't. All his old girlfriends were probably rich airheads that he only met because his parents knew *their* parents. Either that, or they were only interested in him for his money."

"That's a really big thing for you, isn't it? You're jealous that he's well-off."

"God no. I'm not jealous of him in any way. I just can't figure out what you see in him."

"Well, you've never met him. If you met him, you'd know. He's a really nice guy."

"Nice, eh?"

"Yeah."

"Orla, when I was a teenager the *worst* thing a girl could say to a guy was that he was 'nice'. It meant that she didn't fancy him in the slightest and that she was going to pretend that she just wanted to be friends. It's a code-phrase that means, 'Get the hell away from me, you dirty little pervert'. But now you're grown up, and you're settling for a man because he's 'nice'. Where's the fire? Where's the passion? If he's so wonderful, you wouldn't even be *considering* cancelling the date so that you could go to work." He picked up the tea towel and started drying the dishes.

"*You're* the one who said that if he was really interested in me he'd understand that I have to work."

"I know, but that's not my point."

"Well, if you ever get anywhere near the point, let me know in advance so that I can plan a bloody party for it."

For someone who maintained that I changed the subject a lot, Barry was pretty good at it himself: "I was in love with Jemima," he said. "She drove me absolutely bonkers, but I would have done almost anything for her. She's manipulative, and selfish, she's a borderline hypochondriac for God's sake! She argued about everything. I'd say, 'It looks like it's going to rain,' and she'd say, 'No, it doesn't.' And then, if it did rain, she'd give me a nasty look and say, 'I bet you're happy *now*, aren't you?'"

"Barry, she sounds awful."

"I stayed with her for as long as I did because I loved her. I know you're thinking, 'What's to love about her?', but that's not how love works. It's irrational. You don't decide to fall in love with someone, it just happens. And you certainly don't weigh up the pros and cons and think, 'All right, she'll do.' Love is a mugger."

"Love is a mugger?"

"Yeah. Well, that's how I've always thought of it. There you are, walking down the street, and *bam*! There's someone in front of you demanding that you either do what they say, or you're going to get hurt. That's the way love is. For me, anyway. It comes out of nowhere, stops you in your tracks, shakes you up pretty badly, and no matter how it turns out, the rest of your life is never going to be the same again."

"That's a very negative attitude," I said.

"I don't mean that being in love is bad, like getting mugged is bad. I mean that you can't see it coming, but once it arrives, you sure as hell know all about it. So with that in mind, have you ever been in love?"

"Yes, I have. But it wasn't like that at all. I was in love with Des. I didn't fall in love with him at first. It was gradual. I knew him for ages before I realised I was in love with him."

He raised his eyes. "God above! Analogies are totally wasted on you, aren't they?"

"Good ones aren't."

"I wasn't saying that the *person* you love comes out of the blue, just love itself. If you wake up with the sudden realisation that you're in love with the man you're with, that's love. But if you're going through the relationship thinking, 'Am I in love yet? No, not yet. I'm only about forty-three per cent of the way there,' well, that's not love. So with Des, did you get the sudden realisation, or did you one day just *decide* that you liked him enough to start calling it love?"

I didn't answer. Despite what I'd been telling Barry, I'd already come to the conclusion that what I'd felt for Des had been more comfort than love. It had been nice to have someone around I could talk to, someone who shared my life.

Someone to sit with in front of the fire on rainy winter evenings, someone who would be there for me when things were bad.

Someone I could always depend on.

The tears came then.

Barry dropped the tea cloth and came over to me. "Jesus, I'm sorry."

I pushed him away. "You *bastard*."

"Orla, I wasn't . . ."

I didn't let him finish. "Sod you, Barry Sheridan! I give you a place to live and you pay me back by ruining the last shreds of dignity I have left! You won't let me forget what Des did to me, and you want to ruin any chance I might have with Thomas Kennedy!" I opened the door and went out into the hall. "I want you out of here before I get home tonight!"

"No, wait . . .!"

But I was already running up the stairs to my room.

Chapter 21

Pauline went "Yay!" when I walked into the bistro. "You're back!" She was pulling three tables together.

"For tonight, anyway."

"Flanagan said he offered you the job full-time."

"I haven't decided whether to take it or not." I looked around. There was only one occupied table. "It's pretty quiet."

"So far. Are you okay? You look like you were crying or something."

"I sneezed when I was washing my hair and got shampoo in my eyes," I lied.

"Oh, I've done *that*!" Pauline said. She picked up the appointments book and ran her finger down the page. "Anyway, we've got a party of eight coming in at about eight-thirty, that's going to be tough, but apart from that it's just the usual twos and fours. As long as we don't get a whole bunch of spontaneous arrivals, it shouldn't be too bad."

I left her to it, and went into the kitchen, where Mr Flanagan was slicing vegetables. He looked up briefly when he saw me. "Orla. Thanks for coming in."

I took off my coat and hung it on the back of the door, and he glanced at me again. "New uniform?"

"My old one was stolen," I said.

"Oh. Of course."

"It's quiet out there at the moment. What do you need me to do?"

"The desserts." He passed me the day's menu. "The usual, plus there's this new blueberry pie we're trying out. It seems to be pretty popular."

"What's the special?"

"Honey-glazed venison, *avec crudités*."

"No vegetables with that?" I asked. It was a sort of running joke we'd had.

He smiled, his old man's face creasing up. "Not today."

I set about preparing the desserts. This involved taking them out of the fridge and slicing the pies and cheesecakes into as many slices as possible without making them look too small, taking the ice-cream out of the freezer – so that it would thaw a little and we wouldn't need to hack through it with a cleaver like we'd had to on a couple of occasions – and making the meringues. That was my favourite part of the job. It was everyone's favourite part, and the fact that Mr Flanagan had left it for me was a sure sign that he was feeling guilty.

Half an hour later, Pauline pushed her way through the swinging door. "We're up. Tables four and seven." She looked at me. "You can have table four, if you like."

Table four was the "good" table; secluded from the rest of the room, not in a draught, very cosy. We generally put regular customers there if we knew they were big tippers, or new customers if we were trying to impress them.

Table seven, on the other hand, was right next to the door. Customers waiting to be seated could see everything you were eating and listen to your conversations. Unless the place was full, we only put someone at table seven if we didn't like them.

I grabbed my notepad and pen, and walked out to table four. There was a young couple who were clearly very much in love, staring at the candlelight reflected in each other's eyes. Their menus were unopened on their side-plates.

"Good evening," I said. "Are you ready to order?"

"Oh," the man said, and opened his menu. "Um . . ."

"I'll give you a few minutes, if you like," I said.

The girl said, "I know what I'm having. Can I have the Chicken Fandango?"

I wrote this down. "Certainly. Would you like that with fries or a baked potato?"

"Fries, please."

The man said, "What's in the Oyster Cloister? Apart from oysters, I mean?"

It was right there on the menu in front of him, but I answered him anyway. "Diced fresh vegetables, seasoned with a light honey and mustard dressing."

"Any garlic in it?"

"Just a hint."

He looked disappointed. "Oh."

"I can ask Chef to do you one without garlic," I said. With the customers, we always referred to Mr Flanagan as "Chef".

"That would be great, thanks."

"Anything to start?"

They glanced at each other, a look that seemed to be asking, "Do you think we should?" and I knew then that they were on a budget. There would be no massive tip for me from *this* table. I wasn't bothered about that, because pleasant customers are almost worth the tips they don't give you.

"No starters, thanks," the girl said.

"Can I get you anything to drink?"

"Just a mineral water, thanks," the girl said.

"Same here."

"Certainly," I said. I took back the menus and returned to the kitchen. "Chicken Fandango and Oyster Cloister for table four," I said to Mr Flanagan as I was getting the drinks. "Chips with the chicken. Can you make the Oyster Cloister without garlic?"

"I can, but it's not great without the garlic."

"Well, that's the way the customer wants it."

"All right, then. Twelve minutes."

Pauline came in. "Table seven, steak and chips twice."

"I heard you the first time," said Mr Flanagan, who probably didn't realise that it had been years since anyone had laughed at that particular joke. "How do you want the steaks?"

"Both well-done," Pauline said.

"Okay, I'll do my best. Now how do you want them cooked?" Another old favourite.

It was like nothing had never happened: Mr Flanagan cooked and made lame jokes, Pauline and I ran in and out of the kitchen bearing trays.

There were the usual minor problems . . . One customer's credit card refused to swipe properly through the machine, which meant phoning the credit-card company and reading out the number. Another customer knocked a glass of red wine all over the table. Some of it dripped onto her white dress and she seemed to think that we should compensate her for her own clumsiness; she and her dining partner spent the rest of the evening trying to make the table wobble. We had a few last-minute bookings and cancellations, and a couple of late and early arrivals, but nothing serious.

Even the party of eight didn't give us that much trouble. Three of them arrived on time, saw that there was no one else there, and two of them left to find their friends, leaving one to sit on his own looking miserable and eating bread rolls. Then his other friends arrived and they all wondered what had happened to the two who had gone looking for them, so someone else was despatched to track them down.

At ten, Kalim the washing-up boy arrived for his nightly stint, and – as sometimes happens when we're busy – he was forced into a shirt and tie and made to wait on the tables. He didn't mind this at all, because he hated washing-up and looked on serving the customers as a chance to practice his English.

369

By midnight, when the bistro officially closed, I was exhausted. Pauline and I stood by the cash register, watching the party of eight enjoying themselves as we tried to send telepathic messages for them to leave. They didn't seem to want to budge.

Kalim came out of the kitchen pulling on his anorak, then stopped when he saw that they were still there. "Bloody damn!" he muttered. They were *still* nibbling at their desserts and slowly sipping their coffee.

It was then that I made my first management-level decision. I knew that Kalim had to get up early to go to college. "You go on," I told him. "We'll look after their dishes."

"We?" Pauline asked.

Kalim said goodnight and went on his way.

"You can go now too, if you want," I said to Pauline.

She looked at me and grinned. There was no way either of us was going to leave before the party of eight. Even if they only tipped the absolute minimum, it would be worth waiting for.

* * *

I didn't leave the bistro until nearly two in the morning; unlike at home, you can't abandon the washing-up and tidying until the next morning. Everything has to be spotless before you leave.

As he was locking up, Mr Flanagan said to me, "Listen, thanks for coming in."

I wasn't sure what to say, so I just nodded.

"And I'm sorry again about everything . . ." He started

trying to excuse – or at least explain – his behaviour, but I was too tired to listen.

"Can we talk about this some other time?" I asked. "If I don't get home soon I'll fall apart."

"Sure. Do you want a lift?"

"I'll be fine, thanks."

"Well, let me know what you think about coming in full-time."

I wasn't feeling too bad as I headed home. I had money in my pocket, food in my stomach – one of the advantages of working in a restaurant – and that contented feeling you get when you're worn out from good, honest work.

But as I got closer and closer to the house, the situation with Barry started to play on my mind.

Maybe I was too hard on him, I said to myself. He wasn't being mean. In his own strange way, he was just trying to help.

He would have arrived home from work at about ten, maybe eleven. That wasn't enough time for him to pack up his stuff and find somewhere else to live, and I was a little relieved about that. In the morning I'd tell him that he could stay, but there would be conditions: from now on, we weren't friends any more. We had a business relationship, and that was all. There would be no more late-night conversations about our personal lives. He wouldn't be allowed to mention Des or Thomas ever again.

A wave of sadness hit me then; another friend gone. Sooner or later, they all leave. Either you just lose interest in each other, as had happened with most of my friends, or they get married and sort of leave you behind, like

Justin did, or they move away, like Davina, or get married and *then* move like Claire and Killian did. Or they die, like my parents.

Or, like Des, they get you to trust them and then they stab you in the back and tear your life apart.

Maybe it's me, I said to myself. It can't be like this for everyone. Maybe *I'm* the one who has the problem. Am I such a bad friend that no one wants to stick around?

When I turned the last corner I was relieved to see that Barry's car was still outside the house. Okay, I said to myself. If he's still up, I'll lay down the rules.

But as I passed the car, I heard a familiar rumbling sound and turned to look: Barry was asleep in the driver's seat, huddled under a blanket, snoring so loud that it almost sounded like the engine was running.

There and then, my heart melted.

I rapped my knuckles against the window. Barry sat up, startled, and looked around wildly, then he saw me and rolled down the window. "Hi. Sorry, I didn't have time to find somewhere else to stay. I hope you don't mind, but I left my stuff in the room. I got home too late to start packing."

"This is crazy," I said. "You can't spend the night in the car. Come on in."

"Just for the night, then. I'll find somewhere in the morning."

"We can talk about that then," I said.

He got out of the car, locked it up, and followed me up the driveway. When I opened the front door I saw that he'd pushed his key through the letterbox. Without saying anything, I picked it up and handed it back to him. As I was doing so, I touched his hand. "You're freezing," I said. "Do you want a cup of tea or coffee?"

"That'd be great, thanks."

I went into the kitchen . . .

And stopped. There was a large, colourfully wrapped box on the kitchen table. "What's this?"

"Just, you know, a sort of farewell present. It's nothing great, but it should come in handy."

I unwrapped the box. It was a combined telephone handset and answering machine.

"It'll save you having to use your mobile all the time," Barry explained. "Sorry, I couldn't find anything nicer on short notice."

"Thank you. It's . . . very thoughtful of you."

* * *

We sat sipping our tea and not watching each other across the kitchen table.

"So how did it go tonight? Busy?"

I nodded.

"Are you going to go back full-time, then?"

"Maybe. I haven't fully made up my mind yet."

Another stretch of silence.

"I'm really sorry about this morning," Barry said. "I just . . . well, I didn't mean to make things harder for you."

"Barry, I don't think we should talk about it. In fact, I don't think we should *ever* talk about things like that again. If you want to live here, then from now on we're going to keep our personal lives separate. We keep out of each other's way, you don't criticise me or Des or Thomas, or any of my friends, and we'll be fine."

"All right. I understand. And I'm sorry. I think what it was is that you're pretty much the only person I've really connected with since Jemima. I mean, most of my friends think I was wrong to leave her. Half my family won't talk to me, and none of *her* family will. In fact, sometimes it seems like the only one who thinks I did the right thing is Jemima herself."

I didn't want to get drawn into this conversation, but I couldn't help myself. "When was the last time you talked to her?"

"This afternoon. I . . . well, to be honest, I wanted her advice about the situation here."

"You're telling me that you asked your ex-wife what you were going to do about *me*? Jesus!"

"It's not like that. She's always been able to get along with people – except me, of course – and I didn't have anyone else to ask."

"So what did she tell you?"

"She said I was being a complete bloody idiot. She was right. She told me that my problem is that I have all these theories on how everyone else should live their lives, but if I was as good at that as I thought I was, I wouldn't be in such a mess myself right now. She was right about that, too. You ever get those dreams where there's something chasing you, but you can't run fast enough to get away from it? It's like you're moving at not much more than a walking pace, and you *know* you can run faster, but it's just not happening? Well, that's what my life is like. I know I should be able to do so much better, but I just can't seem to manage it."

"You're always falling short of your own expectations."

"Exactly! To misquote Oscar Wilde: some of us may be looking at the stars, but let's not forget we're still in the gutter. But you have to have your dreams . . . without them, what are you?"

"Happy," I said. "Look, I had a similar conversation with Thomas last week." Mentally, I was kicking myself for bringing up Thomas after I'd promised myself that I wouldn't involve Barry in my personal life any more. "If you go through life always wanting more, then you're never going to be happy with the things you *do* have."

"And if you have nothing?"

"But you *don't* have nothing, Barry. Look at me. I lost my job, my money, my boyfriend, the contents of my house *and* my self-respect, all in the space of a couple of days. Shit happens. That's one of the rules of life. Shit happens, and you deal with it. You don't let it roll over you. You don't pretend it's not there. You deal with it as well as you can, because sooner or later things will get better."

He looked at me for a while, then said, "I'm not sure which of us you're trying to convince."

"Both of us, probably." I finished my tea, and stood up. "All right. I'm going to bed. You don't have to move out, but remember what I said about keeping our personal lives to ourselves. You go your way and I'll go mine."

* * *

The next morning, Friday, I was woken by the smell of a cooked breakfast.

It was Barry's day off, so I'd expected him to sleep in. But no, there he was in the kitchen, grilling sausages and frying eggs.

"Morning," he said. "Hungry?"

"Starving. But I'll get my own breakfast, thanks." I didn't want him to forget that the nature of our relationship had changed.

"Don't be daft. Sit down and relax. It'll only be a couple of minutes."

So I sat.

"Sleep okay?" he asked.

"Sure. You?"

He nodded. "Definitely." He slid out the grill, gave all the sausages a quarter-turn, slid it back, then picked up the spatula and flipped the eggs.

As we ate, Barry told me about work the previous day. Nothing exciting had happened, but it was his way of filling the silence. Then he asked me about work. "Have you decided yet whether you're going to go back?"

"I think I will," I said, "but not full-time. At least, not until after the last of the evening classes. And I don't want to have to work every weekend like I used to."

"That's probably the best thing," he said.

I agreed that it was.

* * *

Barry and I kept out of each other's way for the rest of the day. There was a potential minor problem at about six, when he was getting ready for his date, and I was getting ready to meet Thomas; we both headed towards the bathroom at the same time.

He stepped aside. "After you," he said. "I'm not in a hurry."

An hour later, Barry and Thomas finally met when Barry answered the door. I was in my room, admiring myself in the outfit I'd bought that afternoon – a loose black satin top and a long, fairly tight black skirt – when the doorbell rang.

"Oh, hi," I heard Thomas say. "You must be Barry, right?"

"Yeah. Thomas, isn't it?"

I called out, "I'll be down in a minute!" then rushed about making the last-minute adjustments.

When I got down to the sitting-room, Thomas and Barry were sitting as far away from each other as possible, and I got the impression that neither of them had spoken since their introduction.

"Hi," I said to Thomas, who was getting to his feet.

"You look amazing," he said.

"Thanks."

"Stunning, even." Then he went, "Oh!" and jumped. He reached into his jacket pocket and pulled out his mobile phone. "Sorry, forgot to turn it off. Do you mind if I take this? It's my mother."

"No, go ahead."

Thomas went out into the hall to answer the phone.

Barry looked at me. "He's right, you know. You look incredible."

I wasn't sure how to take that; knowing him, that could be the opening of an argument. "Thanks."

"He seems okay."

"I'm glad you think so."

"Good-looking fella, all right."

"Barry . . ."

He put his hands up. "Sorry, sorry! I forgot! I won't say another word."

"What time are you meeting Jennifer?"

Barry jumped up. "Shite! I nearly forgot!" He moved towards the door, then stopped. "He's still in the hall. Is it rude for me to rush past him and go upstairs?"

I wasn't sure about that. "*I* don't know."

He dithered for a few seconds, his hand hovering near the doorknob. He was facing me, about to say something, when the door opened and smacked him in the back of the head. Hard.

"Oh, I'm sorry," said Thomas.

"God, that really hurts!" Barry turned his back to me, gingerly parted his hair with his fingers. "Is there a lump?"

"No, it looks fine," I said.

"No blood?"

"It's not cut, Barry. You'll live."

"Sorry about that," Thomas said.

"Forget it. It was my own fault," said Barry. "Anyway, I'd better get moving. Enjoy yourselves tonight," he added as he went out into the hall.

* * *

"So how's your mother?" I asked Thomas as we drove.

"She's fine. She was asking about you, actually. She wants to know when she's going to get to meet you."

"You've told her about me already?"

378

He nodded.

"But we've only been going out for a week."

Thomas smiled. "She's spent her whole life wondering when I'm going to get married, or at least settle down, so she takes a great interest in my social life. To be honest, I think she's afraid I'll turn out like my cousin."

"How do you mean?"

"He's six years older than me, and he's a confirmed bachelor. Every time we meet him he's with a different girl. I don't think he's had one relationship that's lasted longer than a month. And just between the two of us, he's usually got more than one relationship happening at the same time." He shook his head. "I don't know how he finds the time."

I knew from our previous dates that Thomas had had three long-term girlfriends, and in each case the break-up had been amicable. I wondered if he ever fought with *anyone*.

"Sarah was very impressed when I told her about your approach to life," Thomas said.

"Sarah?"

"My mother."

"You call your mother by her first name? I always think that's really strange. Do you do the same with your father?"

"No, he's always just 'Dad'. When I was younger I started to call him by his first name, but it didn't really stick."

"What *is* his name?"

"Thomas."

"Ah . . . that must have made things awkward when you were living at home."

"A little. But it's a tradition in our family. The first-born son is always called Thomas. If I ever had a son, he'll be called Thomas too."

The way he said that made me think of a movie sequel: *Thomas 2 – The Revenge*. "But what if your wife has her own family tradition, and wants her son called something else?"

He shrugged. "I'll worry about that when – if – it happens."

"So you do see yourself settling down one day?"

"Oh, definitely. I'm as far removed from the bachelor type as you can be. My cousin is addicted to the whole dating scene, but – and please don't take this the wrong way – I hate it. I mean, it's great now, at this stage; you and I know each other, but when I'm just getting to know someone it can be absolutely terrifying."

"You weren't terrified on our first date, were you?"

"A little, yes. I'm always afraid of saying the wrong thing. I imagine that's what Barry's going through right now. You were saying that is his first date since he left his wife, right?"

"Yeah. But I can't see *him* being afraid of saying the wrong thing. He'll just say it anyway."

"Sometimes I think it would be great to have more self-confidence."

"It isn't self-confidence that Barry has; it's just bloody ignorance."

"So you're still not talking to him?" The previous

afternoon – after Barry had gone to work – Thomas had made his daily phone call, and I'd told him the whole story.

"I'm trying not to, but he seems to have a way of drawing me into his conversations. I'm half-convinced that the man's insane. It's no wonder his wife fought with him all the time."

"He doesn't seem too bad to me."

"Oh, he's all right, I suppose."

"He has quite hairy hands . . ." Thomas took one of his own hands off the steering wheel and looked at it. "When I was younger I always wanted to have hairy hands."

I made a face. "Why?"

"Because then girls would know I was a real man, and not a sort of pre-pubescent wimp."

That was the first time I'd ever heard him speak about himself in that way. "Oh. But you're not a wimp."

"Something I learned quite early on is that if a man is polite, has manners and doesn't swear, he's automatically categorised as either gay or a wimp. Or both, I suppose, because some people can't tell the difference. I've been called everything from a mammy's boy to a flaming queen, all because I'm polite." He glanced at me, then back to the road. "That's something else I learned when I was a teenager. If I showed other teenagers respect, they wouldn't respect me in return. You have to treat them with contempt to earn their respect, because they equate arrogance with strength, and consideration with weakness. Unfortunately, that's true for a lot of adults as well."

"I see what you mean. You rarely get a bunch of young men in a pub boasting about how good they are at abstaining from drink, or how they're able to drive below the speed limit."

"Exactly."

"How about your friends, though? How do they see you?"

"My closest friends see me as I am – like you do – but there are a few on the periphery who I'm sure think that I'm some sort of glitch. I don't fit into their view of the world. 'He's a good-looking man who's not married and speaks politely and dresses well and is respectful of others . . . how could he *not* be gay?' Even some of my gay friends are convinced that I'm just fooling myself." He laughed. "A few years ago a couple of friends who had always assumed I *was* gay saw me out with a really gorgeous girl, and they 'outed' me!"

"So did you have much trouble when you were a kid?"

"Not as much as you might think. I was slagged mercilessly, which probably explains why anyone can say anything they like about me now and it doesn't bother me, and I was bullied a few times. I found that the best way to avoid a beating is to just agree with the bully. It doesn't always work, of course, but most of the time it does. If you stand your ground against a bully, you're just giving them exactly the excuse they need to beat you up. I find that most difficult situations like that will just sort themselves out. Actually, that's one of the things that attracted me to you. At the hotel, when that guy confronted you and you just kneed him where it hurts, I said to myself, 'Now, *she's* got fire!' That is, I thought this after my *own* eyes had stopped watering in sympathy. But the point is, you didn't back down or hide behind someone else. Your friend Justin stepped in, of course, but you didn't ask him to, and you still dealt with that guy after he'd knocked Justin over."

"Well, he had it coming," I said. "Though someone told me afterwards that he probably wouldn't have hurt me."

"Regardless – he threatened you, and you stood up to him. I'm sure that he'll think again before he threatens anyone else."

"I hope so."

"So where would you like to go tonight?" he asked.

"I don't mind."

"How hungry are you?"

"Not *too* hungry. I can wait a couple of hours before eating."

"Okay . . . How about we just drive, and see where the road takes us?"

"That sounds nice," I said, then cursed myself for using the word "nice." Ever since that conversation with Barry the word had taken on a whole new meaning. Now, it meant: "I don't care either way but I'm too polite to say otherwise."

But the thing is, it *did* sound nice. Not exciting, no. But pleasant. Life doesn't have to be dramatic and dynamic all the time. Sometimes, you need to take things really easy and just do something, well, nice.

I resolved not to allow Barry's definition of the word replace the real meaning.

After all, Thomas was nice, but that didn't mean that I wanted to be just friends with him.

* * *

Jaye Carroll

Because of work, I didn't meet up with Thomas until the following Monday evening. We went to the cinema to see Hugh Grant and Amanda Jayne Garfield dithering about in a romantic comedy.

"What did you think?" Thomas asked as we were on the way out.

"I liked it," I said. "It wasn't exactly *Citizen Kane*, but it was fun."

"You know, I met him once," Thomas said.

"You met Hugh Grant?"

"No, I met Orson Welles. I was only a kid at the time, and had no idea who he was, but my dad was *incredibly* excited. We were in Los Angeles, and there was some sort of function, I can't remember exactly what it was for. This enormous man with a grey beard and deep, deep eyes was at the next table. My dad grabbed my mother and said, 'Oh my God! That's Orson Welles!' And next thing I knew he was dragging us over to say hello."

"So what was he like?"

"Big, that's all I can really remember. Over the years I've seen all of his films, so now my memory is tainted by that."

"Did you get his autograph?"

Thomas shook his head. "No, Dad was too embarrassed to ask him. But he talked to us for a few minutes. He made a joke about how he was going to make a sequel to *The Third Man* called *The Fourth Man*. I remember Dad laughing like it was the best joke he'd ever heard."

Someone behind us shouted, "Hey, Orla!" and we turned to see Barry and a fairly attractive girl leaving the cinema. "Didn't know you were coming here," Barry said. "Which one did you see? No, don't tell me – the Hugh Grant flick, yeah?"

I nodded. "How about you?"

The girl said, "We've just spent an hour and a half watching Jackie Chan beating up bad guys with different bits of furniture."

"This is Jennifer," Barry said. "Jen, this is Orla, my landlady, and Thomas."

After the handshaking was done, we stood there looking at each other for a few awkward seconds.

"So why don't we all go somewhere for a coffee?" Barry asked.

Before I could jump in with a good reason why we couldn't do that, Thomas said, "Good idea."

* * *

Half an hour later we were in an ultra-trendy Sixties-themed café called The Psychedelicatessen. The walls were plastered with posters of Jimi Hendrix, Barbarella and Bob Dylan, with peace symbols and the word "love" with a heart instead of the "o" in the gaps between the posters, and the staff – the poor bastards – were dressed as what could only be described as "pantomime hippies": long or afro wigs, headbands, flowers painted on their cheeks, tie-dyed T-shirts, flared jeans with patches on the knees. They looked miserable.

Barry and Thomas took our orders then joined the line of people waiting at a sign that said, *"Q here, man!"* while Jennifer and I found a table. As it was pretty late and the place was full, the only available table that seated four was covered with the debris left behind by previous diners.

As Jennifer and I cleared off the table, I wondered what I was going to talk to her about. She was pretty. Not exactly stunning, but pretty. Tall, slim, bottle-green eyes and, I suspected, bottle-red hair. I used a tissue to sweep the last of the spilled sugar onto the floor, and we sat down.

"So, what's it like going out with someone you work with?"

"No one else knows yet," she said. "It's not that we're keeping it a secret, though. We just haven't told them."

"I see what you mean," I said, wondering if there really was a difference. "Still, you're going to be in for some slagging."

"Probably. But, well, who cares? So tell me – any news about Des yet?"

"God, don't tell me *you* lost money to him as well?"

"Me? No. But I know a fair few people who have. You have to admire him in a way – there's not many people who can screw up a whole town."

"That's true. Barry said that no matter what Des does now – he could rescue a whole orphanage full of kids from a fire, or save the world from aliens, or anything – he's always going to be remembered for this."

Then Jennifer said, "Oh, I forgot. Barry said we're not allowed to talk about Des to you."

I shrugged in a sort of "it's not that big a deal" gesture. "I don't know what else he said about it, but me and Barry had a kind of fight. I overreacted a bit."

"Well, if it's any help, I think I know what you mean. The first time I met him I *hated* him. I thought he was being a right bastard."

"So is he a good assistant manager, then?"

She thought about this. "I suppose he is, because we don't notice. Things are running pretty smoothly now. If he was bad at his job, we'd know all about it soon enough." She looked at me for a few seconds, clearly with something on her mind. "Listen . . . Barry won't bring this up, so I think *I* should. How can I put it . . .? Would you have a problem with him bringing me back to your house? It's just that I share a flat with two others and there's no room for privacy."

"Oh. Well, no, not at all. I don't have a problem with that."

Jennifer looked relieved. "Oh, that's great! We were starting to wonder whether we might have to book into a hotel or something!"

I said to myself, "They've only been going out for a few days!"

"How about tonight, then?" she asked. "That would be okay, right?"

I said, "Jennifer, you don't need my permission! Barry's free to do what he wants. I'm surprised he even thought he needed to ask me."

Thomas and Barry arrived then, each carrying a tray containing two cups of coffee and an assortment of heart-attack-inducing cream buns. I got the impression that they'd tried to out-do each other in some bizarre cake-buying macho ritual.

The conversation was pretty light, the four of us talking about the movies we'd just been to see. At one point when Thomas was talking I caught Barry and Jennifer exchanging a glance; he gave her a quizzical look, and she nodded slightly and smiled.

So *that's* it, I said to myself, he asked her to ask me if I had any problems with her staying over.

Suddenly I was seeing Barry in a different light. Before, he was a man who elbowed his way through life, did more or less whatever he wanted, and seemed to have a "take me as you find me" philosophy. He didn't care what people thought or said about him; he spoke his mind and worried about the consequences later.

I always knew that wasn't an totally accurate impression of him, because he had on several occasions shown signs of greater understanding and compassion, but on the whole it had always seemed to me that Barry's approach to life was that if you couldn't take him as he was, then you weren't worth him bothering about.

But now, it seemed that he was tip-toeing around me, like he was thinking, "This is the one person I *really* don't want to piss off."

I realised then why that was. It wasn't because he was living in my house and if he upset me too much I'd ask him to move out.

I also realised that deep down I already knew, I just hadn't admitted it to myself. His jealousy of Thomas was one of the more obvious clues. Barry wasn't jealous because Thomas was good-looking, rich and successful. He was jealous because Thomas had me, and he didn't.

Maybe he was even thinking, "I helped Orla out when things were at their worst. I moved into her place even though it would have been almost cheaper to stay in the local bed and breakfast, where they *did* have a cooker and carpets and doors on the rooms. I brought her out to dinner and kept her company and sympathised and sorted out tricky problems and she *still* ended up falling for someone else."

I didn't know how I was going to deal with this.

Chapter 22

I dealt with it the simple way. The way Thomas would have done. I ignored it and hoped it would go away.

Without being too blatant, I let Barry know that I wasn't interested in him. I made jokes about him being my surrogate brother, about how much like Killian he was at times. I let him know that I thought he and Jennifer were a good match, and I made it clear that I felt the same about me and Thomas.

Over the next few weeks, my relationship with Barry changed a little. At least, that was how it seemed to me. Certainly, he spent less time telling me how I should be living my life. He stopped criticising Thomas, though I was sure that they didn't like each other much.

I started to wonder whether I'd been wrong. Perhaps Barry didn't have feelings for me after all; maybe that was something I'd just projected onto him. He and Jennifer were a couple for about two months, and then – seemingly out of the blue – they broke up.

He didn't tell me the details, just that they "weren't working out," but a few days afterwards I bumped into Jennifer in town.

"He's in love with someone else," she told me, a little sadly.

"Oh. Did he say who?" To myself, I was saying, 'Don't panic! Whatever she says, don't panic!'

"He didn't say anything about it at all, but I could tell."

"That's a shame," I said. "I thought the two of you were good together."

She shrugged. "Yeah, Well, that's how it goes sometimes. How's Thomas?"

"He's fine. You know him. Nothing ever gets him down. So did Barry say anything at all about why he broke it off with you?"

Jennifer said, "I broke it off with him. I just told him that I could see his mind was always with someone else. Like I said, he wouldn't say anything about it. But if you want my opinion? I think he's still pining for his wife. They still meet up every couple of weeks, and they nearly always end up having a row, but I always had the feeling that if he could sort it out with her, he'd drop me like a sack of hot potatoes."

* * *

Barry moped around the house for ages. I did feel sorry for him, but in a way I was relieved; I was getting fed up with listening to them making giggles and bed-squeaks all night every night.

On the other hand, Thomas and I were going from

strength to strength. I met his parents – they were really posh but dead nice – and three months after we started going out, we drove to Tipperary to spend a weekend with Killian and Claire and the kids.

Thomas and Killian got on like they'd been friends their whole lives, and the kids thought that he was great fun. Especially Sean, because Thomas let him climb all over him.

On the Sunday afternoon, Killian took Thomas down to the pub to watch some match or other, and Claire and I brought Sean and Niamh to the playground in the local park. As we watched the kids arguing over who'd had more goes on the swing, Claire and I sat on the only bench that wasn't covered in bird-droppings.

It was the first time we'd been alone together since Des had pulled his diabolical trick.

"Right," she said to me, wearing her "getting down to business" face. "What's the story?"

"Which story?"

"You and Thomas."

"How do you mean?"

"Are you in love with him?"

"I'm getting there," I said. "He's been really good to me."

"Jesus, Orla!"

I stared at her. "What?"

"You really like the guy that much? Seriously?"

"Of course I like him! What's not to like?"

"Orla, he's . . ." She shrugged. "I don't know how to say it."

I sighed. "Go ahead. I can take it."

"No, I don't mean I'm afraid to say it. I mean I don't know how to describe him."

"You don't like him?"

"It's not that I don't like him, but he's . . . I don't know. He doesn't seem real, I suppose. He's *too* nice."

"Too nice. Yeah, sure."

"I mean it," Claire said. "On Friday night when we were all sitting around talking, I was watching you watching him. Haven't you noticed that you always know what he's going to say?"

"What's that got to do with anything?"

Claire suddenly sat up straight and stared at me. "I've got it! You know what it is that he reminds me of? An understudy in a play. It's like the real star is off sick and the understudy has to take over. Or, no, that's not quite it . . ." She made a frowny face as she mulled over the problem.

"You think he's just a substitute for Des?"

"Not for Des specifically. He's . . ." She gave me a triumphant grin. "He's a stand-in! You know how they do it in movies? They get a guy who looks like the star to go through the motions when they're setting up the cameras and lights and all that. Meanwhile the real star is relaxing in his trailer. That's Thomas. Like he's just keeping the 'boyfriend seat' warm until someone better comes along!"

"Thanks," I said. "Yeah, that's exactly the sort of thing I need to hear. Ten out of ten for making me feel good about myself."

"What's he like in bed?"

"For God's sake, Claire! I'm not going to tell you that!"

"Hah! Back in the old days we used to talk about that sort of thing all the time! Well, I bet you anything you like he's strictly missionary. He probably has everything

timed; twenty-five minutes on foreplay, that kind of thing.
I bet he always has on fresh underwear and everything."
She looked as though she was disappointed with me.
"You don't need a bloody robot in your life, Orla. You
need someone real. And you know something else? I
think *he* knows that too. I think he's just waiting for you
to realise that he's not the right one."

"Well, screw you!" I said, a bit too loud; the kids stopped
fighting and stared at us. I lowered my voice. "Oh, sorry."

"They've heard worse. Look, I'm not being mean to
you just for the sake of being mean. But, well, people are
worried about you. Some of us just don't think that Thomas
is the right guy."

"How do you mean, 'some of us'? Who's been talking
about me behind my back?"

She hesitated before answering. "A couple of weeks
ago we got a call from someone who I won't name, but
he's really concerned that you're settling for Thomas because
he's the safe option. He thinks that you're doing your best to
convince yourself that you're in love with him. I think that
too."

"Right. Well, that *does* it! As soon I get home, I'm
telling him to move out. I mean it this time! I've warned
him before about interfering with my personal life."

"It wasn't Barry, Orla. Sure why would he ring us? He
doesn't even know us. But this person does know us and
he said that he thinks you're making a really big mistake,
but he doesn't know how to tell you. He's tried to bring it
up a few times, but you're just not listening."

Whoever had told Claire this obviously wanted it to
get back to me, because if he knew her well enough to tell

her something like that, he certainly knew her well enough to know that she'd never been any good at keeping secrets. "It was Justin, wasn't it?"

Then she caught me out. "Oh yeah, him too. He was down this way about a month ago, dropped in for a chat, and he said more or less the same thing. Him and Mags are really concerned about you. But he wasn't the one I was talking about."

"Then who was it? If it wasn't Barry and it wasn't Justin, who was it?"

"Your next-door-neighbour. Mr Farley."

My jaw dropped open, but I couldn't think of anything to say.

"He said he's seen you a couple of times, and you don't look yourself any more. He said that it looks like you've given up, and just settled for Thomas because you know he'll never hurt you. And Justin said that it's like you're constantly telling yourself how lucky you are to have him, and that's not a good enough reason to stay with someone."

To myself, I said, "Well, Justin's not really in a position to give advice about relationships. If he was such an expert on love, then his wife wouldn't be having an affair."

For one mad second, I even considered saying this to Claire. She'd definitely let it slip and it wouldn't be long before it got back to Justin. That would show him.

But I couldn't do that; we didn't see each other very often these days, but Justin was still my closest friend. I knew I could never hurt him like that, no matter what he thought or said about me.

So I said nothing about Mags' affair with Peter Harney.

There are some secrets you should never tell, and there are some you should never keep. The hard part is knowing which is which.

Some people – like Claire – are terrible at keeping secrets, while others – like Des – are experts at it. Des had managed to keep his plans secret from me and everyone else for a long time. And as we all later discovered, Des also knew all about Mags and Peter Harney.

But if I *had* let it slip to Claire about Mags and Peter, and it had somehow got back to Justin . . . well, things might have turned out differently.

* * *

On the drive back to Dublin from Tipperary, I pretended to be asleep, so that I could go over everything in my head.

The previous night, Killian had taken me aside and said, "Listen . . . he's nice guy, but he's not the *right* guy."

"What would *you* know about it?"

"Don't start with me, Orla! You know your track record isn't exactly spotless, is it? Now, I'm just going to say this once, and I'll never bring it up again, but, well, you can do better than him."

"Killian, aren't big brothers supposed to look after their little sisters? Aren't you supposed to support me? What happened to you that you somehow think your job is to keep picking apart my life and telling me what's wrong with it?"

"My job as your big brother is *not* to support you; it's to protect you. I was right about Des, and I'm right about Thomas. Oh, he won't hurt you like Des did, that's just not in him. But he won't love you like Des did either. Because I think he did love you, you know, despite everything he did. *We* all do too. Me, and Claire, and the kids. We love you and we don't want you to just give up."

"But you don't love me enough to allow me to live my own life as I see fit."

"If you had thought it wouldn't work out between me and Claire, would you have said something?"

"Probably." I didn't tell him that in such a case I'd probably have told Claire first. After all, he was only my brother, but she was my friend.

"But you don't think I should do the same for you?"

"No, because you're wrong. Thomas is a rock, and that's what I need. I've had enough upheavals to last me a lifetime. Look, you know me. I don't want much out of life. I've never been greedy or ambitious. All I want is someone to love, and who'll love me back. Someone who will always be there for me."

Then Killian reached out and cupped my face in his hands, very gently. "Orla ... Mam and Dad are gone. They're not coming back."

"What's that got to do with anything?"

"You're still living in their house. God, I know you better than anyone else does, and I know that sometimes you walk into the house and you half expect to see them there."

"You think that I'm living in the past, don't you? You think that I'm only with Thomas because he's some sort of surrogate parent. That's just crap, Killian!"

"No, it's not. Look, I miss them too. I always will. How do you think I feel when Niamh and Sean talk about their grandparents and I know that they only mean Claire's parents? I'd give anything for them to know *our* parents too. Mam and Dad would have adored them. But the fact is that you're not allowing yourself to let go."

And then the thought struck me that what was really bothering Killian was that *he* was the one who hadn't come to terms with our parents' death; he'd moved away and left the past behind, but I'd stayed and dealt with it. He was the one who needed comforting, not me.

I put my hands on his, and said, "Killian, I understand what you're saying, I really do. But you have to trust me to make my own choices. I'm not a kid any more."

"No, I suppose you're not. Just . . . be careful. I don't want you to get hurt again."

* * *

So I sat there in the car, head back and eyes closed, as Thomas made the long drive home.

They were wrong. They were all wrong about him. Barry, Killian, Justin, even Mr Farley, all wrong.

If I was to apply Barry's theory about the nature of love, then I wasn't in love with Thomas. I liked him, but I didn't love him.

But then, Barry's theory was just that: a theory. Not all theories are accurate.

Love doesn't have to come as a sudden, blinding realisation. Love can come gradually. Friendship is the seed of love; it may not always immediately blossom into an overwhelmingly gorgeous flower, but that doesn't mean that one day it won't.

In the case of me and Thomas, the flower was growing

steadily and strongly, and soon – I was certain – it would begin to bud.

Which was a really cheesy metaphor, but it seemed to fit quite well.

* * *

The next time I saw Justin, I told him that I appreciated that he was looking out for me, but I felt that I should be allowed to choose my own path through life. I didn't need all my friends ganging up on me and telling me to dump the man I was going out with.

It was a Friday morning. He'd called over to the house because Mags was at work and he was bored at home on his own.

"Don't get me wrong. I like him well enough," Justin said. "I just think you're fooling yourself into thinking that he's Mr Right, when he's really just Mr Safe."

"I wonder if there's *anyone* I know who thinks I'm capable of making my own decisions. The only person I know who hasn't tried to give me advice in the past few months is Pauline, and that's because *she* knows I'm not a complete idiot."

"No one thinks you're an idiot," Justin said. "But look at it like this; we were all fooled by Des, and he really hurt you. We don't want that to happen again."

"Neither do I," I said. "But even though you're all sure that Thomas will never hurt me, you still seem to think that he's a bad choice."

"It's not that he's a bad choice, he's just the *wrong* choice. Let's just say, for the moment, that Thomas calls over tonight and he says, 'Orla, I'm sorry, but it's not working out.'"

"He wouldn't do that."

"Let's just say he does. How do you react?"

"I can't react to that, because it's not going to happen."

Justin looked at me for a long time, and I could see that he wasn't convinced.

"I'm telling you, it'll never happen. Thomas wouldn't break up with me."

"How do you know?"

"He just wouldn't."

I pushed a nasty thought to the back of my mind. I was vaguely aware that I'd been keeping the same nasty thought under wraps for a long time now.

It wasn't a big thing. It wasn't important at all.

I could certainly see myself spending the rest of my life without this particular nasty thought ever making another appearance. Okay, so there was a chance that it would sit there eating away at my confidence over the years, but I wasn't willing to face up to it. Deep down, I knew that I *should* let the nasty thought out and really pay attention to it, but I didn't. I was weak.

After all, nobody's perfect.

Not even Thomas.

* * *

Christmas approached, and the people of the town were overjoyed to be able to say, "God, another one! They seem to be coming round faster and faster!" Then Christmas jingled its way past, and the people of the town were even more overjoyed to be able to say, "There's a grand stretch in the evenings."

I decided not to run any more evening classes; as it

was, I was spending so much time in the bistro that I barely had any time to see Thomas. Mrs Darcy, the principal of the secondary school, had told me that she completely understood, that I'd be missed, and that I still owed her for all the art supplies the classes had used. I didn't know whether to be annoyed or pleased that she hadn't mentioned it back when times were tough.

Barry moved out of my house in the middle of March. "I just need a place of my own," he said to me. "Sorry."

"No, I understand."

"And I know that sometimes it's awkward for you and Thomas when I'm there. And you don't really need the rent money these days."

That was true. Not only was I now working an average of five nights a week, but the bank had finally caved – after six and a half months of solicitor's letters and phone calls – and had paid me back every cent they'd allowed Des to steal, plus the interest I would have earned had the money remained in their highest-yielding account.

They hadn't, as I'd hoped, awarded me millions of euros in compensation, but my solicitor was still on the case, still holding out for more. I was sure that was mainly because we'd agreed that the only money she'd get would be thirty per cent of any compensation I received.

"Still friends, right?" Barry asked.

"Sure."

He paused. "So . . . I'll pack up my stuff this afternoon and I'll be gone before you get home."

"Okay."

"So you're not my landlady any more."

I nodded. "This is true."

"Good. That means that the rules no longer apply."

"The rules?" To myself, I said, uh oh, I know where *this* is going. Might as well let him have his say, and tell me how wrong I am to be going out with Thomas. "No, as of now, the rules are gone."

He grinned. "At last! Great! God, where do I even begin? Okay . . . First, I want to thank you for putting up with me all these months. I know it hasn't been easy for you, especially not after that big fight we had."

"Well, okay . . ."

"And you know something? It hasn't been easy for me, either. We were getting to be really good friends, or at least I thought we were, and then I made one mistake and you shut me out." His grin faded. "That hurt. That *really* hurt. It was a lousy thing to do to someone."

"You hurt *me*, Barry. You can't blame me for reacting like that."

"No, I didn't hurt you."

"Yes, you did! You said some really horrible things about me!"

"No, I *didn't*! Look, I've got a good memory for these things: all I did was ask you *how* you knew you'd been in love with Des. I don't know what was going through your head after that, but you treated me like I was the one who hurt you, not Des. And you know something? Remember when it all happened and everyone was blaming you for what Des did to them, because you were the only one they could blame? Well, that's *exactly* what you were doing to me."

"You're wrong about that. I was upset with you because you were saying things to me that you had no right to say."

"Since when is there a limit on what friends can say to each other?"

"But we weren't friends, Barry! We barely knew each other then! You just *thought* that we were closer than we really were, because you were in love with me!"

Barry's face fell. "Come again?"

"You heard me!"

He frowned. "Orla . . . whatever made you think I was in love with you?"

"But you were . . ." I trailed off.

"No, I wasn't. Jesus, is that what all this has been about? You think I fell in love with you in just a couple of days? For God's sake, I'm wasn't *that* starved for affection! Look, I know that for the first few weeks I latched on to you, but that was because I'd just moved here – I didn't know anyone else. I'm not in love with you, Orla. Sorry if that destroys your illusions, but it's the truth. You were a friend, that's all. I was *never* in love with you."

Now, *that* was embarrassing.

* * *

Awkward as that situation was, I got over it fairly quickly.

Pauline helped me get past it, late one night as we were closing up the restaurant. "Look," she said, "maybe it was just you. Maybe you'd been hurt so much by Des that you subconsciously needed some sort of proof that you weren't unlovable."

"You could be right."

"And Barry didn't seem to be too bothered by it?"

"No, not really. He thought it was kind of funny, though."

"Then let it go. There's no point in worrying about something like that. I'm sure everyone's done it from time to time. I know *I* have." She went on to relate a similar story about a guy she knew years before, and how he'd become convinced she'd had feelings for him.

After that, I didn't feel so bad. Maybe it was because after Des I'd developed a much thicker skin. Or maybe it was because Barry wasn't around any more so I wasn't reminded of it every day. But mostly, I think, it was because I was spending so much time with Thomas.

We talked at least once every day, and met each other three or four times a week.

But now and then I still had dreams about Des, and they were a little unsettling, mainly because in the dreams Des and I were often still together and nothing bad had happened. Sometimes the dreams were of specific events that really happened – going out to a movie, or for a meal, that kind of thing – but on a couple of occasions I dreamed that Des had come back and I'd forgiven him. Now, *that* was scary. I've always been amazed at how some women put up with an awful lot of shit from their boyfriend or husband and still want to take him back: "I know he slept with my best friend, but he loves me really!" "He only hit me that one time, and he promised that it'd never happen again." "It was my own fault, really. I should have known better than to interrupt him in the middle of his favourite programme." Yeah, sure!

How can someone possibly have such low self-esteem that they put up with something like that? I knew I'd never forgive Des for what he did to me, and that was nothing compared to what some women have to go through.

* * *

Summer crawled around, reluctantly, and brought with it long evenings and bare arms and the chance for the same people who in winter complained that it was too cold to now complain that it was too hot.

I was still working in the bistro, though mostly I was on lunch-times and weekday evenings. That meant I was able to spend a lot more time with Thomas, and one Saturday evening, late in the summer, he picked me up at the house and said, "I have something to show you."

"Oh yeah? What is it?"

"No, I'm not telling you until we get there."

So we drove out of town, down a narrow winding road I hadn't travelled in a long time.

"This is where the shopping centre would have been," I said as I got out of the car.

Thomas said, "Yep."

We stood and looked over the hedge at a large, empty field. "Pity," I said. "It would have been nice."

"Sometimes things don't go the way you expect them to," he said. "But sometimes . . . sometimes they do."

I turned to look at him, but he wasn't there. Then I looked down, and he was on one knee, and holding out a black ring-box.

"Orla, will you do me the great honour of becoming my wife?"

Chapter 23

It was one of those days that you just know you're going to remember forever.

Thomas, on one knee, gazing up at me. And me, on wobbly knees, gazing back down at him.

This was the second time a man had proposed to me. Des's proposal had been a lot more basic: he'd turned to me in bed one morning and said, "So . . . what do you think? D'you want to get married then?" I'd told him, "Yeah, why not? But not just yet." After that, we hadn't talked about it much, but we'd always had the understanding that one day we *would* get married.

But now I was looking down at Thomas – a man who was a thousand times better than Des – and somehow my reaction wasn't so positive.

I'd been half-expecting this for the past few months, and a couple of times I'd even daydreamed about what it might be like, but now I didn't know what to do.

Thomas was prime husband material; he was good-looking, kind, thoughtful, intelligent and charming – and let's not forget loaded – but there was something wrong, something that didn't fit, and I couldn't quite put my finger on it. Whatever it was, it made me think of a novelty alarm-clock that Killian had bought me for my fourteenth birthday. The clock worked perfectly, but all the numbers were in the wrong place – seven came immediately before ten, which came before three, that kind of thing – and even though with a bit of effort you could use it to tell the real time, everyone who saw the clock would kind of freak out a little bit. My mother used to drape a T-shirt or something similar over it whenever she was in the room, because the clock just "didn't *look* right".

So me and Thomas . . . like the clock, our relationship had all the necessary parts to function reasonably well, but the parts weren't necessarily in the right order. Exactly which parts were out of place I couldn't tell.

As I stared at him, Thomas's arm swayed a little, and I realised that he'd been holding the same position for two or three minutes while my mind went off a-wanderin'.

I grabbed his arm and pulled him to his feet. "Sorry . . . you kind of caught me off-guard there."

"Yes, I'd gathered." He glanced down at the ring, and seemed to be wondering whether he should put it away or offer it again. "Um . . ." He looked at me with his big hazel eyes, and I could sense that he was mentally kicking himself. "I'm sorry, I just thought that this was the ideal time." He snapped the ring-box closed and started to tuck it back into his pocket.

"Thomas, I'm not saying no."

"You're not?"

"I need time to think about it. I mean, if I was going to marry anyone, it'd be you. But – I need time. Given everything that's happened to me in the past year, I really don't want to rush into anything."

Thomas nodded. "Of course. I understand." He stepped back, then took a deep breath and let it out slowly. Then he crouched down a bit to brush the dust off his knee, and smiled at me. "I should have brought the picnic basket and the champagne, shouldn't I?"

"So this isn't a spontaneous proposal, then? You've been giving it a lot of thought?"

"I have." He glanced over towards the field. "I *was* going to hold off for a few more months, but I don't think I can wait that long." He threw me a quick glance, then resumed staring at the field. "No, I shouldn't have said that. I don't want you to think that I'm giving you an ultimatum. Take all the time you need."

I didn't know what to say to that, so I just reached out and took his hand, and we stood side by side, looking out over the fields.

* * *

As I said, it was one of those days that you remember forever.

And not just because it was the day that Thomas proposed.

He drove me home and walked me to the door. I invited him in, but he declined. "It's okay," he said. "I know you need time to think about things."

So we kissed good-bye and he went back to the car, as usual waiting until I was inside before he drove off.

I closed the hall-door and collapsed against it. "What the hell am I going to do?" I said out loud.

I was heading into the kitchen, passing by the phone, when it rang. Instead of waiting for the answering machine to do its job, I picked it up immediately. "Hello?"

"Orla?"

"Who's this?"

"It's me. Des."

The phone slipped out of my hands and clattered off the little table. I was almost shaking too much to pick it up. I put the handset to my ear and I could hear him going, "Hello? Hello?"

"You fucking *bastard*!" I roared.

"Oh, thank God! I heard a bang and I thought you'd hung up on me!"

"Give me one good reason why I shouldn't!"

"Because if you do, you'll never find out what happened."

I swallowed. "All right. I'm listening."

He paused for a few seconds, then said, "You have no idea how many times I've picked up the phone to call you, only to chicken out at the last minute."

"Yeah, my heart bleeds for you. So talk. Why did you do it?"

"I thought I could get away with it."

"That's it? *That's* the reason you nearly screwed up my entire life?"

"Look, it wasn't about you."

"Then what *was* it about? Do you know what I had to go through? I lost my job because Flanagan was one of your investors, and I damn near lost the house because I

409

couldn't pay the mortgage. I had to get a lodger just to pay the bills! *And* you took all the furniture! Half the people in the town still think I had something to do with it! I had mobs turning up on the doorstep looking for your blood but willing to settle for mine! I had the bank trying to pin the blame on me, because you made me a director of your company – without even fucking telling me! I've been verbally and physically assaulted, I even had to have police protection at one stage!" I was aware that I was ranting, but I didn't care.

"I never intended anything like that to happen."

"Why did you do it?"

There was another pause. "Which part, exactly?"

"*All* of it!"

"Okay. You want the whole story, *here's* the whole story. I got into debt. That's all, plain and simple. I'd borrowed some money off some people, and they wanted it back, plus interest. Those bastards at Wagner, Kennedy and Parker kept delaying, and delaying, and the interest was going up and up. I thought I had it all worked out, see. The money coming in from Wagner, Kennedy and Parker – added to the money from the other investors – would have been more than enough to cover the money I owed. If that gobshite Tom Kennedy hadn't been such a prick about getting the money to me, no one would have been any wiser and I'd have been in the clear."

"What are you talking about? Why did you need to borrow money?"

"To buy the land." He said that as though I was being incredibly dense.

"But you didn't *own* the land."

"Yes, I did. Look, remember the first syndicate? We bought the land off Paddy Kane, the farmer? And then we sold it to a private investor?"

"Yeah, some rich woman."

"Well, there was no rich woman. I made her up. That is, I *kind* of made her up. She's real, but she's ancient and pretty much out of it most of the time. I used her name and details and set up an account, but I was the only one who had access to it. So then I borrowed the money off a couple of guys to pay the members of the syndicate. I promised them I'd pay them back two hundred per cent within two years. And because Kennedy kept pissing about and delaying things, well . . . the deadline was long gone and the guys wanted their money back. So I took everything I could from the second syndicate to pay them off."

"So why did you run? I mean, there must have been more in the account than the two hundred per cent."

"Orla, I had a two-year deadline, after which they started putting on interest of eight per cent a month. I borrowed two and a half million off them. You know how much that turns into after eleven months at eight per cent compound interest? Almost six million. There was no way I could have ever paid all of that back."

"But why did you have to steal from *me*?"

"I needed money to get out of Ireland in a hurry, and I needed to be well hidden. These guys I borrowed from . . . well, they're good at finding people. *Very* good. I knew someone who knew someone – you know how it is – and they set me up with a fake ID and a way out of the country. And the only way to get the money for that was . . ." He trailed off.

"Was to steal from my bank account and strip the entire house?"

"Well, yeah."

"Des, ever since it happened I've been calling you a bastard, but that's not right, is it? You're worse than that. You're a coward."

"Orla, if you knew these people –"

"Don't give me that! This is *Ireland*, you know! They're not the Mafia! They're not the Yakuza!"

"You honestly think that Ireland doesn't have its own organised crime? Jesus, Orla! Grow up!"

"Fuck you! Do you have any idea the sort of shit you put me through?"

"Yeah, I do. You just told me. Look, I'm sorry about that. I really am. But I didn't have a choice. The people I owe would have taken it out on you if they thought you were involved."

"So you stripped the entire house and stole all the money from my account, and you did it for *my* benefit? Thanks. I really appreciate that. If the furniture hadn't ended up in Peter Harney's yard, I'd probably never have got any of it back. And that was only the furniture. God only knows where everything else is."

Des paused. "Hold on . . . How do you mean, everything else?"

"As if you don't know! They took *everything*. All my clothes, my shoes, the contents of the presses, all my books and CDs and videos and DVDs, the fridge and the washing machine and the cooker . . . even all the junk in the garage. I came back that Monday morning and there wasn't a single thing left. They even took up the bloody carpets!"

"Seriously? Jesus, they were only supposed to take the furniture! I told them: 'Only take the furniture, leave the rest of it.' I mean, you were always saying that you were eventually going to replace all the furniture anyway, so I thought it wouldn't be that big a deal."

"Well, they did. There wasn't a teaspoon left in the house."

"Shit. I'm sorry about that."

"You're sorry about that, but not about the rest of it?"

"No, I mean . . . Look, at least you got the furniture back, right?"

"Eventually, yeah, most of it. But that's only because someone tried to flog it to Peter Harney."

Almost casually, Des said, "I wonder is he still seeing Mags on the side?"

"How the hell do you know about that?"

"Oh, I figured that out years ago. I saw him coming out of Mags's house one day and he said something about needing tuition with his reading and writing. He said that he was embarrassed about it and asked me not to mention it to anyone, especially not his wife. Well, I knew that was crap straight away, because I happen to know he can read and write perfectly well. But hang on, how did *you* hear about it?"

"Never mind that."

"Does Justin know?"

"God, no."

"How are they doing, anyway?"

"Why should *you* care how they are?"

"Look, just because I – did what I had to do, that doesn't mean I'm happy about it. You think I wanted to leave everything behind? You think I wanted to leave *you* behind? I still love you, you know."

"Well, I don't bloody love you!"

"I don't blame you, really I don't. Jesus, I know what it must have been like but, believe me, it was the only way. If I hadn't taken off, they'd have killed me."

"Maybe they should have. And maybe they still should. God knows there's enough people in this town who are going to string you up if they ever see you again! And I'm first in the queue."

"Orla, I made one mistake. Yeah, it was a bad one, but there was no other way out of it. I couldn't pay them back and they made it clear that if I didn't, they'd kill me. But they wouldn't have done it straight away, though. They said they'd go after *you* first. That's when I knew I had to hurt you too, so that they wouldn't think you had anything to do with it. They probably had people checking you out, you know. Was there anyone strange hanging around after it all happened?"

"They were *all* bloody strange!"

"Yeah, but I mean someone who wasn't just after me because of the money?"

"I don't know. And I don't care. Des, you practically ruined my life! And you did worse to Killian and Claire, and Justin and Mags, and God only knows how many other people!"

Des sighed, then said, "Look. I've got to go. I just wanted to see that you were all right."

"Oh, nice of you to think about me *now*! And where the hell are you, anyway?"

"I can't say. I mean, I'm sure they're still looking for me."

"Well, if they – whoever *they* are – turn up and ask me if I've heard from you, I'm going to say that I have."

"Fine. I don't care about that. They'll never find me anyway. I just . . . I'm sorry about everything. Really."

"Sorry isn't even nearly good enough! Now piss off and never call me again!" I slammed down the phone and stood glaring at it for a long, long time.

Then I picked it up again, and phoned Detective Mason.

Chapter 24

Detective Mason arrived at the house ten minutes later. I'd started to tell him what had happened over the phone, but he'd insisted on making a personal visit.

From the way he was dressed, I could tell that this was his day off: in place of his usual charcoal grey suit, he was wearing faded jeans, white runners and a black *Judge Dredd* T-shirt bearing the words *"I am the Law!"*. When he saw my reaction to the T-shirt, he looked a little embarrassed and said, "It was a present from my girlfriend."

"It's nice to know you're going out with someone who has a sense of humour."

"So about this phone call, then . . .?"

I brought him into the kitchen and put the kettle on. He listened carefully and took notes while I went through my conversation with Des, then asked, "Was there any recognisable background noise? Any unusual sounds that might help us pin-point his location?"

"Nothing that I noticed."

"Traffic?"

"Yeah, there was a bit of traffic all right," I said.

The kettle went *click* and shut itself off. "Tea or coffee?" I asked.

"Coffee, please. Black, no sugar. Did you happen to hear any other voices in the background?"

"Just murmuring."

"Not even a single distinct word?"

I shook my head. "No. Why?" I dumped a teaspoonful of coffee into a mug, and filled it from the kettle.

"Because if you'd heard someone speaking in, say, Italian, then we could make the assumption that he might be in Italy."

"Or in an Italian restaurant."

"True enough. But at least it would be something."

I handed him the mug. "I'm not sure, but he could have been using a mobile phone. Aren't you guys able to trace calls that come in from mobiles?"

"Sometimes. But if he was clever, he'll have bought a cheap phone and only used it for the call to you. We might be able to narrow down his location to within, say, half a mile, but unfortunately that's not going to be of any real use. Still, I'll get on to it. I wouldn't hold out much hope, though. Our resources are stretched pretty thin these days."

"I suppose he could have taken a bus to somewhere far from where he's living and made the call from there, right?"

"If he had any sense, yes. In the meantime, you should get yourself one of those Caller-ID boxes, just in case he calls again."

"I don't think he will."

"From what you said, it doesn't sound likely. Apart from that, how are you doing?"

I couldn't help laughing. "It's been a weird day . . . first, my boyfriend proposed to me, and then I get a call from Des!"

He stared at me for a second. "Thomas Kennedy asked you to marry him? Have you accepted?"

"Not yet. I sort of need some time to think about it."

"I see . . . Anyway, I'll let you know if I find out anything about Mr Mills. And you'll let me know if he phones again?"

"Sure."

"For now, though, I wouldn't tell anyone else that you were speaking to him. We don't have any useful answers for them, and it'll just start up the whole mess again. It would be like picking at a wound that's just starting to heal over, and I don't want to have to rescue you from your own house a second time."

"All right. I wasn't looking forward to letting people know anyway."

The detective didn't seem to be in a rush to leave. He stretched his feet out and crossed them at the ankles, then sipped at his coffee. "So apart from hearing from Mills and receiving a marriage proposal, how have you been?"

"Not too bad. I'm still at the restaurant, but I'm not doing the art classes any more. It was pretty good money, but most of the students only stuck with the course because of Des."

"How do you mean?"

"Well, usually by the time we get to the end of a term

there's only a handful of people left, but the last term I did they all kept coming back, and all they wanted to do was ask me if I'd heard from Des, or how you lot were getting on with the investigation. At least they all stopped blaming me, that's something."

He nodded. "And – if this isn't an indelicate question – how are you coping money-wise?"

"I'm earning just enough at the restaurant to keep my head above water. I've been half-thinking about going back to work as a designer, but I'm not sure all the stress would be worth the money."

"Well, if you do decide to marry Thomas Kennedy, I'm sure you won't be short of a few quid."

"This is true."

"So where would you live? Here, or at his place?"

"I don't know. I haven't really had much time to give it any thought." I looked around the kitchen. "Here, probably. Thomas's apartment is a bit small for two people. Besides, I'm still planning to finish doing this place up one day. I've started a bit here and there, but I just don't have the funds for it any more." I nodded towards the kitchen window. "I think, though, the first thing I'll get sorted will be the garden. I'm going to get rid of the grass, level out the topsoil and divide the garden up into little areas."

"I did the same sort of thing just last year in my parent's garden," he said. "I put down decking just outside the back door, with steps going down to a little barbecue area. Ferns and grasses in planters along the sides. It's the ultimate low-maintenance garden."

"That's what I want. I like the idea of being able to sit

out in the garden without feeling guilty because I've let it get so wild. Besides, it'd be a nice change to do some work on the outside after all the effort I put in on the inside."

The detective knocked back the rest of his coffee, then brought the mug over to the sink and rinsed it. "I'll be on my way, then. Congratulations on the proposal, by the way."

"Thanks."

I walked him to the front door. "So what'll happen now?"

"Now I'll fill out an incident report and add it to the file, and see if anything turns up. To be honest, I wouldn't get my hopes up if I was you." He walked a little up the driveway, then turned back. "Phone me if you need me, Orla. Any time, day or night, all right?"

"Thanks. I appreciate that."

"Or even if it all just gets a bit much for you, and you need someone to talk to, just call me."

* * *

I spent the rest of the day pottering about the house. I washed down the woodwork, rearranged my wardrobe – and as always felt a knot twist in my stomach when I thought about all the clothes I no longer had – and swept the house from top to bottom. And all the while, I was trying not to think about Thomas's proposal or Des's phone call.

That night, I lay awake for ages, because I'd somehow managed to convince myself that Des would phone in the middle of the night.

It didn't happen, of course, and I woke up the next morning feeling more than a little relieved.

The first thing I did was phone my brother and tell him that Thomas had proposed. I hadn't spoken to him much since the night he'd told me that I was making a mistake with Thomas, so I wanted him to know first.

"What did you tell him?" Killian asked.

"I told him I need time to think about it," I said.

"I see," Killian said, sounding relieved. "So?"

"So?"

"So what are you going to do?"

"I'm not sure."

"Do you love him?"

"Yes."

"And do you think that you're going to love him for the rest of your life?"

"I think so."

"Then – go for it."

Next, I talked to Justin and Mags. They were overjoyed for me, as I'd expected. That was because Justin and I had had many long conversations about the subject, and I'd made it very clear to him that I wasn't going to allow him or anyone else to tell me who I should be in love with.

After that, I went next door to see Mr Farley. I'd barely talked to him since I'd found out that he'd phoned Killian to gossip about me, but I'd known him all my life, and I wanted him involved in the wedding.

He seemed pleased to see me when he opened the door. "Orla Adare! How are you?"

"I'm fine."

"And how's Thomas?"

"He's fine too. Um . . . can I come in for a second? I have something to ask you."

He ushered me inside, sat me down and plied me with tea and biscuits. "Now . . . what's on your mind?"

"Thomas proposed to me."

He nodded. "I thought it might be something like that. And have you accepted?"

"Not yet. But I'm going to."

"Well! Congratulations are in order, then!" He pushed himself out of his chair and rooted through a cupboard, then produced a half-bottle of whiskey. "It's all I have, I'm afraid. The champagne man didn't come this morning."

"Thanks, but not for me. I have to go to work in an hour."

He looked at the bottle, and seemed to come to a decision. "Well, you don't mind if I have one, do you?"

"Not at all."

He produced a tiny shot glass and filled it to the rim. "To your health, Orla, and the health of your husband to be, and to your offspring. May they be many, and healthy, and may they give you no trouble whatsoever and move out as soon as they reach the age of eighteen!" He knocked back the whiskey in one go.

I laughed. "So . . . Look, I haven't told anyone else yet that I'm definitely going to accept. Not even Thomas."

He tapped the side of his nose. "I'll say nothing."

"No, that's not what I mean. The thing is, obviously we haven't set a date yet, so it might be ages away, but . . . I'd like you to be the one who gives me away."

He stared at me, and the shot glass dropped from his hand and clattered onto the table. "But what about your brother?"

"I'd prefer you to do it."

"I'm . . . speechless. Speechless, and honoured. I accept. Thank you." He looked like he was about to cry.

I reached across the table and patted his hand. "No, *I'm* honoured. You've always been very good to me. Anyway, like I said, it's a while away yet, but I wanted you to be the first to know."

He smiled. "Even before the groom himself?"

"Ah, I'm pretty sure he knows my answer already!"

* * *

What with planning the wedding and everything, the next couple of months were pretty busy. So busy, in fact, that the anniversary of the day Des left had passed by without me even noticing.

Well, that's not true. I noticed. I tried not to, but it was difficult because whenever I talked to Mr Flanagan or Justin – or pretty much anyone else involved – they made big deal about how much time had passed.

Plus, of course, it was my birthday. I knew that for the rest of my life I'd never really be able to fully enjoy a birthday celebration.

* * *

"Orla, if this is true then you're out of your bloody mind! That's the stupidest decision I ever heard in my life! I promise you, you are really going to regret it! It might not be for a couple of years, but believe me one day you'll wake up and think, 'Shit! I should have listened to Barry!', but it'll be too late."

I raised my eyes in disgust. I wasn't talking to Barry: this was a message he'd left on the answering machine.

I didn't know where or how he'd heard that Thomas and I were getting married, but now here he was, three days before I tied the knot, and he was far too late to do anything about it.

"That's a bit embarrassing," I said to Mrs Diggle, who had accompanied me into the house.

After I'd told Thomas that I would marry him, we'd started to plan the wedding. As old Mrs Diggle had always told me she'd make my wedding dress for me, I'd decided to call over to her house to make peace. She was still upset about Des running off with her money, but that had been over a year before, and she was finally willing to concede that it wasn't my fault. I insisted on paying for the dress, of course, and she hadn't tried very hard to out-insist me.

Now, she just brushed past me into the sitting-room. "Never mind, dear. There's always one. Was that the same Barry who used to lodge here?"

"Yeah."

"Whatever happened to him?"

"He got promoted, and moved to a different store. I haven't seen him in ages."

"Pity. I quite liked him."

"Well, me too. But you know how it is. Sooner or later, everyone moves on."

She gave me her famous thin-lipped smile. "Only if you let them."

My wedding dress was on a mannequin in the sitting-room. It was in there rather than in the bedroom because Mrs Diggle wasn't so great at stairs. The curtains were closed, of course, to keep the light off it and to make sure that no one caught a glimpse of it before the grand unveiling.

Though I do say do myself, it was a truly beautiful piece of work. I'd spent ages designing it, and Mrs Diggle followed my design almost exactly. She may have been rapidly approaching her seventies, but she still knew her way around the old sewing machine. The dress was a pure, dazzling white – I'd expected Mrs Diggle to frown upon that idea, but she wasn't fazed at all – with a bodice designed to look like a corset, long lace sleeves – off the shoulder – and a long voluminous satin skirt that did make my bum look big, but I didn't mind. I'd opted for a shoulder-length veil, and no train – I just couldn't see myself dragging a long train up the aisle.

"Let's see how we're doing, then," she said. The dress had been finished a week earlier, but she said she always made a point of checking it out a couple of days before the wedding, "just in case".

I stripped off my jeans and top, and carefully stepped into the dress. I'd tried it on many times, but I'd never gone the whole way; I'd never worn the dress, the veil and the shoes at the same time. I wasn't sure why, but it just didn't feel right to put everything on together before the day of the wedding.

Mrs Diggle went "Hmm" a lot as she peered at me, made me turn this way and that, checked the seams, made imperceptible adjustments, and finally stepped back. In an accusing tone, she said, "Have you been dieting? It seems to be hanging a little."

"I've been too nervous to eat much," I said. "But I'm not doing it deliberately."

"You've definitely lost a couple of pounds in the past week . . ." She sighed. "It's always the same. Start eating properly again if you don't want to be walking down the aisle looking like your dress was made for someone else. Besides, you're going to need to keep your strength up for the big day."

"I know, I know!"

A key rattled in the front door. "It's only me!" Davina called as she slammed the door behind her. She came into the sitting-room and looked me up and down. "Oooh! Nice!"

Davina had arrived the previous day, full of excitement and presents and news about her life in France. That I was getting married seemed to be almost incidental to her: she was more interested in catching up with all the latest gossip.

She'd been one of my closest friends when I was a teenager, and we'd done everything together. Then in her very early twenties Davina decided that she was moving to France for no good reason – "because I want to," she'd told us at the time. We occasionally wrote to each other, phoned now and then, but I hadn't actually seen her in almost seven years.

She hadn't changed a bit. When we were teenagers, Davina was definitely the leader and the rest of us were the followers. It was always her who arranged where we'd go and what time we'd meet. And when she emigrated, the rest of our little gang had drifted apart; Claire was the only one I still had any contact with, and I knew that was probably only because she'd married my brother.

Mrs Diggle said, "Davina, I want you to make sure

that she eats properly over the next few days. We don't want her looking like the dress is still on a hanger."

"*No problemo,*" Davina said.

"All right then," Mrs Diggle said to me. "You're ready."

I nodded, examining myself in the full-length mirror Mags and I had carried down from the bedroom the day the dress arrived. "I'm ready," I agreed.

"At least, the dress is ready," Davina said.

"How do you mean?"

"Only you know if *you're* ready, Orla."

"I *am* ready," I said.

Mrs Diggle looked at me silently for a while. "Your mother would be in floods of tears about now."

"I know. She never could cope with weddings."

"I remember *her* wedding like it was yesterday. She went through the usual panic beforehand. 'Am I doing the right thing?' and the like. 'What if it's all a big mistake?' and 'Is it too late to back out now?' Well, let me tell you, Orla, the same things I told her. Yes, you're doing the right thing. It's not all a big mistake. And no, it's not too late to back out."

"She really said that? God, it's hard to imagine her having doubts about marrying my dad."

"Most people have doubts, dear. If they don't, then that's the time to worry."

"Why's that?"

Davina said, "If they don't have any doubts, there's a good chance that they're just fooling themselves."

I sneered at her. "Yeah? How many times have *you* been married?"

"A few years ago," Mrs Diggle said, "I made a dress

for a girl – she'd be about your age now – who was being beaten up by her boyfriend. We had to change the dress style two weeks before the wedding because otherwise the bruises would show."

"That's horrible!"

"Yes, it is. And you know something? She had no doubts that she was doing the right thing."

"Maybe she was just too scared of him?"

"She didn't seem scared. I said to her, I said, 'What if he does it again?' And she said, 'He won't. He loves me and that's all there is to it.' She refused to talk about it any more. It was like she'd just decided that it had never happened and sort of cut that part out of her past."

"So she married him?" Davina asked.

"She did. Fool that she was, she went ahead and married a man she knew was going to hurt her again."

"Silly bitch!"

"That's not fair, Davina!" I said. "Maybe she really did love him!"

"Look, if she's going to marry someone who's hitting her, then maybe she deserves it."

"You're not tremendously generous with the old sympathy, are you?"

She sighed and turned to Mrs Diggle. "Am I right?"

The old woman nodded. "I think so." To me, she said, "They say love is blind, Orla, but I've seen a lot of weddings over the years, and let me tell you this: there are times when love is not only blind, it's mentally deficient too. I've seen women in tears as they walked down the aisle, because they didn't want to get married but didn't have the courage to change their minds. So they live in misery because they thought that it would be better than living in shame, or, worse, living alone. I've seen women getting married because their parents thinks that it's a wise financial move. Or because all their friends are married and they don't want to be left out. On more than one occasion, it's been because they've told themselves they have to be married before the age of thirty. So they pick some man they know who has the fewest flaws, and marry him. Or they do it just because they're pregnant, or even because they're not pregnant but they want to have a child before it's too late." She tutted. "People getting married for all the wrong reasons! It breaks my heart, it really does."

"But come on! It's not always like that!"

She looked surprised. "Lord, no! Most of the time people get married because they genuinely love each other. Like you and Thomas. You love him, don't you?"

"I do."

She smiled. "Well then."

"But, you know . . . what you were saying about doubts . . . I do have *some* doubts."

Davina looked up at me. "Oh? What's all this?"

We ignored her.

"Of course you have doubts, dear," Mrs Diggle said. "That's perfectly natural. And I'm sure that over the years there may be one or two times when you think, 'What have I done?' and that's perfectly natural too. You're going to be fine." She walked around me and tugged at the dress here and there. Almost too casually, she said, "But if you're worried about your doubts, then I suggest you talk to someone. Get your feelings out into the open. That way, they won't seem nearly as bad." She stopped what she was doing and looked up at me expectantly. "I'm listening."

"Me too," Davina said.

I shook my head. "No, but thanks. I'll be okay."

"I daresay that Thomas is going through the same thing. It's called last-minute jitters." She stepped back and looked me up and down. "About now, your mother would be hugging you and telling us about when you were a little girl and who you'd thought you were going to marry. And you'd be telling her to be careful so as not to crush the dress."

"It's always like that?"

"Pretty much."

"How many wedding dresses have you made, then?"

She frowned as she thought about this. "I don't know . . . this is the first one in a couple of years, but let me think . . . well, it's been nearly fifty years since I made my own dress, that was my very first one, and it was a couple of years before I started doing it professionally. We used to do at least one a month at our peak. And sometimes I'd have to do one in a hurry, if you know what I mean . . . I'd say that I've made at least three hundred wedding dresses, plus God only knows how many bridesmaids' dresses."

"Wow! That's impressive!"

"I've had the same postman for thirty years," she said, and for a second I thought she'd fallen into her old habit of switching stories with no warning, "and he tells me he hates it when Christmas comes, because most of my brides still send me cards."

After a few last adjustments, she stepped back and

made me turn around one final time. "There's nothing more I can do, Orla. It's definitely finished. This is as good as it's going to be."

* * *

Davina and I walked Mrs Diggle back to her house, and I promised her that Justin and Mags would pick her up in the morning of the big day in plenty of time to get to the church.

We walked back home through the town, and I was very much aware that the next time I passed that way would probably be in the wedding car.

We dropped into the bistro, where Pauline and Steve were busy with the lunch-time customers, but not so busy that Pauline couldn't come over to talk to us. "So you must be the famous Davina," Pauline said.

She nodded. "That's me."

"This is Pauline," I said. "The heart and soul of the restaurant."

"As if. So, are you all set?" Pauline asked.

"Pretty much. You?"

"Yeah. Flanagan's still annoyed that you're not having the reception here, though."

"I *told* him; there's not nearly enough room. Thomas's folks have invited loads of people."

"And they really don't mind paying for it?"

"They insisted."

"Wow. He doesn't have a brother, does he?"

I smiled. "No, he's an only child."

"Listen . . . what if you-know-who shows up?"

"Des?" Davina asked.

431

Pauline gave her a look. "No, Barry."

"Well, I don't think he will," I said. "God, you *still* think that he was interested in me, don't you?"

"I don't know. But say he was . . . suppose he turns up at the church and you know that bit where the priest asks if anyone there knows of any reason that you can't be married . . .? Well, suppose Barry stands up and says that you can't marry Thomas because you don't really love him?"

"But I *do* love him," I said. "You've had this on your mind for a while, haven't you?"

"Yeah."

"Well, it won't happen," I said. "Besides, Killian would probably kill him."

"I suppose you're right . . . I meant to say, your brother and his family called in for dinner last night. God, the kids are dead cute! Niamh was a bit cagey with me at first, though. I think she wanted to be the only bridesmaid. How come they're not staying with you?"

"The kids wanted to stay with their grandparents. Which is probably just as well, because I don't have enough time for them at the moment." I nodded towards Davina. "And someone else is kipping in the spare room."

"Anyway, I'd better get back to this lot. So, what time tonight?"

"How do you mean?"

Out of the corner of my eye, I caught Davina frantically making some kind of gesture to Pauline. I looked from one to the other. "Ah . . .! The two of you are planning something, aren't you?"

They both tried to look innocent. "Such as?" Davina asked.

"Look, I've said a million times that I'm not interested in a hen party!"

Then Pauline said, "Your opinion doesn't count. The hen party's as much for your friends as it is for you."

"Anyway, it's not going to be anything big," Davina said. "We were just going to invite a few people over, order some pizzas, that kind of thing."

"So when did all this happen?"

"She called in a couple of hours ago and introduced herself," Pauline said. "Come on, Orla! I've already booked the night off!"

"Who else are you planning on inviting?"

"Just Mags and your sister-in-law. It's not even really a proper hen party, just a bunch of friends staying in for a few drinks."

Davina grabbed my arm. "Come on! Please, please, please!"

"All right, all right!" I said. "Anything for a quiet life! You promise I won't regret this?"

"You won't," Pauline said.

She was wrong.

Chapter 25

Mags was the last to arrive for the hen party. She looked a little dishevelled, and smiled weakly when I answered the door to her.

"You're late! What have *you* been up to?" I asked, about half a second before I figured it out for myself. I lowered my voice. "Oh. Right. Sorry."

I led her into the smoke-filled sitting-room, which was now littered with half-empty pizza boxes and completely empty beer cans. "You know everyone, right?"

"Not everyone."

"Okay . . . the horizontal one is Claire – my sister-in-law and Thomas's future sister-in-law-squared – and Pauline you definitely know, and the drunk with the evil grin is Davina. Everyone, this is Mags."

"So *you're* Mrs Justin!" Davina asked. "Haven't seen him in years! How's he doing?"

"Great, thanks."

"Sit yourself down and grab a drink," Pauline said. "We're playing a really stupid game."

"What's that?" I asked.

Claire – who was stretched out face-down on the sofa, with her head hanging over the armrest, one shoe kicked off and her hair all over the place – said, "Every time Orla mentions Thomas, you have to take a drink. And if she mentions Des, you have to take *two* drinks."

"So now we're all pissed," said Pauline, "'cept Orla, who didn't even know we were playing."

"Oh, thanks a bunch," I said.

"*Any*way . . ." Claire said to Mags, "you do know me because I met you before. Years and years ago, when you first started going out with Killian, just after me and Justin moved."

"I think you got the names the wrong way around," Davina said.

Claire raised her head. "No, I'm pretty sure I didn't. I think I know my own husband's name, thank you very much!"

"He'd be so proud of you right now," said Pauline. To the rest of us, she said, "Last night in the restaurant it took her an hour to drink one – *one*! – glass of white wine, and now look at her!"

Mags said, "Any pizza left?"

I rooted through the boxes until I found a few reasonably edible slices. "Help yourself. What'll you have to drink?"

"I'd better not. I've got school in the morning. I can't even stay that long." She sat down on the arm of Davina's

435

chair and nibbled at a slice of lukewarm pizza. "So, Orla . . . are you counting the hours?"

"No," I said.

"Yes, she is," Davina said. "She keeps looking at her watch. You know, Pauline, in a few days' time we'll be the only ones in this room who aren't married."

Claire said, "That's ridiculous! The party's not going to go on for *that* long!"

I laughed. "Claire, you're plastered!"

She pushed herself into a wobbly sitting position. "No, *you're* a bastard!"

"I said you were plastered, not a bastard."

"Oh, right. Sorry. You know, I have had a lot to drink, but I don't think it's affected me."

"Really?" Mags asked. "Say 'toast' ten times."

Claire took a deep breath. "Toast, toast, toast, toast, toast, toast, toast, toast . . . How many is that?"

Pauline: "Nine."

Davina: "Seven."

"That was eight," Mags said. "But you've kind of spoiled it now."

"I don't get it."

"Look, we'll do it again, then. Say 'toast' ten times."

This time, Claire managed to get to the end in one go.

"Now what do you put in a toaster?" Mags asked.

"Toast," Claire said. "I still don't get it."

Davina threw a cushion at her. "Ah, you feckin' eejit! You don't put toast into a toaster! You put *bread* into a toaster!"

Claire burst out laughing, as though this was the best trick anyone's ever played. She wiped her eyes, and said, "That was brilliant! Do it again!"

"It kind of only works the first time," said Mags. "You can thank a bunch of eight-year-olds for that one."

"Oh, I forgot you were a teacher," Davina said.

"That's what she meant about having school in the morning," Pauline said. She pushed herself out of the armchair. "Top of the stairs, first on the left, isn't it?" she asked me.

"Yep."

Swaying slightly, Pauline carefully stepped over the discarded pizza boxes and cans. "If I'm not back in ten minutes . . . wait a bit longer."

Claire leaned over and picked up another can of Budweiser. As she fumbled with the ring-pull, she said, to me, "Hey, Orla . . . jimember that time when you came down to stay with us and you went back home and Des had nicked everything?"

"Do I *remember*? It's not the sort of thing you forget! That bastard completely ruined my life!"

She nodded. "An' jimember that you phoned us to tell us?"

"I do."

Claire grinned. "Well, guess what we were right in the middle of doing when you phoned?"

"Don't tell me you were doing the nasty?" Davina said.

"No, we were having sex."

I raised my eyes. "Claire, I really don't want to know that sort of thing when my brother's involved!"

She carried on: "We were coming up to the good bit and then . . . *Ring ring! Ring ring!* We almost didn't answer it."

437

Davina stared at her. "You mean you don't take the phone off the hook before you start?"

"Well, no. Do you?"

"God yeah! I take the phone off the hook and I switch off the door buzzer! *And* I turn off my mobile phone. The last thing you want when you're having a good shag is someone phoning you."

"I have to ask," Mags said. "Why did you bring that up?"

Claire shrugged. "Well, Pauline's gone to the loo and I was thinking how sometimes Killian has to stop halfway through so that he can go for a piss, and you know how it is: you're lying there for ages for him to come back, because first *he* has to wait until –"

I interrupted her. "Stop right there! We all know what you're talking about!"

Davina said, "God, you've turned into a right prude, Orla! You used to be as filthy-minded as the rest of us."

"It's not that. I just don't want to think of Killian having sex."

"He's a married man, Orla. You must be aware that he's had sex on more than one occasion! I mean, they have two kids, right, Claire?"

"That's right."

"And they're both Killian's, yeah?"

"Yep. No doubt about that."

"You've never slept with someone else?"

At that, I stole a glance at Mags. She didn't seem at all bothered.

"God no!" Claire said. "Sure it took us *years* to really get to know what we both like in bed!"

I put my hands over my ears. "I'm not hearing this!"

438

"How about you, though, Davina?" Claire asked. "Are you seeing anyone at the moment?"

"Yeah, I suppose. There's a guy in the apartment block I'm sort of seeing."

"When you say 'sort of' . . .?"

"We just sleep together a couple of times a week. We're not going out or anything."

"That's where you're the exact opposite of me," Claire said. "I could do without the sex as long as I had the relationship."

"You say that now, but say Killian was in an accident or something and couldn't perform. I bet you'd be thinking differently then."

"No, I wouldn't."

Mag said, "How about if it was the other way around? Say you were the one who couldn't have sex . . . would you let him sleep with other women?"

"Not a chance."

"So you'd just let him suffer?"

I decided I didn't want to hear any more of this. I went into the kitchen and filled the kettle. As I was waiting for it to boil, Pauline came in. "Making tea?"

"Coffee. I've got enough to do tomorrow without having to worry about a hangover. Want one?"

"Yeah . . . So what are they up to in there?"

"They're discussing their sex lives. Well, Davina and Claire are. I think Mags is trying to keep out of it. Speaking of sex lives, I meant to ask – have you decided yet who you're bringing to the wedding?"

Pauline had been dithering between two of her many consorts. I hadn't met either of them, but from what she'd told me, one of them was tall and handsome but kind of dull, and the other was short and plain and great fun.

"I asked Eamonn in the end."

"Which one's he?"

"The good-looking one."

"Why him and not the fun one?"

She smiled. "Because in years to come, when you're a grandmother and you're in a retirement home somewhere and all you have left are your wedding photos, you're going to want all the other old dears to be going, 'Who was that handsome man?' and not 'It's a shame that strange little man is in all that photos.' So I was only thinking of you!"

"You know, I believe every single word of that."

Pauline regarded me silently for a few seconds.

"What?" I said.

"I have to ask you this: are you sure you're doing the right thing?"

"Of course I'm sure!"

"Only, I've seen the two of you together a lot, and . . ."

I let out a long sigh. "Go ahead. Say what you feel."

"You say you've never had a fight with him?"

"No. Never."

"Any sort of disagreement?"

"Nothing that I can think of. Definitely nothing serious."

She nodded. "Well, that's good."

"I know what you're getting at. Some people think that it's not a proper relationship unless you're at each other's throats all the time, but with me and Thomas, we just fit together perfectly."

"You and Des used to have occasional arguments, though, didn't you?"

"Yeah, a few. And look how that all turned out."

"And God knows you and Barry used to fight about the most trivial things, and you weren't even going out together."

"Ah, come on now! We weren't *that* bad!"

Pauline gave me one of her "is that what you think?" looks. "For God's sake, Orla, I remember you and Barry having a fight about what time it was!"

"When was this?"

"Last Christmas, when we all went out for dinner and Barry brought what's-her-name along."

"I remember the night, but I don't remember fighting with him."

"Someone said, 'Anyone got the time?' and Barry said, 'I don't have my watch on me, but it's probably about nine-thirty.' Then you – you didn't have a watch on either – you said, 'It's never nine thirty, it's only about nine.'"

"Oh . . . now I remember. And I was right in the end."

Pauline rinsed a mug at the sink, and dumped two spoons of coffee into it, then filled it from the kettle. "Yes, you were right, but it took the two of you ten minutes of loud debating before you allowed someone who *did* have a watch to tell the real time."

"But the point is, I was right and he was wrong."

"Jesus! If you're still gloating about it after all this time, then there's no hope for you! Anyway, that's *not* the point. The point is that you don't fight at all with Thomas, do you?"

"No."

441

She nodded. "And from what I've observed, you don't laugh much with him either."

I dismissed this with a smirk. "Would you give over? Me and Thomas have a great laugh together!"

Before she could respond, Davina came into the kitchen. "I think Claire's about to pass out. Should we phone Killian and get him to collect her?"

"He can't," I said. "He's gone out with Thomas for the stag party."

Pauline and Davina glanced at each other.

"Killian went to Thomas's stag party?" Davina asked. "Seriously?"

"Yeah. Why?"

Pauline said, "Well, I never want to hear you complain about your brother again! Just for the sake of your happiness, Killian was willing to spend a whole evening in Thomas's company!"

I didn't like where I knew this was going. "Why shouldn't he?"

"He can't stand him, Orla. He told me that Thomas is a complete and utter wanker and that he wouldn't bother to piss on him if he was on fire."

"Is that so? Then how come he's always so friendly to Thomas?"

"Because he doesn't want to upset *you*," Pauline said. "Even last night in the restaurant, Killian said that he was just praying that you'd call off the wedding."

"Right!" I pushed my way past them, and into the sitting-room, where Claire was sitting slumped over with her head between her knees, and Mags was flicking through a magazine.

I sat down next to Claire. "Are you okay?"

"I'm feeling a bit off . . . What the hell was in those pizzas?"

"You should know; you're the one who ordered them. Look, I've got something to ask you, okay?"

"Fire away."

"Killian likes Thomas, right?"

She swivelled her head towards me. "Sure he does."

I looked up at Pauline and Davina, who were standing in the doorway. "There you are, you see?"

"In fact," Claire said, "he said to make sure that that was what I told you, if you asked."

Oh God, they're right, I said to myself. "And . . . did he say what you were *not* to tell me?"

"That he's half-hoping that Thomas ends up screwing a stripper at the stag party so you'll have a good solid reason not to marry him." She slapped her hand over her mouth. "Oops. Just don't tell him I said that, okay?"

"I won't."

"Sorry, I'm normally very good at keeping secrets," she said.

"Actually, no, you're not. You're crap at it." I sat back and looked at the others. "Well . . . come on, then! Anyone else got anything bad to say about the man I'm going to marry?"

Davina shrugged. "I haven't met him yet, so I've no opinion one way or the other."

"What about you?" I asked Mags.

"I really don't know him well enough to say, Orla."

"Pauline?"

"Same here."

Davina collapsed into an armchair. "Look, when Mrs Thingy was here today to check out the dress, you told her that you have doubts about the wedding. So come on, out with it!"

I shook my head. "It's nothing important. Just pre-wedding jitters."

Pauline, who was still standing in the doorway, said, quietly, "I think I know what it is. Or at least I know what *one* of your doubts is."

"You barely know him, Pauline! You just said so yourself!"

"But I know *you*," she said.

"Come on, then. Tell me what you're thinking."

"It's something you said before. Well, a couple of things, really. But if you put them together . . . Tell us again about that meeting in the hotel. The one where Thomas was able to prove that Des stole all that money without you being involved."

"Okay. Thomas's company organised the meeting, because they wanted to get everyone together . . ."

"No, I mean after. When that guy attacked you and you kneed him in the balls."

I hesitated before answering. "What about it?"

Mags suddenly said, "Oh God. I know what she means."

"Well, *I* don't!"

Mags said, "I think you do, Orla. I think you've been thinking along the same lines. I mean, I was there when it happened, wasn't I?"

Davina said, "What have I missed? Who did you knee in the balls?"

"Never mind that now," Pauline said. "I'll fill you in later."

I knew, of course, exactly what Pauline and Mags were getting at. It was something that had been niggling at the back of my brain for a long time, but I'd ignored it, convinced myself it wasn't really that important.

Then Claire said, "He's a coward."

I turned to look at her. "Shut up, you! You don't know anything! You're too pissed to even sit up straight!"

"God, *somebody* tell me what this is all about!" Davina shouted.

"All right," said Mags. "I'll tell it, since none of the rest of you were there. The weekend after Des disappeared, Thomas and his company organised a meeting down at the hotel, for all the investors. They really just wanted to figure out exactly what had happened. But a few people thought that they were going to be getting their money back. You have to remember that at that stage an awful lot of them believed that Orla was involved in the whole thing. Anyway, after the meeting this guy came up and started having a go at Orla. Justin tried to get him to back down, but he shoved Justin aside and grabbed Orla's arm. And she kneed him in the balls."

Davina laughed, and pumped the air with her fist. "Yes! Ten points, girl! So where's the problem?"

"There is no problem," I said. "That's the whole story."

"No, it isn't," Mags said. "Because Thomas came rushing over then and asked you what had happened."

Claire nodded. "Yeah. Even though he's mentioned it a couple of times since."

"So?" Davina said. "He's proud of her. There's nothing wrong with that."

Pauline said, "Because when he talks about it, it's pretty obvious that he *did* see what was going on." She looked at me. "Thomas saw that guy confronting you, and he saw Justin get knocked aside, and he saw you defending yourself. When he talked to me about it, he kept saying how just seeing your knee whack yer man between the legs was enough to make his own eyes water in sympathy."

"Look, just shut up!" I said. "This is not important!"

"Yes, it is," Mags said. "He saw all that happening and he did nothing. He stood there and watched this guy attacking you and Justin, and then when it was *safe*, he came rushing over pretending that he'd missed it all."

"He's a coward," Claire said again. "Sorry, Orla, but there it is."

"You know how Thomas is," I said. "He considers things before he acts. Anyway, Thomas and I barely even knew each other at the time. And apart from Justin, no one else jumped in to help me!"

"That sounds like an awful lot of justification," Davina said. "It seems to me that you're –"

I jumped to my feet. "All right. That's it. The party's over. The lot of you can fuck off home right now!" I headed towards the door, and stopped when I passed Mags. "And *you* . . .! Don't you *ever* try to tell me how I should and shouldn't be living my life!"

She swallowed. "Orla, it's not like that."

"Just – just go home, Mags."

I stormed up the stairs to my bedroom and slammed the door.

While I sat on the bed, hugging a pillow, the next few minutes were filled with quiet mutterings from downstairs, with the hall door opening and closing a couple of times, then I heard the stairs creaking as Davina came up, followed by a gentle knocking. "Are you okay?"

"What do you think?"

"Can I come in?"

"No."

There was a few seconds' silence. "Please?"

"All right. Just don't piss me off."

Davina came in and sat down on the edge of the bed. "Sorry."

"Nothing's changed, you know? People are still trying to run my life for me. That's one thing that Thomas *doesn't* do. He's happy with me the way I am."

She kicked off her shoes, then put her left leg up on her right knee and started picking at her toes. "Look, the fact is that my own life isn't in any great shakes. I'm only just earning enough to pay my rent, and I can't seem to hang on to a boyfriend for more than a couple of weeks. Oh, there's lots of guys who want to sleep with me, but that's as far as they want to take it. I know I let on that I've got this great glamorous life in the south of France, but the truth is that my life isn't glamorous; it's just a different kind of ordinary. So I'm not trying to run your life for you – none of us are – but we want to be sure that you're marrying Thomas for the right reasons. Not just because he's the safe option."

Jaye Carroll

"You weren't here when Des disappeared. You don't know what I had to go through!"

"I know that. But Thomas was engaged before, right?"

"Yeah. So?"

"And it ended well, you said. They didn't break up in a blazing row or anything."

"Of course not! Thomas isn't like that. He doesn't fight with people."

"He doesn't stand up to people, you mean."

"Don't tell me what I mean, Davina! I *know* what I mean!"

"I'm sure he's a real wolf in the boardroom, but based on what the others were saying, and on what I've picked up from you, I think you're making a mistake."

"All right, so maybe Thomas did see that guy grabbing me and he just stood there and didn't do anything to help me. So? That doesn't make him a coward!"

Very quietly, she said, "Then what *does* it make him?"

"He's not a coward. Look, he was in charge of the whole project from their side of things. It was worth millions! He wasn't exactly in a position to jump in with his fists flailing and beat the crap out of one of the investors."

"Do you love him?"

"Yes, I love him! He's kind, and gentle, and considerate."

"No, be honest! *Do* you love him?"

"*Yes!*"

"You're lying to yourself, aren't you? I don't think you do love him. You're just settling for him. I think that Des hurt you much more than you'll even admit to yourself. You're taking the safe road now, Orla. The path of least resistance. You know something else?"

I raised my eyes. "God! What *now*?"

"I think that you know you're making a mistake and the only reason you don't want to back out of the wedding is because you want people to remember you as the one who married a nice, good-looking, well-off guy. That way they're less likely to remember you as the one who was completely screwed over by Des."

"You're not the first one to say that. No one seems to be willing to let me make my own mistakes."

"So you think it's a mistake too?"

"No, I was just . . . Ah, piss off!"

Davina suddenly laughed. "Tell you what . . . there's enough room in my apartment in Nice for the two of us. Tomorrow morning we'll get up early and go to the airport. We won't tell anyone what we're doing, we'll just go. You'll get a job there no problem. You still remember some of your French from school, right? So we'll just go. When we get there, you can phone Killian or Justin or someone and tell them that you changed your mind. What do you say?"

"I–I can't just do that. I can't just disappear on him! That's the same kind of thing that Des did to me!"

"Okay, then say – somehow – you could just call off the wedding and there'd be no repercussions. Say you could just flick a switch, and it would all be off. Would you do it?"

"I don't know what you mean," I said.

She didn't say anything to that, but I could see that she knew I was stalling for time.

"I do love him, you know."

"So you keep saying."

449

"He's the one. He's Mr Right."

"Maybe he is. But is he Mr Right Now?"

"What?"

"Postpone the wedding for a year."

"That's crazy!"

"You said his folks are paying for it, and they're loaded. I'm sure they won't miss the money."

I sighed. "Davina . . . really, you're nuts, you know that? Let me tell you what things have been like since Des left, okay? First, I get half the people in the town assuming that I was involved in Des's scam. Then I had Barry move in and spend all his time giving me tons of useless theories and advice. And then I met Thomas and everyone started telling me that he wasn't the right man for me. It's like none of you understand that I have a mind of my own. Everyone's projecting their own thoughts and fears onto me."

"I can see why you might think that, all right."

"I do love Thomas, and in three days time I'm going to marry him. And that's that."

But that *wasn't* that.

Chapter 26

I spent the next morning tidying up the house after the prematurely aborted party. Davina had gone to spend the day with her mother, and I was grateful for that. We'd already agreed that she wouldn't say another word against Thomas, but she was still giving me "knowing" looks.

At noon, I realised that in only forty-eight hours I'd be walking down the aisle.

Only two more days of being a single woman, I said to myself. Two days and then I'll be Mrs Orla Kennedy.

We'd talked about that quite a bit. At first, I'd assumed I'd simply keep my own surname, but the more I thought about it, the more I realised that changing my name wasn't a bad idea; there were still a few people in the town to whom the name Orla Adare would be forever linked to the name Desmond Mills.

Thomas had suggested that we could both combine our surnames, and I could become Mrs Orla Adare-

Kennedy, but I exercised my veto on that one. I've never been able to take double-barrelled names very seriously.

Besides, I kind of liked the idea of my initials being OK.

In the early afternoon, I was vacuuming the hall when Thomas phoned. He sounded a little under the weather. "I drank a bit too much last night. And then I drank another bit too much. Your brother can really put it away, you know."

"Yeah, he takes after our granddad in that regard. So where did you go?"

"We started off in Clooney's, had one there. Then we went across the road to the hotel to meet up with the others. I think we were there for about an hour. Then we went to some other place – had three or four drinks there. After that it's a bit of a blur. Oh, and at one stage there was a stripper too. I think."

My mouth went dry as I remembered what Claire had said the previous night. "You think?" I said, trying to sound amused. "You can't remember?"

"Not really . . . I remember a girl coming in and she was kind of scrawny and not wearing much. But I don't remember if she took off her clothes."

"You didn't do anything you regret, then?"

"I regret trying to match drinks with Killian, but apart from that, I think I'm okay. In the shower this morning I checked myself for bite-marks, scars, tattoos and lipstick-marks, and I didn't find any. So I doubt there's going to be any compromising photos. How about you? How did the hen party go?"

"It was okay," I lied. "Only the five of us, though. How big was your entourage?"

"About thirty at one point. Almost all the guys from the office came. Even my dad showed up for a while. So anyway . . . where do we stand? Anything else need to be done for the wedding?"

"Nothing," I said. "We're all set. Mrs Diggle checked out the dress yesterday, and that was the last thing. I think."

"Great. Everything seems to be going fine at our end. They're going to be setting up the marquee tomorrow afternoon. That reminds me . . . the bad news is that I checked the weather and the forecast doesn't look great: rain is expected."

"Damn!"

"So I think we should postpone the wedding until we're sure of better weather."

For a second, I thought he was being serious. It was a second that played on my mind a lot, later on. For now, I just said, "Oh, very funny."

"You want to know something strange? Now that all the planning and organising is done, I barely know what to do with myself. I shouldn't have taken the whole week off work. I can see that I'm going to be pacing up and down and fretting for the next couple of days."

"You've got the suits?"

"Sarah picked them up this morning. You've paid the caterers?"

"No, they don't get paid until after the wedding. Just in case something goes wrong."

"Such as?"

"Well, if for some reason we had to cancel the wedding. According to the contract, they'll keep the deposit and we're still liable for seventy per cent of the bill, but that's a lot better than a hundred per cent. But that seventy per cent only applies if we cancel after they've arrived. It's forty per cent if we cancel tomorrow, and twenty if we cancel today."

Thomas said, "I'm impressed. You negotiated that yourself?"

"Yeah. But it didn't hurt that I had the name of your company as leverage. It's amazing how quickly people fall over themselves to cut their prices if they think they're making a really good contact."

"So how much is the whole thing coming in at? What's our final figure?"

"Not counting the honeymoon," – Thomas had been taking care of that – "we're talking just over twelve and a half thousand euro."

He whistled. "Incredible! How come it's so cheap? Stephen Parker was telling me that his wedding cost about twenty-three thousand, and his wasn't any more elaborate than ours."

"Stephen Parker didn't have me organising it. This *is* the kind of thing I used to do when I was with Desire and Design, after all."

"We're pretty much all poised and ready to go, then?"

"We are."

He hesitated. "That's great. So . . . how are you feeling about it all?"

"Fine. A little nervous, but nothing too serious. You?"

"You know me: calm on the outside, tumble-dryer-in-a-hurricane on the inside."

"Is it too late for us to just elope and avoid the whole show?"

Thomas laughed. "I've been wondering that myself! Can't you just picture the look on everyone's faces? We'd turn up together and say, 'Sorry, everyone, but there's not going to be a wedding today because we already got married. But stay for the meal anyway.'"

"Or we could just say, 'We've decided not to get married, but we're still going to be together, so consider this a free party.' And we'd tell them that they could even take all their presents back."

"Somehow, I don't think that would make anyone very happy."

"You're probably right."

"Anyway, I'd better get back to nursing my hangover. I've already had three espressos and a litre of Lucozade . . . that might explain all the pacing and fretting. Listen, did Sam Maroto call over yet? He said he'd do it this afternoon."

"Who's Sam Maroto?"

"A solicitor. The company keeps him on retainer."

"No . . . what's all this about? Why would he need to see me?"

"The pre-nups."

My heart was suddenly pounding. "The *what*?"

"The pre-nuptial agreement."

"You have got to be fucking kidding me! There's no way I'm signing anything like that!"

Thomas paused. "But – but everyone does it! It's a standard part of getting married these days. We both sign an agreement that helps to control any recompense or settlements if the marriage doesn't work out. It's standard stuff."

"I'm not doing it."

"Orla, you're going to have to. I mean, *I* know you're not after my money or anything, but, well . . . there's my parents. They've got a substantial amount of assets and capital. If I was their sole beneficiary, it might be different, but they're involved in a number of trusts and charities, and they've set aside a sizeable portion to be set up as a trust fund of their own. It would be incredibly foolhardy of me to get married without having a legal document to protect the family estate. It's not like you're going to get *nothing* if we were to divorce; the pre-nuptial agreement is just there to stop you from getting everything."

"So we're not even married yet and you're already planning for our divorce? Jesus, that's cold!"

"I realise that it's not pleasant, but that's the way things are done. You have to look at it from *my* point of view."

"Oh, I am! From your point of view, it's a bribe for me to stay married to you, right?"

"It's not like that at all."

"Thomas, I'm not doing it! I'm not going to sign any sort of pre-nuptial agreement. Even if the agreement was completely in my favour, I still wouldn't sign it. The only thing I was prepared to sign was the registry book. Why the hell didn't you bring this up before?"

"I didn't think I needed to. I thought it was understood. Everybody does it."

"No, they don't. I can understand movie stars doing it, because their marriages are much less likely to last, but it's not for me. It's not for ordinary people like me."

"Orla, you haven't even *seen* the agreement yet! When Sam gets there, he'll explain it to you in as much detail as you like. He's even going to have his laptop and a printer with him, so if there's any changes – within reason – he can do them there and then."

"And should I get my own solicitor to have a look at it?"

"There shouldn't be any need. This isn't like divorce papers. In this instance, Sam's not just my solicitor, he's *our* solicitor. Trust me, this is the right thing to do."

I took a deep breath and let it out slowly. "Just say, for the sake of it, that I refuse to sign it. What would happen?"

"Well . . . we'd have to sit down and talk about it, like any contract. Hammer out the details and try to reach a compromise."

"What if I wasn't willing to compromise? Say if I just flat-out refuse to sign any pre-nuptial agreement?"

"I can't believe you're doing this! Really, it's not like I'm asking you to sign a pact with the devil! The agreement is just to make sure that you're not marrying me just for my money."

"You know I'm not!"

"Yes, *I* know that, but we need a legal document to back it up!"

"Don't you trust me? You don't, do you?"

"Of course I trust you! Orla, the pre-nup protects you as well as me, you know! I've seen cases where the husband had all the money and could afford the best solicitors, and the wife ended up with nothing, even though it was the husband who called for the divorce. With our agreement, you're guaranteed a substantial income no matter what happens!"

"I don't want a bloody written guarantee, Thomas!"

"Then what *do* you want?"

"I want love! And love should be unconditional!"

"I do love you, you know that, it's just . . . there's more to a marriage than love. A marriage is an agreement that we're going to share every part of our lives together."

"Exactly! The marriage is already an agreement – we shouldn't need any other legal documents!"

"You're right; we shouldn't. In a perfect world, we'd never need anything like this. But it's not a perfect world, Orla. Sometimes things don't work out the way we want them to, and you have to be prepared for that. That's all the pre-nuptial agreement is, you know. It's like . . . it's like putting a first-aid kit into the glove compartment of your car. You hope you're never going to need it, but it's better to have it and not need it, than to need it and not have it."

That made sense, and for a second I almost relented. Then a voice at the back of my mind said: This is my one chance to get out of this wedding. It's now or never.

"Are you still there?"

"I'm here . . . I'm sorry, Thomas. I understand what you're saying, and I can see how it makes perfect sense to you, but it's not going to happen. I'm not going to sign it."

"But –"

I interrupted him. "It isn't just because of the pre-nuptial agreement. I've had – doubts, I suppose – for a while now, and this is just throwing some light onto them. I think that you knew I'd have problems with the agreement, and that's why you didn't mention it before. You thought that you could just slip it in at the last minute, and I'd sign it because it'd be too late not to, right?"

"No, look –"

"Thomas, you're a businessman. You deal with contracts every single day. That's your job, isn't it? You spend your days negotiating over contracts, trying to get the best possible deal. I mean, that's how you did it with the Nine Acres project, right? You kept delaying and delaying, holding out for the best possible deal from Des before you signed the contract. You know, if you hadn't done that, if you'd signed the contract and given Des the money on the original date, he might never have run."

Thomas paused for so long that I almost thought that he'd hung up on me. Or died. "You're blaming me for what Mills did to you."

"No, I'm not. I'm blaming him. I'm just making a point, that's all."

"What point *are* you making?"

"That you know enough about contracts to know how things should be done. And springing a pre-nuptial agreement on me two days before the wedding is wrong. It's unforgivable."

"Forget it, then. I'll call Maroto and tell him to tear up the agreement. We can do without it, right? We shouldn't let something like this come between us."

Again, I almost gave in there and then. "No. Look, I need to think. I'll call you back in a couple of minutes."

"Wait a second –"

"No. You wait. Give me five minutes, okay? That's all." I hung up the phone.

I jumped when a voice from the doorway said, "You all right?"

I turned to see Davina standing there, carefully watching me. "How much did you hear?"

"Everything from 'Say I just flat-out refuse to sign any pre-nuptial agreement?'. Sorry . . . I didn't know whether to back out quietly and go for a walk, or to let you know I was there." She shrugged, and gave me a faint smile. "In the end I decided to be nosey."

I bit my lip. "So . . .?"

"So I say good for you; you didn't give in. Phone the bastard back and tell him to fuck off with himself."

"He just said that he'll tell his solicitor to tear it up."

Davina pushed the door closed. "Would that make you happy?"

"Of course it would!"

"What would make you happier, then? Marrying Thomas with no pre-nuptial agreement, or not marrying him?"

"Right now? Not marrying him."

"There's your answer, then."

Chapter 27

It was Thursday morning: the day I should have been getting married.

I woke to the sound of Davina clattering away in the kitchen, cleaning up from the previous night's impromptu party. It had started when Justin and Mags called over to see how I was. In the middle of their sympathetic hugs the doorbell rang again, and Justin answered it to see Killian and Claire standing on the doorstep looking anxious. Then Davina had phoned Pauline, and she'd come along with her not-boyfriend Eamonn, who brought along one of his mates that they happened to meet on the way. It wasn't long before Davina and Eamonn's friend were snogging in the kitchen and I was the only one there without a partner.

Despite that, though, it had been an interesting night; at first, everyone avoided talking about Thomas, and instead concentrated on what a bastard Des had been, which cheered me up not in the slightest.

Cancelling the wedding had been a painful task, but at

least I'd only had to tell my own friends that it was all over; Thomas said he'd take care of his family and friends. I found out later, though, that he'd actually delegated that responsibility to his mother.

And now here I was, pulling on a pair of jeans when I should have been getting stitched into my wedding dress.

Still, I felt more relieved than disappointed. My life had taken yet another unexpected right turn into the unknown, but this time I was better equipped to deal with it.

Davina was in the kitchen, very slowly doing the washing up and looking miserable about it. "Morning," I said.

"How're you doing?"

"Not bad." I looked around; she hadn't made that much of a difference to the untidiness. "Been up long?"

"A couple of hours." She sighed and splashed at the water with the washing-up brush. "Why don't we just go mad and hire a cleaner to do all this?"

"Ah, it won't take us that long if we really put our backs into it." I found a reasonably clean tea towel and started to dry the glasses. "So how late did Thingy leave last night?" When I gave up and went to bed, Davina and Eamonn's friend had been wrapped up in each other on the sofa.

"About three, I think."

"Made any plans?"

"God no! Sure I'm going home in a couple of days."

There was a familiar knocking on the door. "That'll be Mr Farley," I said. I'd left a note for him the previous day, explaining that I'd called off the wedding.

I went out to the hall and opened the door to see him standing there with a single red rose. "For you, Orla."

"Thank you! Come in, please."

He took off his old-man's overcoat and hung it over his arm. "You're the talk of the town again," he said as he followed me into the kitchen.

"I can imagine. I'm sorry about everything. I know you were looking forward to being the surrogate father of the bride. But, well . . . it just wasn't right."

"I understand. And you know, I'm happy for you."

"Happy?"

"Yes. Because you didn't leave it until it was too late. You didn't take the easy path and just get married and hope it would work out." He rummaged in his coat pocket and found a half-bottle of whiskey. "I don't know about you two, but I think this calls for a celebration!"

I laughed. "Didn't we celebrate my engagement too?"

"Yes, but I don't mind, you don't mind, I'm sure Davina doesn't mind, and I know that the whiskey doesn't mind. Will you join me for a small one?"

"I will indeed."

* * *

An hour later the three of us were well on the way to being drunk. Again. Davina had left the washing-up water to go cold and found several unopened beer bottles, which we rapidly opened.

Mr Farley was in the middle of telling us a story – about a jackdaw that used to perch outside his window when he was a boy – when the phone rang. We ignored it and let the answering machine take over.

It was only when Mr Farley went back next door that I bothered to play the message.

"Ms Adare? This is Detective Mason. Call me as soon as you get this. We've just heard from Scotland Yard that Desmond Mills has been arrested in London. They're extraditing him. He should be back in Ireland in a day or two. His solicitor is maintaining that Mills is completely innocent, that he was forced against his will to take the money, and that you will be able to provide evidence to that effect."

* * *

Detective Mason arrived at the house in a squad car, which must have really amused the neighbours. Following his instructions, I was waiting – coat in hand – at the gate.

He jumped out and opened the passenger door for me. "All set?"

"Yeah. Where exactly are we going?"

"Back to the station. Mr Mills' solicitor is waiting for you there, and he's got a lot of questions to ask you." He ushered me into the car, then went around and got in the other side. He hit the accelerator and we sped off.

"Am I in some kind of trouble?" I asked, fumbling for the seat belt. The last thing I needed was to be killed in a car crash. And in a police car, no less.

He sniffed, then frowned. "Ms Adare . . . have you been drinking?"

"Yep."

"Bit early in the day for that."

"Well, that's not a crime, is it?"

"No. And no, you're not in trouble. But Mills is."

"So how did they find him?"

"He was living in London under a false identity. He probably never would have been found if he hadn't been involved in a minor traffic incident; he rear-ended a car that was stopped at a red light, and the SOCO became suspicious and checked him out."

"The SOCO?"

"Scene-of-crime officer. The policeman who was investigating. Apparently he felt that Mills was acting suspiciously. I don't know what that means exactly. Whatever it was that tipped him off, it was enough for him to investigate further. He checked Mills' ID and discovered it was a forgery. Because of his Irish accent he then checked with us, and found out we're looking for a man named Desmond Mills who happens to fit this man's description exactly. So they printed him, and it was Mills all right."

It was fascinating to see how the other motorists reacted to the sight of a squad car; the road was a sea of guilty faces and sudden deceleration. "Can you put the siren on?" I asked.

"No."

"Well, can we go through a red light, then?"

"Orla, if I put the siren on, it'll be logged and transmitted back to Garda HQ and then I'll have to fill out a report about it. And since there's no specific need for the siren, I'll be fined and possibly have to face a disciplinary hearing."

"Oh." Then I caught a hint of a smile. "You just made that up, didn't you?"

Another smile. "Not a bit."

"On your phone message you said something about me being able to provide Des with an alibi?"

"That's right. According to his story, he'd never had

any plans to take the money. He says he fell foul of a couple of thugs who forced him to do it. I can't see exactly how he expects to fit you into it all."

"God, Des sure knows how to pick his times, doesn't he?"

"How do you mean?"

"Today's my wedding day."

Detective Mason's face fell. "I'm sorry. I didn't know. We can do this some other time."

"I'm not actually *getting* married today; we called it off. Long story. I won't go into it now, but it culminates in me drowning my sorrows a few times. Hence the smell of drink. Forget it. Look, what do I have to do?"

"The man you're about to meet at the station is Mills' solicitor. He's a right shady bastard and he's going to put pressure on you, okay? I don't know his game-plan, but I know what he's after: he wants Mills to come out of this looking like a victim. Now, if that means he needs to make *you* look bad, he'll do it, understood?"

I nodded. "Understood."

The Sierra in front of us came to a rather sudden stop, and the detective hit the brakes. We were right outside McGrath's newsagents, and the driver calmly got out of his car and walked into the shop without even noticing us.

"Arrest him!" I said. "The bastard didn't even bother to put on his hazard lights!"

Detective Mason pulled the squad car in behind the Sierra. "Don't go anywhere, Orla. And don't touch anything."

He got out of the car, and walked around the Sierra

making notes in his little book. He even checked the threads on the tyres.

A minute later, the motorist came out of the shop, newspaper in one hand, car keys dangling from the other, and a Mars bar sticking out of his mouth. He looked like he didn't have a care in the world. Then he saw the police car; he went extremely pale and the Mars bar dropped to the ground.

It was a joy to watch, and I wished I knew how to work the squad car's windows so that I could hear more of the conversation. As it was, I only caught brief phrases like "reckless disregard" and "penalty points".

The best bit was at the end, when Detective Mason told the driver to pick up the fallen Mars bar and put it in the bin: "Littering is an offence," he told him.

We watched as the motorist got back into his Sierra and drove off very, very slowly.

"That was great!" I said. "So . . . Is there going to be a trial?"

"No, but I think I scared him into driving more carefully from now on."

"I mean, for Des. Is *he* going to have a trial?"

The detective pulled out into the traffic, which very kindly slowed way down for us. "There'll be an arraignment first. That's to establish the situation. If the solicitor can prove to a reasonable degree that Mills was forced against his will to take the money – and I'm sure he's going to try – then that's going to change the whole nature of the case. It's not likely, but it's possible that Mills will get away with this. There's also a possibility that he's going to claim that he needs police protection against the people who allegedly forced him."

"Which would in fact *really* protect him against the loan sharks, right?"

"If everything he told you about that is true, yes."

"I'm sure it *is* true," I said.

"With all due respect, Orla, after what he did, I think you'd be incredibly foolish to believe a word he said."

"Good point. But say I refuse to back Des's story up?"

"If you refuse to testify, they can issue you with a summons and you'll be entered as a hostile witness."

"Is that bad?"

"It's bad for them. But I wouldn't do that, if I was you. Just tell the truth as you know it, and you'll be fine."

"Yeah, but what if the truth I tell still happens to get him off the charge?"

"That's irrelevant. It's up to the prosecutor to prove that Mills is guilty, and the evidence is pretty strong. I mean, if he really was being coerced into taking the money – and the story he told you about the loan sharks wasn't true – then why did he set up the company with you named as a director, but not tell you about it? No, I don't think he's going to get away with it."

"What'll happen if he's found guilty?"

"That's almost impossible to say. It really depends on the tactics his solicitor will use. Look, I shouldn't tell you too much, because I don't want anyone to be able to accuse me of coaching a witness, but I will say this: justice is justice, do you understand me?"

"I think so."

"I hope you do. Do *not* let the solicitor pressurise you

into perjury, okay? You tell the absolute truth regardless of the outcome. And when I say he's going to pressurise you, I mean it. That man could talk the hind legs off a whole sanctuary full of donkeys." He sighed. "Orla, regardless of how you feel about Mills, you have to do what's right. Even if it means that he gets off."

* * *

"I'd like a few moments alone with Ms Adare," Nathan Fowler said to Detective Mason.

"Not a chance."

Fowler just shrugged and sat down opposite me. I was nursing my second black coffee in ten minutes. It might even have been nice coffee, but I couldn't tell because Detective Mason had practically force-fed me with Extra Strong Mints to get rid of the smell of drink.

"Hello again, Ms Adare," Fowler said. "You never returned my phone calls."

"You never made any."

He frowned and consulted his notes. "I'm quite sure that I did." He began to list a series of dates and times, all quite recent.

I shook my head. "You're mistaken. I never received any phone calls from you."

Detective Mason cleared his throat loudly, and said, "Excuse me for interrupting, Mr Fowler. It's just that I was wondering if now might be a good time for me to take my lunch. Your famous" – he made quotes marks with his fingers – "'I made a lot of phone calls to you' routine usually lasts about half an hour, right?"

Fowler gazed up at the detective with an "I don't know

what you're talking about" expression, but clearly he did. He flipped through his notes until he reached another page. "Ms Adare, are you now or have you ever in the past been aware that Mr Mills suffers from a mild form of epilepsy?"

Out of the corner of my eye I could see Detective Mason shaking his head very slightly.

"No. This is the first I've heard about that." It also turned out to be the *last* I'd hear about it: the detective later told me that this was another of Fowler's little tricks: plant the seeds early on, just in case you need to reap them later.

"I see. And . . . is it or is it not true that in both the recent past *and* the recent present you entered into a relationship with one Thomas Kennedy, the very same man with whom your former – and I stress *former* – lover Desmond Mills, the defendant, was working on the shopping-mall complex allegedly known as Nine Acres, *regardless* of the fact that the site upon which aforementioned said shopping-centre complex is somewhat larger than nine actual acres in size?"

As I was trying to navigate my way around this question, he smiled smugly and said, "A simple yes or no will suffice."

The detective raised his eyes. "Mr Fowler –"

"Please allow Ms Adare to give her answers, Detective!" He turned to me. "Ms Adare?"

"The answer is yes *and* no."

"I see," he said, and seemed unsure how to continue. "So . . . you admit it, then?"

"I admit that it is or is not true, yes. And thank you for asking."

He said, "You're welcome," then looked a little unsettled, as though he wasn't sure how to deal with someone who wasn't overwhelmed by his wordplay.

"I particularly like your use of the phrase 'the recent present'," I added, cheerfully.

"Indeed." He took a short, sharp breath. "Excellent." Another sharp breath. "Incidentally, I understand that you thereafter regained possession of most of the furniture allegedly stolen from your house?"

"That's correct."

"And it was found to be located in the hardware store belonging to one Mr Peter Harney – is that also correct?"

"It is."

"This would be the same Peter Harney who was shortly thereafter seen to be entering your property with said furniture with a view to returning it to its rightful owner, that is, you, yourself?"

"That's right."

"I *see*!" He said that as though I'd just inadvertently given something away. "Now, don't you find it strange that your belongings ended up in the possession of a man with whom your former lover had had had dealings in the past?"

I was sure that the three "hads" were only in there in another attempt to confuse me. "No, it's not strange at all. He has the only hardware store in town. Look, Mr Fowler, we could play this game all day! Just tell me what you want from me."

He got all indignant. "Play? *Game*? Ms Adare, an innocent man's future is at stake here!"

"If he's innocent, then how come the last time I spoke

to you, you referred to him as a criminal mastermind? You were all gung-ho to track him down then, and now you're defending him. And how come you ended up as his solicitor? How did he choose you?"

"I heard about his arrest and offered my services to him. *Pro bono publico.*"

"Ah, that! Just as you offered your services to me, which were also *pro bono publico*, until you mentioned the usual ten per cent finder's fee." I sighed. "Mr Fowler, I've had a really, really stressful couple of days, so let's just get this over with. As it is, all these little tricks to confuse me are just turning me against you. What do you want?"

"Very well. My client wishes you to appear as a witness in his defence."

"That much I'd gathered. But after what he did to me, why should I defend him?"

"Because he is an innocent man! Accused of a crime he didn't commit! Friendless, alone, forced to go on the run to prove his innocence!"

"He went on the run because he's guilty," I said. "He told me that himself. He told me that he'd borrowed money from some loan sharks and wasn't able to pay it back. He never said anything about someone else forcing him to do it."

He looked at me sombrely. "Of course not. They had a gun to his head."

I couldn't help myself: I burst out laughing. "That's great! Oh, I love that! And now you're going to come up with an explanation for that, too, aren't you? For some strange reason, these people forced Des to phone me and tell me a bunch of lies about some loan sharks, right?"

"So! You admit that they were lies!"

"Mr Fowler, you're not going to be able to trick me into providing Des with an alibi, okay? I may not have studied law, but that doesn't mean I'm stupid. And after everything I've gone through in the past year, you're not going to be able to intimidate me or baffle me with bullshit." Then I leaned closer to him. "Maybe I am only a waitress and not a high-paid lawyer, but I'm smarter than you are. Now, you tell me exactly how I'm supposed to be able to help Des, or I'm walking."

Finally, Fowler caved in. "He wants you to mention that on several occasions he was visited at your home by a number of dangerous-looking men who seemed to have some sort of strange hold over him. He has provided dates, first names and descriptions, and he's sure that you'll remember them."

I pushed myself away from the desk, and stood up. "There was never anyone like that. Either Des or you have made that all up." I remembered something that the detective had said in the car. "Des can't be completely innocent, because he forged my signature on all the business forms. He was up to something right from the start."

The solicitor just stared at his papers for a few seconds. "All right. I understand. We may still need to call upon you as a witness."

"That's fine," I said. "But you should know that I'm never going to lie in court. The truth, the whole truth, and nothing but the truth. Isn't that what you people are supposed to believe in?"

"It is indeed, Ms Adare. It is indeed." He stood up and

gathered his papers together, then reached into the inside breast pocket of his jacket, and pulled out a business card and handed it to me. "In case you have any further questions . . ."

"You already gave me your card."

"This one has my new mobile phone number."

I looked at the card. "And I see that it has your name spelled correctly this time. Congratulations. So are we done here?"

"We are." He turned to the detective. "Thank you for your time, officer."

Once Fowler had left, Detective Mason said, "You handled him well."

"It might have been different if I hadn't met him before. So what's going to happen now?"

"It's possible now that Fowler will encourage Mills to plead guilty, but with extenuating circumstances."

"Such as?"

He shrugged. "Could be anything at all, knowing Fowler. Do you want a lift back home?"

"Yes, please."

* * *

Davina arrived back at the house half an hour after I did. "Orla? You here?" There was a slight tremor in her voice.

I went out into the hall. "Everything okay?"

"I'm not sure. A really weird thing just happened."

"What?"

"I was just coming around the corner and this guy came up to me, and I thought he was going to ask for directions or something like that, but he just said, 'Tell her that if she doesn't want Justin to find out about Mags and Peter, she has to do whatever I tell her to do.' I asked him what he meant, but he just told me the same thing again, and again, to make sure I remembered it. You don't suppose he meant *our* Justin and Mags, do you?"

Chapter 28

So after everything that Des had done, now he was trying to blackmail me.

This did not make me very happy.

"Describe the man who said this to you," I told Davina.

"He was about forty, I suppose. Overweight, glasses, grey hair. He had really fat lips, too. You know? All rubbery and wet-looking."

"Shit. That sounds like Fowler." I explained to Davina what had happened at the police station, and what Fowler's message had meant.

She said, "Your best option is to do as he says. Even if your testimony manages to get Des off, that doesn't mean he'll get away scot-free. The cops are going to start investigating these made-up gangsters who are supposed to have forced him to do it, and the more they dig the more they're going to realise that he was lying."

"Right," I said. "And then they'll know that *I* was lying in court. And that's an offence."

"But if you tell the truth, then Des will mention what Justin's wife's been up to. And he'll definitely mention that you knew about it and didn't say anything."

"I know."

She had a think. "You know what you could do? You could go to Justin and Mags and tell them what's happened, and say that you got this cryptic note, and that it mentions people called Pete and Mags, and you're wondering if it's the same Mags."

"You mean, leave it out there for her to decide what to do?"

"Well, yeah."

"In that case, why don't I just phone her and tell her directly that Des knows about her affair and that he's using that knowledge to blackmail me?"

"That might be better . . . but you'd be putting her in a really awkward position."

"Yeah . . . well, no, actually. It wouldn't be me putting her in the awkward position, it'd be herself. But regardless of that, no matter how it comes out, Justin will find out that I knew and didn't tell him. There's no way I can win."

"And so we're back to you doing whatever Fowler wants, aren't we?"

"That's how it looks. But . . . where will it stop? If I do this, how do I know he won't try to blackmail me about something else in the future?"

* * *

A few minutes later, I was on my way upstairs when Nathan Fowler phoned my mobile. "So you got the message?"

"Yeah," I said. "You know that what you're doing is called blackmail, don't you?"

He ignored me. "What's your decision?"

"I haven't made it yet."

"You have two hours to make up your mind, Ms Adare. If I don't hear from you before then, the deal is off. Understood?"

"Suppose I go straight to the police and tell them what you're doing?"

"Good luck proving it. If you do, however, your friend Justin will definitely find out about his wife's affair. And what's more, he'll find out that you've known all along."

"Look, two hours isn't long enough! There's a lot to consider!"

"The clock is ticking, Ms Adare." He hung up.

I screamed into the phone. "Bastard!"

Davina came out from the kitchen. "What did he say?"

"I have two hours to make up my mind."

"Okay . . . Look, what you should do first is –"

I cut her off. "Sorry, Davina. I've already got my mind reeling without any more advice, okay? I just need some time alone to work it all out."

"Sure. Okay. Right. I'll tell you what, I'll go and see my mother. Give me a call if you need me, okay?"

"Thanks."

* * *

After Davina left I went up to my bedroom and stretched out on the bed, staring at the ceiling as I went over my options.

I could perjure myself and say that there had indeed been some dangerous-looking men hanging around.

I could just go and see Mags and tell her about the situation, and let her deal with it.

Or I could talk to Justin and tell him the whole truth.

A thought occurred to me: I could go and see Justin and tell him a complete lie . . . I could say that Des was making things up in order to throw everything into confusion, and that one of the things he made up was an affair between Mags and Pete Harney.

But I dismissed that idea almost immediately: Des wouldn't make up something like that because it wouldn't help his case in any way.

Then again, I could just go straight to Detective Mason and tell him that Nathan Fowler was trying to blackmail me.

And if I did *that*, then the truth about Mags and Pete would definitely get out. So that brought me back to square one.

I went over it and over it, and it seemed impossible to find a way to prevent Justin from getting hurt.

Unless I did as Fowler said. And even then, how could I trust that Des wouldn't mention the affair anyway? I mean, this man stole everything I owned and now he was trying to blackmail me! How could I trust him at all?

* * *

Killian looked surprised to see me. "Hey . . . how're things?"

I peered in past him. "Is Claire here? The kids?"

"No, their granny and granddad took them off to the zoo."

I breathed a sigh of relief. "Good! It's you I need to talk to, and I don't want anyone to overhear."

"Okay. Come on in."

"No, I'd rather we weren't here. I could do with some fresh air anyway."

So, for the first time since we were little kids, my brother and I went for a walk. We went through the town via the backstreets – I really wasn't in the mood for bumping into people who may have been expecting to see me in a wedding dress – and headed out into darkest suburbia.

"What's on your mind? Still worrying that you did the right thing?"

"No, I know I did the right thing. Listen, I've got a bit of a dilemma. Suppose someone you knew was married to someone else, and you found out that your friend's wife – or husband – was having an affair. And suppose that the person who's having the affair knows that you know, because she – or he – told you, but made you promise not to say anything to anybody. And suppose that someone else knew, and knew that you knew, and wanted to use that . . ." I took a deep breath, and tried to figure out the best way of explaining the situation without giving too much away. Then I changed my mind. "Ah, screw it! Look, the fact is Justin's wife has been seeing someone else for the past few years."

"You're serious?"

"Yeah. I found out about it last year. Remember when I had to stay with someone after Des ran off? Well, I stayed with Mags and she told me all about it. We haven't mentioned it much since, but I know it's still going on. And the thing is, I can't tell Justin, can I?"

He thought about that. "Not really. Who's she having the affair with?"

"Do you know Peter Harney who runs the hardware store?"

"No."

"Oh. Well, that doesn't really matter anyway. Here's the story; I've just spent an hour in the police station. Des was arrested in London a couple of days ago."

Killian laughed and pumped the air with his fist. "Yes!"

"It's not that simple. He's claiming that he was forced to take the money and disappear, and his solicitor is trying to get me to back up Des's claims in court."

"Bastard! So what did you tell him?"

"I said no, but after I got home Davina met the solicitor on the road and he said that she was to tell me that if I didn't do what he said, Des would tell everyone about Mags's affair. Now do you see the problem?"

"Not really."

I started to explain it again, in simpler terms, but Killian stopped me. "I understand what you mean, but I don't know why it's a problem. *Let* him tell Justin. If Mags is doing the dirty on him, it's got nothing to do with you."

"Yeah, but I don't want Justin to get hurt."

"So? It's not you who's doing the hurting, is it?"

"It will be if I let it happen. What the hell am I going to do? I've got to decide between Justin getting hurt and me committing perjury, and possibly helping Des to go free!"

Killian stopped walking, grabbed my arm and spun me around to face him. "Orla . . . get a grip, okay?"

I repeated myself. "What am I going to do?"

481

"You are going to tell the truth, that's all."

"But Justin –"

"Screw Justin!"

"He's one of my oldest friends!"

"I know that. But you're not the one who's having the affair. Mags is. If Justin gets hurt, it's Mags's fault, not yours. Look, Des is just using you again. This time, he's relying on your loyalty to Justin to save him. Hasn't he already taken enough from you, without also taking your honesty?"

I swallowed. "Put like that, yeah. You could be right."

"I am right. But I'll tell you what I'll do . . . I'll remove the problem for you, how's that sound?"

"How do you mean?"

"I'll call Justin and tell him." He pulled his mobile phone out of his jacket pocket.

"No! Killian, that's exactly what I *don't* want!"

He looked at me for a few seconds. "How much choice do you have?"

"What if it was you? What if Claire was seeing someone else? Would you want to find out about it from one of your best friends?"

"I'd be less concerned with how I found out about it than I would be with the affair itself." He handed the phone to me. "Call him. Now."

* * *

I'd told Justin that I needed to talk to him, and I didn't want to meet at his place or my place or anywhere we might meet someone we knew. We needed to be alone, and uninterrupted.

So he'd agreed to meet me in the park, by the swings. It was all very clandestine and mysterious, and I think he rather enjoyed the idea; Justin's always wanted to be a spy.

Killian went back to his in-laws' house, and I sat on the bench in the playground and waited for Justin. I didn't really know how I would explain it to him, or even how much I was going to tell him, but I did my best to convince myself that this was the right thing to do.

Someone suddenly vaulted over the bench and dropped into a sitting position next to me. It was Justin and, without looking at me, he said in a bad Russian accent, "So! You are the one known as The Purple Badger, yes?"

I was about to reply when someone sat on the other end of the bench. It was Mags.

I looked from Justin to Mags and back. "Shit!"

"What's up?" Mags asked.

To Justin, I said, "Which part of 'Come alone' didn't you understand?"

Now they were both looking puzzled. "Is everything okay?" Justin asked. "Er . . . considering what day it is, and everything."

"Do you want me to go?" Mags asked.

"No . . . wait. Give me a minute . . . Okay, here's the story. Des was arrested in London. His solicitor is trying to blackmail me into providing Des with an alibi. Des knows that I'm keeping a secret for someone, and if I don't do what his solicitor wants, he's going to spill the beans at the trial. If that happens, there's some people close to me who are going to be hurt."

"Jesus," Justin said. "Okay, look, you have to be honest. I don't suppose you've talked to the police about this?"

"No. And I don't have much time to make my decision. If I do what the solicitor says, that's perjury. If I don't, I'm hurting someone."

I looked at Mags. She was staring at her hands.

"So what do I do?" I asked.

"Don't let the bastards force you into lying on the witness stand, Orla! That'll make you as guilty as Des is. You just tell the truth and let someone else worry about the consequences."

"Right," Mags said. "Whatever this secret is, it might never come out."

"I'm sure it will," I said. "Seriously. I met the solicitor, and he's going to use whatever he can to get Des off the hook." I looked at my watch. "I've got half an hour to decide. He's going to phone me at home and get my decision."

"Look, how bad is this secret?" Justin asked. "You haven't murdered anyone, have you?"

"No, it's not me. Someone I know has done something they shouldn't have."

"Something illegal?"

"No, not illegal."

"Well, in that case, don't worry about it."

I nodded, and got to my feet. "I'd better head on home, then. Thanks."

"Record his phone call," Justin said. "Your answering machine can do that, can't it?"

"Yeah, but he's going to phone on my mobile. Anyway, he's probably not going to say anything that could be used against him."

They walked with me as far as the gate of the park. "So it's turned out to be a big day for you after all," Justin said, cheerfully.

I gave him a hug, then took Mags aside. "I'm sorry."

Still keeping a smile on her face in case Justin was watching, she said, "You fucking *bitch*."

"It wasn't me. I never told anyone. Des found out about it from Peter."

"I thought I could trust you!" Her fake smile faded and tears began to spill down her cheeks.

"For God's sake, Mags! Don't you think I've got enough on my plate without you blaming me for all this? You're the one who –"

I didn't see it coming: she slapped me. Open-handed, right across the face.

Justin came rushing over. "What the hell . . .?"

Mags pushed him aside, screamed right into my face, "This is all your fucking fault!"

I stared at her. "Mags – don't push me. I mean it."

Justin stepped in between the two of us. "What's this about? Mags?"

"Tell him," I said to her. "Now you don't have a choice, do you? You could have kept your mouth shut and hoped that it'd turn out okay, but you didn't. Live with the consequences, Mags."

I turned and walked away, leaving them to sort out their own problems.

* * *

To put it simply, Justin walked out on Mags. He spent the next couple of days in my spare bedroom – Davina having been despatched back to her mother's house – and he did a *lot* of moping.

And after the moping, came the blaming. It was his own fault for spending so much time away from home. It was my fault, because if not for me he might never have known about it and would still be happy. It was Des's fault for trying to blackmail me.

Eventually, he got around to "It's Mags' fault and Pete's fault" which struck me as a fair and accurate assessment.

It was a week before Justin even stepped outside the house, and then it was only because he was going home to pick up some clothes. He chose a time when he knew that Mags would be at school, and he came straight back and spent another week in the house, moping and blaming.

And all through this, I felt guilty as hell.

It didn't help that towards the end of the second week I received a letter from Argentina:

"Dear Orla,

Decided to go on the honeymoon by myself. No sense in wasting both of the tickets, right? Been interesting so far. Met a lot of nice people. I'm sure you won't mind that I've told them how I managed to be in the honeymoon suite all on my own. And even if you do mind, well . . . that's just your hard luck. Believe me, it makes for fascinating conversation! I've been invited to more parties in the past week than I could possibly hope to attend.

"I keep thinking that maybe you made the right choice. I need to take a long, hard look at my life, and see where I've been going wrong. Who knows: maybe one day we'll meet again, and perhaps things might be different.

"In the meantime, I just want you to know that I only hate you a bit for dumping me. But it's only a tiny bit, and even then I don't actually blame you.

"I hope all is well with you. I'm thinking of staying on here for another couple of weeks, maybe even a couple of months, so if you feel like it, please write and let me know how things are going with you. Any news?

"Love, Thomas."

Justin read the letter after me. "Wow," he said.

"Wow how?"

"Just wow in general. He seems to have gotten over you pretty quickly. A lot quicker than I'm getting over Mags."

I'd half-expected that; Justin somehow managed to twist every topic around so that it came back to him and Mags. "I've told you before, Justin. You don't *have* to get over Mags. Just go and talk to her!"

He shook his head. "No. She slept with someone else."

"Well, go and beat the crap out of him if that'll make you feel better!"

"I've thought about that, but it won't help." Justin had refused to confront Pete Harney about the affair. It wasn't that he was afraid of him, though. It was because Pete's wife still didn't know, and Justin maintained that there was no point in hurting her as well. I didn't comment on that, but I felt he was wrong. Leaving Pete's wife in the dark was exactly the same thing as me not telling Justin as soon as I'd heard about it.

"Did you ever sleep with someone else, then?" I asked him.

"No, never. Though I did have a chance once. The sales conference in Letterkenny last year. I was pretty sure that one of the women was making a pass at me."

"But you didn't do anything about it?"

"Of course not! As far as I was aware, me and Mags were happily married!"

"If you had done it, though, would that have made a difference?"

"I suppose. But the thing is, I didn't. I've never even so much as kissed another woman. But Mags slept with that bastard God only knows how many times. That's bad enough in itself, but what's worse is that she betrayed me."

It would be nice to say that somewhere along the way I came up with a blinder of an idea that helped Justin and Mags sort things out, but I didn't. Just as there are some secrets that you should never keep, there are some problems that you just can't fix.

Chapter 29

Des wasn't at most of the trial himself. That was because one of his victims had ended up in the same prison for a couple of relatively minor offences and he didn't seem to mind adding aggravated assault to his list. Des's left arm and both of his legs were broken.

My own part in the proceedings was minor: Nathan Fowler changed his mind about calling me as a witness since he no longer had anything to blackmail me with, but the prosecutors did call me, to testify against Des. I told them the truth, the whole truth, and nothing but the truth.

The trial lasted less than a week. It had been expected to run a lot longer, but in light of the overwhelming evidence against him, Des apparently instructed Fowler to change his plea to "Guilty".

I never saw Des again, and I didn't want to. Oh, I saw his photo in the papers, and the TV news showed some footage of him being wheeled out of the courtroom under a blanket, but the last time I actually saw him in person was the Friday before I'd left to spend the weekend in Killian's house.

I suppose it's possible that I might see him again in about seven to ten years, depending on his behaviour.

That's assuming that one of his many falls doesn't turn out to be fatal. Apparently prison stairs can be quite slippery.

* * *

Four weeks after the court case ended, I took two bus rides to the far side of the city, and walked into a large, bright, new supermarket, where I eventually spotted the manager talking to a boy holding a sweeping brush taller than he was.

"Look," Barry was saying to the boy, "it's quite simple. The end with the bristles goes on the ground, you go on the other end, and the object of the game is to get the dust and the spilled pasta shells all in one pile. You then put that pile into the bin. And at the end of the week, you win a prize. For legal reasons we have to call that prize 'your wages'. If you don't play the game, you can't win the prize. Get the picture?"

"All right, all right! Geez!" He went about his duties.

Barry looked up and saw me. "I heard about your trial."

"It wasn't *my* trial," I said. "It was Des's."

"Still. So will everyone get their money back?"

"It's not likely, not unless Des decides to spill the beans on the loan sharks and they manage to get convicted."

490

"And I also heard about your wedding. Or lack thereof."

"Yeah, it's been loads of fun back home, let me tell you. Orla Adare dumps a wealthy bachelor only a couple of days before the notorious Des Mills is finally brought to justice. That's enough to keep them talking for the rest of their lives."

"So . . . why are you here?"

"Believe it or not, I kind of missed you. The last thing I heard from you was a message on my answering machine a few days before the wedding."

Barry cringed. "Oh. That. Still, I was right though, wasn't I?"

"You were. So what's been happening in your life lately?"

"You're going to laugh when I tell you."

"Go on."

"I'm back with Jemima again."

I didn't laugh. "Seriously?"

"Seriously. We had a long, long talk about everything, and we both agreed that we need to see a relationship counsellor. So we've been going every Wednesday afternoon for the past few months. And not only that . . . we're pregnant."

My mouth dropped open in shock.

"We're going to have a baby," he said.

"Yes, I *do* know what 'pregnant' means! So when is it due?"

"We're two and a half months along," he said, grinning. "Imagine me being a father! God, the poor kid!"

"No, you'd make a great dad. And I'm happy for you, I really am."

"How about yourself, though? Seeing anyone?"

I laughed. "Are you kidding? I went out with Thomas on the rebound from Des, and look how that worked out! I'm not going to make the same mistake again!"

Barry nodded. "Good for you. Keep your options open. Listen, I've really got to get back to managing the store. Apparently that's what I'm paid for. You know what you should do? You should come over for dinner some night. I'm sure you and Jem would get on great. You could spend the whole evening tearing me apart."

"Yeah, that sounds like fun. Ring me to arrange it, okay?"

"I will."

"I mean it. I don't want to have to try and track you down again in another few months, all right?"

Barry wrapped his arms around me and kissed the top of my head. "I'm glad you're okay. I was kind of worried, you know?"

"Not worried enough to pick up the phone, though!"

He smiled. "I'll talk to Jem, and pick a good night. Sometime next week, how's that sound?"

I told him it sounded great.

* * *

Two weeks later, on a bright, warm afternoon, I was digging up the back garden when Justin pushed open the kitchen window. "Orla! It's the local law enforcement!"

"Oh, what *now*?" I trudged back towards the house, only to find Detective Mason coming out to meet me halfway.

"Afternoon," he said. "Any exciting developments that you haven't told me about?"

"No, nothing."

"You're sure? No blackmail attempts or kidnappings or fencing stolen goods or anything? Only, the lads have been wondering when you're going to be providing us with some extra overtime."

"Nope. Nothing happening, just work and more work and this," I said, gesturing to the half-dug garden. "I've finally decided to get around to it. Justin's supposed to be helping me, but he keeps finding excuses to watch the snooker instead. You don't feel up to giving us a hand, do you?"

"Not today, sorry. I'm still on duty." He looked me up and down, and smiled. "I like your pink wellies."

"They were the only ones I could find in my size. So how's life in the trenches?"

"It hasn't been too bad lately." He nodded towards the house. "So this Justin – another lodger?"

"Strictly temporary. He broke up with his wife and now has no idea what to do with his life."

"It's not anything more serious, then?"

"No . . . Justin's one of my oldest friends. You know how it is."

He nodded. "Understood."

"So how can I help you?"

"You can have dinner with me tomorrow night," he said.

I laughed. "Oh, I'm sure your girlfriend would love that!"

"Girlfriend?"

"I thought you said you were going out with someone?"

"I was, but we broke up a few months back. So what do you say?"

"You're seriously asking me out?"

"I am."

"On a real date?"

"Of course."

I had to bite the inside of my cheek to stop myself from grinning. "You want to go out with *me*?"

He nodded. "Is that so strange?"

"No, not at all but . . . Actually, yes it is. It'd be weird."

The detective smiled. "It'd be great. What do you say? Yes or no?"

"I mean, are you even *allowed* to ask people out when you're on duty?"

"Come on, now, Orla! Yes or no! I haven't got all day. Somewhere there's a crime happening . . ."

I pretended to think about it. "Okay then, I will, but on one condition. You have to tell me your first name. I can hardly go out with someone whose name I don't know."

"I already told you my name. Philip."

"No, you said that was your middle name. What's your real first name?"

He cringed. "You have to *swear* that you're not going to tell anyone else, okay? God, the slagging I'm going to get if this gets out . . ."

I folded my arms and tapped my feet. "Go on."

"First, you have to understand that when my mother got pregnant my father panicked and did a runner. They weren't married. So my surname wasn't Mason to begin with, okay? It was McKenna. Then a couple of years later my mother married my step-dad, Kenneth Mason. So Mason then became my surname."

"Okay. So you're really Something Philip McKenna. And the something is . . .?"

"Jason."

I burst out laughing. "So the name you were born with is Jason McKenna, but now your name is Jason Mason? God, that's great!"

The detective reddened with embarrassment. "Please! Keep it down! So . . . a deal's a deal, right? You'll go out with me, then?"

I tried to say "Yes" but I was still laughing, so I nodded instead. It was nearly a minute before I could talk again. "Thank you," I said, breathlessly.

He smiled. "For giving you a good laugh, or for asking you out?"

"For caring enough to do both. And for looking after me when things were bad."

"I was just doing my job."

"You did it well."

"Tomorrow night, then? I'll pick you up at eight? We'll go somewhere dead swanky." He looked down at my feet. "So don't wear the wellies."

I walked with him through the house and watched as he headed towards the main road.

Justin came out and stood next to me. "So what did he want this time?"

"Justin . . . it's been nearly two months now. I think it's time you left."

"You want me to go?"

"It's not that I don't enjoy having you here. I do, but

you're spending all your time moping around. You need to either go and see Mags and talk about things, or just forget about her. I know you're still in a bad way, but life moves on, Justin, and you have to move with it."

"But what about you?"

I watched silently until Detective Mason turned the corner.

"Orla? What about you?"

I smiled. "Me? I'm going to be just fine."

THE END

Also published by Poolbeg

The Sweetest Feeling

Jaye Carroll

"After five and a half years of marriage, he can't just make a decision like that and expect me to tag along"

Donal is heading off to Finland on a two-year contract leaving June with her adorable but demanding mutt, Hannibal, for company and the promise of weekend trips home.

But when the trips don't happen and his emails don't exactly shout *can't live without you*, it seems that Donal is settling in too easily. At least she can rely on kind-hearted Vince for some brotherly-in-law support.

While June does battle on the emotional front, her boss is waging war in the office. When he drafts in his equally nasty girlfriend, the poisonous Linda, June's future with the company starts to look just a little shaky.

But that may be the least of her problems!

ISBN 1-84223-049-2

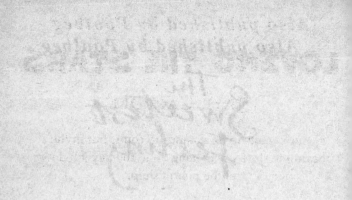

LOVING THE STARS

JAYE CARROLL

Andi wants to be a stand-up comic but in the meantime she's got to hang on to the day job down at the pound shop.

It's not exactly showbiz, but it helps to have a sense of humour when you're trying to sell badly painted ornamental cats and bright blue toilet brushes.

Her love life is a bit of a joke too, but could be a lot better if only Dean, her best friend Ellen's twin brother, would just get the hint. "I think we should just be friends," Andi told him. But, it has been a year and a half and he still expects them to get back together.

When Andi bumps into Tony, an up-and-coming comedian, who just happens to be good-looking, they hit it off immediately and now he wants her to write some material for him. Andi's sure that this will take her a step closer to her dream of becoming a comedian herself.

But the road to stardom is not going to be easy, especially if her disapproving mother and paranoid and panicky older sister have any say in it.

ISBN 1-84223-069-7

If the Shoe Fits

JAYE CARROLL

Twenty-five, single and just a little paranoid, Susan meets Sam. He's everything she wants: good-looking, fun, intelligent and as mad about movies as she is. Out of the blue, happiness has kicked in.

Or so she thinks.
The shoe fits at last and she's going to wear it . . .

Then her boss goes on holiday and leaves her in charge, she suddenly has to find a new place to live, she answers a very odd ad in the Personal Columns . . .

And life doesn't seem such a perfect fit any more

ISBN 1-85371-957-9